DATE DUE

SKYHOOK

SKYHOOK

JOHN J. NANCE

G. P. PUTNAM'S SONS

NEW YORK

This is a work of fiction. Names, characters, places and incidents either
are the product of the author's imagination or are used fictitiously,
and any resemblance to actual persons, living or dead, business
establishments, events, or locales is entirely coincidental.

G. P. Putnam's Sons
Publishers Since 1838
a member of
Penguin Putnam Inc.
375 Hudson Street
New York, NY 10014

Library of Congress Cataloging-in-Publication Data

Nance, John J.
Skyhook
p. cm.
ISBN 0-399-14980-5
1. Aeronautics—Safety measures—Fiction.   2. Computer scientists—Fiction.
3. Sabotage—Fiction.   I. Title.
PS3564.A546 S58   2003   2002031914
813'.54—dc21

Printed in the United States of America
1   3   5   7   9   10   8   6   4   2

This book is printed on acid-free paper. ∞

BOOK DESIGN BY MEIGHAN CAVANAUGH

To all of the members of the James L. Noel Clan—My Extended Family

The Honorable Judge James L. Noel, Jr., U.S. District Judge (1909–1997),
Uncle Jim; Virginia Grubbs Noel, Esq. (1917–2000), *Aunt Jenny*

And My Honored Cousins and "Cousins-in-Law"
James L. Noel III & Melinda Caldwell Noel
Carol Noel King, Esq. & J. Stephen King, Esq.
Edmund Orr Noel & Patrice Oden Noel
William D. Noel, Esq. & Barbara Wick Noel
Robert C. Noel, Esq. & Deanne Moore Noel, Esq.

SKYHOOK

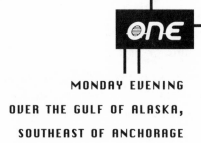

Whoa! What's this thing doing?" Captain Gene Hammond asked.

The chief test pilot's unexpected question snapped Ben Cole upright in his seat, drawing his attention from the maze of computer screens. Instinctively, he pressed the right side of his headset closer to his ear, as if trying to recapture the comment.

"I don't know," he heard the copilot respond.

Ben's eyes flickered to the forward bulkhead of the converted business jet's cabin, imagining the civilian test pilots hunched over their controls in the cockpit some thirty feet away. He felt the Gulfstream pitch down slightly, the white noise of the slipstream rising as the jet gained speed, the unexplained maneuver sharpening the isolation of being all alone in the stripped-down cabin.

"Crown, are you purposely descending us?" Hammond queried the test director by radio link. "I don't think that's the plan."

Ben felt a sparkle of chills as he forced his eyes back to the display, confirming the lowering altitude and rising airspeed.

"Negative," the voice from the Air Force AWACS replied. "Stand by."

The unseen presence of the AWACS, a huge four-engine Boeing, had been reassuring, like a protective parent hovering in the night some ten thousand feet above and several miles behind the Gulfstream. But it seemed dangerously distant. Ben knew that the cavernous interior of the AWACS was crammed full of electronics, a two-star Air Force general, two corporate officers, and a cadre of test engineers, all of them expecting a much-needed flawless performance in the eleventh hour of a top secret program that could make or break Uniwave Industries.

"We're descending at three thousand, four hundred feet per minute, on a course of zero two five degrees," Hammond said. The edge in his voice was cutting into Ben's faith that humans were really meant to fly.

Dr. Ben Cole, a Ph.D. in electrical engineering from Caltech, pulled his eyes away from the computer screens and glanced toward the aircraft windows on his left, all of them black portals into the void of a moonless Alaskan night. He swallowed, and the sound was suddenly deafening.

"We're working on it, Sage Ten," the test director shot back, using the typically innocuous call assigned to the Gulfstream.

"And down here we're definitely locked out," Hammond replied.

Ben fumbled for his transmit switch. "What . . . what's going on up there, guys?"

There was no reply at first, the silence conspiring with the dilation of time to feed the rising apprehension clawing at his insides.

"Stand by, Ben," the copilot replied at last, his voice typically calm and flat. "Your damn program's diving us. You're not doing anything back there, are you?"

"No!" Ben replied, much too sharply. "I got all the right signals when we locked the program link. Nothing's showing wrong here."

The test director's voice was back on the radio, overriding Ben's reply.

"Sage Ten, we're not asking for that descent. The remote control column up here is commanding straight and level. You sure you're locked on our signal?"

"Trust me," Hammond shot back. "We're straight, but anything but level, and we are locked onto the telemetry. About two minutes after we turned over control to you, this started, just when you checked the speed brake. You've got the controls, Crown, and you're descending us through fourteen thousand now."

"No, we're not," another voice chimed in.

The remote test pilot was sitting in a replica of the Gulfstream's cockpit safely aboard the AWACS. The plan called for the remote pilot to fly the Gulfstream by high-speed datalink for five minutes before engaging the automatic program they were there to validate—the program Ben had labored tirelessly to perfect for the previous eighteen months of eighteen-hour days. They were down to the wire now, and the thought of a setback was unacceptable.

"If this continues," the Gulfstream pilot was saying, "we'd better abort."

"Not yet." The swift reply from the test director cut through their headsets. "Hang on, we're . . . working on it."

"Ben?" Gene Hammond's voice was taking on a new level of urgency as he called his on-board test engineer, but as usual, he was trying to wrap his concern in the joking tones of a stressed airman who wasn't about to admit to the pressure he felt. "Ben, now would be a very good time to tell me what your brainchild thinks it's doing. A temper tantrum, perhaps?"

Ben mashed the interphone switch again, trying, and failing, to match the casual tone the pilot had adopted. "I don't know! If they're not commanding the descent from the AWACS, I can tell you it's sure not in the program."

"Is it thinking on its own, Ben?" the copilot added. "You know, making up some solution we don't know about? You're not some secret fan of the HAL 9000 computer in *2001: A Space Odyssey,* are you?"

Ben felt his mind racing through an impossible tangle of technical details in search of a reassuring answer. There was none.

"Maybe we'd better disconnect."

"Crown?" the pilot transmitted without hesitation. "I'm unsafeing the kill switch down here. If we descend through eight thousand, I'm pulling the plug on Winky."

Ben suppressed a tiny flash of resentment. He hated the word the test pilots had coined to belittle the complex automatic system. Winky indeed! Pilots and engineers were always on a collision course, he'd been told, and he was realizing the truth of it as he punched the transmit switch again. "We could try a reset," he added, aware the AWACS above couldn't hear him on interphone. "They could have screwed up something back there in entering the maneuver plan. The test point altitudes, for instance."

"Crown?" Hammond was transmitting again. "We're descending through ten thousand, I'm just short of red-line speed, and your sage advice for Sage Ten would be greatly appreciated right about now."

"Uh . . . stand by," the test director repeated.

There was a pause the length of a heartbeat before Hammond responded. "No . . . too late. We're disconnecting."

Shit! Ben thought to himself. He sighed and sat back, feeling a cloak of disappointment enfold him. There would be corporate hell to pay for a bad test sequence. He wouldn't be the only one in the crosshairs of company dissatisfaction, of course. There were more than sixty software experts working on the top secret system. But it had been Dr. Ben Cole, the young and the bold, who'd risked his fledgling career and his fair-haired status of "wunderkind" to take the lead position at age thirty-four.

Ben felt the Gulfstream undulate through some mild turbulence. *They're pulling out,* he told himself, letting his mind disconnect for a few seconds, entering one of the tiny distractive mental loops that always helped him recharge.

Whatever happened, he would be employable. He could still work most anywhere he wanted to, and maybe he could even throttle some of his eternal ambition in favor of doing a little living. He'd had no life at all for the past two years in Anchorage. He'd been too busy to even have a girlfriend, although he'd dated a few local women and taken an occasional touristy side trip.

I know almost nothing about Alaska, he thought, resolving, as he had a hundred times before, to take a four-month vacation when this push was over. Maybe he could see some of Denali National Park on foot. He wasn't much of an outdoorsman like his dad had been, but the fond memories of camping and hiking the Rockies in his teens with his dad as guide were always hanging there as a Valhalla to be re-experienced. He was sure he could figure out the basics of camping. After all, pitching a tent was just an applied engineering problem.

More radio chatter caught his attention, and Ben forced his mind back to the matters at hand, expecting to hear a decision to reposition to try it again.

". . . up there? I'm getting nothing here," Hammond, the Gulfstream pilot was saying. Ben's eyes went to the screens, wondering why the altitude readout wasn't showing the level-off. They'd disengaged at eight thousand, hadn't they?

"We're trying to break the link up here, Sage Ten, but the computer's not responding."

Ben recognized the test director's voice. What did he mean, "not responding"?

He heard Gene Hammond's voice snap back an answer as he came forward in the seat, instantly reengaging. "Crown, we're dropping through four thousand at the same descent rate, same heading. Do something!"

The altitude readout on his screen showed three thousand two hundred feet, its numbers unwinding.

"Ben! Can you hear us?" Hammond was asking, his words implying a previous call Ben had missed. A rush of adrenaline filled Ben's bloodstream as he answered, his voice sounding a bit strange.

"I'm here."

"Do something, dammit! Help us disconnect."

"Use the guarded disconnect switch," Ben replied.

"We did. It doesn't work," the pilot said as the copilot chimed in, his voice taut with tension. "One thousand five hundred. It's flying us into the water. What now, Ben?"

"The guarded switch won't work?" Ben repeated blankly, his mind in a daze. How could anyone think under such pressure? The readout in front of him was still whizzing downward as he reached forward and keyed a disconnect command into the computer, sending it just as rapidly through the telemetry link to the main processor aboard the AWACS.

"One thousand!" The copilot had dropped all pretense of calm now, his voice up a half octave.

"I'm . . . pulling . . . but . . . I can't override," Hammond was saying through gritted teeth.

"Five hundred!" the copilot intoned. "Oh, God . . ."

Ben thought of reaching for the keyboard again to try the same disconnect sequence, but something was yanking him down hard in his seat as the Gulfstream's nose came up without warning, spiking gravity and making him feel incredibly heavy before returning just as rapidly to the normality of a single G.

And suddenly they were level, the sounds of excessive speed bleeding off in the background.

"Jesus Christ, Crown!" he heard Hammond say on the radio. "It just jerked us level at—"

The copilot finished the sentence. "Fifty feet. On the radio altimeter. We're holding at fifty feet, three hundred knots."

"What's your status, Sage Ten?" the test director asked.

"Our *status?* We're into hyperventilation down here, if that's any clue," the pilot responded, pausing. Ben could hear a long breath. "The damn thing almost killed us! Whatever the heck is going on in that silicon psycho's little mind, it wants to fly at fifty feet, and I still can't disconnect it."

"But . . . you're level?"

"Yeah . . . for now. Otherwise we wouldn't be having this chat.

But we're just a hiccup from the water and there's land somewhere ahead. Ben? Get this goddamned electronic octopus off my controls!"

ABOARD CROWN

Aboard the AWACS, Major General Mac MacAdams dared to let his breath out as he glanced quickly at the grim faces around him. All of them had been listening on small Telex headsets and unconsciously pressing in behind the pilot sitting at the remote controls as the Gulfstream had dropped toward the ocean.

The test director looked around at Mac and shook his head in shock.

"What the hell was all that about?" the general asked. He could see the test director, Jeff Kaminsky, jaw muscles working overtime as he struggled to answer.

"I don't know, General. Stand by." He triggered his transmit button again. "Sage Ten, we're going to pull the circuit boards on the computer up here and disconnect you."

"NO!" A voice from the Gulfstream cut in.

"Who's this?" Kaminsky demanded.

"Ben Cole. Don't pull any circuit boards! If your computer's doing this and you get the wrong board first, it could pitch us down."

Kaminsky glanced at the general in puzzlement as he answered. "You know what's causing this, Dr. Cole?"

"No . . . but . . . I'm guessing. The problem may be down here, but it may not."

"How about killing the radio links between us, then?" the test director asked.

"Wait on that, too," Ben Cole replied. "I'm working on it from here."

"Sage," Kaminsky said, "we're still showing you at fifty feet, three hundred twenty knots."

Hammond's voice growled back at them. "Yeah, and Winky is

goosing my throttles to max thrust. Would someone check up there to make sure there's not an island ahead or something?"

A shout marked Ben Cole's return to the channel. "Okay! Our computer's the culprit. Go ahead and shut down the radio link."

Kaminsky mashed one of the intercom buttons and relayed the order to another engineer at a console ten feet away. "Shut it off. All right, Dr. Cole, the link is history. Are you released?"

There was a long pause before the pilot's voice returned from the Gulfstream.

"No," Hammond said. "Dammit, it's still locked up. Ben? What the hell's going on back there?"

The channel fell silent for several long seconds as one of the test engineers on the AWACS rose quickly from his position and came forward, pushing in alongside the general and Kaminsky. Mac Mac-Adams noticed the man first. The haunted look on his face meant a new emergency. The general put his hand on the test director's shoulder and turned him toward the worried subordinate.

"What?" Jeff Kaminsky snapped.

"There's a . . . problem ahead," the test engineer said.

Kaminsky's attention was shifting slowly to the engineer as he kept one eye on his readouts. "Spill it," he said.

"Ahead, on my radar, about forty miles, there's a big ship."

Jeff Kaminsky swiveled around to look the engineer in the eye. "What do you mean, 'big ship'?"

"Sage Ten is at fifty feet," he said. "I know this part of the Gulf, and this target's big."

"He's in Sage's way? A big ship?"

"Yes, sir. Dead-on collision course. He's on a heading of one hundred twenty degrees, about a right angle to our guy."

"He's big enough to have a superstructure fifty feet above the water line?"

"If it's a supertanker out of Valdez, yes. The hull will be higher than that. If he hits, he'll broadside the hull. Even if he misses, he'll hit one of the ridges on Hitchinbrook Island twenty miles farther."

The general caught the tech's shoulder. "You're saying it's a *loaded* tanker?"

The man nodded. "He's a loaded thousand-foot-long supertanker southeast-bound making eleven knots on my scope, coming out of Hitchinbrook entrance to Prince William Sound. Ships like that usually stand at least seventy feet above the water when loaded," the engineer said, wondering why the general turned suddenly and disappeared.

Jeff Kaminsky sighed and nodded, then turned back to his screen. "Keep me informed," he said, regretting the utter uselessness of the remark.

"Sage Ten, Crown," Kaminsky said. "How're you doing on the disconnect?"

The chief software engineer Kaminsky had met several times replied, his voice taut, "I can't just kill the computer without knowing which channel I'm dealing with."

"Dr. Cole? Listen to me. You've got about two minutes maximum to knock that thing offline and give your pilots control again."

"I'm trying . . . stand by," Cole replied. "I may need more than a couple of minutes. I'm running a critical diagnostic."

"You don't have more than that, Doctor. You may just have to yank the plug, so to speak. Reset the computer or something drastic."

"What's going on?" Hammond cut in. "Why two minutes?"

Jeff Kaminsky sighed quietly to himself as he decided how much to say. "There's . . . a possibility of an obstruction ahead of you. It's imperative you either change course or climb, within . . . a couple of minutes."

Some twenty feet to the rear in the AWACS cabin General MacAdams replaced a handset and pointed to a window on the communications panel as he caught the attention of a young sergeant.

"Quickly and quietly dial me up on UHF frequency three twenty-two point four."

"Yes, sir," the sergeant said, punching in the numbers and giving a thumbs-up.

Mac plugged into the console and toggled the radio to transmit.

"Shepard Five, this is Crown."

The reply was instantaneous.

"Shepard Five."

"Max speed and lock him up. Inform me when you're within firing range."

The lead pilot of a flight of two F-15 fighters from Elmendorf Air Force Base in Anchorage gave a brief acknowledgment. Mac could imagine them going to afterburner, the two fighters accelerating to more than twice the speed of sound in an emergency dash across the eighty miles separating them from the slower Gulfstream.

Mac forced his mind away from the horror of the situation and focused instead on being grateful for having the foresight to launch the two fighters as a precaution against something unforeseen that might threaten civilian interests.

That "something" had occurred. One *Exxon Valdez* oil spill was enough.

"You have both targets on radar?" Mac asked the sergeant, who nodded toward his screen.

"Yes, sir."

"Give me decreasing range, down to six miles."

ABOARD SAGE TEN

Ben Cole felt his mind accelerating to a speed he'd never experienced as he worked through the logic of the problem, eliminating possibilities one by one, struggling hard to make sure nothing he triggered would cause a sudden pitchdown. He was aware of the radio discussion about an object in front of them, but it was a shadowy snippet of information rumbling in the background. The main event was unfolding all around him, but a part of his consciousness was perversely standing to the side, exhilarated to be watching himself trying to master such a complex problem.

The software commanding the Gulfstream was his, and there were only a finite number of possible reasons it wouldn't release, half of which he'd already eliminated. The remaining ones, however, were even more complex, involving safety procedures to use in case of radio link failure. The system was supposed to be able to fully control an Air Force jet anywhere over the planet.

Seven down, four to go! Ben thought, feeling the timeline stretch even more. He had a minute left. It was a numbers game now, but he should have plenty of time.

"Ben, dammit, talk to me!" Gene Hammond was saying over the interphone. "We're getting something on the radar ahead, about thirteen miles."

He took his hand away long enough to punch the interphone transmit button. "I'm working on it. Hang on."

"We don't have much time, Ben! In about a minute we're going to merge with whatever the hell that is."

He forced himself to ignore the pilot and stay focused. There was an additional possibility he hadn't considered. Should he take time and probe it? That hadn't been in his plan ten seconds before.

No! Stay with what you were doing, he chided himself, tuning out the pilot's voice booming in his ear again.

"Ben, old boy, what say we just reset that damn computer of yours and let the two of us up here deal with the consequences, okay? The possibility of a sudden pitchdown won't really matter much if we don't regain control."

More silence.

Two possibilities left. Has to be one of them.

More keystrokes, his fingers flying with nimble certainty over the keyboard.

"Ben, dammit, disconnect the thing NOW! *Please,* Ben. Your tip depends on it. Ben? For crissakes answer me! *BEN?*"

One more. Murphy's law dictates the solution will be the last one I try.

He fired off the final string of orders, but nothing changed, and the realization was a sudden slap. He'd been wrong, it wasn't any of them.

What now? Maybe a power supply lock! Oh, Lord, let it be power supply.

"Ben, I'm sending the copilot back to either get you on channel or kill you. Please, guy, shut down that damned computer now! We've got eight miles left."

Ben could hear the forward cabin door being yanked open as the copilot burst through.

"Ben? What the hell are you *doing?* Pull the plug!" the copilot yelped, but Ben shook his head before looking up suddenly. "I don't believe this," Ben said.

"What?" the copilot asked, even more alarmed.

"It won't respond!"

ABOARD CROWN

For several critical minutes General MacAdams had stood in silence watching the Gulfstream's radar target close at 340 knots on the huge thousand-foot-long supertanker. The Coast Guard had confirmed the identity, but warned there was no time for the tanker's captain to change course.

Mac felt himself running the alternatives over in his mind again and again, but the equation always yielded the same result.

"Eight miles to go, sir," the sergeant said quietly.

MacAdams sighed and raised the microphone to his mouth, hesitating before pressing the transmit button. "Stand by, Shepard. Launch on my command only."

"Roger, Crown. We're still locked, range twenty miles, and we're slowing."

The sergeant was intoning the decreasing range as he watched the general for any indication the impending deaths of the three men below could be averted.

"Six point five. Six point four. Six point three . . ."

The general sighed and punched the transmit button again.

ABOARD SAGE TEN

The copilot had spotted a crash axe along the cabin wall and grabbed it before arriving at Ben Cole's side. "Show me where to whack it! We're down to seconds."

"No need," Ben replied. He reached over with one hand and toggled the interphone. His other hand reached for a single switch on the side of the main computer tower. "Hang onto your controls. I'm disconnecting."

There was an immediate jump in G forces as the pilot yanked the jet into a climb.

ABOARD CROWN

"Shepard, this is Crown. On my mark . . . *NO!* Hold it."

The sergeant was shaking his head energetically and pointing to the radar screen. "I've got an altitude and course change, sir."

"Negative launch, Shepard. Safe your weapons. Acknowledge."

"He's coming up fast," the sergeant was saying as the fighter lead replied.

"Roger, Crown, negative launch. Weapons safed. Standing by, and we have the target climbing steeply."

"Jeez Louise," the sergeant chimed in. "He's climbing like a . . . a . . ." The sergeant glanced up nervously at the general, who smiled back in relief as he shook his head. "Climbing like a striped-ass ape? Don't worry, I've heard just about all of them."

"I was gonna say a homesick angel."

"Sure you were," MacAdams chuckled, taking a very deep breath as he tightened his grip on the mike and pressed the transmit button to send the F-15s back to Elmendorf.

ABOARD SAGE TEN

When the copilot had returned to the cockpit, Captain Gene Hammond, the chief test pilot for Uniwave, turned control over to him and came back to talk to Ben Cole, unsure whether to hug him or punch him out.

"So, Ben, what happened with Winky?"

"I . . . really wish you wouldn't call it that."

He could see the pilot's features harden in a flash of anger.

"When a stupid piece of silicon tries to kill me, I'll call it anything I damn well please. Now what the hell happened?"

"I don't know."

The pilot looked perplexed as he gestured to the array of computers. "But . . . you said you needed time, and you disconnected it successfully."

"No, I said I had to check to make sure it wouldn't plunge us nose down if I turned the computer off, which is what I finally did. I had to check a series of . . . of readouts. The program was holding the latching relays closed, but in a complex sequence, and I don't know why."

"You don't know what went wrong?"

"No."

"You don't even know if the problem will repeat?"

"No."

"But you told General MacAdams we're through for the night. You do realize the company brass were listening, don't you?"

"Yes."

Hammond sighed and shook his head. "Then God have mercy on all of us, Ben. At best, we've got one more shot at a test flight to make this salable, and I'll bet with MacAdams right now we're hanging by a thread."

"I know it," Ben replied quietly, his mind already chewing over the chances of finding and fixing in time what might be a single glitch in a software program of more than six million lines of binary code. With any luck, he thought, he could complete the job by the time he reached the age of seventy.

But Uniwave would need the problem solved in forty-eight hours.

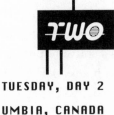

*I*n a high-rise condo overlooking Vancouver's west end, the incongruous sounds of barnyard animals wafted through the carefully decorated interior and scratched at the exposed ear of the sleeping owner, the abrasive vibrations subtly turning a strange dream to the bizarre.

April Rosen opened one eye and tried to focus on something coherent as her mind grappled with the possibility that pigs had found the twenty-third floor, bringing what sounded like a flock of chickens and geese along for good measure.

She pushed herself up from the bed and blew a curtain of jet-black hair from her eyes as she turned, half expecting the TV to be the culprit, her mind spinning up rapidly and eliminating possibilities one by one.

The TV sat dark and silent in the built-in credenza, yet the pigs persisted.

April threw off the bedcovers and slid to her feet, disconcerted by the cacophonous concert, unaware that she was gloriously naked in front of a wall of uncovered floor-to-ceiling windows, with several of downtown Vancouver's high-rise offices across the way.

What in the world is that noise? Annoyance was replacing shock, her ears guiding her gaze to the bedside, where a new electronic alarm clock sat, happily spewing the wake-up call from hell. She leaned over and examined it, turning the volume down before sliding the switch to "off" to stop the clucking and snorting. The clock was supposed to play soothing noises such as surf and babbling brooks. Nowhere in the little owner's manual had there been anything about babbling animals.

April sighed and made a mental note to reread the instructions. She stood and stretched luxuriously, stopping suddenly when she realized she was putting on a skin show. There were guys with high-powered binoculars already zeroed in on her condo. She'd caught some of them several times before with her own set of binoculars.

April swiftly dropped to her knees and fished on the bed stand for the remote control that closed the curtains, waiting for Vancouver to disappear before standing again. She picked up a purple satin robe from the floor, where it had slid off the end of the bed during the night, and put it on, tying the belt deftly around her waist.

A motion detector clicked on and a small electronic chime echoed pleasantly through the condo, announcing that its tiny silicon brain had just activated her preloaded coffeemaker and raised the thermostat two degrees as it tuned the music system to light classical. The strains of Mozart's Clarinet Concerto radiated from the hidden ceiling speakers, and she glanced up involuntarily with a smile. Classical was a touch of elegance, even when the apartment was a mess, which it seldom was. The music blended with the rich colors of the collection of paintings she'd spent far too much on, original oils by local artists. She walked into the living room, enjoying the uncurtained, panoramic view of English Bay spread out in front of her. She never tired of seeing all that beauty, and was glad she'd made the decision to mortgage most of her salary and buy the corner unit.

April loved being the newest staff vice-president of Empress Cruise Lines, but she was equally pleased that on such a beautiful morning, she didn't have to be in her office until early afternoon.

I can have a leisurely breakfast, read the paper, go jogging, or all of the above.

There was one more waking ritual before coffee, and she moved to her computer to figure out where her parents were today.

April typed in her password before triggering the world map and opening the appropriate program, initiating a high-speed connection with the Internet. She could picture the small satellite antenna she'd paid to have installed on top of Captain Arlie Rosen's aircraft after he'd reluctantly given in to the idea of being actively tracked by his daughter. The GPS-based system sent a burst of radio energy to an orbiting satellite every sixty seconds, reporting its position wherever they were.

"That's all it is, Dad," she'd said, hands on her hips as she stood alongside his beautifully refurbished World War II amphibian aircraft at the dock in Seattle months before. The interior resembled the parlor of a luxury yacht, with a bedroom, living room, galley, and bathroom, and her folks used it at every opportunity.

"You're spying on your mother and me, right?" her father had accused.

"Wait . . . hold it," April had replied, laughing. "That's my line!"

"What do you mean, your line?"

"When I was a little girl—"

"You're still a little girl."

"Dad! When I was just starting to car date and you wanted me to take a cell phone with me, I accused *you* of spying on *me*."

"Yeah, well, you were right. We *were* spying on you. You were dating boys, for crying out loud."

"No, Dad, you said the phone was for emergencies."

"And you believed me?"

"Yes, because you were right."

Arlie Rosen had turned to her mother, who was trying unsuccessfully to suppress her laughter.

"Rachel? Our daughter admitted her father was right about some-thing. Record the moment and then do CPR. She's obviously ill."

"Dad . . ."

He'd smiled at April then, his silver hair framing his well-tanned face, looking every inch the reliable veteran 747 captain, as he shook his head in defeat. "Oh, all right, if it'll make you feel better. Just no cameras or microphones inside listening to whatever we're doing."

"Don't worry. It just reports your position."

"Position?" he'd repeated. "Which ones? Missionary, doggie . . ."

Rachel Rosen had swatted him on the shoulder as April turned a deep shade of red. "Now . . . see . . ." she'd said, fumbling for words, "that's something I don't expect to hear coming out of my father's mouth."

April chuckled at the memory. She waited for the computer pro-gram to report the latest latitude and longitude of the Rosens' Grumman Albatross and let her eyes fall on the small video camera on top of the screen. Several of her friends now used computer-mounted cameras, too, and they enjoyed being able to see each other when talking over the web, especially her best friend Gracie in Seattle, 150 miles distant. Unfortunately, she'd accidentally left her camera on and connected to the Internet a couple of times, and once she'd been mortified to find that she'd been broadcasting for a whole day and had inadvertently become a popular webshow. She'd disconnected in embarrassment as a small counter had flashed on the screen proudly reporting that nearly ten thousand web surfers had clicked in to watch her moving around her condo. The camera had even had a bird's-eye view of her bed, making her embarrassment all the more acute.

The world map now assembled itself on the screen, then snapped to a closer view, framing Alaska. The track of the Albatross's flight from Japan the previous week appeared along with small flags mark-ing each stop. April looked at the track from Anchorage. The trail of blue position dots showed they'd flown down Turnagain Arm and crossed the small range of mountains near Whittier before setting a course for . . .

What's this?

A small chill climbed her back. The blue dots did not extend to Sitka, or Juneau, or any of the other places they were planning to visit. Instead they marched to the southeast for almost a hundred miles, past a tiny dot of land called Middleton Island, then turned northwest, toward Valdez. The last dot was somewhere south of the entrance to Prince William Sound and the Valdez area, maybe sixty miles out to sea.

She zoomed the screen and ordered the program to show the time each report had been sent.

They're probably still in flight, she told herself.

But the last transmission had come during darkness the night before. At 10:13 P.M. local, they had been in flight at 140 miles per hour at an altitude of less than a hundred feet and on a heading of 320 degrees, and after that, the little reporting unit had fallen silent.

April sat back and tried to suppress her growing concern. There were a million possible benign explanations. The unit itself could have failed. They could have had an electrical failure in the airplane. She knew they could still fly and land safely even if that were the case, but wasn't that open ocean? Her dad had always said that landings in open ocean were far more difficult and dangerous in a seaplane.

Something's wrong. April sat forward and grabbed for the portable phone as she stood and began pacing, a habit that always drove Gracie to distraction. April entered her parents' Iridium satellite phone number from memory and waited for the clicks and squawks to end in a ringing sound.

"The Iridium customer you have called is not currently available," a voice intoned. She disconnected and tried again, harvesting the same result.

The lure of coffee and breakfast completely forgotten, she returned to the computer and launched a search for the FAA's regional facility in Anchorage, punched the resulting number into the telephone keypad, and worked her way through several people before receiving a definitive no.

"We have no record, Miss . . . *Rosen?*"

"Yes. April Rosen."

"No record of any accidents or incidents last night, or calls for help, or even an emergency locator transmission."

"You would know if one had been received, right?"

"Well, someone would. You say that's an old Albatross, right? They could easily land out there on the water."

"I know, but—"

"That's why the Navy built them. Not as effective as the old PBY Catalina on open ocean, but they can handle it. The Coast Guard used them for years as—"

"Excuse me," April interrupted.

"Yes?"

"My dad always files a flight plan. Is there any record of his flight plan and where he was going?"

"VFR or IFR?"

"He's . . . an airline captain. Very experienced. Usually it's a visual flight plan, I think, because they stay so low."

"Okay. Hang on, and I'll check."

He put her on hold and returned several minutes later. "Miss Rosen . . . April . . . apparently your dad didn't file a flight plan. Anchorage Flight Service tells me there's nothing on the computer."

"That's really unusual."

"I'm sure they're just fine, but if you're still worried, I'll give you the number of the Coast Guard's regional command post, and you can double-check with them."

April wrote down the digits absently, her mind racing around the entrance to Prince William Sound for an explanation and a reassuring image of her parents floating and fishing or making love or whatever else they might be doing. She thanked him and disconnected before turning to the computer to send an e-mail to Gracie in Seattle, routing it to Gracie's beeper, cell phone screen, and office and home computers simultaneously.

Sir, they're waiting for you."

Will Martin, chairman of the board of Uniwave Industries, forced himself to turn away from the pleasant vistas of wooded countryside spread out beyond his office windows and glanced at his secretary of six years.

"What, Jill?"

"Did you get my computer message that the teleconference is ready?"

"I'm sorry, no," he said, permitting himself to notice the lovely contours of her body as his mind replayed a little fantasy about her, a repeated private indulgence that always ended with a flash of fear that she might someday decipher his thoughts. "You . . . say they're already waiting?" he added.

Jill nodded. "Yes. Shall I tell them you'll be right in?"

He smiled back at her and nodded in return, his mind still on the sexy fantasy and wondering if prurient thoughts ever crackled behind her professional facade. He watched her as she turned and left the office, a gentle wave of femininity singularly unburdened by the corporate anvils weighing him down.

Martin turned to pick up a stack of papers and messages on his desk, feeling the strong tug between what he wanted to do and what he had to do.

He wanted to run, but running had never been in his nature.

He wanted to study the expensive paintings on the wall, or watch the squirrels playing in the trees outside, or contemplate the sweet taboo of making love to his secretary—*anything* to avoid the intense apprehension he would have to skillfully hide in a few minutes from the others.

Martin willed his hand to scoop up a stack of papers on his desk that pertained to the critical black project they'd agreed to build for the Air Force more than three years ago. Back then, all he'd feared were the heavy security procedures the company would have to follow. He'd never questioned their ability to produce the so-called Boomerang Box, the heart of the Skyhook Project, a system designed to safely land by remote control a military aircraft whose crew had been disabled. The system had made good sense, but within months, the task of completing it had rapidly become a nightmare of delays and technical insufficiencies.

Will Martin moved toward his office door, but the urge to stop and turn back was irresistible. Once more he stood quietly, memorizing the details of the peaceful vista outside his window.

The conference could wait a few seconds more.

The new teleconferencing suite had been complete for less than a month. The entire setup—from the long, rectangular mahogany table to the wallpaper and state-of-the-art video equipment—had been leased to Uniwave by a company called Simulight, a rapidly growing corporation that was wowing Wall Street and changing the idea of teleconferencing from a novelty to a necessity. The suite had cost Uniwave practically nothing, and Martin was proud of that deal. Since he had dearly wanted the technology, and Simulight had dearly wanted their business, it had been a win-win situation.

Martin walked into the room wearing his trademark air of seriousness and nodded to the six senior executives who would be sitting with him on the Raleigh-Durham side of the table. The room itself was twenty-five feet long by what appeared to be sixteen feet, but in fact the real width was only eight feet since the room was divided in half lengthwise by a solid panel of high-definition liquid crystal glass. The team in Anchorage appeared in living color, sitting on the other side of their half of the table in the composite room, which was adorned with matching paintings, wallpaper, and even matching coffee cups and pitchers. He had entertained the idea of trying to buy Simulight, but his board had vetoed the idea, which was a shame, he thought. The new technology would eventually make billions by setting the worldwide standards for teleconferencing, but his board was too panicked about whether Uniwave itself could survive.

"We all here?" the chairman asked the assemblage on both sides of the screen, surveying the nodding heads and noting the fear in the eyes of those in Anchorage. It would be a challenge getting the truth out of the Alaskan group, he thought. They were well aware their jobs were on the line.

Maybe, he thought, *I should have entered the room a little more pleasantly.*

Martin cleared his throat and the conversations ceased.

"Okay, team. We're in deep excrement here and up against the deadline. What happened last night, why did it happen, and how are we going to fix it and retest it in the next forty-eight hours? I also need to hear any lingering concerns anyone might have over the system's safety before we give it to the Air Force and ask for our check." All but two of the Anchorage contingent appeared ready to bolt from the room in fear. *Tone it down,* he warned himself, as he pointed to the senior project manager in Anchorage.

"Joe? Why don't you give me the basics."

Joe Davis scooted his chair forward and narrated the sequence of events over the Gulf of Alaska the night before, describing Dr. Ben Cole's ultimate solution, which had been to simply turn off the main computer.

"So, Ben's computer was the culprit?" Martin asked. "Not the software?"

"We think so. We're running all kinds of diagnostics. Have been all night. Our best guess right now is a hardware fault of some sort."

Martin could see the look of alarm on Ben Cole's face. He turned to him. "Ben? You look upset."

"Well . . ."

"You agree with Joe's assessment?"

Ben shot Joe Davis a worried look before answering. "Ah . . . turning the computer off did unlatch the relays, Mr. Martin, so, technically . . ."

"Your on-board computer was sending signals to lock the aircraft in its control, right?"

Ben nodded without enthusiasm.

"But," Martin continued, "why was it diving you to fifty feet and then skimming the water?"

"We don't know," Ben answered cautiously.

"Well, hardware or software? Or both?"

There was a flurry of activity to one side of the suite in Anchorage and a woman entered with a note for Joe Davis, withdrawing quickly. Martin saw a broad smile spread over Davis's face as he shared the note with the others and gestured for the chairman's attention.

"I think we've got it!" Davis said, looking at Ben. "Our guys just found a bad circuit board in Ben's computer aboard the Gulfstream, and it's the board that governs pitch and altitude as well as the latching relays for the flight controls."

Martin smiled and exhaled as he flashed a thumbs-up gesture. "Great!"

But Ben Cole was not smiling, and the chairman noticed.

"Ben? You look unconvinced."

"Well . . ."

"Spit it out."

Ben pursed his lips and smiled as he shook his head. "I hate to be the skunk at the party, and, of course, I haven't seen what they found, but I really think we need to finish looking through the program to make sure there's nothing else going on."

"Ben," Joe Davis began, reaching a hand toward his sleeve, but Ben Cole's eyes were locked on Will Martin's across the transparent divide of the screen.

"Leave him be, Joe," Martin ordered quietly. "Everyone gets their say here. Go ahead, Ben."

"Well, first, we shouldn't try to fly the acceptance test tonight, just in case I'm right. If we blow this one, as I understand it, we blow the on-time acceptance."

Will Martin was nodding slowly as he watched the young engineer and made quiet note of the perspiration glistening on his forehead.

"Okay," Ben continued. "This has nothing to do with the fact that we almost died in that Gulfstream last night. I just want to make sure we get this right, and the logic here—that it would be just a circuit board and not involve the software—really scares me. And after all, we've been moving awfully fast."

"So you think it could be software. Isn't the software your responsibility as lead engineer, Ben?" the chairman asked. His words and tone were gentle, but the implication was devastating. Here was the chief software engineer for the project giving his boss a "no confidence" rating on two years of his own work, and in the eleventh hour.

"Yes, Mr. Chairman," Ben managed, "but what happened last night was too precise—the fifty-foot altitude, I mean—to be explained by a fried circuit board, in my opinion."

"Is that a guess, Ben, or do you have some hard evidence?"

"It's all guesswork, Mr. Martin, until we find a faulty line of code . . . but it's good guesswork. Bad circuits don't stop a jet at precisely fifty feet. At least, I don't think they would. Look, I'm sorry—"

"You made reference a second ago . . . what'd you say? That we've been moving too fast? What do you mean by that, Ben?"

The fact that Joe Davis was looking at Ben Cole with a frozen expression had not escaped Will Martin's attention.

"What I mean, or meant, sir, is that we've been under tremendous pressure on this project, and while I know everyone's done their best to get it right the first time, the truth is, this is a very complex software program with millions of lines of code, and I'm worried that we haven't fully tested it yet. At least, not enough to deploy."

"Okay, thanks for the caution," Martin began, nodding dismissively at Ben Cole as he straightened his back and surveyed all of them in turn around the table. "Here's the deal, folks. By the contract, we have until Saturday night to hand this system over to General MacAdams and proclaim it ready, or two very undesirable things are going to happen: One, we don't get paid the little green government check for one hundred ninety-three million dollars this company has to have by Wednesday to avoid default and stay afloat, as well as pay your paychecks. Two, we go into contract penalty clause territory for late delivery and start losing two hundred fifty thousand dollars per day, which is a million seven hundred fifty thousand a week. We can't afford either occurrence. We've lost two other contracts this year, as you know, our bond ratings are in the toilet, we've used up all but a pittance of our credit lines, and we're down to the crunch. So, if we're not sure we can be safe, we don't fly. But if there's any way we can patch the situation together sufficiently so we can be safe and still dazzle MacAdams and get this damn Boomerang Box system accepted, I say we find a way to do it. Now. Tonight. We need creative thinking, but with lightning speed. Understood?"

There were nods in all directions with the sole exception of Ben Cole, who was looking ill as Martin continued. "We add whatever safeguards we need to make absolutely sure the damn thing doesn't misbehave tonight, and then we fly it and sign off the final acceptance test. MacAdams is ready. I've already talked to him and assured him that we'd have an answer on what the problem was in a few hours, and now we've got it. A bad circuit board in a single computer. And, Ben?"

Ben Cole looked up, startled. "Yes, sir?"

"If you're still worried after tonight, you and your team can keep looking for the glitch. It'll take the Air Force three weeks to gear up to install the first black box on a real airplane anyway. That should give you time."

"Mr. Martin, I don't want to be a roadblock," Ben Cole began.

"Then don't," Martin said, flashing a perfunctory smile. "Let's find a way to get this accomplished."

"Sir," Ben began, but Martin cut him off.

"Ben, I need solutions overriding cautions now. Are you really prepared to tell me there's no way to safeguard the system against diving the Gulfstream during the test, or once again failing to release the controls, once that circuit board is fixed?"

"Well, no . . . the circuit board was probably . . . almost surely . . . the reason we couldn't disconnect. And I can rig a protective circuit that we didn't have last night to prevent any dives or turns. . . . But this is almost certainly a compound problem. I mean, there's a software logic problem somewhere. We wouldn't have leveled at fifty feet otherwise."

Will Martin got to his feet and looked across the electronic divide.

"You were aboard the Gulfstream last night, weren't you, Ben?"

"Yes, sir."

"And . . . that must have been a pretty terrifying episode for a non-pilot."

"I think it was terrifying for the pilots, too, sir."

Martin looked at the table and nodded before snapping his eyes back to Ben's.

"When something shakes you that badly, it can affect your judgment. I understand that's where your passion is coming from regarding tonight's test flight. That's why I want you to sit this one out. Stay home. Have a beer, watch TV, chase your wife to the bedroom, and let someone else from your team fly the test."

Ben started to protest but the chairman had his hand out in a stop gesture. "No, I mean it. In the aftermath of last night's problem, you're not going to be as cool and focused as you should be. Hell, I wouldn't be either."

Will Martin turned and left the room, leaving Ben Cole searching for a reply as Joe Davis leaned over and put a hand on his shoulder. "Come on, Ben. Cook up that protective circuit you mentioned, pick your crew for tonight, and go home."

"Joe, this could be a disaster," Ben began, but the project manager waved him away.

"We've got our orders, Ben. Let's get moving. We're not going to let it be a disaster." The older man picked up his coffee cup and hurried away, leaving Ben alone in the teleconferencing chamber. The screen went dark, making the enclosure suddenly feel half its size, and Ben looked at it in a quandary. A half dozen things he should have said to Martin were echoing through his mind, including the useless but vital fact that he was no longer married.

But Martin should have remembered that, Ben thought. He'd flown to Anchorage two years before for Lisa's funeral.

FOUR

April scooped up the receiver on the first ring and snapped off an urgent hello, instantly relieved to hear Gracie's voice on the other end.

"Okay, the Coast Guard's launching a search for your folks."

"Thank God!" April Rosen sighed as she massaged her temple and sank onto the edge of her bed. "I couldn't get their headquarters in Juneau to do anything, since the FAA claims Dad didn't file a flight plan and no one's heard a distress call." She reached for a Kleenex as the tears escaped her self-control. "Where are you?"

"In my sensory deprivation chamber. My windowless baby-lawyer office."

"How'd you get the Coast Guard to listen?"

There was a chuckle on the other end and April pictured Gracie O'Brien leaning back in her plush leather office chair. April had surprised her with the expensive chair when her best friend landed the coveted junior associate position with the mega law firm of Janssen and Pruzan.

"Well, I had a little help from one of the senior partners, Dick

Walsh," Gracie was explaining. "Dick put pressure on the right people in Washington, D.C., for me."

"Wow. You work with someone that powerful?" April asked.

"You could say that. Until last year, Dick was the Secretary of Transportation, and they kind of own the Coast Guard. Now he plays golf and calls in favors."

"However you did it, thank you. Oh. You did give them the coordinates of the last fix I got, right?"

"No, April Rosen, I told them to look for your folks somewhere in the North Pacific where the waves are blue and fish swim. Of *course* I gave them the coordinates. They're launching both a C-130 and something called a Jayhawk chopper out of Kodiak, which is only two hundred miles away, so they'll be all over the area in a couple of hours. It's just a matter of a little waiting time now."

"I'm pacing a hole in the floor up here."

"April, I'm sure your mom and dad are okay. I just feel it. After all, you said yourself that there's been no distress call and no emergency locator beacons heard in the area, and you know those beacons are picked up by satellite almost immediately."

"I know, but . . ."

"This is premature panic, Miss Icewater-In-Her-Veins Newly Minted Cruise Line Vice-President. Take a deep breath."

"Seriously, I'm scared, Gracie," April replied. "I'm sorry. I know I'm overreacting, but I love my folks and this is exactly why I paid for that GPS tracking system Dad didn't want . . . so I could make sure they had help if anything happened."

"The day's clear up there. If your folks are floating around, they'll find them."

"Think so?"

"*Yes*, I think so. But I also think that when they're found, they'll be aboard the Albatross tied up to some obscure pier with a dead battery waiting for a passing boat and boinking their brains out in the meantime."

"*Gracie!*"

"Well, your parents are pretty lusty. You know that."

"Yeah, I know. They embarrass me."

"That's their mission as parents. Especially yours. I just hope I still feel that lusty at their age. Of course, it would be nice to be married to a male of the species by that time, too."

The comforting, familiar banter trailed off for nearly half a minute until April broke the silence with a sigh. "Gracie?"

"Yeah?"

"What . . . do we do if the Coast Guard can't find them?" she asked, the words constrained by the sudden lump in her throat. "What if . . . something terrible's happened?"

"April, *listen* to yourself! Who was the wise young woman who recently advised a certain panicked, unemployed female law graduate to hang in there and keep applying? I seem to recall her telling me, and I quote, that the saddest people of all are those who refuse to take risks and pursue their dreams."

"You were probably listening to some sappy New Age priestess on a twenty-five-watt talk show," April replied, chuckling in spite of herself. "Was she selling crystals?"

"As I recall," Gracie said, "this little girl had dark hair, big boobs, and answered to the name of April. And her parents were having a ball flying all over creation, scandalizing their uptight daughter and pursuing *their* dreams."

"My parents are juvenile delinquents," April said, laughing and crying at the same time. "And if I get them back safely, I'm going to kill both of them!"

"Okay, now you're scaring me, April. You're sounding like *my* parents. I think the phrase is 'anal retentive.' Yeah, that's the ticket. You're definitely anal retentive."

"I am not."

"Uh-huh."

"And my boobs aren't that big, either."

"Right. Tell that to all the men who can never stop talking to your chest. I've had a raging inferiority complex since I was twelve years old because of your enormous boobs."

"Cut it out, Gracie!"

"April, just hang tight. Seriously. I'll call the second I know anything."

"They're going to call you?"

"No, they're going to call the former Secretary of Transportation, who'll call me the second the Coast Guard confirms that Captain Arlie and Rachel are just fine."

"Gracie?"

"Yes, ma'am?"

"Say a prayer, okay?"

"Already have," Gracie said quietly.

COAST GUARD DISTRICT 17 AIR OPERATIONS CENTER
KODIAK, ALASKA

The pace of operations in the Coast Guard's Kodiak Air Station command post had been at high pitch for the previous hour as two C-130 rescue aircraft searched the area south of Prince William Sound, steadily reporting their progress. With an HH-60 Jayhawk helicopter inbound to the search box at 140 knots, the two C-130s had divided up the standard search pattern and begun flying separate back-and-forth grids south of Valdez, the crews carefully searching the waters on both sides for any sign of a downed aircraft, oil slicks, or survivors. The first hour had ticked by with no results, leaving the officer in Juneau who had refused April Rosen's request feeling somewhere between smug and relieved as he monitored the radio traffic and waited.

"Just a panicked woman with political clout," he'd grumbled to another officer when the order had come from Washington, over-ruling him and ordering the search.

A report from one of the C-130s that two people had been spotted in the water in a small survival raft quickly changed the equation. With the Jayhawk minutes away and homing in on the C130's coordinates for the rescue, the Juneau-bound lieutenant commander glued himself to the telephone link with Kodiak.

"The chopper has two survivors aboard, a male and a female, semi-responsive, both in exposure suits and both extremely hypothermic with extent of injuries unknown. We're stabilizing and transporting to Anchorage Providence immediately."

SEATTLE, WASHINGTON

Gracie O'Brien thanked her senior partner profusely when he relayed the flash from Coast Guard headquarters and then dialed the Kodiak, Alaska, phone number he'd passed to her. She felt her heart pounding as she waited. Rachel and Arlie Rosen were family. She'd practically grown up in their home.

The duty officer answered and she fired a rapid string of questions at him, hurriedly taking down the vital information and confirming the names.

"What happened to their plane?"

"We don't know. All we're sure of is that they're both semi-conscious, they were found in a life raft and wearing exposure suits, and they had to be lifted out of the water in rescue baskets. But there've been no reports of aircraft wreckage or debris in the water."

"You say they're hypothermic? They're both going to make it, aren't they?"

"Well . . . I can't give you a diagnosis, ma'am. There was some mention of possible back injury to the male."

"Back injury? Was the word 'paralysis' used?"

"Well, I don't know. There's been a lot of radio conversation, ma'am. No one's going to know anything until they get to the hospital."

"But, you do think they're stable enough to make it?"

There was a deadly silence on the other end of the line.

"Lieutenant, are you still there?"

"Ma'am, you're kind of putting me in a corner here. I really can't tell you anything more of substance."

Gracie took a deep breath. "I see."

"Those are cold waters out there, and if they were in a plane crash, that inevitably involves a lot of force and impact. Best just to say that we found them alive, and beyond that, I don't know."

She thanked him and disconnected, rolling the right words around in her head. She'd always been a terrible liar, and April could usually tell in a second when she was leaving something out or coloring reality. Gracie jabbed at the speed-dial button for April's Vancouver condo and repeated the primary details as fast as she could when April answered.

"Oh my *God!*" April gasped. "Are they hurt? How bad?"

"They're going to be okay, April, but they lost the plane and they've been in freezing waters for a couple of hours. They evidently had time to get into exposure suits and blow up a raft, so that's something. The Coast Guard says they're being flown directly to Providence Hospital and should be touching down any minute. April? You okay?"

"Yes," a tiny voice replied.

"Okay, I'll call your brothers. Have you talked to them?"

"Yes. I talked with Dean and left a message for Sam. Sam's in Phoenix or somewhere."

"I'll call his cell phone. Are you dressed?"

"Huh?"

"Focus, April. Are you wearing anything but a stunned expression?"

"Ah, no. I mean . . . I'm not dressed."

"Then put on some clothes, throw a toothbrush and your emergency face kit in a bag, catch the taxi I'm going to order, and head for Vancouver International. Call me from the cab as soon as the driver pulls away from your building."

"Okay. Oh, Lord, Gracie! They *crashed?*"

"Your folks are going to need you there in Anchorage as soon as possible. I . . . can't come immediately. I'm under the gun here."

"That's okay."

"I'll arrange a ticket and send the cab. Can you be downstairs in ten minutes?"

"Yes."

"Hey, kiddo, they'll be okay. Pull yourself together."

"I'm together, Gracie. Really. Thank you. Let me ring off and get dressed."

Gracie replaced the receiver and thought in silence for a few seconds, her mind constructing dark conclusions about the physical condition of Arlie and Rachel Rosen. Had he said paralysis, or had she?

Dear God, let them be whole and intact!

Gracie forced herself to yank up the receiver and start punching in numbers. She had to scramble a cab to pick up April and get her an immediate flight to Anchorage.

INBOUND TO ANCHORAGE

The past few hours of Arlie Rosen's life had passed like a strange dream. There had been helicopters and cold, stinging ocean spray, and when he'd tried to turn over and go back to sleep, the dream got more intense with shouting and flying baskets and hands pulling at him. Now a new sensation was coursing through part of him, pins and needles and an icy hot feeling amid the cacophonous noise of an engine, which he finally decided must be real.

The dream had something to do with his aircraft, but what it was, wasn't clear. He wondered if Rachel would roll her eyes at the bizarre nature of the story when he told her about it in the morning.

Rachel!

Wait . . . wasn't she in bed next to him? Was he home? No, home wasn't that loud, or cold. He recalled being very cold, and she was, too. He should ask her . . . if he could just roll over and hold her.

But rolling over seemed strangely difficult. His body wouldn't respond.

Arlie forced his eyes open and looked to the left, past the hovering face of someone in an orange flight suit. Strange. Why would he dream about an orange flight suit? This dream was getting really weird, and he could see Rachel lying down a few feet away with people hovering over her, too.

"Rachel?" Arlie was pretty sure he had called her name, but he hadn't heard his voice. Yet Rachel was moving her head and looking in his direction.

That's okay then, he concluded, trying to smile back at her as he drifted off to sleep just as the door to the helicopter was yanked open by a waiting team of med techs.

FIVE

Major General Mac MacAdams had listened for twenty minutes to an unctuous presentation by Joe Davis on why the central feature of Project Skyhook, the so-called "Boomerang Box," was ready for Air Force acceptance.

"Joe, let's cut to the heart of the matter here, okay?" Mac interrupted.

"Certainly, General."

"You and your folks do a great production number, you know. Great graphics, video, sound, and fury. All that's missing is a soft-shoe routine with top hats, and, of course, a truly functional system I can approve."

"Sir?" Davis looked alarmed, and Mac smiled at his discomfort and sat forward.

"Joe, for God's sake, don't you think I've been around this business awhile?"

Davis sat back in his swivel chair on the other side of the boardroom, his feigned confidence rapidly leaking away.

"Well, of course I know you're a very experienced guy . . ."

"Joe, look at me. Cut the bullshit, okay? When I made brigadier general and a four-star pinned on *my* star, he shook my hand and said, 'Congratulations, General MacAdams, no one will ever tell you the truth again.' I've always been determined not to accept that tendency on the part of subordinates, and I'm sure as hell not going to accept it from a contractor I need to be able to trust, okay?"

"Yes, sir," Joe Davis replied, his face a fine shade of gray.

"Something happened last night that threatens this entire project, and you're not going to happy talk your way out of it. You know it. I know it. Your guys on the Gulfstream know it, and in fact I imagine they're working themselves into a frenzy right now trying to solve the problem. Right?"

"Well, yes, they're working on it."

"We nearly lost those boys last night, Joe. If nothing else had worked and that Gulfstream had slammed into a supertanker, we'd be facing another version of the *Exxon Valdez*." He decided to bypass the fact that two sidewinder missiles had been seconds away from launch on his command. "If that had happened, Skyhook and Uniwave would be history, and my career would be history, just to name the threshold victims."

Joe Davis took a deep breath and nodded. "I know that, Mac. I was really scared when they couldn't disconnect, but it was . . ."

"And I hear you about the bad circuit board. That was the initial problem. You've made that point. And I know your guys are out there at the Gulfstream right now on the ramp trying to add a second disconnect circuit in case something strange happens again tonight. But, Joe, there are no emergency disconnects in the Boomerang design. This little box is supposed to bring back a B-52 or even a B-2 if the pilots on board can't, or won't, do it themselves. We don't want a way for anyone on board to disconnect. That's part of the main safety logic, in case someone ever goes nuts up there. You *know* the reasons for this black project, for God's sake."

"Of course I do."

"We're not installing an emergency disconnect on the actual

deployed system, and if we need one to buttress the test, then the test fails."

"But, Mac, it's a safety issue."

"Absolutely. No, go ahead and install it tonight, but understand that if you use it, the test is over."

Davis was trying to hide the fact that his hands were shaking slightly and his voice had become raspy with stress. The two other Uniwave project employees in the room were sitting in shocked silence, and trying to look invisible.

Mac MacAdams thrust himself out of the chair and turned to the far end of the carpeted, secure meeting room, his lean, uniformed, six-foot frame towering over the much shorter Davis.

There were framed pictures on the walls, Mac noted. He'd never really noticed them before, but they were the type of evocative aviation images that stirred the heart of a pilot on a primal level. Mac let his eyes rest on one for a few moments, following the amazing vortex of disturbed water trailing a low-flying B-1 in terrain-following mode buzzing a lake, an image painted so realistically it looked like a photo.

"Joe," he began, still facing the wall before turning back to the project director. "Here's the deal. You either lay all the company's cards on the table right here, right now, or I'll almost guarantee you non-acceptance. Understood?"

Davis's hands were out in a beseeching gesture. "Mac, please! I'm trying to level with you."

"Really? Then explain to me where in that presentation anything was mentioned about the possibility of a logic glitch in the program? Why'd the system drive that Gulfstream down to precisely fifty feet and hold it there, Joe? You think I'm an idiot? That's not hardware, that's software, and we're not going to waste each other's time explaining why we both know that. Look, I'm not unsympathetic to your position. I'm interested in keeping our major defense contractors healthy, and I'm certainly aware that you're hanging by a thread as a company with this project. But what happened last night is not as simple as you're trying to make it. So, either I get answers by six P.M. this evening, or the acceptance test is off until next Monday at the earliest, and you're into contract penalty territory."

"Six?" Joe Davis looked as if he'd just been handed a death sentence.

"I'll see you back here, in this room, at six sharp. And, Joe, have Dr. Cole in here as well as the two Gulfstream pilots."

"Dr. Cole isn't going to fly tonight's test."

"Why not?"

"Ah . . . scheduling conflict, I think."

MacAdams straightened and pointed toward the table. "Have him in here, Joe. That's not an option." He turned and swept out of the room before Davis could reply.

ELMENDORF AFB RECREATION AREA

Ben Cole slowed his pace along the jogging path overlooking Runway 05 and cocked his ear, trying to identify the extra sound rising above the roar of a departing F-15. As the waves of noise from the powerful engines subsided, an electronic warble pulsed into prominence and he stopped to dig out his cell phone and check his message.

"Don't bother," a female voice said from a few yards behind. Ben turned, startled to see Lindsey White, his immediate supervisor under Joe Davis, approaching down the path. "The message is from me asking where I could find you."

"Lindsey! I guess you can find me here." He glanced at the very same words on the screen and put the phone away, aware that the grey and white fur parka she was wearing had nothing to do with exercising. "I take it you're not joining me for a run."

She smiled and shook her head as she came up beside him and tossed back her shoulder-length hair. "My policy is to run only when being chased."

He smiled briefly and motioned toward the north. "Can we walk?"

"Sure."

They began moving down the north path in silence before Lindsey spoke.

"You weren't planning on obeying orders and staying home tonight, were you?"

He glanced over at her, but she was watching the path. "No. I know the system better than anyone, and . . . it's my responsibility."

"But, you're nervous?"

He looked at her again, this time waiting until she met his gaze. "Lindsey, I'm terrified."

"We shouldn't be talking out here in the open about a black project, so minimize your lip movements and keep your voice very low," she said, brushing lightly against his side. "You know they're installing a second emergency disconnect switch?"

"Yes, which is still dependent on the computer. It'll only work if . . ." His voice trailed off.

"If what?" she prompted.

He leaned toward her slightly as they walked, wondering if there really was surveillance equipment sophisticated enough to intercept words spoken softly through stiff lips. "Lindsey, I've tried to tell everyone that whatever went wrong last night is more than a bad circuit board. It's somewhere in the software code, and if it happens again, remember that we've given this system a whole bunch of pathways to choose in taking over complete control of the airplane."

"Ben, wait," she said suddenly as she stopped him. "I'm not making a pass at you or issuing some sexual invitation, okay?"

"What?" he said, his voice sounding like a stammer.

She moved against him. "We've got to be very careful not to be caught talking in the open about this, so . . . this is merely a method of looking somewhat innocuous while whispering."

"What is?"

"Here," she said, taking his arm and pulling it to her waist. "Put your arm around me. Hold me close like we're two lovers walking along, and we'll alternately whisper in each other's ears."

"Oh. Okay." He complied, sheepishly at first, relishing the feel of her through the wolf-fur coat and forcing himself back to the subject. "As I was saying, Lindsey, what this system is all about is taking over complete control of the jet. So, until I've found the problem, we can't test it without running a huge risk. I left the team back there crunching numbers, but I had to get out here to think."

"I didn't track you down to scold you, Ben," she whispered, "but we've got a corporate mandate, and you're already planning to violate Martin's direct order. I figured that out when I couldn't find anyone preparing to fly tonight in your place."

He was shaking his head, then remembered to lean toward her ear. "I can't let anyone fly in my place, Lindsey. If anything happened, I could never live with someone who's taking my place getting hurt just because Martin doesn't understand."

She stopped and caught his shoulder, turning him toward her and studying his face. "My God, Ben. You really expect to die tonight, don't you?"

He turned away, but her grip was firm, and he finally met her eyes once more. "I . . . think there's a good chance."

"Look, if you're really that worried—"

"Lindsey, you ever have that dream where you're running from the monster but you can't seem to move?"

She nodded.

"Okay. This morning, Lindsey, with Martin telling me we've got to do it, regardless, and Joe scared to death of General MacAdams, I mean . . . it was obvious that no one was listening."

"I am, Ben."

"But, can you stop this?"

She pulled back and looked him in the eye again. "Convince me."

"Sorry?"

"Here. Sit." There was a wooden bench adjacent to the path and she guided him to it and sat backward, beside him, her left arm snaking around his chest, his left arm kept discreetly in his lap. He felt a jumble of conflicting instincts as she leaned her head to his shoulder, almost cheek to cheek, and chuckled. "We may start some serious boy-girl rumors around here, but you've got my undivided, nonjudgmental attention. Now, convince me."

On the adjacent runway and just out of view behind a row of trees, an Air Force C-141B pilot had run his engines to takeoff power and was beginning his takeoff roll, the rumble washing over them as Ben waited, enjoying her nearness.

"In a nutshell," he said at last, "the computer program leveled us at fifty feet because that corresponds to the difference between the actual and the standard barometric setting. In other words, if the altimeter setting had been precisely twenty-nine, ninety-two inches of mercury, we would have hit the water."

"So, you've found the glitch?"

"No. I just understand what the program's goal was. I don't know what part of the program came to that conclusion or how it set that goal, and that's where the danger lurks. The second the system was engaged, it began descending us. It wasn't a dive, Lindsey, it was a controlled descent, which means the program logic planned it. But how in the hell? I *wrote* that program, and there's nothing in it that would give it the power or the basis to make such a decision."

"But, the program can descend an airplane for landing."

"No, the program is supposed to keep the airplane safe while a live pilot using the remote cockpit makes all the decisions on altitude, airspeed, configuration, and everything else. This . . . this thing was thinking for itself! Now, how the hell can I find and cure *that* if I don't have a clue what I'm looking for?"

Lindsey fell silent for a few seconds.

"Ben, you're not telling me this program has written its own fuzzy logic, are you? You're not saying it's making decisions on its own?"

He shook his head and glanced up for a second before answering, tracking the progress of a golden eagle soaring effortlessly in the crisp air overhead. She heard a tired sigh in her ear. "I don't know what to think. Maybe . . . just maybe there's a garbled line of code in there that made it behave like it was coming up with its own solution, but I just don't know."

"We have four days to the deadline," she replied. "And the general has forced a meeting tonight at six where he'll be demanding a full explanation. If we slip the schedule for twenty-four hours, will it make a difference?"

He snorted and began to chuckle.

"What?" she probed, partially turning toward him, a move that nuzzled his neck and sent a small chill of pleasure up his back. Lindsey smiled involuntarily at the smell of his cologne in her nostrils. "Tell me."

"Well," he said, "it's like a warden asking the condemned if he'd like an extra day to give the governor more time to call. Yeah, an extra day would give me more of a chance to find a solution."

"Is there anything else we can do to make sure the unit can't crash the test plane?"

He nodded, partially turning toward her. "Yeah, but MacAdams will never approve it, and it would take some fancy jury-rigging of hardware."

"Meaning?"

"An emergency disconnect T-handle to physically pull the computer-controlled servos off the control cables. Otherwise, we're still at the mercy of the program."

Lindsey patted his shoulder before disengaging. She stood, then leaned back down, her lips to his ear. "Okay, Ben. Joe may fire me for this, but we're going to get you that extra day, and we're going to install that emergency T-handle before we fly."

"And if Martin says no?"

"We'll do it anyway. If you're too worried to fly, I'm too worried to let you."

He turned his head a bit too quickly, and his nose brushed hers. The tantalizing proximity caused him to look into her eyes for a second, wondering how she'd respond if he kissed her.

But she was already pulling away, smiling as she did so.

April Rosen closed her cell phone and tried to focus as the streets of Anchorage flew by essentially unseen. She was vaguely aware that the landmark Anchorage Hilton was in view in the distance, but her mind was already at Providence Hospital, as she recalled Gracie's words from the cell phone conversation when she'd stepped off the flight.

"There's a Dr. Swift, April. He's like a parrot saying 'fine, fine, fine, they're fine,' but he won't give details because my name isn't Rosen. So I think your mom and dad really are fine, but when you get there, give him a cracker and make him define the word in clinical detail."

"Okay," was all April could manage.

"April? Really, they're going to be okay. You got a grip?"

"I'm gripped," she'd replied with a small, forced laugh. The three-hour flight after the connection from Vancouver through Seattle had been an agony of worry and waiting, even though Gracie's unexpected appearance at the Seatac Airport gate had helped tremendously.

"I'm not here, you didn't see me. I'm actually at the office working my buns off in the law library," Gracie had instructed as she'd guided April to the outbound Alaska Airlines gate for the flight to Anchorage.

"How did you get out here to the gate to meet me without a ticket, Gracie? They don't let people out here anymore, do they?"

"I bought a ticket," Gracie had explained. "I'll cash it in later."

April looked up suddenly, realizing she was in Anchorage. The man behind the wheel glanced at her with concern. "Are you okay?" They were passing Chilkoot Charlie's and half a block evaporated before she completely returned to the present and looked at him. "I'm sorry?"

"I didn't mean to interrupt your thoughts. I just wondered if they'd told you anything about your folks. On the phone just then."

April shook her head as she looked at him, letting the image register. In the airport he had been just a needed male with a hand-printed sign bearing the name Rosen. But now his image coalesced into an athletic young man in his thirties, sandy hair, large, powerful hands lightly gripping the wheel, and big brown eyes watching her.

"You lift weights, don't you?" she asked, jolted by the stupidity of her question in light of her mission.

He merely smiled and looked sheepish. "Yeah. More in the winter to avoid terminal boredom."

"The answer is no," she said.

"I'm . . . sorry?" he replied.

She was shaking her head. "I can't get any details out of them other than that my mother and dad are stable. Hello? What the heck does 'stable' mean?"

"Actually, it means they're not in any serious danger and their condition is steady and not deteriorating."

The words brought her attention back to him. "You a doctor?"

"No. I was an emergency-med tech while in college."

"Oh."

"Ambulances, mainly."

"I want to thank you, by the way," she said, her eyes forward again. "I've been very rude just using your help and hardly even saying hello." Her voice was coming out flat and metered, as if she were in a daze, which, she thought, wasn't far from the truth. "I don't even recall your name, I'm embarrassed to say."

"That's okay, April. It's Kimo." He caught her puzzled expression and smiled.

"Kimo," she repeated. "Is that . . . Hawaiian?"

He laughed easily. "No, just an old family name. I'm part native."

"Well, Kimo . . . thank you very much."

"You're welcome," he said, dodging a large truck that had stopped too quickly in the middle of the roadway. "And no apologies are necessary. Gracie explained everything."

"How do you know Gracie?"

She watched him skillfully negotiate an icy corner before looking back at her. A large smile had spread over his face. "Gracie and I were classmates in law school at the University of Washington. She's . . . one incredible gal. We studied together, but she was just plain frightening, she was so sharp and . . . I don't know . . . energetic."

"Gracie is that, all right."

"I once called her a gerbil on steroids, and I think she kinda liked that."

"Did you two date?" April asked, trying to keep the conversation going as a shield against the incredible anxiety she was feeling. There was a roaring deep inside her yelling silently at him to step on it, and only her slightly forced questions were keeping it from bursting out as a scream.

Kimo chuckled. "Lord, I wish. Gracie's a beautiful, desirable woman. But . . . she was my study partner, and . . . we just kind of ended up platonic."

"Bummer," April managed as she spotted Providence ahead.

She heard him laugh softly. "You have no idea."

The entrance to the hospital slid up to her door and she threw him a quick smile and a thank-you, took the piece of paper with the

number of his cell phone, and bolted inside, almost daring someone
to stop her from going straight to room 312 East.

Arlie Rosen heard his daughter's voice before he could open his
eyes. He raised his hand in greeting as she came in and ran to hug
him, her face glistening with tears.

"Daddy! Thank God!"

"It's okay, baby. I'm okay."

She pulled away and looked him up and down, relieved to see him
shift his legs under the sheet.

"Everything's working, Dad? All your parts are still here?"

He smiled and nodded. "Yeah. If I recall, that was the first question your mom asked." He shifted position suddenly and winced.
"Ow. I gotta remember not to do that." There was a large butterfly
bandage on the right side of his forehead and she leaned over to
touch it carefully.

"What's this, Dad?"

"Just a scratch." His voice was low and slower than normal, she
noted, his pacing a bit leaden. An IV bag was at work, but she saw
no casts or traction devices.

"Where *is* Mom?" April asked, looking at the empty bed next to
him and feeling a momentary panic until she remembered he'd already referred to Rachel in the present. Arlie focused on the question and waved away her flash of fear.

"She's fine. They just took her down for an X ray, but she's in better shape than I am. Don't worry."

April blinked back tears of relief and held her father's hand as a
nurse slipped quietly into the room and introduced herself.

"Would you like to speak with your parents' doctor, Ms. Rosen?
Miss O'Brien said you would."

April followed her out to the corridor, where a tired-looking,
silver-haired physician was working on a set of charts. He put his pen
down and turned, offering his hand at the nurse's introduction.

"They're still thawing out," Dr. Swift explained, "but all signs are
stable. Your dad has a nasty contusion on his forehead and, I suspect,

a light concussion. Your mom may just have a few bruises, but that's it. They were very lucky. When the chopper crew started warming them up, their body temperatures were in the upper eighties. There wasn't much time left."

The memory of the abortive search request to the Coast Guard officer in Juneau a dozen hours before replayed in April's head.

If Gracie hadn't been successful, she thought, *they would have died.*

"When can they go home?" April asked, slowly regaining her balance.

He shrugged. "Contrary to popular belief, we don't kick everyone out instantly. I'd say tomorrow morning, if they're feeling up to it. I would prefer to keep them overnight because of the head bumps and hypothermia."

She thanked him and started to turn when he stopped her. "Oh, Ms. Rosen? Your friend Gracie has called me several times from Seattle."

"Several?" April said, grinning at him.

"Okay, about ten times. She's my new best friend, and persistent enough to be a head nurse. I think she wants a call from you when possible."

April thanked him and punched in Gracie's number on her cell phone, handing it to her father as she returned to his bedside. He initiated the speakerphone function and placed the phone on his chest.

"Gracie! How's my favorite surrogate daughter?"

"Well, *I'm* fine, Captain R, but how the heck are you and Rachel? And what happened? You two scared us to death."

Arlie chuckled, taking time to breathe before answering. April sensed motion and looked over to see two men, one in a business suit, the other more casually dressed, standing uncomfortably just inside the door.

"Gracie," Arlie was saying, "I haven't had time to go over this with April yet, but . . . we lost the Albatross somehow."

"I'm so sorry, Captain," Gracie replied, as April got to her feet and covered the small distance to the two men. "May I help you?"

April asked, already aware that the taller of the two, a man in his early thirties, was fumbling with something that looked like a wallet. The leather case opened, and she read the words "National Transportation Safety Board" before realizing that the other man was holding up a similar wallet with the familiar logo of the Federal Aviation Administration.

"George Mikulsky, NTSB field investigator for Alaska," the young man was saying. She took his offered hand without enthusiasm, acutely aware that her father's voice was filling the room as he began to describe the accident to Gracie.

The FAA inspector appeared to be in his fifties and humorless, a severe expression on his face. He offered his hand as well. "I'm Walter Harrison," he said, without changing expression.

"Gentlemen, let's step out in the corridor and give my father some privacy for a few seconds here," April said, ushering them out and pulling the door closed behind her, muting Arlie's words. "What can I—can we—help you with?"

Mikulsky and Harrison glanced at each other without expression before the NTSB investigator broke the brief silence.

"Well, there's apparently been an aviation accident here involving your father and mother, and the loss of their aircraft, and the NTSB is required to investigate all air accidents."

"I'm aware of that," April replied, her voice flat and cautious, her demeanor automatically protective. "And you want to interview my father, right?"

"Yes, ma'am. Dr. Swift said he was physically able to be interviewed."

"This is a routine thing, Miss Rosen," Harrison added a bit too forcefully.

"You know, I just got here myself," April said. "I've hardly had time to hug him, and I haven't even seen my mom yet. Couldn't this wait?"

Harrison was shaking his head as Mikulsky answered. "If he was physically unable to talk to us, of course it could, but we've got some basic questions we need to have answered, and the sooner the better.

After all, this involved a major Coast Guard search-and-rescue operation. We'd appreciate your cooperation."

April glanced at the nurses' station, sharing a brief nod with the nurse who had first greeted her before turning back to the two men.

"Okay, you know what? Let me go talk to my dad for a few minutes and make sure he feels up to it. I shouldn't be making the decision for him."

"We'll wait out here," Harrison replied.

She pushed open the door and let it close behind her, waiting for a lull in the conversation between her father and Gracie.

"Dad . . . Gracie, hold it a second," April interjected, explaining who was waiting and what they wanted to do.

"I should be there," Gracie said immediately from Seattle.

"Why, Gracie?" Arlie asked.

"It's the feds, complete with enforcement authority, Captain, that's why. Maybe we should call the Air Line Pilots Association to send someone."

"It's not an airline matter, Gracie, and I didn't do anything wrong. So, hey, it's our government, and I pay most of their salaries, so I'll talk to them."

"Ho-kay, Captain. But if you need me, I'm right here. And if they ask you when you stopped beating Rachel, clam up and call me."

Arlie chuckled. "I'm sure it will be just a pro forma thing, Gracie. But I appreciate your being cautious."

"April, you there?" Gracie asked.

April turned off the speakerphone and pulled the cell phone to her ear. "Yeah."

"Monitor that interview, lady, and cut it off if there's anything you don't like in their tone. Take notes, too."

"Should I tell them to go away?"

"No, that just antagonizes. I just don't trust the FAA to be fair."

"That's an awful commentary."

"I know. And it was your dad who taught me that."

SEVEN

TUESDAY, DAY 2

PROVIDENCE ALASKA MEDICAL CENTER, ANCHORAGE

The fact that George Mikulsky of the NTSB had produced a small tape recorder and asked permission to tape the interview prompted April to pull a tiny five-hour digital recorder from her purse and do the same, a move that sparked a clear flash of anger from the FAA inspector.

"Do you object to my recording the interview?" April asked Harrison. "Especially since you're recording it, too."

The FAA inspector forced his expression back to neutral.

"No. Not a problem. No reason you shouldn't," he said, his conciliatory tone too forced.

They gathered in the hospital room with Harrison and Mikulsky sitting on gray metal chairs by the right side of Arlie Rosen's bed, and April sitting on the other side. Both men had shaken hands with Arlie before sitting, Mikulsky making more of an effort to smile and be friendly.

"Okay, Captain Rosen," George Mikulsky began, "this is not a deposition, it's an informal interview, but it is on the record, which is why I'm recording it, with your permission. Now, would you just take us through what you recall of last night, beginning with take-off, and including route, altitude, flight plan, radio calls, et cetera."

"I'll do my best, fellows. I'm still pretty fuzzy."

"Your plane's tail number was November Three Four Delta Delta, correct?"

"Yes."

"And it was current on all airworthiness certificates, inspections, airworthiness directive items?"

"She certainly was. I'm also a licensed A and P mechanic. All logs are current, but they're in the plane—wherever it is."

Mikulsky made a note and nodded. "Sorry, Captain. Go ahead. How did the flight start?"

Arlie described a routine takeoff from the smooth surface of Anchorage's Lake Hood, just north of Anchorage International Airport. He remembered a lazy climb to six thousand feet as they flew down the channel known as Turnagain Arm and crossed a low ridge of mountains to fly over Whittier and out to sea.

"It was dusk, and my intention was to make Sitka, and the weather report was favorable for visual flight. In other words, clearly VFR. That was true until we were about sixty miles east of Whittier. Then I had to start descending and cutting more to the south over Montague Island on more or less a direct GPS course toward Middleton Island in order to avoid the cloud layers lying more to the north. Once we'd cleared Montague, I decided to keep stepping down over the water until we were cruising at a thousand feet. I've got a great . . . had a great moving map GPS, so I knew we were clear of any land. But by the time we'd passed Middleton, I realized we were in a sort of trap, and I told Rachel this wasn't going to work and began trying to raise Anchorage Center for a pop-up instrument clearance."

"You're instrument-rated?" Mikulsky asked, drawing a puzzled frown.

"You're asking if I'm instrument-rated?" Arlie replied incredulously.

"Yes, I believe that's what I asked you," Mikulsky said, a slightly officious tone bleeding into his words.

Arlie chuckled. "Son, I'm a Boeing 747 captain for a major airline, with thirty thousand hours and an airline transport pilot rating. Last time I checked, you couldn't get an ATP without having an instrument ticket."

"Oh. Yeah," George Mikulsky said, his face reddening.

"How long have you been with the NTSB, George?" Arlie asked.

April could feel the rising tension in the room as the inspector shifted in his chair and Mikulsky drew back. "I've been with NTSB for four months now."

"Are you a licensed pilot?"

"Captain Rosen, why don't you let me ask the questions here?" Mikulsky said, his voice taut.

Arlie smiled the characteristic smile Gracie always described as irresistible. He readjusted himself on the bed as if girding for a small battle before replying. "George, the reason I asked you that question is because there are certain things I need to explain in more detail if you're not a pilot than I would need to explain if you were. I'm sorry you take offense at the question."

"No, I'm not a pilot yet, but that doesn't matter," Mikulsky snapped, making an exaggerated note before continuing. "I'll tell you if I'm unfamiliar with something. Let's please get back to your narrative."

April and Arlie exchanged a cautionary glance.

"Okay," Arlie said, resuming the narrative. "I'm at a thousand feet, I'm not getting a response from Anchorage Center, the clouds are getting lower ahead, and it's almost dark. I've only got a few coastal lights way off to my left, and I have only one choice left other than turning around, and that is to pull out my satellite phone and try to call Anchorage Flight Service by phone. But the visibility is deteriorating too fast, so I told Rachel we'd better turn around and divert back to the northwest into Valdez, and she agreed. I—"

"You had your sectional maps out and available?" Walter Harrison asked, interrupting.

"Yes," Arlie replied carefully, fixing Harrison with a none-too-friendly look. "I characteristically use maps when I go flying, in addition to my dash-mounted moving map GPS system, and my backup handheld GPS. Do you want me to list the charts?"

Harrison quickly shook his head no.

"Very well. I punched Valdez into both GPS units, which gave me a course of something like three three zero, which won't work because of the mountains, so I headed northwest to fly up the channel and decided I was safe for about ten miles north before I'd have to either climb in clear conditions, or turn back to the west toward Anchorage to stay visual. Just to make sure I had the required clearance below the clouds, and since I was over open water, I descended to a hundred feet on the radio altimeter. The sea state was fairly choppy. I'd estimate the waves at five to seven feet, and I didn't want to land in rough conditions like that in open water."

"You could still see?" Mikulsky asked.

"Yes. It was still dusk, and I was in the clear beneath the cloud layer. That's why I could see the waves below. This is open ocean, you understand, in international waters."

"Okay."

"So, we're motoring along on a course of about two hundred ninety degrees and it looked a bit clearer to the right, so I came right to about three-twenty, and we're getting close to the decision point, with a cloud deck still overhead, when all hell broke loose for no apparent reason."

"How much fuel did you have?"

"Nine hours', George. Fuel's not an issue here."

"Okay."

"I'm holding the controls steady at a hundred feet and a hundred forty miles per hour when I unexpectedly run into a fog bank that seemed to come out of nowhere. Everything goes gray outside and I, of course, transition to the instruments and am just starting to climb and turn around to get out of it when there's this loud metallic snap, or clang, or something, and I lose a prop blade on the right side. At least, that's what it felt like, because the ship instantly starts shaking, which it would with a missing prop blade. Not only that, it must have just missed the cockpit as it broke away, because there's this incredible whooshing noise along with this instant, horrible shaking."

April watched her father as he spoke, his eyes far away, his mind reliving that terrible moment as he talked.

"The controls suddenly feel like they're going to beat me to death, they're shaking and rattling so bad. Only a split second has passed, but it's clear I'm going to be fighting for our lives. The old girl heaves to the right, and I yank the yoke back to the left and hit the left rudder, working to maintain my instrument scan at the same moment the right engine comes off its mounts. Somehow there's a huge ball of flame on the right, probably from a breached fuel tank. I figure we'll explode before I lose control, but there's just this raging orange glow. I yank the feather knob for number-two engine and try to get the fuel cut off as Rachel yelps and turns to look. 'We're on fire!' she reports to me like she's trained to do, and I'm thinking it's damned lucky she's a pilot, too. I don't need panic at a moment like this, I need all my efforts to keep the airplane in the air and level, which is getting to be a real challenge. I goose the left engine up to max power and I've got almost full left rudder, when we hit something . . . I don't know . . . probably low-level mechanical turbulence off the mainland several miles to the northwest. Whatever it is, it's the last thing I need because it just flips us to the right like a toy, despite full left aileron and full left rudder. I'm just hanging there in an impossible position with ninety degrees of bank and no lift, for just a heartbeat, but it's enough to lose most of my hundred feet of altitude. I've almost got her back to wings level when the right wing or the right pontoon digs into the waves, and I can't pull her out. Suddenly we're cartwheeling and there's water and cold and screaming metal and the most amazing noises. When the motion stops, I'm still conscious, and, incredibly, there are still lights glowing in the cockpit, although we're filling with water. I look to the right to find

Rachel, and thank God, she's conscious, too, and wide-eyed and working to release my harness. It's obvious the bird is sinking, not floating. I mean, I've got cold water to my knees. Somehow Rachel gets herself and me out of the seat belts and opens the hatch in the top of the cockpit, and we swim out just as the bird goes down."

"You mean, sinks?" Mikulsky asked.

Arlie nodded. "I can tell you, the icy cold of that water is beyond description. We were both instantly wide awake. And there was another small miracle: One of the emergency life rafts had apparently worked as it was designed to do and popped out of the wing locker I'd engineered. The raft came up right next to us, and we pulled ourselves in and got the survival kit aboard—I bought the kind with the survival suits—and we somehow wiggled into them, soaking wet and freezing. I tried to find the emergency radio, but we were struggling and thrashing around so wildly to get the suits on, my guess is I knocked the damn radio overboard. The wind was cutting, the waves were mountainous . . . much higher than I expected . . . with the spray blowing everywhere. The wind . . . my God, the wind was howling like a monster, and I remember thinking that the satellites would at least pick up our ELT, emergency locator beacon, within ninety minutes. I could hang onto that, you know? I just assumed the ELT was working, but I didn't know for sure. I did know that we were okay for a while in the survival suits, but then, we got them on while wet and cold, and I knew we couldn't hold out indefinitely. I tied a line between Rachel and myself to make sure we didn't get separated. I told her our ELT would bring help fast, but the night got deeper, the fog got thicker, and we tried to huddle together and maintain warmth, but we were both shaking so hard and getting numb, and then . . . then there were a bunch of weird dreams, and I guess now that some of them may have been the helicopter picking us up."

Arlie stopped talking and looked at the two men, who were sitting transfixed and breathing hard.

George Mikulsky suddenly realized the narrative had ended. His body jerked slightly as he sat up. "Ah . . . okay. The emergency transmitter. The emergency transmitter beacon was never picked up, Captain."

"Really?" Arlie responded. "Then how . . ."

"The tracking unit, Dad," April said. "It dutifully sent me your position just before you went in. When I woke up, I checked my computer readout and realized you'd never arrived anywhere. The tracking unit saved you."

"Mr. Rosen," Walter Harrison began.

Mikulsky turned to the FAA inspector and held up an index finger. "Captain Rosen," he corrected, flinching slightly at the murderous look Harrison flashed at him.

"Very well, *Captain* Rosen," Harrison continued, "let's talk about the absence of a flight plan, your weather briefing, and your altitude."

"Excuse me, but I filed a visual flight plan with Anchorage Flight Service by cell phone before departure."

Harrison had been leaning forward in the spartan metal chair. He sat up with an expression of extreme skepticism. "Did you, now?"

"Yes."

"Well, did they acknowledge that it had been filed?"

It was Arlie Rosen's turn to cock his head in disbelief as he looked at Harrison in silence and cleared his throat. "Mr. Harrison, when a senior airman tells you he's filed a flight plan, visual or instrument, it's usually a pretty good bet he knows the difference between just discussing it and filing it. You're not talking to a student pilot here. Yes, I got confirmation verbally. That's how we do it."

"I'm well aware of the procedures, since I helped write them," Harrison snapped back. "Point is, Captain, there was no flight plan in the computer at Anchorage Flight Service. There's no record you even called them."

"I assume you searched for not only our tail number, but under any other possible variations in the number in case the briefer made a mistake entering it? You do realize, don't you, that they don't list their calls in the computer by pilot name?"

Harrison ignored the verbal slap. "There was no flight plan in the computer, Captain, which is why no one missed you until your daughter figured something was wrong."

April had been listening to the exchange with rising alarm. Mikulsky's extremely stiff questioning had been bad enough, but Harrison was openly hostile. April rose to her feet and noisily scooted her chair back to interrupt.

"Okay, Mr. Harrison, you know what? My father's just been brought in from a near-death experience, and if you can't even question him with respect, I think we'd better end this."

"That's okay, honey," Arlie said as he gestured to April to sit. "Mr. Harrison is an FAA inspector, and it's his job to be openly skeptical to the point of perceived hostility. Right, Walter?"

Harrison had been doing a slow burn in silence. He made a small snorting sound and shook his head. "I do not attempt to be purposely skeptical, Ms. Rosen," he said, glancing suddenly at April, then back at Arlie. "Nor am I hostile. But a fact is a fact, Captain, and the fact is that whatever calls you say you made, they do not show up on the record, and Anchorage had no flight plan on you."

"Which, if true, would mean a major failure on their part," Arlie interjected. "Which, by the way, is anything but unprecedented. Flight service stations lose flight plans every day, and you know it. And that's aside from the fact that, as you also well know, a VFR flight plan is not required, merely recommended. I always file one if I'm not going on instruments. Always. No exceptions."

"When you're flying privately, Captain, and you don't have an airline dispatcher to do things for you, do you often depart without a weather briefing?"

April was on her feet again. "Okay, that's it. The interview's over."

Arlie turned to April and shook his head slightly. "Honey . . ."

April froze, reading her father's resolve, then nodded reluctantly but remained standing.

"Now, Walter," Arlie began again, "before you get your knickers in a knot over this flawed assumption, I would assume you're aware that cell phone companies keep records, too. Have you bothered to check to see whether there's a record of a call to flight service, which there will be?"

"No."

"Well, perhaps you'll want to be judicious enough to stand down on your tone and your very hostile attitude until you do. Fact is, I got my weather briefing, filed my visual flight plan in great detail, and followed all the FAR's and normal procedures."

"And you lost your aircraft because you lost a propeller while dragging the waves at less than a hundred feet."

Arlie Rosen took a deep breath. April could see his jaw muscles twitching as he tried to maintain control of his temper, which was approaching his personal red line.

"Walter—"

"Excuse me," Harrison interrupted with a snort, "I'm doing *you* the courtesy of using your formal airline title. Kindly do *me* the courtesy of calling me Mr. Harrison. You don't know me, and I resent first name usage."

George Mikulsky shifted uncomfortably in his chair, wondering how to regain control, but Harrison was ignoring him.

"Why don't I just call you *Inspector* Harrison, then?" Arlie asked, as sarcastically as he could manage. "Or would you prefer 'Your Excellency'?"

"Mister will do fine. Here's what I want you to answer. You say you kept dropping lower to stay in visual conditions. You were operating under part ninety-one of the Federal Air Regulations, right?"

"Yes."

"Okay. So how far above you were those clouds, Captain? I assume you know the regulations for visual flight."

"The clouds were more than the required five hundred feet above me," Arlie shot back, his voice hardening. "And, yes, I know the regs, as I'm sure you do, *Inspector* Harrison. Under FAR part ninety-one point one fifty-five, the rules for visual operation are that the requirement for cloud clearance when flying in visual conditions at or below twelve hundred feet is a minimum of five hundred feet below, one thousand feet above, and two thousand feet lateral clearance, with a nighttime visibility requirement a minimum of three statute miles, all under the new Class G airspace. I miss anything?"

"No . . . other than how it was that you could have been so close to the water in deteriorating conditions and still think you were in compliance with the FARs when it was dark and you admit you couldn't see anything."

"*What?* I certainly did not admit—or say—that I couldn't see anything, until I entered that fog bank at the last second. That was unanticipated. I had full legal visibility until then."

"Well, Captain," Harrison continued, "you say you think you lost a propeller blade, but isn't it possible the clouds were just pressing you down and you kept descending and didn't realize how low you were until you dug a wing into the water?"

"Hell, no!" Arlie Rosen snapped upright in the bed, wincing at the pain in his head as he fixed the FAA inspector with his eyes and leveled a slightly shaking finger at him. "Get this straight, Harrison. I was doing precisely what I said I was doing, where, when, why, and how I said I was doing it! Who the hell do you think you are to come in here and throw some cockamamy accusation at me without the slightest foundation to back it up?"

Harrison chuckled and began closing the small steno pad he'd been holding. There were no notes on the page.

"Good offense is always the best defense, eh, Rosen? Don't worry. I'll get the facts if you were scud-hopping, as I believe you were."

"*Scud*-hopping?"

"I've seen it a thousand times. Overly cocky airline pilot in a private plane pushing the visual limits. You were in a seaplane, after all, and the FAA's nowhere around, and you want to get to your destination, and you don't give a damn how low the clouds overhead are as long as you can stay airborne and see the water below."

"That is absolutely not true! Not to mention the fact that if you're so damned experienced, you know that pilots who do that do it because they aren't instrument-rated and have no alternatives. I had an alternative!"

"Yeah, well, I understand you have to cook up a good cover story for your insurance company, but it won't wash with the FAA."

"What?" Arlie said, his face reflecting shock.

April moved toward the bed and into the line of fire between her father and the FAA inspector, her palm out to the man in a stop gesture. "That's enough out of you, sir! Get the hell out of this hospital room."

"Miss Rosen, I wasn't talking to you," Harrison replied, his eyes on Arlie.

"You watch your tone with my daughter, buster," Arlie said. "And, like she said, get the hell out of here."

George Mikulsky had stood up in obvious confusion, his eyes wide as he tried to figure out how to disengage himself as quickly as possible from the extreme discomfort of the mess his FAA companion had made of the interview. But Harrison moved to the end of Arlie's bed, physically blocking Mikulsky, his finger leveled at Arlie Rosen.

"Hey, chew on this, *Captain* Rosen. I don't give a damn how big an aircraft you fly or how many hours you've logged sitting in an overstuffed armchair eating first-class meals and pretending it's real pilot time, nor do I care about your obscenely inflated paycheck. But here's a news flash, hotshot. You still have to comply with the rules, or we take your license away. And you want to know what I think?"

Arlie shook his head. "Not bloody likely, asshole!"

"Dad . . ." April cautioned, but it was obviously too late.

"Yeah, good, let's start with the name calling," Harrison sneered. "Very mature response for a thirty-thousand-hour cappie making five times what he's worth."

"Five times . . . Okay, you rancid, pontificating little windbag. This is a jealousy thing with you, isn't it? What the hell happened, United turn you down for a pilot job twenty years ago, so you joined the FAA?"

There was a momentary waver in Harrison's expression, but he stifled it quickly. "I looked up your records, Rosen. You're an alcoholic. You were drinking, weren't you?"

"WHAT?!" Arlie yelped.

"I understand you were in United's alcoholic program a few years back."

"That was ten years ago, and I honorably completed that program!"

Harrison walked toward the door, turning back as he opened it.

"Oh, I'm sure you filled all the squares, Rosen. But we all know there are dropouts. It's painfully obvious you were flying that Albatross last night drunk as a skunk and scud-hopping to boot. When I find the proof that you were drinking and flying—and I will—we'll get your reckless tail permanently grounded." Harrison moved through the door, his back turned.

"Come back here you little son of a bitch!" Arlie bellowed at Harrison as he tried to swing out of bed and found his legs trapped by the tightly tucked sheets. "I'm *gonna have your ass fired, Harrison!*" he yelled through the door at Harrison's back as George Mikulsky retreated after him.

"Dad! Calm down!"

"Goddammit! *Goddammit!*" He was shaking with fury, his face beet red.

"That's not helping!"

"I *can't believe* that little shit! THAT WAS OUTRAGEOUS!"

"Dad! Your language is outrageous!"

"Where's the damned phone? Get me that phone, April. I'm gonna call the entire congressional delegation and have that bastard cashiered!"

"Dad! Take a deep breath and think this through."

"What? Why?"

"You told me yourself, never antagonize an FAA inspector."

"*Me* antagonize? You were right here!"

"Dad, please!"

The door was opening again and the noise riveted Arlie's attention as he tensed for another round, but a wheelchair entered instead with Rachel Rosen aboard.

"Mom!" April said as she ran to hug her. Rachel returned the hug, her eyes on the murderous look in her husband's eyes.

"What's going on here?"

"It's . . ." April began, but Arlie blurted out the basics of the acidic exchange with the FAA.

"Good grief, Arlie, they control your license!" Rachel said.

"Dammit, you think I don't know that?" he replied through gritted teeth.

Rachel left the wheelchair and walked somewhat unsteadily to her husband's side, gathering him to her breast until he hugged her back and stopped snarling.

April watched the seamless move with admiration. Her mother always knew precisely what to do to calm him down, while issuing orders with a flick of her eyes, which she did now in April's direction. April understood instantly. Rachel wanted a sedative for her husband and a strategy session in the corridor as soon as possible. Damage control was obviously going to be necessary, and April silently raised her cell phone and mouthed "Gracie," eliciting an affirmative nod from her mother.

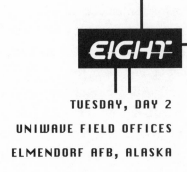

Lindsey White struggled to hide the fact that her stomach was churning and concentrated instead on the neatly arranged bric-a-brac adorning Joe Davis's impeccable desk. She hated confrontations, and it had been difficult to maintain the facade of rock-solid conviction as he ranted, begged, bullied, and finally whined against the news that tonight's acceptance test flight had to be canceled.

At last he ran out of words and plopped himself back in his suitably impressive desk chair with a look of defeat.

Almost.

"Lindsey, how can you sit there for . . . for five minutes—"

"Ten."

"Okay, ten minutes, then, and say absolutely nothing?"

"You were doing the talking."

"Well, hell. I had to. Somebody has to talk or it's not a conversation."

She shook her head.

"There," he said, coming forward in his chair and pointing at her with his index finger as he sighted along it with one eye. "You're doing it again."

"What?"

"You know I hate long silences, so you stay quiet knowing I'll keep talking until I talk myself into whatever you want."

"Pretty efficient method, isn't it? Especially when I'm right and you know it."

Joe shook his head and looked out the windows bordering the south side of his office as he scratched absently at his stubbly chin. He wasn't a bad fellow, Lindsey thought, just scared of his own shadow. He'd been a very sharp electronics engineer for Uniwave, advancing project after project and promoted as a reward each time, until they'd elevated him to a job at least one level above his maximum capability. A small half-full jar of Maalox sat on his credenza, and what little hair he had left was rapidly going to gray. Joe, she knew, was now a full hostage of the high pay, benefits, and stock options of his position, and since the possibility of losing all that was his greatest terror, any suggestion from the corporate leaders in North Carolina attained Ten Commandment status in his mind. He had, Lindsey was fond of saying, achieved a status of profitable agony.

Joe sighed finally. It was a long and exhausted sound of capitulation, made worse by a very small whimper inserted at the far end of the coda.

"All right, Lindsey, I'll make the call."

"Good."

"But you'd better stand outside and be ready to jump back when my severed head comes rolling out the door."

"I'll just put your hat on it and send it home to Betty in a box. With a little formaldehyde and a big Mason jar, you'll make a great conversation piece."

"Very funny."

"Hey! Your metaphor."

"Cole really thinks another twenty-four hours will do it?" Joe asked, returning to Ben Cole's conviction that failing to cancel the planned evening acceptance flight would be tantamount to murder/suicide.

"He hopes so. But as I said—"

Joe waved her off. "Yeah, yeah. I know. No guarantees."

"Joe, this is the small voice from Morton Thiokol in 'eighty-six, trying to tell the grand pooh-bahs of NASA not to launch the *Challenger*."

"Yeah, I get it, Lindsey."

"I hope so, Chief. Because this is one of those O-ring alerts you ignore at everyone's peril."

Lindsey stood and left the office, pulling the door closed behind her, aware that Joe Davis had begun punching in the North Carolina headquarters number like a condemned man mounting the gallows.

Less than 150 feet away on the second story of the high-security-project building, Dr. Ben Cole clapped a hand on the shoulder of one of his team and tried to smile.

"I want to keep everyone working until we lift off this evening."

"So, you're still going to fly tonight?" the man asked.

"No, he's not," Lindsey White's voice replied from the hallway as she walked up, explaining Joe Davis's agonized acceptance of the twenty-four-hour delay.

"Thank God," the same team member said, noting the relief in Ben Cole's eyes as he returned to the lab, leaving Ben and Lindsey in the hallway.

She shoved her hands into the pockets of the faded letter sweater she was wearing and cocked her head, looking into his tired eyes.

"You okay, Ben?"

He nodded with more energy than he had. "Now I am! The delay's approved?"

"Yep."

"You're truly a woman of your word, Lindsey."

She laughed. "Well, I couldn't let you climb on that aircraft feeling doomed."

"Did he put up much of a fight?"

She shook her head and rolled her eyes. "Not a subject for polite company."

"Okay."

"Now, the real question is, are you making any progress?"

Ben had been leaning against the door frame to the lab but he pulled his lank body back to a standing position and shrugged as he glanced at his watch. "I honestly don't know, and I guess I'm still summoned to the meeting at six?"

She nodded. "Unavoidable, unless he cancels."

"I think, with the extra time and that manual T-handle, I can guarantee we won't get hurt physically, but I'm going to need every minute between now and tomorrow evening to make sure the system will pass the test."

"But you can do it, you think? Realistically? Or . . . are you still guessing?"

Ben sighed. "Yeah, I'm still guessing. It's in there somewhere, and now . . . I've got to think how to best use the extra time."

One floor away, Joe Davis replaced the telephone handset and wiped the perspiration from his brow. The chairman had been none too happy, but far less furious than Joe had expected, and the one-day delay had been approved.

"Get it right the first time, Joe," Will Martin had cautioned.

The phone rang again, this time with the chief test flight mechanic.

"Joe, we've got a big problem with that modification you wanted."

Joe Davis sat back and began rubbing his eyes. "Yeah?"

"This is a civilian aircraft, and we can't put a modification in like that—a physical modification—without bringing in our FAA liaison for approval."

"What the heck are you talking about?" Joe asked. "The aircraft is on an experimental certificate. We can do anything we want. We're a secret black project, for God's sake."

"Joe, remember the exemption they gave us? It's usually pro forma, but we have to have our FAA lady sign it off to be legal. We can't bypass the rules."

"Well, then just yank our FAA chick in here and have her sign it off."

"Hey, Joe, a little respect, okay? That 'chick' is a very capable woman."

"Yeah, a very capable female you've been trying to lay for six months now, right, Bill?" Joe Davis snapped, aware his sarcasm would hit home. Bill Waggoner was married, but clearly in lust with the female maintenance inspector.

Waggoner's voice dropped to a frosty, cautious register. "I resent that accusation, Joe."

"Well, sorry the truth hurts, old boy. What's her name? Sandra?"

"Yes."

"Just get Sandra in and get it approved."

"I can't do that. She's in Oklahoma City for training for a week."

"Then get a substitute."

"Jeez, Joe, there are no substitutes with the required top secret clearances and need to know! You, of all people, should know that."

Joe nodded to himself, doubly irritated at the rebuke. "Oh, yeah. Look, if we could get Sandra to a scrambled, secure line out at Tinker Air Force Base down in Oklahoma City . . ."

"No, Joe. She's a straight shooter. No way would she sign off on a physical modification without personally inspecting it."

The explosion had been slow in coming, but it gathered now to a thunderclap riding the pressure and frustration of the last few hours.

"Goddammit, Waggoner! We pay you to come up with solutions. You want the plane to go down?"

"Of course not. What a stupid thing to ask."

"Then install the friggin' disconnect so we can keep them safe, and we'll get it formally approved when Miss Sandra comes back."

More silence.

"Bill?"

The sound of someone clearing his throat on the other end of the line was the only response at first.

"Bill, answer me, dammit!"

"This is for the record, Joe. Neither I, nor anyone working for me and under my control, is going to finish installation of that T-handle disconnect or any other physical modification without the appropriate FAA approval. That's not negotiable. I have a fiduciary—"

"You'll do exactly what I tell you to do, Waggoner!"

"No, Joe, I won't. I'm a licensed mechanic with responsibilities that run beyond you and Uniwave. You want to fire me? Fine. But I've read my contract very carefully, and I know precisely who has the appropriate security clearances and who I can talk to to protest an illegal order, so don't try threatening me."

"You want to collapse this company? Is that what you're up to?"

"You know better than that, Joe."

"Godammit, Waggoner! I *should* fire your ass."

"Go right ahead. I'll be in General MacAdams's face within the hour with a full explanation."

More silence as the standoff intensified, broken finally by the capitulation Joe knew was inevitable.

"All right, leave it unfinished," Joe said quietly, wondering how on earth to tell Lindsey White and Ben Cole without losing the final acceptance flight. Perhaps there was another way, he thought. The emergency disconnect was for the sole purpose of making Lindsey and Ben Cole feel better, but the extra twenty-four hours would give Cole time to solve his problems without needing the manual disconnect. Therefore, the backup disconnect was unnecessary. There was no need to discuss it—or highlight its absence.

The brief pang of moral conflict was no match for the engine of Joe Davis's drive for economic and corporate survival. It was a small, manageable risk at best, and he could live with it.

NINE

Gracie O'Brien parked her silver 1982 Corvette in the marina parking lot and turned off the engine as she listened impatiently to the fellow law associate on the other end of her cell phone. The call had lasted all the way from 4th and Broad in downtown Seattle to her parking place, and he was still droning on.

Twenty minutes of jabbering for two minutes of content! Gracie grumbled.

She adjusted the headset connected to her cell phone. "Jeff? Hey, JEFFY? Yeah, sorry to yell. Look, I understand the problem. I'll be in at six in the morning and we can hash it out then, if that's okay with—"

The other lawyer began again, but she was ready for him.

"JEFF! FIRE! EARTHQUAKE! BAGELS!"

"Wha . . . *what?*"

"Just checking your hearing. Don't you ever breathe between sentences? I couldn't get an edge in wordwise."

"Yeah, so I've been told," he replied.

"Tomorrow, Jeff. Give it a rest for tonight."

She waited for acknowledgment of the ungodly report time before ringing off and extricating herself from her gleaming sports car.

The 'Vette had been her first big indulgence after landing the job with Janssen and Pruzan. A $105,000 starting salary made it more than possible. She'd always wanted a Corvette. "Tom Cruise and me!" she'd told April countless times since the movie *Top Gun* had become her favorite rental.

"We both feel the need for speed."

"Gracie, he rode a motorcycle in *Top Gun*."

"Doesn't matter. It went fast, like a 'Vette."

"Look, Corvettes are, what, fifty thousand?"

"New, yes. I'm talking a pre-loved 'Vette," Gracie had explained, sounding hurt. "This baby's six thousand, one owner, perfect silver paint . . . and all mine."

"What do you mean, 'all mine'?" April had asked.

"I already wrote the check. I knew you'd approve."

That was a year before, and her only regret in the intervening year was having too little free time to drive it—plus the two-hundred-dollar speeding fine she'd earned by blowing past a Washington state trooper at somewhere over 110 miles per hour.

"He actually asked me for my pilot's license," Gracie had laughed when telling April the next day.

"Oh, no. You didn't?"

"Of course I did! I pulled out my private pilot's license and handed it to him. Your dad would have been proud."

"I'm surprised you're not calling from the county jail."

"He actually started laughing."

"But he still wrote the ticket."

"Yeah, and I batted my eyes and thought sexy and everything, just like you taught me, Rosen. I keep telling you, it doesn't work with me."

"That's because you keep talking. It wrecks the mood."

Gracie chuckled at the memory as she pulled her briefcase from the front seat, closed the door, and paused to rub a smudge off the window before heading for the boat she called home.

The Corvette had elicited enough of a yelp from April, but Gracie's maverick decision to buy and live on an expensive yacht north of the downtown Seattle area had stunned her whole extended family.

"Is it *safe* to do that?" April had asked.

"It's safe, and it's calming, and I've got earnest money on a ten-year-old fifty-eight-footer with a great master bedroom, salon, galley, and everything for about the price of your Vancouver condo."

Gracie paused now at the entrance to her slip, admiring the lines of her ship, as she liked to call it. It was a fifty-eight-foot Carver, moored stern-in to the dock.

She closed the gate behind her and walked the twenty yards to her floating home, unlocked the door and tossed her briefcase onto a chair before putting her headset back in place to call April. She punched in April's cell number, rolling over the details of their last conversation. That had been hours before, and while Arlie and Rachel were obviously doing fine physically, the news that NTSB and FAA representatives had shown up for an interview had worried her for the past two hours—and the silence from Anchorage wasn't helping.

"Hello?"

"Where are you, Rosencrantz?" Gracie asked.

"Just leaving the hospital. I was going to call you, Gracie," April said. "I think we've got a problem." Her voice was tense as she related the details of the contentious interview and the attack by the FAA inspector—as well as Arlie Rosen's angry response.

"You're kidding? Our captain came unglued?" Gracie asked in alarm.

"Completely. Name calling and all. If the FAA man wasn't already intending to cause trouble—and he obviously was—he'll be hell for leather to do so now. He came in with a chip on his shoulder."

"Okay, I need to find an air-law specialist, and fast. Someone with experience defending pilots from the FAA."

"Gracie, you think this is going to come back to bite Dad?"

"Well, you tell me. Did the FAA guy mention alcoholism?"

"Yes."

"Did he accuse the captain of flying drunk, and say he was going to recommend what they call 'certificate action'?"

"Yes. In so many words. He didn't say 'certificate action,' but he meant it."

"Then we've got a big, thumping, hairy problem. How are they otherwise?"

"In a bit of a daze. I don't think it's hit Dad yet that his baby's lost. He loved that Albatross so much."

"That may be the least of his problems."

"He's going to want to find a way to salvage her, but when an airplane's been immersed in salt water—"

"April, I need you to focus now. Tell me as much as you can remember about the details of that interview, and exactly what the captain told those guys."

"I'll e-mail it to you in a few minutes."

"What, your notes?"

"No. I recorded the whole thing digitally, and as soon as I get to the hotel—I've booked a room at the Anchorage Hilton—I'll e-mail it to you. I loaded the program on your laptop when I bought this recorder last month."

"Oh. I forgot. Cool. But, you mean you can e-mail it directly from the recorder itself?"

"No. I'll use my laptop."

"Your laptop? You have your laptop in Anchorage?"

"Of course."

"You mean you took the time to grab your computer along with your girl kit when you left Vancouver?"

"Gracie, that's what I grab *before* I pack the girl—" She stopped abruptly. "Why am I repeating that? You know I hate that phrase, 'girl kit.' It's just stuff to make me feel good and look good."

"Yeah, I know. So, how long will your folks be staying in the hospital?"

"Overnight, at least."

"Okay, now, how are *you* doing?"

April sighed audibly. "Oh, I'm close to tears of mixed relief and grief. Thank God they're okay, but who needs this, y'know? Lose the airplane, get the FAA after you . . . not a fun thing."

"Can you take a few days off to get them back home to Sequim?"

"Yes, but I've got ships coming in I have to meet in two days. Dean will be here in the morning. You're going to look for a lawyer?"

"Aside from the one I'm looking at in the mirror? Yes. In the morning, first thing. Is it okay if I call the captain and Rachel? Are they up to it?"

"They'd love to hear from their terminally cynical surrogate daughter." April gave her the bedside number. "Gracie, Dad wasn't drinking. You know that, right?"

"I'd stake my life on it."

"Those were pretty ugly accusations."

"Hang in there and have faith, April. Really. We'll get it fixed, you and me."

"Think so?"

"Hey, that's what kids are for."

TEN

TUESDAY, DAY 2
UNIWAVE FIELD OFFICES
ELMENDORF AFB, ALASKA
AROUND 8 P.M.

The computer screensaver appearance of Lisa Cole was momentarily unnerving. The emotions instantly triggered in Ben Cole by his deceased wife's beautiful face bordered on the uncontrollable, which was why he normally approached the act of looking at her picture with great care and preparation.

But suddenly Lisa's image was there on the screen, his favorite shot of her, hair blowing happily in the stiff wind of the Pali, the historic pass in the saddle of Oahu's volcanic ridgeline separating Honolulu from the Kailua area on the northeast shore. That had been a wonderful day, he recalled, and she'd delighted in having the forty-knot wind threatening to scandalize him by billowing her skirt to indiscreet places as he tried to take her picture. She'd loved the resulting shot. Her "Marilyn" imitation, she'd called it.

His mind started down the same, dark path, reliving the news two years before that his beautiful wife had been broadsided in traffic and killed by a drunk driver. Ben forced himself back to the question of how her picture had suddenly appeared.

And just as quickly he realized the mistake, if it was a mistake. He'd inadvertently triggered a long-dormant little program he'd created—a "macro" in geek-speak, he used to say—that randomly looked for pictures on his hard drive and displayed them without warning as the screensaver of the day.

"Keeps you from downloading porn, I promise you that!" he'd joked with the other engineers.

Somehow he'd reactivated the program, and the first shot it found was Lisa's.

He left her image on the screen, taking a bit of comfort in the idea that in a strange way she was watching over him, and he could certainly use the support.

Ben sat back and debated the merits of making a new pot of coffee or continuing to work. The welcome cancellation of the scheduled meeting with General MacAdams had helped defuse a little of the killing pressure they were under, but when word came that MacAdams had slipped the final test another twenty-four hours—giving them two whole days to find the problem—he'd sent his exhausted software team home for a much-needed rest.

"Are you coming, too, Ben?" one of them had asked.

"Yeah. Absolutely," he'd fibbed. "Be right behind you."

He had little choice but to stay and work into the night. Taking top secret work home in any form was a massive violation with potential jail time attached.

Ben stood and moved to study the half dozen electrical relays his team had hastily wired together in imitation of the prototype system in the Gulfstream. He checked the connections, then moved to an adjacent computer that had an exact copy of the program that had almost killed him the night before. Ben entered the "start" command from memory, watching the various messages on the screen reporting the progress of the program as it went through the sequence of closing the relays to physically take control, exactly as it would happen in the real airplane.

There were a series of snapping sounds, and Ben nodded to himself after glancing toward the table.

Okay, that's right, he thought. He entered a new series of commands, and still more clicking and snapping resulted, again precisely in accordance with the way the program was supposed to work.

All right. Let's see if you can obey the command to sit and roll over, he thought, loosing another string of keyboard commands. The appropriate response after a few seconds would be the snapping of four relays indicating the system had let go of the flight controls.

Instead, the lights in the lab went out.

What the hell? Ben thought. The computers were still running on backup power, but all of the overhead lights and individual workstation lamps had gone dark, and there had been no snapping noises.

Ben grabbed a small flashlight and moved to the relay table, confirming that they had not released.

The room lights go out but the relays won't let go? This makes no sense.

There was a noise at the door to the lab and he looked up, trying to make out who was standing in the darkness of the doorway.

"Hello?"

"Ben, go home," Lindsey White's voice said.

"Lindsey! I've just had a partial power failure in here."

She was moving toward him, carefully negotiating the spaces between the desks and workstations until she was standing next to him. There was a sudden burst of light as she triggered a large flashlight beam directed upward at her face, like a camper in a tent telling ghost stories.

"Go ho-o-ome, Doc-tor Cole!" she said, adopting a comically spooky voice.

"Okay, Lindsey," he chuckled.

"Here thar be software beasties!" She snapped the light off, chuckling as well, her normal voice returning. "And circuit breakers for the ceiling lights."

"*You* did that?"

She nodded, and he could see her smiling in the dim light. "Yep. If I can't get you out of here one way, I'll do it another. Go home and get some sleep."

"Scared the heck out of me, Lindsey. I was just running a system test."

"Well, if I have your word that you'll get out of here in the next ten minutes, I'll give you your one-hundred-ten-volt alternating current back to play with."

"Spoken like a true electrical engineer."

"I love it when you talk dirty," she said, moving back toward the door. "Seriously, Ben."

"Okay. Promise."

"Good. We've got two days and a new T-handle. Good night."

"Good night, Lindsey," he said, thankful she hadn't asked for a progress report.

The lights came back on and Ben moved to the test computer screen to reset the program, remembering the absence of snapping noises.

Wait a minute, he thought. *They never disconnected. The program has paused with the problem clearly apparent.*

His excitement was mounting by the moment. If he could freeze the program with specific knowledge of which line of code had caused the program to freeze and be unresponsive, and copy it precisely that way, he could zero in on the problem within an hour or two.

He stood back from the table, his heart beating faster as he considered the options. He knew Lindsey was serious. Undoubtedly she would check back with security inside an hour to make sure he'd processed out.

But he couldn't leave the search until morning. A thousand things could happen to the uncounted electrons zapping around the interior of the computer's silicon memory. The key to the solution was in his hands, and he had to act now.

Ben pulled out a notepad and scribbled down the computer commands that would copy precisely what he needed from the stopped prototype program. He double-checked it to make sure there was nothing apparent that might crash the program or garble the files, then triggered the process.

The sound of hard drives whirring to life reached his ears as he monitored the information on the screen. The download continued for two very long minutes before the final confirmation blinked on-screen. Ben transferred the downloaded files to a CD and sat down at his computer desk in deep thought. It would be professional suicide to leave the building with the CD or any computer-storage medium. But Ben had always known about an uncovered hole in the system. He'd monitored it carefully to prevent anyone else from finding or using it, but there was a way to get the master hard drive to send anything to one particular serial port on one solitary computer in the lab. He pulled out his cell phone now and looked at it, trying to recall whether its "system" might be actively intercepted by counterintelligence security apparatus.

No, he concluded. *Highly unlikely.*

He pulled out a cable from his briefcase and connected it first to the serial port of the computer, then to the bottom of his cell phone, dialing the special number to his home desktop computer. He entered the appropriate commands until he had a clear channel to a restricted area of his hard drive's memory, and triggered the transfer. He sat in rising apprehension as the computer began the process of sending the top secret program digitally over his cell phone to his personal machine at home.

"Dr. Cole?" a male voice asked without warning.

A cold fear gripped him as he jumped involuntarily. "What? Who's that?"

The voice had come from the doorway, and Ben looked up to see a security guard he knew strolling in, immediately destroying his glib confidence that he was doing something no one could detect. Ben was sure sweat was visible on his forehead. He tried not to swallow or sound as guilty as he felt.

"Ms. White asked me to come make sure you kept your word and went home, Doctor," the guard said with a grin.

Ben sighed audibly. "You scared me, Jerry!"

"Sorry about that. You do look a bit shaken."

"I thought I was alone."

"Nope. You got us rent-a-cops here, too."

"Give me a second and I'll be ready," Ben said, deftly cancelling the return message on the computer screen that the upload was complete. He secured and shut down the computers one by one, feeling a predictable pang as he dumped Lisa's image before grabbing his overstuffed briefcase and turning toward the guard with a smile.

"Okay. That's it."

"Haven't you forgotten something, Doc?" the man said, an expression on his face Ben instantly read as accusatory.

"I . . . I don't think so."

The guard walked toward the computer Ben had used for the download and picked up the cell phone. The download modem cord dangled from the bottom.

"Well, well, well. What have we here?"

A wave of nausea consumed him as he watched the guard hold out the cell phone with the cord still attached and shake his head in smiling disapproval, like a cat playing with his doomed mouse.

"I . . . ah . . ." Ben began.

"It's one thing to get the battery all charged up, but if you forget to take it home, you still can't use it," the guard said with a smile. "It's always the obvious things that get you engineering types."

Ben took the phone from his hand and quickly disconnected the download cord, stuffing them both in his briefcase. "You're so right, Jerry. Thanks! I was expecting an important call in a little while and I didn't want my battery to die in the middle of talking to her. You know."

The guard put a fatherly hand on his shoulder, guiding him to the door.

"Ms. White's instructions were specific. Remove Dr. Cole's fatigued body from the premises no matter how much he protests. I always follow a lady's requests. Well, almost always."

Ben swiped his badge at the security entrance and cleared his handprint and retinal scans before waving goodbye to Jerry and climbing into his car, the guard's words echoing in his head. *It's always the obvious things that get you,* Jerry had said.

But what could he be missing that was obvious?

ELEVEN

April had been battling to ignore the sound of the alarm clock for the previous ten minutes. She gave up and pulled it to her. She'd left a wake-up call for 8 A.M., but it was 5:50.

Dean, one of her two brothers, was due in at 10 A.M., and she had to get to the airport as well as make a half dozen calls back to Vancouver. And, if her folks were to be released by mid afternoon, there were airline tickets to Seattle to arrange.

April turned out the lamp on the bedside table and pulled a pillow over her head to try to recapture sleep, but it was no use. After less than ten minutes she sat up abruptly and tossed the pillow across the room in frustration, wide awake. Something was rolling around in her mind and she couldn't quite capture it.

Okay. I'll try the shower.

Anchorage was hunkered down under a slate sky on a particularly frigid morning when she slid out from under the bedcovers and padded over to the window to look out. She thought about her state of undress, but her silk robe was back in Vancouver, and besides, there were no high buildings across from the Anchorage Hilton.

April pulled the curtains back to an otherwise exhibitionistic extent and folded her arms beneath her breasts as she watched a flight of four Air Force F-15s landing at Elmendorf one by one. She waited until all four had crossed the threshold and disappeared onto the runway before heading for the bathroom and inserting herself into the comfortable cocoon of hot water and white noise, letting the spray block out all but her thoughts.

Long, hot, luxurious showers had always been her best thinking time, something her brothers had never understood—especially when they had to wait endlessly for their little sister to release the bathroom.

But the never-ending supply of hot water in a major hotel was a wonderful luxury, and she'd taken advantage of such opportunities all her life—so much so, Gracie was fond of saying, that her name had become a permanent feature on the environmentalist hit list of international water wasters.

April closed her eyes and tried to remember what it was about the conversation with her mother the night before that was bothering her so. She'd left the hospital around seven and checked into the hotel, then had gone downstairs for a quick sandwich. But her mother was already ringing her room phone by the time she returned. Rachel Rosen needed to go over everything in great detail once more, and it had been therapeutic for both mother and daughter.

Something, however, had been bothering April ever since.

Okay . . . Dad said the prop threw a blade and everything started shaking wildly.

She let her mind replay her parents' narratives.

Mom said Dad's description of the prop blade must be right because there was this incredible noise, just as he said.

She turned around, letting the cascade of water inundate her face, standing in thought a few more minutes, melding her memory of the Albatross with their description of the moment.

April's eyes fluttered open as an alternate possibility popped into her head, a slightly bizarre thought that propelled her out of the shower and into a bath towel. She glanced at her watch, calculating the distance to the airport and wondering if there was enough time for a critical errand before her brother arrived.

ANCHORAGE AIR ROUTE TRAFFIC CONTROL CENTER
ANCHORAGE, ALASKA
8:05 A.M.

April wheeled the rental car into the entrance of the FAA facility and stopped at the guard shack, ready to show her driver's and pilot's licenses. As a pilot, it had taken little more than a phoned request and a quick background check to secure the permission needed to visit the windowless radar rooms of the center. Pilots were always welcome, they told her.

April left her car and walked to the entrance, where the man she'd talked to was waiting with an outstretched hand.

"Ms. Rosen? Jay Simpson."

"Yes. Thanks so much for arranging this at the last minute."

"My pleasure," he said, his eyes appraising her in a way that validated his words. "You said you wanted to sit and watch a sector for a little while, right?"

She nodded. "That's what I didn't get to do at the Seattle ARTCC."

"The one in Everett?" he asked, obviously testing her.

"It's actually located in Auburn," she said, smiling at his pleased reaction.

Simpson handed her a clip-on security badge and led the way through a series of heavy doors into the subdued light of the main control room. The room was lined with glowing computer-generated screens tracking virtually all airborne traffic over the state of Alaska.

"You already know the basics about our airspace?" he asked.

April nodded with a smile. "I know you work traffic from south of Ketchikan all the way to above seventy degrees north, Kotzebue and Nome and the Bering Strait on the west, and Canadian airspace on the eastern border."

"You got it," he said, handing her a small brochure. "That'll give you the statistics if you ever need them." They moved up quietly behind one of the control positions and waited until the male controller finished handing off a Russian Aeroflot passenger jet to an adjacent sector. Simpson tapped the controller's shoulder and the man turned and rose from his chair with a smile as Simpson handed April a headset and plugged it in.

"I'm Rusty Bach, Miss Rosen," the controller said.

"April, please. Are you any relation to the author? Richard Bach?"

"I wish, but no."

She could see no evidence of a ring on his left hand, which, she figured, partially explained his enthusiastic reception of her visit.

"Have a seat, April."

She let him guide her through the intricacies of the sector of airspace he was working, quietly pleased it covered the Valdez area and the sea lanes to the south. A steady procession of Alaska, Delta, and American Airlines flights, along with foreign airliners, Air Force jets, and private and corporate flights were all moving in various directions across the screen, tagged by tiny "data blocks" giving information on altitude, speed, and heading.

April noticed another controller quietly plugging into the same position to watch over their shoulder. Safety backup, she figured, and probably a standard procedure with a visitor present.

"How low can an aircraft still be tracked by your radar out here?" April asked. "Let's say . . . here."

"Well, you're pointing to the area over the water east of Whittier," the controller replied. "We can track targets pretty well down to eight hundred feet over the water out there. Sometimes less."

"But if they're very low, such as a hundred feet or so . . ."

"Then we can't give them flight-following services, you know, keep them clear of other traffic, because we can't see them. They become stealth aircraft. Maybe we'll get an occasional transponder hit, but that's all."

They talked between radio calls, and she let the conversation drift to other areas before asking one of the key questions that had sparked the visit.

"Rusty, I understand you record virtually everything these scopes see, and in the case of an accident, you can reconstruct what was showing at the time. Right?"

He smiled. "That's a bit oversimplified, but it's essentially correct. If it formed a target on this screen, it'll be on the tapes, digitally. Why do you ask?"

She smiled her most alluring smile and felt an instant, resonant response. "I've flown out there in a seaplane before, really low," April said, "and I wasn't able to reach you guys to even ask for flight following. I remember wondering if you could see me, or if the radar tapes were at least watching me."

He shook his head, doubly eager to impress her now. "I sure wish we could. But we can't. Now . . . there *are* a lot of military radar sites around the state, and there's the Coast Guard's vessel-traffic radar in Valdez, which can see you down to the water. But we can't use those signals."

"Yes, but about the tapes you do have; you keep those for months, right?"

He raised a finger, his eyes on a flight approaching the edge of his sector. "Alaska Three Twelve, descend now and maintain one-one thousand. Anchorage altimeter three-zero-two-two."

The voice of the commercial pilot boomed through her headset and she reached up to turn down the volume. "Roger, Anchorage, Alaska Three Hundred and Twelve out of flight level three-three-zero this time for one-one thousand. Beautiful day out here south of Anchorage, Center."

"Thanks!" Rusty replied, laughing. "I really needed that, stuck as I am in a windowless room."

"Sorry," the pilot responded. "If you like, we could *describe* it to you."

More laughter.

"Negative, Alaska Three Twelve," Rusty was saying, "but you can tell the next guy. Contact the Anchorage Center now on one twenty-two point six."

The pilot repeated the frequency change as Rusty turned back to April, trying hard to keep his eyes above her neckline. She glanced at her watch, feigning surprise as she got up to go, thanking him profusely.

But Rusty gently caught her sleeve and pressed a business card in her hand.

"My number. Just in case, you know, you want someone to show you around," he said. The hopeful look in his eyes was unmistakable, and she smiled and patted his shoulder.

"Thanks, Rusty. I'll keep that in mind."

*A*s the comely female visitor departed, the controller who'd been shadowing Rusty Bach unplugged and moved to the far end of the room to a small workstation. He keyed in his password and called up a series of databases, paging back to the flight plans from two days before. The information he was searching for eluded him, however, and he collapsed the screen and pulled a phone to his ear instead, to punch in the number of the acting facility chief.

"Ralph? Ed here. Something odd. Maybe it's nothing, but . . . thought you might need to know." He described April's questions in detail, and the area south of Valdez that had seemed to interest her.

"What's your point, Ed?"

"Okay, you recall the search-and-rescue effort out there yesterday morning, just about the same place?"

"Yes. They found survivors of what I guess was an old Grumman that went down the night before."

"Right. You know the name of the captain? I can't find a flight plan."

There was hesitation on the other end. "No . . . not offhand. You think her visit was connected?"

Ed snorted and shrugged his shoulders. "Don't know. I just get curious when someone starts asking how long we keep tapes, can we see to the waterline, and that sort of thing. Kind of what a smuggler would ask, you know?"

"Yeah . . . or a seaplane pilot."

"Could be."

"Forget it, Ed."

"Okay."

*I*n an office one floor away, the acting facility chief replaced the receiver for a moment and checked a phone number on a business card he'd stuffed in his pocket, then raised the receiver and punched in the number. He thought better of it then and hung up, recalling that all government phones were subject to monitoring. Instead, he pulled out his personal cell phone and entered the same number.

TWELVE

*I*n the mind of the marginally overfed yellow feline named Schroedinger, the fact that the human with whom he shared his house had yet to feed him had risen to the level of an issue demanding immediate resolution.

Schroedinger made a smooth leap from the floor to the desk where Ben Cole's laptop computer was blinking dutifully through a procession of pictures, some including the image of Lisa—the long-absent woman who used to be in charge of keeping him fed and relatively content.

Ben's head was down on the desktop, his hair a mess, his elbows splayed out on both sides where he'd shoved papers and journals aside, some falling to the floor. He was sound asleep, and Schroedinger wasn't impressed. Ben had a bed, and that's where he should have been sleeping. When he was in it, he usually arose in time to serve the proper amount of food and water. But when Ben didn't spend the night in his own bed, Schroedinger knew his breakfast would be seriously delayed.

Carefully, he padded over to Ben's face, boosting the volume of his purr to its highest intensity. At least this morning there were none of the empty bottles that had occasionally heralded an even deeper unconscious state, and an even later meal.

Schroedinger extended a paw, keeping his claws carefully retracted as he patted Ben's closed eye with no response. You had to be careful with humans, he'd found. They became unmanageably agitated over the smallest of things, and their eyes were very sensitive.

He patted again, but there was no response—other than the obnoxious, rhythmic buzzing sound that humans made when they slept. Once more he tried, moving closer this time and pushing against Ben's face with the top of his head before using his move of last resort: a loud, protesting "Meow!" delivered right in his human's ear.

"Wh . . . What?"

Ben Cole snapped upright, a look of complete confusion on his face as Schroedinger stepped back and repeated his verbal protest, expecting immediate compliance with the business of feeding the resident feline.

Instead, Ben was up, looking at his watch and making upsetting noises.

"Oh *dammit!* It's . . . jeez! Ten after nine! How in the world?" Ben turned back to the desk and realized where he was, and where he'd been. "I was only going to rest a few minutes!" He'd put his head down just past six, after working through the night, and now this. His team would have arrived back at the lab at seven and well noted the absence of their leader by now. This was deeply embarrassing. Sleeping late was a personal failure.

Ben grabbed for the phone to call the lab, cautioning himself at the same moment that explaining his tardiness by admitting he'd worked all night could spark a major security investigation. After all, he could take nothing home at night but his mind. So if he was working late, what was he working *on?* The possibility that a midnight-oil session might involve illicitly removed materials was well understood by Uniwave's security department, especially since they were operating under the incredibly stringent military requirements of a black project.

Ben heard one of his programmers answer the line. "Gene? Yeah, Ben. Hey, I'm really embarrassed, but I took some cold medicine last night and . . . I guess it must've really knocked me out. I just woke up."

There was a chuckle from the other end and relayed assurance that they understood, but only Ben could forgive Ben, and that wasn't happening.

"Let me hit the shower and I'll be there by, ah, ten or so."

"We're fine, Ben. Take it easy. You needed the rest."

Ben replaced the receiver, feeling an overwhelming need for coffee as he touched the laptop's mousepad with intent to shut it down. The pressure to run to the shower and then dash to his car was intense, but the reality that he'd downloaded forbidden classified information to his hard drive was scaring him. The computer files would have to be fully erased with a special program before he could leave the house.

The screensaver slide show had dissolved, leaving in its place the final report on the search Ben had launched at 5 A.M., for a line-by-line comparison of two versions of the Boomerang Box's master program. He started to save the message for later, but realized with a start that it, too, would have to be erased.

Once more he glanced at his watch in agitation, shoving an even more disgruntled Schroedinger aside as he plopped back in the desk chair to scan the report before erasing it. There was no reason it should show anything different from the four or five dozen comparison searches he'd made during the night, each of which had turned up nothing.

If there's anything wrong with this damn program, I can't find . . .

Ben felt his mind snap to a halt and change direction as he returned to the top of the screen and realized what he was seeing.

What in the world?

Unlike each of the previous searches, this one had yielded something. There were long lists of numbers, each of them representing a specific line of computer code, and each significantly different from any of the code lines on the original completed master program. He knew almost every line of the original version and had instructed the computer to compare the version of the program he'd used aboard the Gulfstream with the original control version.

And now this.

Ben paged down the list, passing a hundred lines before realizing that more than two thousand lines were different, or new, and all in one section. He ordered the computer to show him the raw machine language on several lines he'd selected at random, fully expecting to see something familiar. Perhaps his workstation had gone into some kind of loop and just repeated a rogue line of code several thousand times.

No . . . it's all different! he concluded, trying to decipher what kind of program the code represented. There were shorter off-the-shelf sub-routines throughout modern computer programs, but none of what he was seeing corresponded to any of the standard ones, and some of what he was looking at appeared to be written in a machine language he'd never seen, if that were possible.

Ben glanced at his exasperated cat and pointed to the conundrum on the screen.

"What do make of that, Schroedinger?"

The yellow tomcat meowed again and took a few steps toward the kitchen, lowering his already low opinion of human intelligence as he realized that Ben was failing utterly to get his priorities straight.

A slow whisper of trouble worked its way into Ben's mind, beginning with the realization that someone had purposely inserted unauthorized instructions into a top secret defense program. But who? And why? And what? A virus, perhaps? That was a worrisome thought. In the first few seconds of his mushrooming understanding, the muttered possibility that someone was playing a trick was shouted down by the voice of reason. No, this wasn't a trick or an accident. Whoever had added the sophisticated lines had obviously been try-

ing to fix something, an explanation at once eclipsed by the roar of
reality that all legitimate additions had to have his personal approval.
That final fact triggered an inescapable shout of alarm in his head.

*Oh my God, this is sabotage! And this is the version of the program that
nearly killed us the other night!*

Ben realized he was shaking, perhaps as much from waking up too
fast with too little sleep as from fear. He forced himself to sit back
down and concentrate.

*This could still be an error. Don't be too hasty. Stray lines get into pro-
grams all the time, and we've patched the hell out of this one, and my original comparison copy comes from, what, eight months ago.*

Maybe he was overreacting. After all, the new code could be
something as mundane as an encrypted recipe for brownies. It wasn't
necessarily responsible for the failed test and the locked system two
nights before.

Another horrific thought crossed his mind, and he tried to shake
it off. What if one of his own team were some sort of renegade foreign agent?

Impossible. I know my people better than their mothers know them.

The background checks had been witheringly thorough, yield-
ing embarrassing details ranging from youthful sexual exploits to
sometimes disgusting personal habits. His own file had shocked him.
Apparently, the National Security Agency had employed agents in his
preschool and had been inside his '54 Chevy during his first, fumbling
attempts at lovemaking in the back. They even had her name right.

No, he knew his people. There were no moles.

Ben felt his pulse slowing as he focused on how little he knew
about the puzzle he'd discovered. He couldn't go off half-cocked,
but then again, he couldn't just erase the evidence and go to work as
if he hadn't found it.

*Maybe I can erase it here and just replicate it there. After all, at the lab,
all the files are available and authorized.*

He entered the preliminary keystrokes to destroy the entire series
of files, and paused with his finger over the "enter" button. He had

the evidence in front of him. What if something happened to his data at the lab and he couldn't duplicate it? The urge was strong to punch the button and remove all possibility of prosecution for what had, after all, been the criminal act of breaching a top secret project. But he had a responsibility to find out what this was all about.

Ben pulled his finger away and carefully hit the escape key to cancel the process. Regardless of the enormous personal risk, he had to keep the files until he could duplicate them legitimately at the lab.

A dozen ideas on where to store the thousands of lines of the anomalous code marched through his thinking, and he settled on the least probable, entering the appropriate commands before erasing all traces of the downloaded program files.

One single number remained, and he memorized it before removing it from his laptop. He headed for the shower, pausing to dump some food out for his unhappy cat and wondering if he could hide his agitation when he walked in the door in a half hour.

THIRTEEN

WEDNESDAY, DAY 3

ANCHORAGE INTERNATIONAL AIRPORT

April hated the airport security procedures that kept friends and family from going to the gates. She'd always loved being the first to catch the eye of someone she'd come to meet as the passengers rounded the corner of the jetway. Now she was forced to join the throng of hopefuls waiting for inbound passengers outside the security perimeter, and it seemed an indignity. Still, she managed to spot Dean as he came into view down the concourse, pouncing on him the second he emerged from the security portal.

"Hey, bro!"

"Hey, sis!" He hugged her, a weary look on his face. "How're they doing?"

"They're doing okay, considering what they went through. You know the Albatross was destroyed?"

"You told me on the phone last night, remember?"

She nodded. "I'm not sure what I've told anyone."

"Any physical problems?"

"Bumps, a few contusions, and a mild concussion for Dad, but overall, they're okay."

"That's a huge relief."

"It's just hard to picture their airplane sitting on the bottom of the ocean."

He pointed the way toward the front of the airport and they began walking in that direction. "You said last night there were other problems and you'd tell me when I got here," Dean prompted.

She gave him a detailed rundown of the encounter with the FAA and NTSB as they walked to her rental car in the airport garage.

Dean sat in silence for a while in the right front seat as his sister wheeled them out of the airport drive for the trip across town to the hospital. She waited for him to break the silence.

"April, you said you've got Gracie looking for a lawyer for Dad, right?"

She nodded.

"Which means you think he's going to need one."

"If you'd seen the hate in the eyes of that FAA inspector, Dean, you'd have no doubt. I don't understand what the man's problem was. I mean, most FAA people I've met, including inspectors, are just good, hardworking folks, but this guy . . ."

"He was giving you attitude?"

She grimaced and shook her head. "Not you, too?"

"What?"

"I *hate* the misuse of that word, Dean!"

"What are you talking about?"

"What you just said. 'He's giving me attitude,' that's nonsense. Gracie and I go around about this all the time. Attitude, attitude. *Everyone* has an attitude at any given moment, but that sort of stupid misuse makes it sound like just having one is bad. Talk about the bastardization of English!"

Dean had a hand up, laughing. "Okay, okay. I will refrain from colloquial usage in the future."

"That's not even colloquial. It's just plain guttural."

"But your point was," Dean continued, "that this FAA inspector had an agenda, and the destruction of Arlie Rosen's license to fly airplanes was on it?"

"Something's up with him, that's certain."

"And that's one of the phrases *I* hate," Dean chuckled. "'Up with,' as in 'whazzup wid yew?'"

April turned the car into the hospital entrance.

"Touché. Point well taken. And we're talking obliquely about a certain nephew of mine, right? Little runt who pretends to like rap and answers to the name of David?"

"Ah, yes," Dean said. "The teen monster of Bellevue. Night of the living bored. Now six feet tall, by the way, and his linguistics are atrocious."

"Like, you do realize, like, don't you, that he's, like, just trying to irritate his, like, dad?"

Dean smiled as she braked smoothly to a halt in front of the main entrance. "I seem to recall, little sis, that you were the unchallenged champion in that department in our family."

"I reformed," she replied, looking hurt. "It was a brief rebellion."

"Yeah, such as the time in high school you flew to Europe during a school break without telling anyone."

"Amsterdam."

"That's still in Europe, last time I checked."

"Dean," April said, her hand up to stop him. "Something about Mom and Dad's memory of yesterday is bothering me."

"What do you mean? You're not suggesting they're coloring the truth?"

She shook her head vigorously. "No, no, no! But something about the way they both remember the beginning of the accident sequence doesn't make sense."

"So, what are you thinking? Something else happened? You said that he said a propeller broke."

"I'm thinking that I want to ask you a favor."

"Sure."

"Let me just drop you off here to go take care of Mom and Dad while I . . . do a little research. Find out when they're going to be released and call me."

"I can, but why don't you just come back here when you're through? I'll need to arrange a hotel—"

"Dean, they'll be released this afternoon. Didn't I mention that?"

"No. Today?"

"Yeah. Isn't that great?"

"Well . . . of course, but . . ."

"Unless something's changed in the last hour."

He looked off balance.

"I'll be on my cell phone," she added. "When we're sure of the release time, I'll arrange the flight home."

"I hate to say this, April, but if they're okay and they're getting out of here in a few hours and flying home, why am I here?"

"In other words, why did the extremely busy Boeing executive have to cancel some really important appointments when little April could drop everything and take care of it?"

He nodded. "Okay, that did sound pretty selfish."

"They're really shaken up, Dean, and they need our support. They need to see you here. They can understand why between you and Sam, only one of you might be able to race up here—"

Dean held his hand up to stop her. "I'm sorry. I make this mistake more often than you know, thinking of you as still being in school, not the vice-president of a corporation."

"Times change, bro."

"Imagine that! My little sister a corporate officer."

"Yeah. Strange, isn't it? Look, call me when you know the projected release time, okay?"

He opened the door and hesitated, turning back to search her eyes. "What are you concerned about, April? Is this something to do with the broken propeller?"

"Maybe. I don't want to go into it yet. I just need to know more."

"All right."

"And please, Dean. Don't say anything to Dad. He's upset enough."

"So . . . where are you if they ask?"

"Tell them I'm using the opportunity of being in Anchorage to check up on one of my company's cruise ships. That way, Empress pays for my airline ticket."

Dean smiled. "You've always known how to speak Dad's language."

"Don't start with the 'airline pilots are cheap' thing again."

"No, no. Not cheap. Just . . . cost-conscious."

"And generous to a fault. Dad's living proof of that." She waved goodbye as he closed the door.

*A*pril turned the car north toward the downtown area, her mind on the city's relatively small port facilities and the Coast Guard's Marine Safety Office. She'd had difficulty locating anyone to talk to when she'd called them an hour before. A Lieutenant Hobbs had finally agreed to meet with her, and she found him in his office now, receptive but slightly suspicious.

"What, exactly, do you want to know, Ms. Rosen?" Hobbs asked.

April explained the loss of her parents' plane and her need to find a radar site that might have seen what happened. She passed him the crash-site coordinates.

"Why do you need to see radar tapes?" he asked.

"Because I think my father's airplane may have hit something on the water two nights ago, like the superstructure of a passing ship. If the fog was thick enough, the crew might not even be aware of it. Propeller blades are relatively fragile compared to nautical structures. Just a tiny touch could break a blade off and leave almost no marks on the structure below."

"If he clipped a ship because of flying too low, isn't that negligence?"

She shook her head and explained the difference. "It's not a violation to accidentally fly into fog. It's what you do in response that counts."

She could see Lieutenant Hobbs glance around carefully before coming forward in his chair to pull out a small pad of paper. He opened an ornate Mont Blanc fountain pen, noting April's curious expression. He glanced at the pen, then back at her.

"A gift from *my* dad," he explained. "I told him I needed a basic word processor and he gave me this. He's a professional comedian."

"Aren't all parents?"

"No . . . I mean, he really *is* a professional comedian. He lives in Vegas, was on the old Carson show a bunch of times, and still shows up on Leno every now and then. He's had a good career."

"I don't recall a comedian named Hobbs," April said.

"There's a divorce and a name change in my background," he replied. "I'm going to check with our radar guys for the time period involved and see what they have in the way of vessels in that general area, and whether I can get you a copy. I'll also check on what ships might have been in the vicinity."

"How long will it take?"

He was already on his feet, the interview obviously over, his discomfort at discussing the subject showing. "I'll call you."

She paused at his office door and turned back. "One more question. Can the Coast Guard bring the wreckage of our airplane up from the bottom?"

Jim Hobbs shook his head. "No. But why would you want to salvage it? The aircraft is undoubtedly totaled."

April nibbled her lip for a few seconds in thought. "My dad's propeller threw a blade. I need the remains of that propeller hub to prove it happened in flight." She felt a chill as he shook his head.

"Won't help you. Hitting the water could snap off a propeller blade. Water's like concrete above a hundred miles per hour."

She returned to the rental car too deep in thought to think about where she was heading, and realized she needed a few moments to figure out the next step. What could she accomplish in Anchorage in person that she couldn't do from Vancouver?

April braked and pulled to the curb suddenly, deciding to park and get some coffee while she called Gracie. The sudden change of course prompted an angry honk from the minivan driver behind her, but she waved at the man with a smile as if he'd done something friendly. April put the car in park and got out, oblivious to the dark blue sedan that had pulled out of the parking lot several car lengths behind her and was now moving to the curb as well, the occupants' eyes carefully following the raven-haired young woman ahead.

normally, teamwork delighted Ben Cole, even when performing under the sword of a make-or-break deadline. A lab full of happily collaborating professionals was always a joy of intellectual synergy—except today. For the previous four hours, dealing with the constant communication of his team when he wanted to work alone had created perhaps the most agonizing challenge of his professional life.

"I'm sorry, but I've got to go sit down and work quietly for an hour or so," Ben said at last, triggering no objections as his people continued their intense efforts, going back and forth over the various ways the program might have failed.

At any moment, Ben figured, one of his team was bound to make the same discovery he'd made, stumbling onto the thousands of lines of inserted, renegade code. If not, he would have to make the "discovery" himself and pretend to be astounded.

First, however, he needed time alone in his office, which was little more than a larger cubicle in a "cubeville"collection of partitions on one side of the lab. He retreated there now and entered the necessary access codes, quickly retrieving the comparison copy of the program from a half year before and entering the now-familiar commands to run a general line-by-line comparison with the latest version. The supercomputer began working as Ben sat back and waited for the results, which finally flashed on the screen: "No differences."

He leaned forward, wondering where the lines of code could be. *What did I screw up?*

He checked the dates on the program copies and started the comparison again.

Once more it yielded no differences.

Ben felt his pulse accelerating. There was no doubt he was working with the very same copies he'd illicitly transmitted home the day before. He opened the machine-code list on the latest version and entered the memorized line number which should take him straight to the first section of the illicitly added computer codes. But that particular line came up completely normal and identical to the original program.

This can't be!

He ran through the lab's secure program files, checking several more developmental copies and finding nothing out of the ordinary before sitting back, a cold sweat forming on his brow.

It isn't here! But . . . I didn't just imagine it. If I saw what I saw and I still have the evidence safely stashed away, and these are the copies they came from . . .

There was only one remaining explanation, and the realization coursed through his veins like ice water: Someone had electronically entered their main databank and erased the renegade lines of computer code. Hacking from outside was effectively impossible. Only someone within Uniwave could be responsible.

Ben stood up and looked through the opening of his cubicle, watching his team members for a moment as his thoughts raced around the problem of what to do and who might be responsible. The main evidence was gone, and he'd come within a finger stroke of destroying the only remaining record before leaving his house.

But that remaining record was no threat to whoever was behind the sabotaged code, and they had to know it. Ben shuddered at the symmetry of the dilemma. He was checkmated. If he revealed what he'd found, his career would be over and he'd end up in a federal prison somewhere. But if he didn't blow the whistle, the saboteurs would succeed, probably causing the crash of all aboard during the final test flight in the Gulfstream, himself included.

He thought about going straight to Joe Davis and reporting the existence of the renegade code, and then pretending to "find" it missing when he brought Joe back to the lab.

Impossible, Ben concluded. Without the concrete evidence he had but couldn't reveal, there was no way he'd convince Joe or Martin or anyone else in authority to stop the re-test and risk bankruptcy.

"Ben?" Gene Swanson had been standing next to Ben for several minutes, invisible to him, wondering where Ben's mind was. "You okay? You looked zoned out there," Gene said.

Ben sighed and rubbed his brow as he tried unsuccessfully to laugh. "Yeah. I do feel a little strange."

"You said you were taking a cold medicine . . . maybe it's a virus and not a cold. Not that a cold isn't a virus, but . . . you know what I mean."

"Yeah." Ben smiled at him and clapped a hand on his shoulder in an ineffectual attempt at reassurance as a desperate possibility coalesced in his head. "I'm, ah, going to run out to the aircraft and check a few things, Gene. Where are we in the process?"

"We've found nothing," Gene replied, a puzzled expression crossing his face. Ben held up a finger.

"Ah . . . no one removed any sections from the master code for testing or anything this morning, right?"

Gene Swanson looked stunned. "*Removed?* You mean, without authorization?"

"No, I mean . . . maybe a test copy or something."

"What are you asking, Ben? None of us would do that."

Ben shook his head again. "Just a thought, and obviously a silly one. I know you know this, but we're under such pressure, if any of you find any section of the master code that's been contaminated in any way, isolate and copy that section and wait for me to get back, okay?"

"Well . . . sure. We would anyway."

Ben left the lab as Gene moved back to the main test stand.

"What was that all about?" one of the other programmers asked.

"Frankly? I think Ben's losin' it."

$\mathcal{T}$he short drive to the secure hangar where Uniwave's Gulfstream was housed took less than five minutes, but processing through the security entrance took an additional fifteen since the name "Ben Cole" was not listed on the approved roster for that precise day and hour. First Lindsey, then Joe Davis, had to get involved by phone, verbally approving his visit after questioning why he needed to be there.

"Just checking a theory about the programming," Ben explained.

"Yeah, but, Ben," Joe Davis replied, "you bring the central hard drive back with you after each flight. There's nothing out there to see."

Ben glanced over at the security officers and smiled, rolling his eyes at the shared agony of dealing with bureaucratic machines.

"Joe, I could ask you the same thing in reverse. Is there something out here I'm not supposed to see?"

"No. No, of course not." There was a hesitancy in Joe Davis's voice, but it didn't register in Ben's thinking.

"Well, I'm chief software engineer, Joe, and the computer out here still has software embedded in it, and I'd like to look at it. Why is that a problem?"

"It isn't, now that you've explained yourself," Joe replied. "You should let people know, Ben. Don't just show up. It makes our security people very nervous."

$\mathcal{T}$he Gulfstream sat freshly washed and sparkling in the lights of the windowless hangar as Ben walked to the entrance and climbed aboard, pausing to look to his left into the technical complexity of the cockpit. Somehow the Gulfstream had reverted to the exciting, friendly, safe environment he'd always considered it, almost as if the nightmare of the uncontrolled descent two nights before had never happened.

There were technical manuals open on the copilot's seat, and the captain's seat had been pulled back to its full extent.

Must be the T-handle installation, Ben mused as he let his eyes roam over the area left of the captain's rudder pedals, where the emergency disconnect T-handle was supposed to be. He could hear voices in the hangar and hurried footsteps apparently approaching the entry stairs.

The telltale signs of a new installation were there, all right, along with the manual disconnect handle, which would physically knock the autoflight relays away from the flight controls if the computer glitched again. It was a comforting feeling to see the little handle, and he knew the pilots would equally appreciate having a way to pull the computer's silicon hands from their throat if anything else went wrong.

The footsteps were coming up the Gulfstream's entry stairs behind him, and Ben casually took note, letting his eyes rest on the engineering plans laid out on the copilot's seat. They were obviously the installation instructions for the emergency disconnect T-handle. The word "copy" was stamped in the upper left-hand corner over the more detailed engineering identification box, but it contained another stamped word he couldn't quite make out.

Ben could hear someone approaching the top of the stairs as he reached out and moved the top page to get a better look at the papers.

"Anyone here?" a male voice asked from the entryway, distracting him.

"Yes. Ben Cole. I'm in the cockpit."

A heavyset, worried-looking man moved in behind him and leaned over, snatching the engineering papers off the copilot's seat.

"Is there a problem?" Ben asked, twisting around and looking up to catch the man's eyes.

"No. I just left these . . . maintenance papers here," he said.

"I'm Ben Cole, chief software engineer," Ben said, extending his hand as he got to his feet.

"Ah . . . Don Brossard," the man said, reluctantly shifting the papers to his left hand and meeting the handshake.

"You're maintenance?"

Ben saw Brossard's eyebrows rise visibly. The man nodded, his eyes darting to the entryway with a clear desire to bolt and run. "Yeah. Sorry . . . I've got a . . . a conference." He pointed toward the far door of the hangar.

"Understood, but before you go, let me ask you a question about that emergency disconnect handle you just installed."

Brossard nodded. "Yeah?"

"Is it operational yet, and have you tested it?"

"I'm sure that . . . whatever they're supposed to do has been done. You'll have to ask the chief of maintenance about that. I'm just supposed to bring these papers."

"You're not doing the installation?"

"Not if it's complete. Look, I'm sorry, Mr. Cole, but I've gotta run. Nice meeting you."

Ben watched him descend the steps and hurry out of the hangar before moving back into the spartan cabin and running a series of tests on the computers in search of a stray copy of the main Boomerang program.

After an hour of careful probing, it was obvious it was wasted effort. Ben stood and moved back toward the front entry door and the cockpit, visualizing the final flight test and wondering if the two pilots would be able to pull the new T-handle fast enough if the program went nuts again. It was prominent enough and large enough to get a hand around easily, and judging from the complexity of the engineering drawings he had seen, it had obviously been carefully conceived.

Something about the plans snagged his memory, but he couldn't quite put his finger on it. Ben looked around to see if anyone was observing him, but the hangar appeared empty. He leaned into the cockpit out of curiosity and decided to sit down in the surprisingly comfortable captain's seat, his eyes on the red T-handle.

Ben let his left hand close around the cool metallic mass of the red T-handle as he absently wondered how much force was required on the specially installed device to actually pull the autoflight servos free of the control cables somewhere below in the Gulfstream's belly. He pulled gently on the handle to gauge the resistance, unprepared for the response, as the T-handle came off smoothly in his hand, effortlessly trailing a loose length of cable.

Ben raised the handle to eye level, feeling a flash of guilt for breaking something that shouldn't have been touched, before realizing with a start that the cable had been loose for a very specific reason: It had never been attached to anything.

He threaded the cable back in and replaced the T-handle, recalling the strained encounter with the maintenance man, who had apparently been trying to retrieve the T-handle installation order before Ben Cole could find it. Lindsey had promised him the disconnect would be installed, but if the installation was complete, this was a placebo, a dummy device for show only.

There had been a word stamped in the information block of the papers Ben had seen, and he tried to pull up the visual image of it now, wondering if it was a growing paranoia or reality working to convince him the word he'd seen was "canceled." If so, Lindsey had lied to him.

He scrambled out of the seat and almost fell down the Gulfstream's airstairs in his hurry to leave the hangar as fast as possible. There was a parking lot across the road adjacent to the base exchange and he found a spot and parked, letting the engine idle as he tried to think through the growing puzzle.

Am I being watched? he wondered, glancing around. *Why would they lie about the emergency disconnect? Or could the installation just not have been complete? No. If it were incomplete, why send a nervous maintenance guy to snatch the plans away?*

He recalled the delay getting admission to the Gulfstream hangar in the first place, and his suspicions coalesced.

Davis! He tried to talk me out of getting aboard because he didn't want me to find out they'd canceled the disconnect. Davis and Lindsey are in on this together, but do they have anything to do with the renegade lines of code and their disappearance?

Lindsey's smiling face returned to his thoughts, along with the very pleasant memory of her hair brushing his face the day before, that invigorating wave of femininity now drying into the brittle reality that she had merely been using him. He felt betrayed and helpless.

The memory of the terror two nights before when their jet dove toward the ocean and skimmed the surface returned. That icy fear was all too familiar, like the childhood dream of trying to run from the monster but being unable to move an inch. The memory of those few moments of panic and indecision was enough for a lifetime. Going up again was okay as long as they had the manual disconnect, but without it, and with dangerously unknown lines of code appearing and disappearing in the master program, the possibility that the next test would be fatal was growing at almost the same speed as the conclusion that he was helpless to stop the disaster.

He pulled out his cell phone and dialed the lab.

"I'm . . . really feeling lousy, Gene," Ben said, keeping his voice even. "Unless you seriously need me back there to look at anything new, I think I'm going to go home and go to bed."

"Go home, Ben. Nothing new to talk about."

He punched the disconnect button and put the car in reverse. He had no doubt that he was little more than a pawn now, and just along for the ride.

Could I be wrong? There was little hope of that. But the question of why hung in the air as he put the car in gear and moved out of the parking lot.

I've found him, April."

"Who?" April replied, still fumbling for control of the cell phone she'd yanked from the holster on the side of her purse as she tried to steer.

"An aviation lawyer we can trust. He's in D.C., and he's making calls at FAA headquarters to see if he can head off any problems with that inspector Harrison."

"That's good news, Gracie."

"No guarantees, but he's one of the best. He's spent two decades battling the FAA enforcement division's demonstrated desire to revoke every pilot license in America, and to the extent they can be scared of anyone, they're scared of him. He charged a three-thousand-dollar retainer, which I've already sent."

"Gracie! Thank you. I'll pay you back as soon as I return."

"I'm really seriously worried, as you can tell."

"Dad will deeply appreciate your doing that."

"So how is our captain?"

April related Dean's arrival and her trip to the Coast Guard in lieu of staying at the hospital. "Dean called a few minutes ago. Mom and Dad will be released by four, and we leave for Seattle at six."

"Tell me about the Coast Guard," Gracie said.

"Okay. The Coast Guard is a military-style organization placed under the control of the Department of Transportation with a mission that—"

"April!"

"Well, you do that to me all the time."

"Yeah, but that's how we're supposed to do it. You set up the joke and *I* deliver the punch lines. Okay. Tell me what you found out from the Coasties."

April outlined the conversation with Lieutenant Jim Hobbs and the fact that he'd called just fifteen minutes before to arrange a meeting. "Gracie, something's obviously making him cautious. He wants me to meet him at a Starbucks nearby. I'm trying to figure out what that means."

"Perhaps he likes coffee."

"No, really. He said he was calling on his cell phone and that he'd have a civilian parka over his uniform, and he said not to mention to anyone that I was meeting him."

"Well, at least he wasn't asking you to join him for a serious discussion at the Happy Bottom Motel."

"He's married, Gracie."

"I keep telling you, Rosen. You leave this wide wake of interested males behind you. That's why I can always find you in a crowd."

"Where are *you* right now, O'Brien?"

"Still in my office under a ton of briefs."

"The legal kind, I assume?"

"There you go again, stealing my lines. You headed over to meet him now?"

"Yes. And are you going to meet us at Seatac when we arrive?"

"Absolutely. But this time I'll be one of the pathetic supplicants waiting outside security with the rest of the unwashed masses. Call me after your Coast Guard rendezvous, will you?"

"I will."

There was a long pause from Seattle. "It may be important to sal-vage the Albatross, April, regardless of the expense."

April nodded before remembering Gracie couldn't see the ges-ture. "I know. I have the disturbing feeling that the believability of Dad's story rests on the broken propeller blade, and if so, we may have no choice."

Lieutenant Jim Hobbs was waiting just inside Starbucks when April arrived. He joined her in line and insisted on paying before motioning her to the most remote table.

"Why the cloak-and-dagger routine?" April asked, smiling and enjoying the warm, caffeinated aroma of the place.

Hobbs glanced around carefully, satisfied that no one seemed in-ordinately interested in them. He met her gaze. "Here's what I *can* tell you. Yes, there were ships in the area. Yes, our radar out of Valdez did track what was probably your dad's aircraft. But—and I haven't seen any readouts or copies of what's on the radar tapes—I'm told the targets did not intersect. The only other thing I can tell you is that I believe those tapes are in the public domain, but you may need to file a Freedom of Information Act request to get them."

"They're stonewalling?"

Jim Hobbs smiled thinly and glanced around, mentally tracking the various people in the store. He turned back to her. "Let's just say this. Even in the most innocuous situations, the Coast Guard is insti-tutionally nervous about letting civilians see their radar tapes. Sec-ond, in this case, there's way too much official interest in the very same tapes for this to be routine, and before you ask"—he held up a hand to stop the question he saw coming—"I don't know who's be-hind that special interest, but it means I'll deny that I ever talked to you about it. I was never here."

"Why are you? Talking to me, I mean?"

He smiled nervously. "Because you're a damsel in distress, and I'm a sucker for pretty women in need of aid and comfort. I guess that's why I joined the Coast Guard to begin with. I thought 'Baywatch' was an accurate portrayal."

"Babewatch was in California. This is Alaska."

"The recruiter lied," he laughed. "And then I got married," he said.

By arrangement, April left first, motoring back to the hospital, where her brother and parents were waiting for the trip across town to the airport.

Arlie and Rachel Rosen both refused wheelchairs when they reached the Anchorage airport, but the deep bruises from the crash were forcing Arlie to move with uncharacteristic care as they went through security on the way to the gate, where he insisted on standing in line himself.

"Dad," April tried, "don't you want to sit? There's no shame in that. You and Mom went through a terrible ordeal."

"I'm fine, honey," he said, forcing a smile to hide the pain he was obviously feeling. A shaft of light from the low-hanging sun on the southern horizon cut through the glass of the terminal and illuminated his face, and April fought a sudden wave of sadness at how old and weathered he looked. She'd always thought of him as indestructible and ageless, a dynamo who held off the effects of aging by simply refusing to participate in the process.

But the orange Alaskan sunlight was telling another story, and she purposely refrained from glancing at her mother for fear the same truths would be reflected there.

"We'll start looking this weekend for another Albatross," Arlie Rosen was saying, as much to himself as to April. "It'll take quite awhile to re-create the interior, but with the insurance, it should be straightforward."

"How much recuperation did the doctor say you'd need before you get back on the schedule at United, Dad?" April asked.

Arlie snorted and smiled. "The kid doctor was really serious about that. He said maybe a month, but he has no idea what he's talking about. Pilots are tougher than that. I'll see my FAA flight doc next Monday and get re-cleared immediately."

"Dad, you told me yourself you have enough sick leave to probably sit it out until retirement. Why not use it?"

Arlie reached out and placed the palm of his hand on her head, his infectious smile riveting her. "Now, once more April, let's get this concept down. Repeat after me. Retirement is bad. Retirement is not our friend. Your father does not play well with retired people."

"You've got four years left before—"

He quickly placed his index finger against her lips, shaking his head to expunge any mention of the hated age-sixty mandatory retirement rule. "We don't use cusswords in this family. 'Retirement' is a damn cussword!"

"You just love to fly, don't you, Dad?" Dean said, joining the exchange.

Arlie smiled and nodded as he snaked an arm around Rachel's trim waist and pulled her close, bumping hips. "There are two things I love to do more than anything else in this life. When your mother's too tired, that leaves flying."

"When was I ever too tired?" Rachel replied, looking mischievous.

April rolled her eyes at both of them. "You two are embarrassing me again."

"Yeah," Dean chimed in. "Me, too, for God's sake."

Arlie turned to his wife and winked. "Rachel, what say we start making out right here and really scandalize these two prudes we raised?"

"Dad," April interjected, "no one says 'making out' anymore. And . . . we need to talk about serious stuff."

Arlie grinned and patted Rachel's rear as several other passengers turned to look. "This *is* serious stuff. That's why I married her."

"Dad!" April said through gritted teeth. "Okay, look. Admit it, both of you. I'm adopted, right? I was left by gypsies? Gracie's got to be your natural child."

Arlie was still chuckling, but wincing involuntarily from the pain around his ribs as he put a hand on April's shoulder. "You said we need to talk. What about?"

She filled him in on the profile of the Washington lawyer Gracie had retained with her own money.

"I appreciate that," Arlie said, "but tell Gracie that nothing's going to come of that stupid altercation with whatshisname from the FAA."

"Harrison."

"Yeah. He's a bastard, but there's virtually no evidence I was doing anything wrong, and the NTSB will shoot him down if he tries to allege reckless operation."

"Gracie's not so sure."

"Gracie's trained to worry about everything, April. It'll be all right."

"You've never had an FAA violation, have you, Dad?"

He shook his head, looking mildly startled that his daughter would ask such a thing. "Of course not. Good grief. Not even when I was slipping into alcoholism, which was on my off time. Flying drunk was one thing I never, ever did, for many reasons, not the least of which was my number-one basic fear."

"*You* have a basic fear?"

He nodded, the smile fading. "Fear of *not* flying, April. Fear of losing the right to fly," Arlie said, his face suddenly gray and his words dead serious. "There's no way . . . *no way* . . . that I could ever take that."

SIXTEEN

WEDNESDAY, DAY 3

IN FLIGHT

LATE AFTERNOON

General Mac MacAdams waved off the offer of a stiff drink and refocused his attention on dialing the secure satellite call he was placing to the Pentagon.

"Would you like a Coke or something then, sir?" the flight steward asked.

Mac shook his head. "No, thanks. Wait . . . on second thought, do you have a diet version?"

The sharply dressed young sergeant smiled and flashed him a thumbs-up before turning back to the galley momentarily. The diet Coke appeared within seconds, and the line in D.C. was still ringing.

Mac sighed and looked around the interior of the Air Force Gulfstream 5, one of the newest executive transports assigned to the 89th Presidential Airlift Squadron at Andrews near Washington. It was the closest he'd ever come, he figured, to experiencing the type of plush transportation corporate leaders were so used to. Not that a Gulfstream 5 wasn't a top-of-the-line corporate-level aircraft, but mere two-star generals had an uphill climb finding major corporate positions after retirement. Board positions in public companies, maybe,

but the real plums required four stars on the shoulders of freshly retired general officers, and he just wasn't sufficiently political to wait
around for, or engineer, the extra promotion.

A female voice answered on the other end and Mac pressed the
phone closer to his ear and identified himself.

"Yes, sir," a secretary was saying. "The general's expecting
your call."

There was a short wait before the familiar tones of his immediate
commander, a four-star general, came on the line.

"What's the story, Mac?"

"We're fine, Lou," he said. "I'm not letting Uniwave know that,
of course, since there's still a test flight they've got to make, but I'm
ready to sign off on Boomerang."

"All the problems solved?"

Mac chuckled into the phone. "Not by a long shot, but it'll clean
up nicely. We had a weird problem two nights ago that could have
been a disaster, but they found the glitch and Davis and his people
have finally explained it to my satisfaction. An internal communications thing."

"We've got to be on schedule with this, Mac. The White House
is pressing us hard to get it approved and deployed on time, which is
a little strange, given the pure military nature of the program."

"No accounting for the political world, Lou."

"Amen."

"I'm in flight right now and hustling my tail back there for that
very reason, to get this thing stamped and sealed at the final briefing
in the morning. I assume the list of attendees will be the same as we
discussed?"

"Bad assumption."

"Really?"

General Lou Cassidy sighed on the other end. "I just found this
out ten minutes ago, Mac, but the Secretary of Defense has post-
poned the acceptance briefing for two days. It'll be Friday now."

"But . . . that's right up against the deadline."

"Can't be helped. The secretary is requiring everyone to be there, beginning with himself, the joint chiefs, our mild-mannered Air Force secretary, and the other key uniformed players, and they can't all make it in the morning. In fact, the secretary is in London."

Mac sat in thought for a few seconds. "Okay, if we've got two days, let me keep this plane and crew and take them back home. I can use the time better back in Anchorage."

"Suit yourself. Just be here on time. I can't unveil and approve this without my project commander."

Mac replaced the receiver and got to his feet as the copilot came out of the cockpit. "Ah, just the man I was coming to see."

"Yes, sir?"

"Turn us around, please, Lieutenant. Back to Elmendorf. You fellows will lay over for forty-eight hours, and then we'll try it again. The meeting's been postponed."

The copilot's face fell slightly, but he nodded without protest and returned to the cockpit as Mac sat down next to his aide, Lieutenant Colonel Jon Anderson, repeating the news. "I know these boys were expecting to be home tonight, but it can't be helped."

"Just as well, sir," Anderson replied, watching the boss raise an eyebrow. "We've got something going on I need to brief you about."

"What's up?"

"Sir, do you recall yesterday I mentioned that we had learned of the loss of a civilian aircraft, an old private amphibian, that went down in the general vicinity of where our test flight was Monday night?"

"Yes. And I asked you if we could have had anything to do with it, and you said no. You're not telling me there's a change in that assessment?"

"No, sir. But there's more you need to hear."

"Go on."

Anderson outlined the basics of the Albatross's loss and what the NTSB had discovered so far. "They're pretty sure the airline pilot who owned it just got sloppy, tried some scud-hopping, got too low, and caught a wingtip."

"What's your point, Jon?"

He sighed. "I'm not sure there is one, sir, other than to keep you completely in the loop. But things are unfolding a bit in Anchorage. The man's daughter flew in yesterday, and so far she's visited the FAA and the Coast Guard, apparently looking for radar tapes that might show the track of her father's aircraft."

Mac sat forward. "Radar tapes?"

"Yes, sir."

"What's she trying to prove?"

"That her father wasn't negligent, I suppose. She thinks one of his propellers may have hit a ship in the fog, causing the crash. That's why she went to the Coast Guard. They reported that over to us."

"Did they help her? Did they . . . give her any tapes?"

He shook his head.

"How about the FAA air traffic control people?"

Again the lieutenant colonel shook his head, this time with a mild smile. "She hasn't asked for the Coast Guard tapes directly yet, but we expect she will."

"What's her name?"

"April Rosen. She's an American, living in Vancouver, Canada. Twenty-six years old. A young corporate staff vice-president for one of the U.S. cruise ship lines that's based there."

Mac nodded. "And *did* her dad hit a ship?"

"Probably. But the FAA thinks he was just being reckless."

"But . . . what's worrying you, and now me, is that any of those radar tapes could reveal our test aircraft's presence in the same area and at a very low altitude. That could spark questions we don't want, especially not at this late date."

Jon Anderson was nodding. "Yes, sir. My concern exactly. Our security people have been watching her, and from all indications this young lady is sharp and very persistent, and I believe she poses a threat to the program."

"That's a premature conclusion, Jon. I mean, she can think whatever she wants and ask as many questions as she wants. What would worry me is her getting hold of any real evidence leading to some cage rattling and maybe some media action, and before we know it, they're stumbling onto our sideshow and getting a few foreign intelligence services interested. Can we somehow help this young woman secretly without tipping our hand? You know, silently make sure she gets what she needs in terms of radar tapes without revealing our presence?"

Anderson sighed and chewed his lip. "I don't know, sir. We don't know what's on those tapes. But you need to know that the FAA's apparently become a wild card in this." He outlined the hospital-room confrontation between Walter Harrison and Captain Arlie Rosen.

"How do we know about this, Jon?" Mac asked, cocking his head slightly and draining the remainder of the diet Coke. "I assume we don't have surveillance cameras in every hospital room in Anchorage."

"That would be an interesting thought, sir. Scary, but interesting."

"I'm watching you, Anderson," Mac said, pointing two fingers at him with one eye closed in mock seriousness.

Jon Anderson laughed and shook his head. "We found out by pure chance. The representative of the National Transportation Safety Board is a friend of one of our program security men. They play racquetball together, and I'm told the NTSB guy was very upset about the interview and very talkative."

"Loose lips."

"Sorry?"

Mac laughed. "Oh. An old World War Two expression. And before you ask and insult me, the answer is no, I'm far too young to have been in World War Two."

"I have a career, sir. I wasn't about to make any snide comments . . . that your hearing aid might pickup."

"I heard that! The actual phrase was 'Loose lips sink ships,' and it's still valid. That's why it's so damned hard to run a black project in the middle of a civilian community. I'm amazed we've done as well as we have in the past three years, with only one significant security breach."

The cabin steward appeared silently with another diet Coke and

Mac took it as he shook his head, his eyes falling on a striking twilight painting of the Washington Monument mounted on the aft bulkhead of the cabin.

"I suppose I don't have to say, Jon, that we need to watch both this Harrison character and Ms. Rosen very carefully."

"No, sir, you don't, and our security people will."

"I worry about security being handled by our"—he mouthed the words as if they were sour—"office of special investigations. I don't want any cowboy lieutenant in civilian clothes getting excited and riding off to do something illegal. But . . . have them harvest each and every one of the original radar tapes from FAA, Coast Guard, Navy, and whoever else might have electronic evidence of our test flight that evening. Set them up in the briefing room back at Elmendorf for tomorrow."

"General, what do we do if the Gulfstream does show up on one of those radar tapes?"

Mac smiled and shook his head. "Why, there was never any Gulfstream in the area to begin with, was there?"

"Ah, no, sir."

"Right. So how could it possibly show up on whatever tape we send back?"

Anderson nodded. "Understood."

"Actually," Mac added, "we'll see the raw data radar return on all of them, I suspect, but without a data block generated by a transponder, which we kept off, it's just another unidentified aircraft flitting around the state. I don't want to see anything that might lead Ms. Rosen to think we were involved with her father's plane." He paused and peered closely at Anderson, who had lowered his eyes. "There isn't any possibility of that, is there?"

"No, sir, of course not. But I had already figured you'd want those tapes. I'm ready to move on it." Lieutenant Colonel Anderson began to get up but Mac caught his sleeve, studying his eyes.

"Jon, just a second. You're sure that we could not have had anything to do with the loss of that Albatross?"

The colonel finished standing and shook his head vigorously. "No, sir. Absolutely not! The coordinates I have for where that ditching, or crash, occurred are a long way away from the surface track of our test Gulfstream."

"But," the general said as he raised a finger, "you *were* concerned enough to check."

There was a momentary twitch in Anderson's expression, and Mac noticed. "Jon, look at me. As I told you when you became my aide, I've got to know everything you know, without exception. You withhold anything from me, no matter how noble the intent, and I'll personally ride your shredded ass out of the Air Force. Understood?"

"Honestly, sir, I'm telling you everything I know, and I would never—"

Mac cut him off with a single look of warning and a raised index finger. "Just get the tapes and set up a secure viewing room for zero eight hundred in the morning."

SEVENTEEN

Schroedinger had spent all afternoon mulling the indignities of the morning and was unprepared for yet another assault on normalcy when Ben burst through the door hours ahead of the schedule.

There were no actual words formed in Schroedinger's mind to define his discomfited response, merely a disgusted consciousness of the continued attack on the predictability of his world. He would need to find a way to demonstrate his displeasure to Ben, he decided. And there were many options available to a creature with claws in a house with furniture.

"Hi, fellow," Ben said as he breezed through without so much as a session of ear scratching. Schroedinger watched him charge across the den and pull various things from a desk drawer, things Schroedinger had sniffed before and found uninteresting. Ben, it seemed, liked to pay far more attention to his things and his computer than to his cat, and in a feline frame of reference, such an attitude was simply inexplicable.

The 3,500-square-foot home Ben had purchased for Lisa and

himself three months before her death was tucked into a new subdivision on the flanks of the Chugach Mountains bordering the east side of Anchorage. All the way back from the base Ben had been fighting the image of Lisa standing before the picture window in the upper-story den with their real estate agent, squealing with delight at the sweeping view of the city. The decision to buy had been made on the spot, and the night of delighted lovemaking that followed had been a thank-you of sorts.

Ben had tried repeatedly to get the image out of his mind. It inevitably triggered a deep sadness, and a feeling that had been growing precipitously of late, the simple longing for feminine companionship. It was the same disturbing instinct Lindsey had inadvertently twanged the day before.

So much for that, Ben thought, bitterness overlaying his thoughts of Lindsey. She'd used him, *was* using him, wagging her shapely tail to keep him under control.

That's unfair, he corrected himself. *She wasn't making a pass. It was me who was thinking prurient thoughts.*

Nonetheless, the sudden loss of trust in what had appeared to be a growing friendship hurt.

The refrigerator yielded a poor selection limited to bottled water and a few soft drinks, and he opted for the water before moving to the living room, aware that he couldn't recall the details of the drive home. He plopped in the big easy chair Lisa had insisted he buy when they moved in, and wondered who would mourn him if he crashed on the upcoming test flight.

Phyllis, his only sibling, would be momentarily hysterical when the news reached her palatial North Dallas home. With their folks gone, Phyllis would arrange the funeral and make all the requisite noises, but in the end, they had never been close enough as adults for his passing to alter her life.

The flight! There was no doubt that whoever had contaminated the basic program would strike again, and this time succeed. Someone wanted the program to fail and Uniwave to go under. There was no doubt that he and the two pilots would die. And he would be condemning someone else to perish in his place if he elected to stay on the ground.

He glanced over at Schroedinger and smiled, puzzling the cat even more. He needed to make arrangements for Schroedinger, and that thought triggered an image of Nelson, who would be the only Alaskan genuinely saddened by his passing.

Dammit! Nelson had left a message the day before on his voice mail and he'd forgotten to get back to him. Ben came out of the chair with enough haste to startle Schroedinger. He found his hand-held database PDA and located Nelson's cell phone number, then punched it into the portable handset.

Nelson Oolokvit was contemptuous of the label "Eskimo." Ben remembered his explosion one night at a clumsy question from a California tourist with a dilettante concern for Native Americans.

"If you call me an Eskimo one more time, sister, I'm gonna find an uulu and gut you!" he'd raged, waving a beer in the woman's face. "Go find yourself a frozen Athabascan to patronize! I'm from Kotzebue. I'm Inupiat. I've never lived in a damned igloo, and I know better things to do with a female than rub noses with her, okay?"

"Who's this?" a voice was saying on the other end of the phone as Ben snapped back to the present. The voice was slightly clipped and accented, the aftereffects of American English overlaid on a childhood of his native tongue.

"Nelson?"

"You called his phone and you're surprised to get him?" Nelson said, chuckling. "At least I answer my phone, unlike some other people who let machines do it for them." The sounds of a raucous bar filtered through from the background, voices talking loudly over an even higher volume of a country-and-western song. It was Shania Twain, her words coming through like a coda to the conversation.

"Okay, so you've got a car. That don't impress me much!"

"Nelson, this is Ben."

"What? It's too damned loud in here. Who?"

"Ben. BEN COLE."

"Oh. Ben. Hello. Where are you?"

"At home."

"Well, get your scrawny computer geek ass down here to Charlie's and join me for a few beers. I'll even buy you a Guinness if you'll actually drink it this time."

"Charlie's? Where's that?"

"*. . . don't get me wrong, yeah, I think you're all right . . .*"

"Chilkoot Charlie's on Spenard. Where the hell else can a guy find a good brawl and sawdust on the floor?"

"I thought you hated Chilkoot's."

"Yeah, but I have to check on 'em every now and then."

"*. . . but that won't keep me warm on the long, cold, lonely night . . .*"

The absence of Lisa and his own familiarity with cold, lonely nights momentarily eclipsed the image of Nelson waiting for a response.

"*So whadda you think? You're Elvis or something?*"

"Ben? Are you still there?"

"Yes, Nelson. I just . . ."

"Something's chewing on you. I can tell. Get in your car and pick me up here. My car's in the shop."

Ben knew better. Nelson's car had been in the shop for the past decade, which meant up on blocks since a disgusted Anchorage judge had tired of his drunk driving convictions and created a new taxi patron by permanently revoking his driver's license.

"Okay. I'm on the way, Nelson."

"*Whatever. That don't impress me!*"

*I*t took less than twenty minutes to pull up in front of the infamous bar. Nelson was already on the sidewalk waiting, and he climbed in, smelling of peanuts and beer and pointing west.

"Turn around. Head for Lake Spenard."

"Why?"

"We need to go boating."

"Nelson, you don't own a boat . . . do you?"

"Of course. Turn around."

They reversed course and parked on the eastern side of the lake by a grassy bank where a ramshackle wooden rowboat sat chained and padlocked to a tree.

"Hey, I'm not going out in that thing."

"What thing?" Nelson asked, following Ben's index finger. "Oh. Of course not. I wouldn't either."

"So . . . where's your boat?"

"In here," Nelson replied, walking to an old toolshed standing at a slight angle some five feet from the shoreline. He worked with the padlock for a few seconds and pulled the creaking door open to take out what appeared to be a large blue duffel bag. He extracted a folded-up mass of vinyl from the bag and pulled a string, standing back as an inflatable boat took shape.

"I won that two years ago," Nelson said proudly, pointing to the boat. "First thing I ever won. And I'm fifty-nine this year."

"Really?"

"Or fifty-six. I'm not sure. Somedays, twenty-eight."

Ben locked the car and gingerly lowered himself into the two-man craft, taking one of the aluminum paddles Nelson offered and following his lead as they pushed off.

"We have to hug the shoreline to stay away from the planes," Nelson said, nodding toward a Cessna 180 on floats just beginning its takeoff run down the lake.

"How much daylight do we have left?" Ben asked.

"About an hour, I think."

They paddled around the bend into a calm part of the waterway and Nelson shipped his paddle and turned around.

"Okay, Benjamin. What did you want to tell me?"

Ben laughed. "What makes you think I want to tell you something?"

"I know you, Ben Cole. As my people would say, you have a good heart, and it is heavy."

Ben smiled. "And you, sir, have good insight."

"I also sing well, but it's never kept me fed. Now tell me. The doctor is in."

"There are many things I can't tell you, because of the place I work."

"I know. Go on."

Ben outlined the dilemma of trying to find a problem in the massive computer program he'd written, only to turn up evidence of sabotage that was then erased. Ben kept away from the specifics, holding back, he hoped, anything considered classified, but even mentioning the possibility of a secret project could still get him in extreme trouble. "Talking around" top secret information was forbidden.

His words tumbled out, quietly at first, but impassioned, about the betrayal of a woman he liked and respected, even though she was his boss; the shock of realizing that someone or some group wanted the project to fail; and the reality that if he flew the last test flight, he would probably not be coming home.

"Maybe that's my destiny, Nelson," he said after a long pause. "Maybe it's time to join Lisa, you know? God knows I've just been using work as an excuse to avoid living again."

"Or dating."

"Yeah."

"Or even recreational screwing, which you probably haven't done for at least two years."

"Thank you so much for pointing that out."

"You're not a monk, Ben. You're not even Catholic, as I recall."

Ben shook his head. "My family was mainstream Presbyterian, whatever that means."

"And now you expect some ancient Inupiat wisdom from me, right?"

Ben laughed and sat back, inadvertently rocking the boat. "No, I just wanted to talk to a friend."

"Well, that's good, because I don't dispense tribal wisdom. You have to be licensed to do that."

"Aw, heck, Nelson," Ben said, trying hard to grin, "I expected incense, rattles, drums, and a sweat lodge."

"*Sweat* lodge?" Nelson replied, looking thoroughly alarmed. "Hollywood's warped your mind, Ben. That's American Indian! Down south. Your basic Blackfeet, Ogalala Sioux, Cheyenne, and such." Nelson's broad face broke into a huge smile. "I mean, we understand the concept, but I'm a card-carrying Inupiat, remember? The guy with the hooded parka and the long lance chasing polar bears and whales? Next you'll be expecting me to don a feather headdress."

Ben chuckled, the momentary flash of humor a transitory replacement for the sadness Nelson could see reflected in his eyes.

They let a long period of silence pass.

"Ben, you think you've given up, but you haven't."

"No?"

"You called me, right?"

"Maybe I called to say goodbye, Nelson, and to thank you for being a good friend. And while I'm on the subject, if anything does happen to me, would you please take care of poor old Schroedinger?"

"Sure. I like old man Schroedinger."

Ben cocked his head. "Why *do* you always call him 'old man'?"

"Very, very old soul in that cat's body. Who knows? Could be Archimedes, Caesar, or even Elvis."

Ben snorted. "Well, now that's enough to give me nightmares."

Nelson raised a finger, using the thickest native accent he could manage. "'Dere are more tings in heaven and earth than you have dreamt of.'"

"Inupiat?"

"No. Shakespeare. Hamlet, to be precise. Act one, scene five." Nelson's eyes were on an approaching DeHavilland Beaver as the single-engine floatplane flared and merged ever so smoothly with the glassy surface of the lake, the resulting spray kicking up from both pontoons as it settled in and slowed. He was shaking his head. "Ben, you're still looking for answers, and that's the right thing to do, because you're not a quitter. So don't tell yourself to quit. There is an answer right in front of you somewhere, and even if you can't find it, you can't give up, because it will eventually find you."

"Good words, Nelson, but . . ."

"There is always an answer, Ben. Keep looking. You're the software master. You can create something that can unlock anything the program locks up, no matter how critical the moment."

Ben nodded, his mind racing around the problem again, looking for a new perspective and finding nothing.

Nelson picked up an oar. "Time for you to get back to work."

"Now, how do you know that?"

Nelson Oolokvit widened his eyes until they were about to pop out and raised both hands above his shoulders, flexing his fingers in a cartoonish attempt to look scary. "Ancient Eskimo wisdom!"

Ben chuckled. "I thought you weren't licensed *or* Eskimo."

"I'm not. It's bootleg advice. And it's worth exactly what you paid for it."

*I*t was past eight when Ben reached his front door, which had an etched-glass center panel. He stopped cold. The porch light was on, but he had no memory of throwing the switch before he'd left.

He tried the door and found it locked.

There was a back door and a side entrance through the garage, both alarmed with the security system he'd installed a year before, and inside, reflecting in a hall mirror, he could see a little red light indicating the system was still armed.

Ben looked around, spotting no one. Maybe, he thought, he'd actually thrown the switch before he'd left and forgotten. After all, he'd been very distracted. But just to be sure, he circled around the back of the house, stopping at the sight of what appeared to be a set of footprints just off the concrete walk.

Once again, small sparkles of fear began climbing his back as he knelt down to touch the muddy indentations. The ridges were soft, but that could mean anything. He could find no other tracks and no muddy traces on the walkway.

The back door and side doors were secure, and a search of the ground beneath every window turned up nothing. Ben returned to the front door and entered the hallway, canceling the alarm system and querying it for previous entries or alarms. The last reported event had been the time he'd left and armed the system.

So much for that, he concluded. *Maybe I'm just getting paranoid.*

He gave Schroedinger a quick pat on the head and went directly to his computer to upload the programs he'd hidden, suppressing another flash of anxiety as he waited to see if the renegade computer files were still there.

Thank God! The endless lines of computer code popped onto the screen, just as he had saved it. Mute evidence that he hadn't imagined it.

Right in front of me, huh? Ben thought, recalling Nelson's words. *He could be right. I didn't have time to fully examine this stuff.* He thought for a few minutes before sketching out in his mind a methodical way of searching the thousands of lines of arcane code. First he'd look for lists, and then patterns, and if that failed, there were a host of other things he could try in an effort to decipher precisely what the author was trying to accomplish.

Ben entered the first of the search routines and pressed the "enter" key, matching the flurry of activity on the screen as the search routines began. He started to get to his feet when a message flashed into prominence: "Requested list found."

A numbered list appeared on the screen, coalescing slowly as the computer translated the code into English, presenting him at last with a comprehensive listing of most of the airlines in North America, complete with their two-letter identification codes and what appeared to be the registration and serial numbers of each airplane in the respective airline fleets.

What the heck is this? Ben thought as he paged through the listings. This was a military program. Why were commercial airlines being referenced in a military computer program? He reminded himself that he was exploring an unauthorized addition to the main program.

Ben suppressed thoughts of more sinister possibilities and got to his feet, forcing himself to go to the kitchen and calmly fix a pot of coffee, while the search routines continued.

He was in the process of grinding the coffee beans when a snippet of the conversation in Nelson's inflatable boat suddenly popped into his mind, and he lifted his hand from the grinder switch, restoring silence to the kitchen. Ben could hear the soft whirring sounds of the computer's hard drive in the den as his thoughts rose to a dull roar in his head. *Wait a minute. Wait just a minute! Nelson said something about the computer locking up . . . something about the program locking up. How on earth could he have guessed that? How could he know I was dealing with a program glitch that had locked up the computer in flight?*

Ben felt the room undulating slightly. First the commercial airliner list, and now this. Had he said something, anything, that might have clued the affable Alaskan in to what had taken place two nights before? Of course, computers locked up all the time. But . . .

No! Ben concluded. *There's no way he could legitimately know that. He must have surmised it from something else I said.*

EIGHTEEN

April glanced at the clock as a plume of dust caught her attention a quarter mile to the south at the entrance to their road. The outline of a postal service jeep was bouncing toward the house.

She turned back toward the cliff side of her parents' home, toward the Strait of Juan de Fuca separating Vancouver Island from the Olympic Peninsula, taking solace in the magnificent view for a few more moments. A large freighter was passing in the distance, perhaps five miles out in the main channel, headed toward the open Pacific forty miles to the west. She thought about picking up the omnipresent binoculars for a better look, but the mail truck was already crunching gravel in the driveway, and she turned instead toward the front door.

"I have a certified letter for Arlie Rosen," the postman told her, straining to read the print on the small green card taped to an official-looking letter.

"Can I sign for it?"

"No, ma'am. Only Mr. Rosen."

"Captain Rosen. Wait here," April said, closing the door and walking around the corner into the spacious kitchen, where she looked at the letter with a sinking feeling. It was from the Federal Aviation Administration.

Better I sign for it than show it to Dad just yet, she decided, faking his signature and returning the card to the postman. She took the letter back to the kitchen and sat on one of the stools, thankful her parents were still in bed. She started to open it, then decided to grab her cell phone instead, punching in Gracie's cell number.

"I'm scared, Gracie. It's from the FAA and it was certified."

"Oh shit, in the vernacular," Gracie said. "Have you opened it?"

"No."

"Open it."

"Do I have to?"

"Yes, you have to. Somebody has to. It's probably an invitation to some sort of check ride or evaluation or a notice of potential violation."

April sighed again. "I was hoping the D.C. attorney we hired had been able to fix things."

"Well, maybe he has. Open it, please, and read it to me."

April used her index fingernail to neatly rip through the top edge of the envelope, pulling the single sheet of pedestrian paper from within. The blue logo of the FAA was imprinted on the sheet along with the text.

"Oh, God, Gracie! Oh, God!"

"What?"

"It's a 'Notice of Emergency Revocation.'"

"Oh, no!"

"Yes. Dammit, Gracie, this will kill Dad."

"You're sure it says 'revocation'?"

"I'm sure. They're accusing him of . . . wait . . . this is ridiculous . . . flying while intoxicated, reckless operation of an aircraft, and violation of visual flight rules. What do we do?"

"You have a fax machine there, don't you?"

"Yes. Fax it to you?"

"And to the lawyer in D.C." Gracie relayed both numbers.

"What do I tell Dad?"

She could hear Gracie sigh on the other end, and the lack of a rapid comeback accelerated her fears. "April, you realize this also grounds him at United?"

"Yes."

"So . . . I don't know what to tell you, except that now the fight begins."

"Gracie, can I get you on a speakerphone to help me tell him?"

"Better that we pull the lawyer in on this as well. His name is Ted Greene. Give me a few minutes and I'll call you back to arrange it. Keep that damn thing hidden from your dad until then."

"I'll try. I was going back to Vancouver this afternoon, but now . . ."

"He's going to need you there, April, for a bit at least. This is going to be a heavy blow."

"I know."

"Stay put. I'll call you back."

"He's never had an FAA violation in his whole career. Did you know that?"

"April, it's going to be okay."

The letter was becoming opaque through her tears as she nodded, then remembered to speak. "Okay."

The phone rang within ten minutes with Gracie on the other end.

"Mr. Greene? Are you there?"

"Yes," a male voice announced in the electronic distance of his Washington office.

"All right. April? We're on your cell phone with the speakerphone feature, right?"

"Yes."

"We'll hold while you go get the captain."

April moved to her parents' bedroom feeling like an executioner. Rachel Rosen was already up and greeted her daughter from the alcove of their bathroom, but Arlie was still lying in bed.

"Dad?"

He looked grim, she noticed.

"Hi, honey."

"I . . ."

"The postal service never comes at this hour, you know."

"No, I didn't."

"Which means it was a registered letter, which means it's from the FAA, which means it's very bad news."

April looked at the letter in her hands as she slid onto the side of the bed and nodded. "I've got Gracie and our aviation lawyer, a Mr. Greene, on the phone. They want to talk to you."

"Let me see the letter," Arlie said quietly as he lifted it from her hands and opened it, scanning the text before handing it back and nodding to the phone. His face was ashen, but his voice was steady.

"Okay, April. Put them on."

OFFICES OF JANSSEN AND PRUZAN,
SEATTLE, WASHINGTON

Gracie O'Brien ended the conference call between Ted Greene and the Rosens and immediately redialed Greene's Washington office.

"I need a straight assessment, Mr. Greene."

There was a long sigh from D.C. "Well, to be blunt, we've got a hell of a mess here."

Gracie felt her heart sink. On the conference call, Greene had said all the right and cautious things a good lawyer should say to a new client at the start of an unknown legal journey, but she'd expected a slightly more optimistic lawyer-to-lawyer statement.

"They're gunning for him, Gracie. I mean, FAA tends to get that way, as we both know, when it gets to enforcement actions. But I couldn't get even the most cursory cooperation in Captain Rosen's case. It's as if they've made an agency decision to go for broke and destroy him."

"What can we do? I mean . . . Okay, that's a dumb question for co-counsel to ask."

"No, not really. The nexus of their righteous indignation is the theory that Captain Rosen simply flew the aircraft into the water, negligently. Everything else stems from that. But the drinking charge is very serious, and could be disastrous. Now, if the hospital did a blood test when Rosen was admitted, a zero blood-alcohol result would help."

"You need me to call Anchorage?"

"One of my staff is already on it. Keep your fingers crossed."

"I will. He wasn't drinking."

"The charge that he violated visual flight rules is hogwash, but it may be the most dangerous one of all, since they can create havoc by saying that he flew too far into instrument conditions without a clearance. I listened carefully to the recording of that hospital interview, and Captain Rosen, unfortunately, left the door open a crack for them with the way he described the conditions."

"But, he tried to turn around."

"Not soon enough. They'll say he spent too much time on the radio calling for an instrument clearance."

Gracie was tapping a pencil against her blotter in a frantic beat. "Oh, damn, damn, damn. You say the reckless charge is the worst?"

"Their word and interpretation against his."

"But what about the propeller?"

"That, unfortunately, is what I'm leading up to. We need to recover enough of that wreckage to at least show the prop blade is missing. That's our best defense. Of course, they'll claim it came off on impact with the water, but I seriously doubt that will sway a hearing examiner. We need that wreckage, regardless of what it costs to salvage it."

She rubbed her head and sighed. "I'll get to work on it."

"Gracie, I know you're a family friend. How long does Captain Rosen have till retirement? Is early retirement an option?"

"Not only no, but hell no. He's only forty-nine. He'll fight to his last penny, and even when they retire him someday, he'll be flying privately. I fully expect to see him flying into his nineties."

"First we have to get his license back."

"And there is, I assume, no chance of getting this so-called emergency revocation reversed quickly?"

"None whatsoever."

SEQUIM, WASHINGTON

Answering the home phone on the first ring was an unconscious habit, and April pulled the receiver to her ear unprepared for the slightly familiar male voice on the other end.

"Mrs. Rosen?"

"Ms. Rosen. Who is this?"

"Walter Harrison of the FAA. I have a message for Captain Rosen."

"You need to talk to his team of lawyers, Mr. Harrison. You won't get away with this outrage, by the way. I'd plan an early retirement if I were you."

There was a malevolent chuckle on the other end. "In denial, are we, Ms. Rosen? Well, you want to believe that dear old dad couldn't be drinking, and I understand your misguided loyalty. But I've found the proof, no pun intended."

"What the hell are you talking about?"

"He visited a liquor store in Anchorage just before the accident, which means the charges are valid and his days of imperiling passengers are over. Undoubtedly the empty bottles will be in the wreckage. A fifth of bourbon, two bottles of vodka—the alcoholic's friend—a bottle of Jamaican rum, and a very fine cognac. All that booze was purchased an hour before departure from Lake Spenard, and he signed the credit card receipt himself."

He paused, but April was too stunned to reply.

"I know you think I'm just a little worm, Ms. Rosen. But the truth is, your father's a dangerous drunk."

"You go to hell!" she snapped, slamming the phone back in the receiver and feeling her entire body quake. She lifted the receiver to call Gracie, then replaced it again, a cancerous doubt creeping into her mind. Why would he buy that much liquor? Why would a recovering alcoholic buy *any* liquor? She felt the growing need to find him, talk to him, and reassure herself, but he was nowhere to be found in the house. A light showed through the window of the detached, barn-like garage, and she pushed through the back door to find him on a stool in his woodworking shed.

"Dad?"

Arlie Rosen looked around at her, trying to smile through an expression of utter despair. There was an object on the workbench in front of him, and April realized with a twinge of fear that it was a bottle of Jack Daniel's, blessedly unopened.

"Dad, what are you doing out here?"

He sighed, a long, ragged sigh, and tapped the workbench. "Looking my old enemy in the eye, April."

"Dad, you're not thinking . . ."

"Of drinking?" he finished, chuckling at the rhyme. He shook his head and picked up the bottle with his left hand, turning it slowly. "No, honey. I'm just wondering why that little FAA bastard hates me so. Because I had a bout with the bottle ten years ago? Or was I right about his being a rejected airline applicant with a vendetta?"

"He called, Dad."

"Who?"

"Harrison." She related the conversation, watching her father's expression harden.

"That isn't true, Dad, is it? You . . . weren't in any liquor store, were you?"

He looked away, nearly a minute passing before she heard an answer. "Yes, dammit." He snapped his eyes back to her. "Your mother is witness to this, April. The liquor was not for me. We entertained on the airplane often when we were moored someplace, and I was planning to see some friends in Sitka on arrival."

"This doesn't help us, Dad."

"I wasn't drinking!"

"It's okay, Dad."

"No, it's not. Forget the stupid liquor charge, what matters is, my reputation's just been assassinated, my plane is gone, I could have killed us, and even your trust has been shaken, and . . ." His right hand flailed the air as he fought the emotion.

"It's okay, Dad," April prompted.

"April, I'm a senior airman. I should have turned around immediately. I should have climbed. I should have seen that fog bank, gotten a better weather briefing . . . *something*, goddammit! I'm in command, and I do not have the luxury of making mistakes!"

"Dad, you're human."

"No!" he said, raising his index finger, his eyes flaring. "No, I can't hide behind being human. I'm an airline captain. I'm required to be perfect, or at the very least to keep my own stupidity from . . . from . . ." Arlie hurled the unopened bottle of bourbon at the concrete wall of the shop where it shattered loudly as he finished the sentence. ". . . crashing my aircraft!"

She tried to move to him, but he was already off the stool and out the door, striding across the manicured lawn toward a grove of trees on a high embankment overlooking the strait.

April watched him go, utterly unsure what to do, her mind maliciously replaying teenage memories of finding empty bottles of vodka in strange parts of their house before he enrolled himself in the airline's alcohol program. She had never smelled liquor on his breath back then. True alcoholics could be very difficult to detect.

And the Anchorage purchase had included vodka.

NINETEEN

THURSDAY, DAY 4

ELMENDORF AFB, ALASKA

8:40 A.M.

"**T**here. What's that?" General MacAdams orbited the shadowy radar return on the screen with the red dot from his tiny laser pen.

"Not sure, sir," a sergeant replied. "This is from one of our air-defense sites."

"Looks like a fast-moving target to me," Mac added.

Sergeant Jacobs, an AWACS air-traffic control specialist normally charged with keeping fighters and tankers headed in the right direction, approached the screen, scratching his chin before turning back to the man operating the liquid crystal projector.

"Run it again, Jim."

Once more the picture came to life, and once again the shadowy target appeared, disappeared, and reappeared on subsequent sweeps of the radar beam.

Jacobs turned to the general. "Well, sir, of seven tapes, that's the only hint I see of an unidentified fast-mover where your guy descended below two thousand feet. *All* the tapes show the skin paint return of the jet until . . . *here.*" He used his own laser pointer to highlight a spot considerably west and on the left margin of the screen. "But this is the only tape I've seen that was getting hits on him while he was within a hundred feet of the water."

"And we're all in agreement that there's no other conflicting traffic visible?"

Everyone in the room nodded except for Lieutenant Colonel Anderson. "Ah, General, there's still the Coast Guard tape we haven't seen."

"Sir," the sergeant interjected. "There is one other target on this tape that's of interest. It's intermittent and running north, where your jet is running east. We had him intermittently on the AWACS tapes, too. While our Gulfstream is coming in from the left side of the scope, this fellow's coming in from the bottom . . . the south. He first appears down here, and the radar is picking up his transponder squawking twelve hundred, the visual flight code, and his altitude is coming through as two hundred feet. Now that's, as I say, at the bottom of the screen—remember the top is oriented to north—and at this point it's about twenty miles south of the estimated position of the Albatross crash site. I'm assuming this is the Albatross, right here where you see this smudge. That's the faint radar return, and it's northbound."

"Could that be that ship we talked about?" Mac asked, then winced and corrected himself. "Of course not. Sorry. Dumb question. The tanker was southbound."

"Yes, sir, and this northbound VFR hit is probably going at least a hundred knots, so it sure as heck isn't a ship."

"But, the two don't intersect, do they?" Mac asked with some alarm. "The track of our Gulfstream coming in from the left crosses or will eventually cross the northbound track of the target you believe is the Albatross, but will they be there at the same time?" Mac was sitting forward now, his concern rising until the sergeant shook his head.

"No, sir. I projected their respective tracks, and with the time-line information we have on the Gulfstream from the flight data recorder, they come close, but miss by several miles."

"Good."

"Provided, sir, that the Albatross doesn't change his heading."

"But, you'd see a change, right?"

Jacobs was shaking his head no. "Well, he probably didn't change course, but we only have a good track on him until about ten miles south of the estimated crash site, and then he apparently dropped too low, or something happened to his transponder, because we have no hits on him after that. That means we can only project his subsequent flight path, but when I do, it misses your Gulfstream by miles."

"Do we have that Coast Guard radar tape?" Mac asked.

"Yes, sir. Racking it up now," the sergeant answered.

Once again a series of computer-generated images filled the screen, this time of surface vessels in the form of large targets crawling along sea lanes into and out of Prince William Sound. Jacobs consulted a briefing sheet sent with the tape and studied the screen for a few seconds before highlighting an area south of Valdez.

"Again, this is approximately the crash site, sir, based on rescue data cross-referenced to emergency locator data, corrected for . . . I guess they call it the prevailing currents. It pretty well matches the projection of the Albatross's flight path from the previous tape."

"How close can we come to a time for the crash of that Albatross?" Mac asked.

Jacobs was shaking his head. "Unknown, sir, from the data I've got."

Mac was on his feet, stretching as he pointed to the screen. "Sergeant, run that through on fast forward and see if you see anything we need to see. We'll be pacing around the hallway."

Mac and Anderson had barely reached the Coke machine down the corridor when the sergeant stuck his head out the door.

"General? You gentlemen need to see this." They followed him back inside.

"Remember, this is a surface radar," the sergeant said. "It's not like our aviation radars that really can't effectively track someone below a thousand feet."

"Understood," Mac said, more impatiently than he'd intended.

"Okay," the sergeant said. "Watch this target appear from the south margins of the coverage area. See it moving north?"

Mac nodded.

"How fast?" Anderson asked.

"I estimate around a hundred twenty to a hundred forty. The Coast Guard system doesn't put data blocks on air traffic. Here's that huge tanker over to the northwest of the target, about eight miles at this point. And you can see several other sizable vessels down here in the same vicinity the Albatross is approaching."

"Okay. So you believe that's the . . . whoa!" Mac said as a new target rushed in from the left side of the screen at twice the speed, its radar return a crisp white blotch closing on the northbound track of what had to be the Albatross. "Slow that down," Mac commanded.

The tape was slowed to quarter-speed, the respective radar tracks showing the Albatross and the Gulfstream closing on each other every four seconds with each sweep of the radar beam.

"Our guy is running without lights, of course," Anderson muttered, and Mac nodded. "We weren't supposed to be just fifty feet over the water, or out of our own control area."

"There's the oil tanker," Jacobs added, using his laser pointer. "If you extend the Gulfstream's track dead on another five miles, it intersects the tanker."

"What's that?" Mac asked, flashing his own pointer on the screen at a spot north-northeast of the Albatross, but barely a hair's breadth south of the approaching Gulfstream's west-to-east track.

"That's another ship, I think," Jacobs replied. "The Albatross will pass to the west of it. Looks like a large enough return to be a large freighter or cruise ship."

"Good Lord," Mac said, his eyes on the screen. "Our Gulfstream's going to barely miss whatever it is."

Jacobs was nodding. "Sir, look at this. Remember we couldn't track the Albatross on the other tape inside ten miles? Look at him here at eight miles out on the Coast Guard tape. He's changing course. Right here. See? He's changing course to the east by . . .

twenty degrees. That completely alters the equation. He's now headed squarely for that freighter, and . . . the point at which the Albatross's projected flight path will cross our Gulfstream's flight path has moved east, and . . . I'm trying to figure out the time, but they're going to arrive at that intersection about the same time."

General MacAdams, Lieutenant Colonel Anderson, and the two sergeants watched transfixed as the targets converged on each other, the Albatross's radar return disappearing for several sweeps of the radar beam as it approached the unidentified new ship, then reappearing brightly on the north side of the ship just as the Gulfstream's target crossed the same point.

"Here the Gulfstream seems to be in a right turn," the sergeant said.

"He was climbing. He'd unlocked the computer and pulled up."

"Okay, the Albatross continues on for two sweeps of the radar and then appears to slow and get more faint . . . finally disappearing, probably when he sinks."

"Again, please," Mac asked as the tape was rewound slightly and the point of convergence played once more.

After the fourth repetition Mac sat back and shook his head, his mind accelerating into the problem. "Oh, shit."

"Yeah."

"Dammit, Jon, you said they weren't that close."

"I . . . told you, sir, the best I had at the time. That isn't the same position the Coast Guard plotted as the crash site."

Sergeant Jacobs was consulting the note sent with the tape. "They apparently noticed this too, sir. They've got the corrected coordinates on this note. And . . . remember I warned you that my projections were based on no turns."

Mac waved them down. "Don't worry, fellows, I'm not looking to blame anyone for anything. But now we've got a potential problem."

"The tapes don't have to leave here alive, General," Jon Anderson said.

"Not the point, Jon. The FAA's trying to string up that pilot and this shows he could have hit not one but two objects out there."

"Well, what was he doing that low, y'know?" Anderson asked. "He's flying a bloody seaplane, Jon. You have to get low to find the sea. No, the question we've got to grapple with is whether or not there's any chance the Albatross hit our Gulfstream."

They looked at the sequence again, rolling it back and forth past the same spot until Mac shook his head. "Jon, was the Gulfstream inspected for any damage?"

"I . . . don't know, General. I assume they'd find any damage when they got back here and did their normal post-flight inspection, and I assume the pilots would have heard any collision. Metal to metal in an airplane isn't subtle."

Mac glanced at him with a smile. "Tell me about it. I survived a glancing blow from pieces of an exploding surface-to-air missile in my F-105 just south of Hanoi in 1973. The memory of that noise still scares the . . . scatology out of me." He pulled himself back out of the chair as he glanced down at Anderson. "We're going over to the hangar immediately. I want inspection stands and lights."

Jon Anderson stood as well. "Sir, we'd better warn Joe Davis what we're looking for."

Mac was shaking his head. "No. No explanations." He turned to the sergeant. "And no leaks to Uniwave, understood?"

"Yes, sir."

"Okay. By the way, Sergeant Jacobs?"

"Yes, sir."

"Well, it's a real shame, Bill, about that accidental erasure on the Coast Guard tape," Mac said with a set jaw, looking the man in the eye.

"Sir?"

"I say . . . it's a real shame that when that particular tape was returned to the Coast Guard, it had accidentally been bulk erased. Right?"

Sergeant Jacobs's eyes fluttered open in sudden comprehension. "Oh! Yes. Yes, sir, I'm . . . terribly sorry about that."

"Just normal human error, I suppose," Mac said, giving the man a tired smile, which was tentatively returned.

Lieutenant Colonel Anderson was already in the hallway as Mac paused in the doorway and turned back to the two men. "This isn't dishonesty per se, gentlemen. Keep that in mind, please. This is a black project, and there are things we have to do that are for solid reasons of national security."

"Yes, sir."

"Oh, and Jacobs, one other thing?"

"Sir?"

Mac motioned him over and issued a verbal order quietly in his ear, outside the hearing of the other man, before waving a quick farewell and joining Anderson, down the hall.

TWENTY

April pulled the tarp from the wings and cockpit of the small Piper Cherokee Cruiser and began folding it as her dad had taught her. Once again she felt a familiar rush of excited anxiety, a feeling that sparkled through her every time she flew, the flash of adrenaline triggered by the knowledge that flying an airplane by herself was a form of tightrope walking in which only she was responsible for the outcome. She inhaled sharply, breathing in the invigorating aroma of freshly cut hay from an adjacent field and remembering so many afternoons of flight training with her dad. Flying, to Arlie Rosen, was a form of breathing, and he'd instilled the same feelings in his daughter, and later on in Gracie. Dean was another matter.

The exhilaration was suddenly overshadowed by a wave of guilt. She was, she realized, getting ready to enjoy something her father could no longer do.

April stepped back a few paces and looked at her father's four-seat Piper 140, a tiny, basic craft. He was a senior 747 captain, yet he was no longer licensed to fly even something this small.

The nightmare precipitated by the FAA had forced her last-minute decision to fly to Seattle from the small airport in Sequim, a proud little airfield built by a family friend and former Braniff captain named Jack Sallee.

The conversation with her mother had been quick.

"Mom. I'm taking the Cherokee and flying over to confer with Gracie. Dad's up there sitting on the ridge. I think he needs you."

Rachel had shaken her head. "I know when he needs me, honey, and it's not yet. I'm watching."

April described the scene in the workroom, explaining the broken fifth of bourbon, in part to alleviate the fear her mother might feel if she opened the door and smelled the liquor. She nodded silently.

"Mom? Did you know about the liquor purchase in Anchorage?"

"Yes. It was for the planned party in Sitka and another get-together in Ketchikan."

"And he wasn't . . ."

"No."

"You were there the whole time, right?"

She nodded, but her eyes had shifted away, and April felt a shiver of apprehension.

"Mom? You were there every minute, right? He couldn't have slipped?"

"I was there."

April could see the troubled expression on Rachel's face. "Mom, what?"

Rachel sighed and studied her hands for a few moments before looking at her daughter. "They won't believe me, April. I'm his wife. And I was asleep."

"In flight?"

She nodded. "In the right seat. I kept a pillow up there."

"You don't recall the crash?"

"I was asleep until everything began coming apart. It was a blur. But . . . I'd seen no signs of any drinking."

"Oh, God, Mom, then he really doesn't even have an eyewitness."

"Are you taking your things, April?"

"What? I . . . hadn't thought . . ."

Rachel was nodding. "Take your things. You may need to go back to Vancouver from there. The plane can stay at Boeing Field. I can fly it back later."

"I," rather than *"we,"* her mother had said. It was an acknowledgment of how serious the situation really was.

April borrowed the old jeep to get down the two miles of road to the airport. She hurried now through the preflight, replaying in her head the cell phone conversation with Gracie.

"If I fly over there in a few hours, can you take time to pick me up at Boeing Field?" she'd asked. "We have some things to discuss."

"Of course," Gracie had replied. "Call me when you get in."

"You sure this isn't jeopardizing your position?"

"I talked to my senior partner this morning, April. He's approved a certain amount of pro bono work. Not unlimited, but enough to be your father's basic lawyer. And, I'm working on the salvage thing."

"You said we had to recover the Albatross, right?"

There was a long sigh from Seattle. "Yes, I think it's going to be the key, regardless of cost. But we've got another potential problem. Until this drinking thing is resolved, I doubt the insurance company is going to pay for the Albatross."

*A*pril ran through the laminated checklist items and fired off the Cherokee's engine, staying focused on the process of taxiing and doing the appropriate runup before allowing herself to notice how beautiful the day had become. Sequim was often called the banana belt of the Puget Sound area because it sat in the rain shadow of the northeast shoulder of the Olympic Peninsula, which generated more than 240 days of sunshine a year—while the rest of Puget Sound sat more often than not under a veil of gentle fog and mist.

A fresh westerly had cleared the entire region, and the sky was cobalt blue as she stood by the Cherokee and used her cell phone to file a visual flight plan to King County Airport, which was also known as Boeing Field. April loved landing at Seattle's original airfield. There was always an inherent thrill in settling onto the runway in the tiny Piper in sight of dozens of brightly colored Boeing jets awaiting delivery on the western side. She looked forward now to the same experience.

The Cherokee lifted off at sixty-five knots and climbed steadily, soaring over the blue waters of nearby Sequim Bay, south of Port Townsend, and across the Hood Canal. The runway at Boeing Field kissed the tires of the little single-engine all too quickly, ending a conflicted hour of trying not to enjoy the beauty unfolding before her as she searched for ways to help her father.

With the unfolding legal problems, the physical peril of the crash had been all but forgotten. The bruises her parents had suffered were trivial compared to the emotional blow her dad had taken with the complete revocation of his pilot's license. The potential financial impact alone might be ruinous. Captain Arlie Rosen's two-hundred-thousand-per-year airline salary would be on hold for however long it took to regain the legal right to fly, and with the evidence that the FAA was amassing and purposely misinterpreting, that might be never.

April had phoned her arrival time to Gracie just before takeoff from Sequim, and, as she taxied in, she could see her longtime friend standing beside another small single-engine, waving as she spotted the familiar Cherokee.

The image brought a smile to April's face. Gracie was always complaining that she couldn't attract the male of the species, but they both knew it was a joke. Gracie was an extremely attractive young woman, and a bundle of energy. Her petite five-foot-three frame next to April's taller five-foot-eight had made them a distinctive team in high school, especially since Gracie insisted on playing every sport her friend took up, including basketball.

April braked to a halt and looked at Gracie's outfit more closely. Stylish, but pushing the limits for a major lawfirm, April decided.

Black heels, a silk blouse tucked into a tweed mini-skirt and a partially opened matching blazer. The male-grabbing visage was topped
off by Gracie's exceptionally full mane of reddish-blond hair blowing in the five-knot breeze.

Gracie came over and carefully climbed up on the wing to open
the door as April ran the shutdown checklist and secured the cockpit.

"It's good to see old Double-Oh-Seven-Whiskey again," Gracie
said, referring to the N6007W registration number of the aircraft
she'd soloed in several years back.

"She still flies nice. Slow, but steady."

"I see my booster cushion is still in the back."

"Well, you always did insist on seeing over the rudder pedals."

"You hungry?" Gracie asked.

April shook her head. "I think I had something for breakfast, but
I'm not even sure I could tell you what. Not much appetite."

"Yeah, I hear you. I forgot to eat before leaving the *Queen Mary*
this morning."

"You've named your boat the *Queen Mary* now?"

"No, no. That's just how it feels."

April unfolded herself from the cockpit as Gracie backed down
to the ramp, carefully using the toes of her high heels on the boarding stand.

"I wouldn't mind coffee while you wolf something down," April
said as she followed Gracie off the wing and into the private terminal. She left a fuel order and her cell phone number before proceeding to Gracie's Corvette. They drove around the field to a faded
coffee shop near the Museum of Flight, where they found a booth,
and Gracie began pulling things from a small briefcase.

"Okay, April. Here is a briefing sheet with all the information,
names, places and potential prices you'll need to pursue booking a
salvage operation, also a floppy disk with the same files on it for your
computer, and your airline ticket."

"My . . . *what?*"

"You're going back to Anchorage on Alaska's one P.M. flight.

You'll meet this afternoon with the guy I think can do us the most good. Took me a few calls to find him. I'd come with you, but . . ."

April looked stunned, and Gracie was more or less enjoying the moment.

"I'm flying back to Anchorage? But . . . I have a job I have to get back to."

"Already talked to your senior vice-president, Niles Dayton. He said to tell you he sends his deepest condolences. He's got the two ship arrivals covered and will call if he needs anything, and said to tell you to take whatever time you need."

"Niles Dayton said all that?"

"He did."

April cocked her head suspiciously. "And what, exactly, did you tell *him* to elicit such a gracious response?"

"Oh, nothing much. Actually, I was talking to Hugh Wellsley, and he patched Niles Dayton into the call, and I might have mentioned something about the publicity value for Empress Lines."

"Publicity value?"

"Sure. Loyal daughter and Empress vice-president embarks on noble mission to save a valuable World War Two warbird from the ravages of saltwater. The *Anchorage Times* reporter will meet with you tomorrow. He's excited. Of course, he'll be more excited when he sees the girl on the other end of the name."

"Wait just a minute here. You arranged *press* coverage? Gracie, I'm not sure that's a wise idea."

"He loved it. So did Hugh."

"*Hugh?* How do you know Hugh?"

"You introduced us at a party last fall, remember?"

"Oh, yeah," April replied, suddenly shaken by the thought that an interview could lead to the drunk flying charge blowing into the public arena.

"We've got to get that bird off the bottom, April," Gracie was saying. "At the very least we have to prove that the prop came off. Ted Greene is ready to march on the FAA the moment we get hard evidence. There are no guarantees of success, but it's just remotely possible he could talk some sense into the enforcement division."

"But, you really think . . . Does *he* think it's wise to go public with this?"

Gracie nodded. "Alaska is a rarified aviation environment, and there will likely be a negative backlash against the FAA for moving so fast without evidence. Lots of Alaskans are pilots, as we both know." Gracie looked at her watch. "There's more to tell you, but I'd better get you over to Seatac."

"Gracie, there's something I have to tell you," April said, studying her coffee cup before meeting Gracie's eyes. "The night of the accident, Dad bought some liquor for a planned party in Sitka. That worm Harrison called me. He knows."

Gracie sat back hard in the booth. "Oh, God, no!"

"Dad wasn't drinking, Gracie!"

"He might as well have been," Gracie said slowly. "Because this may kill us."

TWENTY ONE

THURSDAY, DAY 4
ANCHORAGE, ALASKA
EARLY AFTERNOON

T he lobby of the Regal Alaskan Hotel had been designed to resemble the interior of a rough-hewn national-park lodge, but the hotel itself was anything but remote. The structure occupied the south end of Anchorage's Lake Spenard, which each summer claimed the title of the busiest seaplane base in the world.

April alighted from the hotel's airport shuttle van and unzipped her white parka as she entered the lobby, hardly noticing the array of mounted game trophies on the walls. Deer, elk, moose, and a selection of smaller animals were everywhere, but only the fire burning in the huge river-rock fireplace caught her attention.

She'd tried to fight off depression all the way from Seattle, but the dark bow wave of reality had been slowly winning. Arlie Rosen had not fallen off the wagon. Her mother would have known. She shoved the other disturbing aspects of Rachel's responses to the back of her mind and tried to close them away.

The phone call she'd made to her mother in flight hadn't helped.

"He's taking this very hard, April."

"Try to get him to go to a counselor, Mom."

"I am trying. And he's refusing. He says he'll handle it, but . . ." April could hear her sigh deeply on the other end. "I've never seen your father this despondent." The worrisome report had made the short drive to the hotel a blur of thoughts and renewed determination to extricate her father from the FAA-imposed purgatory consuming him, and her. But salvation would only truly come from raising the wreckage of the old warbird. If every one of those Anchorage-purchased liquor bottles could be found still stowed and unopened, the FAA's case would fall apart.

Okay, where's my pilot?

April surveyed the lobby, noting the huge, stuffed eight-foot-tall Alaskan brown bear in a glass case by the front desk. The hapless former bear had been posed by a taxidermist in all its grizzly ferocity, and even though it was long since deceased, April realized she was automatically giving it a very wide berth.

She walked toward the fireplace, spotting no one even remotely fitting the description of a bush pilot. She sat in one of the big chairs adjacent to the roaring fire and reread the note from Gracie.

> April—You'll be met in the lobby by Scott McDermott, whom I hired to fly you in his Grumman Widgeon over to Valdez to meet with a salvage operator named Jim Dobler, who will have a plan figured out when you get there. He's been recommended by one of our major clients whom I happened to be talking to today by phone to one of his drilling rigs in Venezuela. My client's a billionaire and very friendly. I know he owns a big ship repair and salvage operation in Mobile, Alabama. He said this was too small a job and too far north for his people to take on, but he said that Dobler's a trusted friend, and he promised to lean on him to help us, which he did. The object is to get a diver down to position a harness around the Albatross, then use a barge-mounted winch to haul it to the surface and tow it slowly to shore, if it stays intact. He can do all that. Keep me posted. I'll be in the office late and on the cell. Go, girl. Love ya!

The aroma of something more pungent than wood smoke was assaulting her nose. She recognized it as cigar smoke and turned to track it to the source, a long, Churchill-size stogie a man on the far end of the couch had just fired up. She wrinkled her nose in disapproval, but either he wasn't looking or was pretending not to notice.

That figures, she thought. He had unkempt sandy hair and an abbreviated handlebar mustache, as well as a weathered brown leather jacket and a dirty, blue, oil-stained parka he'd draped boorishly over an adjacent chair. *Your basic bush-class Alaskan,* she concluded, rejecting the idea that he was merely some homeless male who'd wandered past hotel security. The ring on his right middle finger and the expensive boots he was wearing leavened the overall impression somewhat.

But to her mind, the cigar was a fatal flaw.

Why on earth would a woman want to get intimate with someone like him? she mused.

April cautioned herself that, objectionable or not, he'd seated himself around the fireplace first. *But he's stinking up the whole place with that thing.*

"Excuse me," April said, giving in to her irritation.

"Yes?" the man answered without looking at her.

"Would you mind not smoking that in here, please?"

"Yes, ma'am," he said, taking an even deeper drag on the cigar and blowing the smoke out slowly. "As a matter of fact, I *would* mind not smoking this in here." He grinned at her. He was in his thirties, she figured, and obviously an arrogant maverick. "After all, this is the smoking section," he said. "That's why they have ashtrays here."

April tried to suppress her surprise. "They allow smoking here?"

"Yes, ma'am. This is Alaska. We aren't very po-litically cor-rect up here," he said, emphasizing the first syllables. He grinned at her, flashing surprisingly perfect teeth as he pulled on the cigar once more.

April rolled her eyes and stood up, moving away from the fireplace seating as she punched the number Gracie had provided into her cell phone.

"Puffin Flying Service," a male voice answered on the second ring.

"This is April Rosen. I believe a Miss Gracie O'Brien arranged a charter from Anchorage to Valdez for me today?"

"That's right, Miss Rosen. It's all ready for you."

"Yeah, well, I was told the pilot would meet me in the lobby of the Regal Alaskan, and I have yet to find him."

"I know for a fact he's there," the man said, his voice echoing slightly, which was puzzling. She checked the volume of the cell phone's earpiece, but it seemed normal.

"Have you talked to him? Where exactly is he?"

"Well, in a way I've talked to him, because he is me, and I know I'm here waiting for you. I'm your pilot."

"You're *here?*"

"Yes. In the lobby."

April scanned the front desk and the entrance to the bar as well as the staircase without success.

"But *where?* I don't see you."

"Right this second I'm watching a very attractive lady who hates cigars talk on her cell phone."

This time the echo of his voice in her free ear was too loud to ignore, and April turned toward the fireplace. The man with the handlebar mustache was grinning as he waved his cigar at her and nodded toward his cell phone.

Oh, great! she thought, punching off the call. She waited for him to approach, taking his offered hand reluctantly as she tried to ignore the firm grip and slightly calloused feel of his palm.

"Do you always treat your clients this rudely?" she asked.

He chuckled. "Just having a little fun. April, is it?"

"Miss Rosen will do fine," she replied, a frosty edge in her voice.

"All right. Miss Rosen, then," he said evenly.

"I'm not flying with an armed incendiary device. Understood?" she said, pointing to the cigar.

"It's actually a Cuesta-Rey number ninety-five, but if you insist . . ."

"And I do."

"Then I'll be glad to put it out of your misery." He pulled a black tube from his pocket and carefully inserted the still-burning cigar before screwing the lid in place.

"What are you doing?" April yelped. "That thing's still on fire."

"This is a new toy. It keeps a burning cigar nice and fresh for later," he said, grinning at her, "although I'm sure you think a fresh cigar is an oxymoron."

"Where's your aircraft, Mr. McDermott?"

"*Captain* McDermott, if you please," he said with mock seriousness. "Or, you can call me Scott. Your choice."

"Very well, Captain. Where's your plane?"

"Off the back deck of the bar, Miss Rosen." He offered his arm. "May I escort you?"

"You may not. Just lead the way."

"You have baggage?"

Just you, she thought, barely stifling a strong urge to voice the comeback that popped into her head. Gracie was obviously a bad influence. She nodded instead and pointed to a shoulder bag and a wheeled overnight bag, which he picked up after putting on his parka. He motioned her out through the Fancy Moose bar onto the terrace and the concrete walkway that was slick with Canada goose droppings all the way down to the water.

The small, six-seat 1952 Grumman Widgeon amphibian Gracie had chartered was tied up to the hotel's tiny dock. Two small engines sat atop the wing, close into the fuselage, making the diminutive flying boat almost an abbreviated version of her father's Albatross.

McDermott opened the side door along the left flank and loaded the bags before stepping back to let her maneuver herself inside and up between the seats into the right seat of the cockpit. He followed, securing the door and handing her a headset.

"Now, Miss Rosen, this aircraft can take off and land on water, and—"

She had her right hand up to stop him. "I'm a licensed private pilot with an instrument rating. And, I've got a floatplane ticket. So please don't try to snow me."

McDermott looked hurt. "What makes you think I'd do such a thing?"

"Oh, I don't know. Let's just call it instinct."

She saw him studying her eyes for a few seconds before chuckling and turning his attention to pulling an ancient, yellowed checklist from a sidewall pocket. He plopped it in her lap and pointed to it.

"If you're a licensed pilot, you're working crew, and in this case, you're my copilot, whether you're paying the bill or not."

"Okay."

"You read the checklist, follow my instructions, and speak up the instant there's anything you think I should know."

"Like, how to treat a woman and a client?"

"Well, what I had more in mind was a dramatic reading of the before-starting-engines checklist." He arched his eyebrows in an attempt to look innocent, and the effect was too comical to ignore. In spite of herself, April started to chuckle. She tore her eyes away from him and looked at the checklist, clearing her throat and adjusting the microphone before speaking. "Very well. In the beginning, 'twas a dark and stormy night. Master switch?"

"Now, that's dramatic," McDermott said, grinning. "And my line is, 'On.' "

"Preflight?"

"Complete."

"Control locks?" April continued to the end of the checklist items and watched as he cranked both engines.

The takeoff from the glassy surface of the lake was quick, the Widgeon lifting off smoothly at eighty miles per hour and pitching up rather dramatically as McDermott banked to the east and began climbing, topping the Chugach Range at ten thousand before setting a course directly for Valdez. The engine noise was deafening, and April spent the time concentrating on the beauty of the passing terrain, aware that McDermott was sneaking long looks at her, running his eyes along her body when he thought she wasn't looking.

Male chauvinist porker, she concluded, forcing her thoughts back to the challenge of raising her father's aircraft.

The focus was the propeller on the Albatross's right engine. She hoped, when they pulled it to the surface, only two of the three propeller blades would still be in place, and the third would be either partially or completely missing. The conclusions would then be obvious and ruinous to the FAA's case. A thrown blade in flight would horribly unbalance an engine, creating an unbearable vibration sufficient to tear the engine off the wing, or lead to the loss of the aircraft.

Nearly thirty minutes had passed when April felt the engine power being reduced. She glanced over to see McDermott's hand on the throttles and gave him a quizzical look. He pointed to the right as he banked the Widgeon in the direction of a break in a thin deck of cumulus clouds and descended through them. "Valdez is just below," he said.

They came through the bottom of the cloud deck and a spectacular scene of green and gray mountains capped by continuous glaciers emerged all around them. April felt herself gasp involuntarily. The deep blue of the oceanic inlet from Prince William Sound east into Valdez was spread beneath them, and she realized McDermott's hand was reaching past her chin, his finger pointing at something on the right as he banked the amphibian.

"Over there is the tanker terminal. Opposite side of the bay from the town."

"That's the south side?" April asked.

He nodded. "That's where the *Exxon Valdez* loaded up before sailing into history."

"I see."

"And on the far end, ahead of us, you see those washed-out structures? That's the original town of Valdez, which stretched and dropped below sea level in the 1964 Alaskan earthquake."

"So, where's the town now?"

"Back to the left. They rebuilt the whole thing."

McDermott throttled back and extended the flaps as he studied the water condition below and looked for an indication of wind. He satisfied himself it was blowing from the west and turned the Widgeon back in that direction as he called for the "descent" and "before landing" checklists.

April finished the checklist sheet and stuffed it in the side pocket as they descended rapidly toward the water with the engines back to idle. McDermott set up the last portion of his glide and brought the power back in, touching down smoothly in the lee of the town dock on the back of a lazily rolling wave.

"I've watched my dad do the same thing," April said.

Scott McDermott was nodding as he glanced in her direction. "Incredible terrain, right?"

The prickly meeting in Anchorage momentarily forgotten, she responded, "Absolutely! Nice landing, too."

"Thanks," he said, bringing the power back in to stay on the step as he high-speed-taxied through the calm waters toward the dock.

At the dock, a thin, older man in an oil-stained, olive-drab army parka was waiting for them, two tie-down lines in his weathered hands. Scott McDermott asked April to get out of the seat so he could duck under the copilot's side of the dash panel and through a tiny passageway to pop out of the forward hatch on the nose in time to catch the lines. They secured the aircraft and he turned to help April out of the cabin into the icy chill of a stiff wind.

"You must be Mr. Dobler," April said to the man on the dock.

The man grinned, extending his hand, his voice warm and gravelly. "Well, if I must be. Hi, I'm Jim."

"And I'm April. And this is . . ." she started to say, arching a thumb in McDermott's direction as he leaped to the dock from the nose of the Widgeon.

Jim Dobler interrupted her. "I know this scruffy young seadog all too well, April," he said, taking McDermott's hand and pumping it as he slapped his shoulder with his other hand. "Lieutenant Commander McDermott. As skipper of this dock, I grant you permission to come aboard . . . even though you failed to ask."

"Lieutenant commander?" April repeated, looking at Scott Mc-Dermott for the slightest confirmation that he could have ever been in a military unit.

"You didn't know you were flying with a highly decorated Navy carrier pilot, April?" Jim asked.

Several Gracie-class replies flitted across her mind, but she was too off balance and outnumbered to use them.

"No, I didn't."

"Mustache fooled you, huh?" Scott McDermott said with a laugh.

"Among other things," April replied, her hands involuntarily on her hips. She forced herself to cross her arms and took a deep breath. "Where can we talk?"

Dobler led them to a small, insulated office on one side of the dock, dominated by a potbellied stove that was keeping the interior all but oppressively warm while perfuming the air with little wisps of wood smoke. He shucked his coat and McDermott followed suit, noticing April's hesitation as she held her white parka and looked for a non-greasy place to put it.

"Here," the pilot said, nodding to a peg in the far corner. "That one's clean."

She thanked him and relinquished the coat, accepting a cup of coffee as they pulled up chairs around the stove. "Cold out there," she said, sampling the slightly oily smell of the shack's interior.

"This is a heat wave compared to the dead of winter," Jim chuckled, picking up a notepad. "Now, all I know so far, April, is that you need an old Albatross raised from the bottom about sixty miles south of here."

She pulled out her tiny laptop and read off the last geographic coordinates to be transmitted by N34DD, and then ran through the facts of the crash, noting with alarm the number of times Jim Dobler glanced at Scott McDermott with a worried expression.

"What?" April said during one such aside.

"Sorry?" Jim asked, apparently surprised she'd noticed.

"You two keep exchanging mission-impossible glances."

Scott McDermott was looking away and trying not to laugh as Jim simply looked caught.

"Well, that's not exactly . . ."

McDermott turned suddenly and cut him off, talking through a broad grin. "He's not reacting to this job, Miss Rosen, but to one we tried together a number of years ago."

"Oh. What was that?" she asked.

Both Jim Dobler and Scott McDermott exploded in laughter, Jim's slide into uncontrollable mirth beginning with a sound somewhat like the venting of an overstoked steam engine.

"Okay, guys, this is getting intimidating," April said, fighting the urge to laugh at their laughter. McDermott was doubled over and Jim had tipped his chair back on two legs, his eyes closed, as his laugh accelerated into a high giggle.

"Okay!" Scott said, his hand up in a stop gesture. "All right! We've got to get serious here."

Jim closed his mouth and swallowed the remaining yaks, letting silence return between them for a second before uttering one additional word.

"Glub!" Jim said, sending both of them into more gales of uncontrollable laughter, this time joined by a puzzled April.

When they'd regained some semblance of self-control and were actively engaged in wiping away tears, April cleared her throat. "Any chance you two comedians are going to tell me what that was all about?"

Jim was nodding, but Scott spoke first.

"A small barge sank in the channel several years ago, just after I got off active duty, and this genius decided he needed a partner to claim it and salvage it, and I signed on to help him find the wreck and position his barge and raise the thing. I flew him out there. We mapped the area, brought his barge out and hooked on—"

"Then proceeded to sink my barge with its own crane," Jim

added. "Turns out we were hooked onto the wrong wreck. We just cranked that sucker right under."

Scott was giggling again. "Yeah. Davey Jones Dobler here hooked the wreck of a thousand-ton freighter that sank thirty years ago and tried to hoist it with a six-ton crane."

She was shaking her head. "And this is a confidence builder?"

"We've learned our lesson, April," Jim said.

"Okay, now how soon can we get out there and start looking for my father's airplane?" she asked.

"Well, first we need to check on whether we need an environmental application, and—"

"A *what?*" April asked.

"Environmental application," Jim replied. "There was fuel and oil aboard that airplane, right?"

"Yes, but . . ."

"Well, remember this is environmentalist alley, and I can't even sneeze in the open without five permits."

"How long will that take?" she asked, apprehension creeping into her tone.

Jim Dobler sighed. "It just depends on where the airplane came to rest. If it's inside protected waters, it could be anywhere from a few weeks to never, depending on what the state and the federal government decide to do."

"I can't wait that long!" She explained the urgency, and the fact that Arlie Rosen was losing large sums of money every day.

"Miss Rosen," Scott said, "around here, compliance with environmental rules is very important to your economic health."

Jim was nodding. "If I pull your aircraft up without a permit, April, and it spills a drop of anything but Perrier, the Environmental Attack Agency will harpoon me, and the media will accuse me of killing birds and polar bears and God knows what."

"That's crazy! The airplane's down there leaking as we speak."

"I know it, but we don't write the rules. Touch a tree around here and they chase you down with court orders and Uzis."

"Miss Rosen," Scott McDermott began, but she cut him off and turned to look him in the eye.

"It's all right. You can kill the 'Miss Rosen' thing now and call me April. I was just ticked at your attitude back in Anchorage."

"Yeah?" Scott replied, turning to grin at Jim. "She doesn't like my attitude."

"Hell, Scott, no woman this side of Atsugi has liked your attitude since you escaped from the Navy," Jim said.

"Oh, *that* cuts, Mr. Dobler, sir!" He turned back to April. "And just for the record, Miss Rosen—April—it so happens there was nothing wrong with my attitude in Anchorage."

"The heck there wasn't!" she snapped, looking at him incredulously.

"The heck there was!" he countered. "I wasn't the sweet young thang that came flouncing in the door of an Alaskan hotel in high heels and a high-fallutin' coat from needless markup, telling the scruffy locals not to smoke in a smoking area."

"I never saw the sign. And the coat is from Nordstrom's, thank you."

"Okay, children," Jim interjected. "Maybe we should get back to the subject."

Scott reached over and offered the same large hand she'd shaken so reluctantly in Anchorage, and April took it, this time with more enthusiasm.

"Look," Scott said, "I do apologize for being a bloody boor."

"Accepted."

He held her hand for a second and cocked his head. "You know, you're, like, totally welcome to counter the 'boor' part at any time."

"I'll get back to you on that," she said.

He nodded as she let his hand go and turned back to Jim. "You said if the airplane came down outside of some boundary, the rules don't apply?"

"Well, maybe. These coordinates may be outside of restricted waters, and, if so, permits probably won't be needed."

"Can't we go try to find the wreckage at least? I understand you have side-scanning sonar to help locate it."

Jim nodded. "A crude form, yes."

"And we've still got daylight. Can't we start?"

Jim shook his head. "Well, see, I've got a problem. The engine's down on my tug. They're working on it, but it won't be ready until tomorrow. And I only make fifteen knots at full throttle, which means it'll take at least four hours to get there."

"April," Scott McDermott interjected. "Tell me exactly what you're trying to accomplish."

"What do you mean? I'm trying to raise my dad's plane."

"Time is obviously critical, but what do you need to discover in that wreckage?"

"Oh. Right." She explained the need to prove a propeller blade had broken away in flight. "And, there are certain items I need to re-cover from inside the airplane, if they're still intact." The image of shattered liquor bottles flashed through her mind. If even one wasn't intact and sealed, Gracie had warned, the FAA would never let it go. She ignored a cold chill and tried to smile.

"Okay." Scott turned to Dobler. "You've got underwater cameras, don't you, Jim?"

"Sure. I've got your basic fish cam, your little cameras, your big cameras, and even your fancy steerable cameras for underwater hull inspections."

"And they all operate on battery, or one hundred ten volts?"

"Yes. But—"

"And I know you've got one of those little Honda generators."

Jim was nodding.

"Good. This can work. And there's obviously a hatch on the nose of my plane. So why don't we go out to those last known coordi-nates with the video gear and the generator, drop a camera over the side, and see what we can see. It'll take all of thirty minutes to get there."

"It's open ocean, Scott," Jim said, looking alarmed.

"Hey, I can handle it. I used to land impossibly large jets on a pitching carrier deck at night for a living. Compared to that, landing in open ocean in a Widgeon is a piece of cake."

Dobler scratched his chin and nodded. "It's not you I'm worried about."

"You mean your stomach?"

Jim nodded as Scott looked at April and gestured toward the veteran mariner. "He can take twelve-foot seas in a dinghy without a problem but he gets seasick whenever my airplane is in open waters."

"It moves funny," Jim said.

"And he's a pilot to boot," Scott added.

"I guess I'll be okay, Scott. I've got those wristbands."

"I'll keep it as smooth as a baby's . . ." Scott paused, glancing at April, who rolled her eyes and shrugged.

"Oh, go ahead. I know you're dying to."

He flashed her a broad smile. "Baby's behind! Thanks. That felt better."

"I can just imagine," she said.

"April, one thing," Jim said. "Even with the right coordinates, the chances of finding the wreckage quickly are slim. We could be wasting our time. I'll almost certainly need the side-scan sonar to locate it, and that's mounted on my boat."

"I understand," she replied, "but I'd really appreciate it if we could at least try right now."

Both men checked their watches as if on cue before Jim got to his feet with a loud grunt. "Aw, hell, why not," he said, winking at April. "Nothing else going on."

"You'll be okay, Jim. I guarantee it."

"Yeah," he grumbled, as he headed out the door to assemble his gear. "Like I haven't heard that before."

THURSDAY AFTERNOON, DAY 4

UNIWAVE FIELD OFFICES

ELMENDORF AFB, ALASKA

*H*ey, Ben?"

Ben Cole jumped off his chair and let out an involuntary cry as he scrambled to his feet, his heart racing.

"Jeez, Ben, it's just me," one of his team said, her eyes wide. "Sorry if I scared you."

He tried to laugh and keep his hand from migrating to his heart, which was still pounding.

"Whoa! Sorry for that response. I was way deep into a problem."

"Apparently," she said, shaking her head. "You asked for these folders tracking what we've examined so far. We're eighty percent complete."

"And . . . no luck?"

"Not a thing out of place that we can find."

"And no new theories?"

She shook her head. "I think we're all of a mind that, provided the last twenty percent shows no sign of contamination, the program is golden and it had to be the circuit board. Somehow it was just partial to flying fifty feet above the water."

Ben nodded, suppressing the burning desire to explain why that simply wasn't possible.

"I heard you were going to use some Cray time this afternoon?" she said, referring to the Cray SV1 Supercomputer in Uniwave's North Carolina headquarters, which had to be accessed through a fiber-optic link.

"Just testing a wild theory."

"What is it?"

"Embarrassing, if I'm wrong, which I probably am."

"Okay," she replied, handing him the folders and swinging out of his cubicle.

Ben checked his watch. The Cray reservation was for 4 P.M. Anchorage time, which was in less than ten minutes. He thought about the fact that he'd allowed himself nothing to eat since morning, and filed it away. Food he could take care of later. This was far more important.

He picked up the folder carrying the disks he'd been carefully programing for three hours and quickly left the offices through the side door, not wanting to talk to anyone else.

The previous night had been a never-ending series of short naps broken by hours of pacing around the house. He'd tried to think through a growing list of disturbing problems, starting with his rising concern about whether he'd revealed too much to Nelson Oolokvit.

By 5 A.M., with no magic answers forthcoming and the shroud of depression looming over him once more, Ben had sat down at Lisa's prized cherrywood desk in the living room and pulled out the last six remaining sheets of the heavyweight Crane stationery she'd bought so long ago in an attempt to be socially proper. He'd found his aging fountain pen and inserted an ink cartridge before composing his thoughts and inscribing a simple will, formally providing for Schroedinger and leaving all his worldly goods to his sister, Phyllis. A brief letter to Phyllis followed. She had dutifully produced three children—two girls and a boy—for the severe, federal-bureaucrat husband she'd married—a man who spent his life deeply worried that somewhere, someone might be having fun. Ben loved his sister and the kids, but couldn't stand to be around someone anal enough to take offense when a brother-in-law's thoughts were out of what he considered to be proper order. Phyllis could use or dispose of his personal effects as she saw fit, but it was important to Ben that anything he left her and whatever cash could be squeezed from his house and savings accounts remained her separate property.

He had put the final touches on the letter, and then the will, before realizing that the first rays of dawn had already begun to redden the eastern sky.

Ben had showered and dressed for work, amazed that he could face the probability of his own death with such calm. The test flight was scheduled for 8 P.M., and there was virtually no doubt in his mind that something terrible was about to happen. The one bright spot, Ben had chuckled to himself, was his creative plan for getting the renegade code back into his office computer to examine.

"This is a 'Well, duh!' revelation, Schroedinger," Ben had told the cat as the yellow feline supervised Ben's preparations for departure. "Uniwave security is very careful what we take out of the building, but they couldn't care less what we bring back in. So I'll simply walk through security with this disk."

Schroedinger was unimpressed, but Ben had spent extra time holding him and scratching him behind the ears anyway, and was preparing to get up when the tomcat surprised him by moving forward and placing a raspy lick on his face. Ben had picked him up to hug him back, not even caring about the cat hairs that would inevitably make his nose itch the rest of the day. It was worth it, he had concluded. Somehow Schroedinger had seemed to understand that this was a different sort of goodbye.

Ben brought himself back to the present as he walked down the Uniwave hallway, detouring through another corridor in order to bypass Lindsey's office door, hoping to avoid contact. She wouldn't understand why he was so hurt and angry, and she'd probably given no thought to the possibility he might find out the T-handle she'd promised was a sham.

Good, he thought. *No sign of her.*

He continued to the far side of the building and slipped into one of the telecommunication suites equipped with expensive computers hooked into the distant Cray. Six minutes remained before his scheduled session, and he spent the time carefully uploading the program disks he'd prepared before sitting back in thought to reexamine his logic.

The renegade code had been in the Gulfstream's on-board computer three nights before, and it had almost killed them. He was sure of that now. A circuit board malfunction simply wasn't enough to explain the jet's actions. Someone had planted the code, then—when Ben had come too close to the truth—that same someone had pulled the code out of the master program and sanitized all the remaining copies to make it appear as if it'd never existed. That meant that whoever it was enjoyed open access to his lab, the computers, and the building!

But he'd not only seen the renegade code, he had a copy of it. All three thousand–plus lines of the code were on one of the uploaded disks with instructions to the Cray to compare the dizzying mass of computer instructions with every type of so-called sub-routine the Cray could reference. He'd already taken the code apart and put it back together several times, as well as compared it with vast libraries of software codes, but he'd failed to figure out what the set of instructions was trying to get the computer—or the aircraft—to do.

The Cray was his last shot. With its massive ability to compare trillions of bytes in tiny flashes of time, it was his best chance to unlock what someone had obviously gone to so much trouble to create.

The computer screen flashed on, indicating his hard-connection to the Cray was up, and he inserted the disk and triggered the sequence.

Ben sat back, watching the changing numbers on the screen that heralded the increasing percentage of completion.

Twenty minutes elapsed before a gentle electronic beeping recaptured his attention and pulled his eyes to the screen. He read the words casually at first, then leaned forward, reading them again in disbelief.

My God, the renegade code is a basic form of fuzzy logic. The computer was trying to think for itself!

That could explain the descent, he figured, and perhaps even the precise fifty-foot altitude. But there was still the problem of the commercial airline database he'd found embedded as a table within its lines of code. Why an airline database? What possible legitimate function could be served by that?

Ben downloaded the information to another disk and shut down the fiber link with the Cray, then stuffed everything in his leather folder and left. There was no choice now, he decided. Dan Jerrod, Uniwave's security chief, had to be informed that something that smelled very much like sabotage was in progress.

Jerrod, by all accounts, was incorruptible. An ex-FBI agent and ex-Marine who'd taken on the job of Anchorage director of security when the project started, Jerrod was also rumored to have been in the intelligence field. By all accounts, he took his responsibilities very seriously, working to educate and counsel Uniwave's staff on the right ways to handle a massively classified project rather than just trying to catch them in security indiscretions.

Ben found Jerrod in his office and explained the discovery of the renegade computer code, strategically avoiding any reference to having transmitted it home.

"Those three thousand lines of code were there in the middle of the master program when I left the other night. But when I came back the next morning, they were gone from the master and all copies. Someone had meticulously removed it. I knew better than to come alert you without evidence, so . . . I waited until I could reassemble it from backup records." Ben handed the disk across the desk and explained what the Cray had found.

"Doctor, are you saying that the illicit computer code is a program for artificial intelligence?"

"Not as such. I mean, whoever wrote it didn't intend for the machine to 'come alive' or start arguing with us, or anything so science fiction. But there's a forerunner of what will someday be artificial intelligence, and it's called 'fuzzy logic.' That's the ability of a computer program to analyze data and make an unpredictable decision based on what, for a better phrase, would be its qualitative assessment of that data."

"Okay, Doc, you've utterly lost me."

"It's a type of program I can't imagine us using in a precise military system where our task is quite clear and finite: Give a remote pilot the ability to bring an Air Force aircraft home in an otherwise unrecoverable emergency."

"But you mentioned civilian airline data. What's that about?"

"I don't know, and it's really scaring me. I'll tell you flatly as the chief software engineer on this program, there is zero reason for having or needing such information in this project. Whoever put it there had something else in mind, and—"

"You're thinking terrorism, aren't you?"

"How can I not? A strange fuzzy logic code, airline tables and information, none of which should be there. And, I'm fairly convinced it was that damned fuzzy logic code that nearly killed us the other night by diving the airplane."

"You say you've got a final test flight tonight that's terrifying you?" Jerrod asked quietly.

"Yes. I mean, I can verify beforehand that this . . . this renegade code is gone, and I think we'll be safe from having the same thing occur for the same reasons, but whoever did this to begin with is still on the loose, and if the point is to destroy this program and maybe the company, they can't let that test succeed."

"So, they'll find some other way . . ."

"To kill us, literally or figuratively. Yes."

Jerrod drummed his fingers on his desk. He was a man of medium build, penetrating eyes, and a steady gaze, who still favored Marine-style haircuts and a no-nonsense air, but his words were surprisingly reassuring.

"With you watching the software, and me watching everything else, Doctor, whoever it is will not succeed tonight."

Ben felt an illogical flash of relief. Jerrod might be amazingly effective, he thought, but he couldn't be everywhere stemming every risk.

"So, what should I do?" Ben asked.

"Maintain normal routine and appearance, but prepare to make sure that the . . . what did you call it?"

"Renegade code?"

"Yes. Make sure it doesn't climb aboard the aircraft with you tonight."

"Okay. I'll get out there early."

"And let me caution you as you already have sensed, that this is the highest level of security concern. We could have, for want of a better description, a hostile mole inside our own organization. It's not impossible."

"What?" Ben asked, his alarm evident.

Jerrod had his hand up to calm him. "What I mean is, discuss this with absolutely no one else, regardless of clearance, regardless of normal need to know. No one at Uniwave. No one in the Air Force. No one at home. Not even your dog."

"I have a cat, or rather, I'm owned by a cat."

"Understood. Not even your cat."

"Okay."

"Actually, the funny thing is, I'm dead serious. There have been instances in which pets have been bugged because intelligence operatives knew their targets talked to their pets."

"You're not joking, are you?"

"Nope. There can also be bugs in a home, if not surgically implanted in the cat or the cat's collar. Look, we'll talk in a few days. But only you and me." Dan Jerrod rose from his chair and shook Ben's hand. "You did the right thing, Doctor."

Ben left Jerrod's office and headed down the corridor feeling a chill of latent guilt. There was a momentary urge to turn back and ask Dan Jerrod if the name Nelson Oolokvit rang a bell, but he squelched it.

Behind him, Dan Jerrod stood for a few moments in the door of his outer office watching Ben Cole until he disappeared around a far corner on the way back to his lab and office. Jerrod checked his watch, mildly surprised to find it was already 4:15 P.M. He had too much to do before 8 P.M. to be standing around, and the unspoken self-admonition propelled him back inside as he closed the door and decided to sweep his office for clandestine listening devices before making the calls he now had to make.

Cole was a lot more astute than he'd first concluded.

TWENTY THREE

Those waves look enormous!" Jim said from the second row of seats as Scott McDermott worked the control column of the little Grumman, holding the speed just above a stall and looking for the right crest to settle into.

He glanced at April and grinned. "This is challenging enough for an amphibian like this bird—where the hull itself is the boat—but can you imagine an open-ocean landing in something like a little Cessna on pontoons?"

"No," she said simply, not wanting to discuss it. She felt a serious, visceral need to keep her eyes on the rolling sea ahead, and her hands locked in a death grip on the framework of the copilot's seat she was occupying. Engaging him in a broader discussion than basic survival would require more concentration than she could give just now.

April knew that Scott McDermott was trying to shake her up. It was an adolescent effort, but he was obviously still wallowing in the pubescent "Hi girls, I fly jets!" mode—a warped and juvenile state of mind to which young military aviators were often heir, and one primarily distinguishable by a pathological presumption of dazzled female response.

"Okay, this wave looks like a winner," Scott said, working the rudder to sideslip the Widgeon a few degrees to the left. "Nope," he said, as he quickly goosed the overhead throttles and pulled up to evade the wave just beginning to break suddenly, the white foam passing so close beneath them that April caught herself worrying that her seat cushion might get wet.

Once more he lined up on a moving wave crest, this one not as large as the last.

"These are three-foot seas?" Jim fairly bellowed at him. "They look like ten!"

"Naw, they're within limits," Scott replied. "Here we go!"

This time he found the exact position he wanted and pulsed the yoke forward just enough, setting the bottom of the Widgeon's hull into the crest at a little over seventy knots and kicking the rudder left at the same moment, riding with it as he throttled the engines back and held on, waiting for the flying boat to make the uncomfortable transition from aircraft to watercraft as the hull let itself be sucked into the sea and the pontoons on each wingtip made contact.

"Whee-e-e-e!" he said, the exultation prompting April to roll her eyes. Slowly she began to regain confidence in her immediate survival. All her seaplane landings as a pilot had been on smooth water in high-wing single engines on floats, which meant that three-foot waves looked mountainous.

In the air, the Grumman Widgeon had merely bounced through any turbulence it encountered, but now it was a seasick machine, wallowing in all three axes at once as Scott idled the engines and checked his GPS, pointing north.

"We're two miles northwest of the coordinates you gave me," he said to her, holding the map. "Exactly where I wanted to be."

She was nodding, having agreed that the Albatross would have had to come down within sixty seconds of the last satellite burst from her little GPS-based tracking unit, and at 140 knots, that translated into a bit more than two miles.

"What can I help you with?" she asked.

"Go back and open the main upper hatch on the door. Get the little Honda generator going and stand by to plug in the video cords."

She lifted herself carefully out of the copilot's seat and squeezed past him to get to the back, well aware that Scott McDermott would be appraising her shape in the tight-fitting jeans she'd changed into. She'd pulled out a heavy blue sweater to wear over a white blouse and exchanged her beautiful parka for a heavily insulated leather jacket. Jim had insisted on giving her a spare, greasy work parka, and with the cold wind now whistling through the small cabin, she was glad she'd relented.

He waited for her to get to the back, then worked his way under the forward panel to open the nose hatch as Jim pulled the underwater camera apparatus from a plastic shipping container and hooked it up. He passed the camera forward as he prepared a reel containing three hundred feet of umbilical cord.

Within ten minutes, Scott was back in the captain's seat of the Widgeon while Jim stood in the open nose hatch, and April occupied the copilot's seat, holding the color monitor on her lap as the stabilized camera began its towed journey along the bottom.

Scott inched the engine power up enough to maintain a three- to four-knot speed on the GPS readout as he maintained a southeast course. The TV camera was hanging approximately five feet above the sandy bottom some 250 feet down, its tail fins keeping the housing steady while the joystick—which April was controlling—pivoted the lens left and right. The camera platform carried a powerful searchlight that stabbed into the inky cold blackness below.

Rocks and seaweed were interspersed on the screen with darting fish and startled crab scurrying out of the way. A small tiger shark swam by and disappeared with an almost aggravated flip of its tail as the camera routed a huge halibut.

"Jim," Scott called out. "That halibut has to be a hundred pounds!"

"Damn," he replied. "Now you've made me hungry, and here we are without a flight attendant."

The cold marine air was cascading in through the open nose hatch and out the rear hatch, chilling April thoroughly. She pulled her parka around her a bit more tightly, zipping the lower portion as she breathed in the fresh sea air.

The sun was already very low on the southwestern horizon, its fiery orb cupped by the hills of Montague Island to the west. It was a strange feeling, she thought, to know that only three days ago her mother and dad might have died where she was now floating. It was also strange to think that she had awakened in Sequim less than fifteen hours before with no plans to be in Alaska, let alone in a seaplane trying to catch some glimpse of underwater wreckage. And it was nothing short of surreal that N34DD was somewhere below them now in the murk. The reality of just how difficult it might be to find her began to sink in.

"How long do you think we can keep looking before we have to start back?" April asked Scott, whose eyes seemed to be fixed on the horizon to the right.

"About two hours. I don't want to take off in the dark." He leaned under the forward panel. "Hey, Jim. What do you make of that boat at three o'clock?"

"Where?" Jim asked, his voice distant, even though he was standing in the bow hatch only two feet in front of the windscreen. "Hard to hear you up here."

"The boat off the port bow about a thousand yards," Scott repeated.

"What about him?"

"What's he doing?"

April watched Jim turn and look carefully, his weathered face catching the sun in silhouette. She saw him squint and look more closely before turning around.

"You have those field glasses, Scott?"

"Stand by," Scott responded, leaning into the cabin and wrestling a large pair of binoculars from a case. He leaned under the forward panel and handed them to Jim, who began scanning the distant boat. For almost a minute he said nothing. April tried to keep her eyes on the TV screen in her lap, but found herself distracted again by Jim's leaning down into the hatch to be heard.

"He's faking. He's pretending to be a commercial fisherman, but that's not a fishing rig, and he has no nets in the water."

Scott glanced at April, a flash of concern on his face.

"I don't understand," she said.

"Neither do I," Scott replied, ducking under the panel again to look up at Jim.

"Is he moving this way, or does it look like he has any interest in us?"

Jim was nodding before April heard him speak. He lowered the glasses. "He's taken an interest in us, all right. He's making straight for us at maybe ten knots, and they've got glasses on us, too."

"Wait," April said, straining to see details on the boat with her un-aided eyes. "Could he just think we're in trouble, landing out here like this?"

"Possibly," Scott said, climbing back into the left seat and looking over at her. "See anything down there yet?"

April shook her head. "We're still in sight of the bottom, but there's nothing that looks like metal, and I can only see maybe ten or fifteen feet ahead of the camera."

"Whoa!" Jim yelped from the nose hatch, the binoculars once again trained on the approaching boat. "There's another craft behind the first one, closing very fast."

"Can you tell anything about it?" Scott asked, but Jim was already nodding with a strange look on his face. "Yeah, kind of hard to mis-interpret that angular red stripe on the bow."

"Red stripe?" April began, the image popping into her head of Lieutenant Hobbs and the Coast Guard logo in his field safety office in Anchorage.

"It's a Coast Guard cutter," Jim added. "Making maybe twenty-five knots."

"Chasing that other boat, then?" Scott asked.

"No. He's making right for us. Better pull out that marine-band portable from my kit back there."

April kept her eyes on the TV screen, praying for a glimpse of something that resembled an aircraft. The rapid approach of the Coast Guard boat had triggered a very uneasy feeling, and she scolded herself silently for the petty panic. But logic wasn't overriding the reality of feeling as if she was about to be caught red-handed doing something very wrong.

Once again Scott scrambled out of the left seat and into the back of the Widgeon, rummaging around in Jim's bag until he pulled out the portable marine-band radio. He switched it on and handed it forward through the hatch.

The first call from Jim brought an instant response.

"Aircraft in the water, this is the United States Coast Guard Cutter *Point Barrow.* Heave to and prepare to be boarded. You are in restricted waters. Repeat, prepare to be boarded. You are in restricted waters."

Jim Dobler started to respond, then looked back at Scott McDermott in confusion, finally handing the radio back through the hatch.

"You're the skipper of this craft, Scott. You'd better talk to them."

He took the handheld and pressed it to his mouth as he tracked the approach of the cutter, which was looming larger with every minute.

"Coast Guard Cutter *Point Barrow,* this is United States registered aircraft November Eight Seven One Bravo. You are hailing us. We will wait for you, but be advised that neither our current aviation charts nor airmen notices as of this afternoon have announced this position as restricted waters. We are not fishing. Repeat, we are not engaged in any activity involving fishing. Over."

The message from the cutter's bridge was the same, and Scott shrugged as he swung the Widgeon around to the northwest and prepared to shut down the engines.

Jim sensed the turn and was leaning down in the hatch. "Scott, don't turn too rapidly or you'll foul the camera line."

"We're stopping?" April asked.

"No choice. Out here, they're the sheriff. You ever spot anything?"

She shook her head. Scott moved the engine mixture levers to the full lean position and the two radial engines coughed to silence, leaving only the noise of the Honda generator in the back of the cabin. April could see the camera settle to the bottom with a slight jar, the image of disturbed sand shooting up briefly in front of the lens caught in the light.

"I'm going to haul her up, Scott," Jim said, glancing at the cutter, which was now less than a quarter mile off and looming large, its hundred-fifty-foot length becoming intimidating to anyone sitting in a seaplane at wave level.

The TV screen was still on and April saw the camera jerked off the bottom. Without the stabilizing influence of the tow line pulling the platform's tail fins to steady it in one direction, the camera began to turn, the light shining to the left more and more, picking up the outline of something in the distance. April looked closer, squinting at the screen.

"Is the videotape running?" she asked.

"Yes. Why?"

"I . . . I'm not sure what I'm seeing. It looks metallic," she said.

Scott looked at the same image and immediately leaned forward. "Jim! Stop pulling. We see something to port."

"Can you go over that way?" she asked.

Scott nodded and reached for the mixture, prop, and throttle levers and flipped on the starter for the right engine, which coughed to life with one turn. As the Widgeon began moving he kept a heavy foot on the right rudder to try to guide it as he brought the left engine to life.

"In this direction?" he asked April, who was nodding energetically.

The sound of the same Coast Guard crewman's voice on the hand-held registered their instant alarm that the quarry was starting up.

"Aircraft November Eight Seven One Bravo, you have been ordered to heave to, and that means stop your engines. That is an order. Stop your engines."

Scott grabbed the radio with one fluid motion. "We're only maintaining stabilizing headway. We'll shut down when you're close enough to throw a line."

The crewman repeated his order as Scott jerked his head back and forth from the screen to the compass.

"That's it! Scott, that's the Albatross!" April cried.

"Are we close enough?"

"Yes! Can you stop?"

The engines wound to a halt.

"Give Jim some guidance," Scott said. "Should he pull it up, let it down . . . what?"

"Ah . . . up a little, Jim," she said.

Scott repeated the order.

The cutter was slowing now, and in his peripheral vision Scott could make out several crewmen on the bow readying lines and a boarding party, though how they were planning to board such a tiny floating aircraft was anything but clear.

"I can see the left engine, but . . . it's the other one I need," April said, leaning down toward the under-dash panel hatch. "Jim, can you twist it left somehow?"

Slowly the image changed, the camera rotating left imperfectly, but with enough clarity to see a twisted mass of metal where the right engine would normally be mounted, and large gashes in the wing beyond.

"My God, number-two engine dropped to one side on the mounts and the prop blades ate into the wing!" she said.

"April, we've got to get that videotape out of there. They may confiscate it."

"Can you . . . can you wait? I'm getting a better shot every second."

Scott scrambled out of the seat and into the back, positioning himself at the small portable mini-cartridge VCR.

A voice amplified by a bullhorn could be heard clearly now in the cabin, ordering them to stand by for two crewmen to come over by raft and inspect the aircraft.

"Come ahead, lad. We're not doing anything illicit over here," Jim was bellowing back.

"What are you doing out here?" the officer asked.

"Testing a new underwater video system. I'm getting ready to pull it up now."

April was watching the right wing slowly come closer. The engine had somehow dislodged, or shaken itself free from its mountings, but rather than drop off the Albatross entirely, it had lurched to the right and let at least two of the propeller blades eat into the leading edge of the wing and the fuel tank like some sort of bizarre buzz saw. The sight of it was both fascinating and sickening.

How on earth did they get out of there alive? she wondered. They couldn't have been more than seconds away from exploding in midair.

"April! Tear yourself away and record the latitude and longitude coordinates on the small GPS. Precisely! Every decimal place, and triple-check your work."

She grabbed a pen and did so, folding the resulting piece of paper and putting it in her parka, then thinking better of it and stuffing it down her bra.

There was a boat in the water now with an officer and a crewman aboard, and they threw off the lines and began motoring toward the Widgeon.

"April, if there's something restricted around here, they may want to confiscate this tape. I need to end this now."

"Okay," she said. There were other scrambling sounds in the back before she heard the generator die and saw the picture go dark.

"Tell Jim, as quietly as possible, to pull the camera up."

She relayed the word and watched with admiration as he seemed to be merely shifting position while actually winding in the line with the camera on the other end.

"What does he mean, restricted area?" April asked as Scott came back forward.

"I don't know. There was nothing on the charts. I doubt there's anything he can do legally, but I'd say that other boat was watching the area for them. So something's going on."

The small boat pulled alongside the bow, and Jim helped the young officer aboard and down to the interior of the cramped cabin.

"Who's the master . . . or pilot in command?"

"That's me, Scott McDermott," Scott said as he shook his hand. "That's Jim Dobler who helped you in, and this is April."

The Coast Guard lieutenant nodded in response. "I don't understand the problem here, Lieutenant," Scott said. "I checked all the notices to airmen and my charts are current, and there are no notices about steering clear of this area."

The Coast Guardsman held his palm up. "Look, this is not an arrest or anything, but we've got an unannounced military operation going on out here, and the word didn't get out, but it's our job to spread it anyway. So we're going to have to run you off."

"But, what's going on out here? I'm ex-Navy. You can tell me . . . or not. I guess that doesn't cut any mustard."

"Well . . ." The officer smiled. "Since you're Navy, you know I can't tell you unless you have both a current clearance and a need to know, and I'm not even sure I have a need to know."

"Okay," Scott said. "I'll pretend to understand that."

"Look, since you had a camera in the water, I've got to ask you whether you were videotaping anything, and whether you saw anything but fish."

"One gigantic halibut we'd all like to eat, a lot of fish, a shark, and crabs were what we were seeing. We did have a tape in there about the time you showed up, but we had only started to run it. I doubt there's anything there."

"Then I'm sorry, but . . ."

"You need the tape, right?"

The officer nodded. "You'll get it back in some form. Let me get your address."

"Look, where else should we be avoiding you guys? I mean, are there any other unmarked areas we should stay out of? It would be better to tell me. I'm not great on intuiting these things."

The lieutenant chuckled as he glanced at April, letting his eyes linger on her a bit before turning back to Scott.

"We had boats out to bar entry to this area, but apparently the brass didn't think about a seaplane."

"Apparently." Scott reached back and started the generator, turned on the VCR, and ejected the tape from the machine before turning it all off again and handing the tape over. April felt her heart sink as she saw the transfer.

"That's the only one?" the officer asked.

"Only one in there," Scott replied. "It's a new toy for Jim, and we were helping him try it out."

The lieutenant looked Scott in the eye for a few seconds, gauging his answer and whether there was any reason to probe further, then nodded. "Okay. Mr. Dobler, Mr. McDermott, Ms. Rosen? You're all free to go." He turned and squeezed his way out of the plane and back into his boat.

Jim had the camera hauled in and secured, and Scott fired the engines before the cutter crew had finished hauling out their boat. The takeoff was made in relative silence, the long rays of the setting sun just disappearing as they flew up the channel. Forty minutes later, Scott opted for a landing on the hard surface of the Valdez airport rather than risk the water in the dark.

They were waiting for a taxi back into town when Scott sat down on a log by the edge of the tarmac and handed something small and plastic to April.

"What's this?"

"The VCR tape."

"What? I thought you gave it to—"

"I gave him the one that was in the machine. This was the one I ejected from the machine before he came aboard." She could see an almost ear-to-ear grin in the subdued light of a nearby sodium-vapor lamp.

"I don't believe this! Thank you!"

"So . . . that make up for the cigar?"

"Yes," she said without hesitation.

"And. . . . maybe I could take you to dinner?"

"Let's not get carried away."

"The mind boggles at the possible replies to that statement, April."

"Seriously, thank you!"

"Think that's enough?"

"Sorry?"

"To help your dad? Is the tape enough?"

Jim was seating himself on the same log, having listened to the exchange.

"I don't know," April replied, "but something besides negligence knocked that engine off its mounts, and I think this tape will show that. I can't tell you how relieved I am."

"We can take a better look at the tape when we get back to my place," Jim said. "Also, there's a small hotel in town, April. I mean, I'd be honored to have you stay at my house, in my so-called guest room, and I'd even kick Junior here out on the streets to accommodate you, but it's really not fit for a lady."

"Hell, Jim," Scott laughed, "it's not fit for a pig, though I'm not complaining. But I'll be happy to share my space." Scott winked at her and waited for a response.

"Now that you mention it, the hotel sounds nice," April said with an even expression. "Wouldn't want to crowd you, or see you sleeping in the street." April opened her cell phone and started to dial

Gracie's number, but a beeping noise greeted her when she pressed the "send" button.

"Damn. No signal."

A pair of headlights cut through the twilight and turned toward the airport road in the distance.

"Here comes our taxi," Jim said. "Probably the only fare he's had all day."

"I may still need to raise the wreckage," April said suddenly.

Both men looked around at her, but Jim spoke first, shaking his head. "You know, the honor of a boarding party from the Coast Guard usually leads to courtrooms and big, ruinous fines. I'd say we were pretty lucky today, but we stumbled onto something. With all due respect and apologies, April, I don't think raising that bird's going to be possible until they get through with their war games and clear the area and give the okay. I'm sorry."

The silence grew as the cab moved closer, and April heard Scott McDermott sigh deeply.

"What?" she asked.

"It's not war games," Scott said.

"No? What, then?"

"They're trying to keep us, and everyone else, away from what we just found."

She sat in silence for a few seconds looking at him. "My dad's *plane?*"

Scott nodded.

"No, that can't be it. It took political pressure just to get my folks rescued, and the Coast Guard already told me they weren't interested in raising the wreckage or having anything to do with it."

"They knew you were out there with us," he said flatly.

"Why . . . why on earth do you say that?" April asked.

The car was turning the last corner before reaching them as Scott sighed again.

"When that lieutenant left, he told Mr. Dobler and Mr. McDermott, and one Ms. Rosen that we could all go."

"I remember. So?"

"So, I introduced Jim and me by our first and last names. I never mentioned your last name."

The sound of tires crushing gravel and bright headlights prompted Jim and Scott to get to their feet. April remained sitting, thoroughly stunned, as Scott reached out to help her up. There was the sound of a car door opening.

"That you, Jerry?" Jim called to the driver as he squinted into the headlights. "What took you so long? And get those damned lights out of our eyes!"

The passenger door opened, and someone stepped around the front of the car.

"This isn't Jerry, Jim. This is Trooper Joe Harris of the state police. Coast Guard says you folks may have a tape that belongs to them."

TWENTY FOUR

notification that the final acceptance test flight had been post-poned one more time came in the form of a note Lindsey White left on Ben's office computer.

At first Ben didn't see it when he returned from Dan Jerrod's office. It was a folded piece of paper literally taped to the upper right side of his computer monitor, and it was a measure of his current state of distraction that he could miss it for more than an hour. That hour had consisted of stressing out over ways to deny the would-be saboteurs a means of recontaminating the master program on the test flight.

The delay note, when he found it, was tantamount to a stay of execution. All of which meant that Schroedinger would get fed in person for at least one more evening.

The team was growing exasperated with him, Ben could tell, though no one had been bold enough to say anything. His extreme distraction, moodiness, fatigue, and otherwise un-Ben-like behavior was prompting equally uncharacteristic group behavior in response. The room fell silent now when he walked in, and he could feel their eyes following him. Where normally he was a full member of his own team, suddenly he was an oddity, and more of an annoyance than a team leader. That recognition, however, was doing little to cure the underlying malady of frustration and fear.

Ben reread Lindsey's message, wondering what had prompted this new postponement.

Am I somehow out of the loop and don't know it? he wondered. It depended on who had made the decision, and that almost certainly would have come from above Joe Davis.

The basic fact remained, of course, that he did not know who fit the description of enemy. Lindsey and Joe had lied about fitting the emergency disconnect to the Gulfstream. "Hey, Ben," they could have said, "there's some major problem in getting that installed in time. Would you agree to fly without it?"

Ben snorted, startling himself, as he wondered what his answer would have been. He was too compliant, too cooperative to have said no. But they should have asked, because now they, too, looked like the unseen enemy.

He wandered out to talk to his team members and listen to their exasperated admission that after three days of feverish work they'd failed to find a single glitch in the main program. He refrained, of course, from revealing what the Cray had helped him find. Dan Jerrod's admonition wasn't the only reason. It came down to the lonely reality that no one was beyond suspicion.

When all the research team members had left, Ben sat in silence trying to order his thoughts. Perhaps Jerrod *could* protect them tomorrow when the test flight finally occurred. Sharing his suspicions with Jerrod had lifted his spirits, but there were too many unanswered questions to feel comfortable.

A wave of fatigue rolled over him, and he sat at his desk and put his head down to rest for a few minutes, drifting off into a troubled jumble of dreams.

RESEARCH TRIANGLE
RALEIGH-DURHAM, NORTH CAROLINA

Will Martin had been alternately pacing his office and staring out the
window for the better part of the morning as he fielded phone calls
and tried to stay focused. The delays in Anchorage had passed critical,
but pressing Joe Davis any more was certain to be counterproductive.
There was little he could do now but wait and hope and watch the
clock before the day began with a security briefing from Todd Jenkins, his corporate security chief. The possibility, however remote, of
a major security breach at the most critical moment in Uniwave's history had easily captured his undivided attention, but with the daughter of a grounded airline pilot asking too many questions and the pilot
himself hiring lawyers, the threat of a breach was real.

"The name is Rosen?"

Todd Jenkins, the head of Uniwave's corporate security department, nodded.

"Yes, and it's getting more complicated by the hour, with the man's
daughter pushing at the Coast Guard and the FAA for answers."

"What does she know?"

Jenkins had shrugged. "Dan Jerrod's people are watching," Todd had
replied, referring to the Anchorage-based security chief for Skyhook.

Will had leaned forward and leveled a piercing stare at Jenkins.

"I need you in the field. I want you shadowing the situation, too,
in person. I don't trust Jerrod to react in time. This is too serious a
situation to take lightly, Todd. Congress is looking for victims among
black projects, and if this grounded pilot manages to blow our cover,
even a successful flight test won't save us. I mean, this is survival."

Jenkins had nodded and said nothing before taking his leave. His
greatest challenge had been to keep a large smile off his face. With
twenty-eight years in the CIA covert operations, being confined to
a desk job had been killing him.

TWENTY FIVE

*m*ajor General Mac MacAdams walked from the JCS meeting room with General Lou Cassidy after finishing the top secret briefing on the Boomerang system.

"Surprised, Mac?" Cassidy asked when they were back behind his office door.

" 'Flabbergasted' would be a good word, Lou. I expected we'd have at least a month for the first installation, but fifty units installed within the next ten *days?*"

"Right from the Oval Office, Mac. Can we do it?"

Mac nodded. "Well, yes . . . physically. I mean, part of the planning quite a while ago was to have black boxes made up and ready to receive final circuit boards and hard drives for immediate installation."

"Great thinking, too. I'm still impressed that you got it down to the level of such industrial simplicity, with over a year to test all the subcomponents."

"Thanks. The parallel effort out of Wright-Patterson has been handled very efficiently. My latest count shows the entire C-17 fleet, one hundred eighty C-141s, and all the operational C-5s have completed the hardware retrofit."

Cassidy nodded. "Just slide the little sucker in the bracket, turn the cyberlock, and she's operational."

"With codes as secure as the President's launch code."

Cassidy nodded. "I think it was a much better idea to have the same established office that handles the nuclear codes choose the codes for Boomerang. One-stop shopping with proven security."

"Are we ready for the bomber fleet? Do we really want to do that?"

Cassidy shook his head. "No. We have another system planned for which you have no immediate need to know."

"Yes, sir," Mac replied, glad that he hadn't been handed one more weighty responsibility on the spur of the moment.

Cassidy leaned forward. "Mac, really good job in there, by the way."

"Thanks."

"You're headed back to Anchorage?"

Mac nodded. "Immediately. A few loose ends have to be sewn up, including tonight's final acceptance test, but otherwise, we'll make it work."

Cassidy showed him to the door, and Mac collected his aide from Cassidy's outer office and headed down one of the maze of corridors past a portion of the Pentagon's rebuilt western side, which had been hit in the 9/11 attacks.

Lieutenant Colonel Anderson caught his sleeve at one point. "Sir? The car will be waiting on the north side."

"I'm going in a different car, Jon."

"Sir?"

"You take the car you arranged. I'll take the other one."

"Okay. We go separately."

"Yep," Mac said, rather enjoying the confusion on Anderson's face as he tried to keep up.

"If it makes a difference, sir, I did bathe and use deodorant this morning."

"At long last!" Mac joked. "But you still can't go with me."

"Very well, sir. But I assume plausible deniability," Anderson said.

Mac stopped him and turned to put a hand on his shoulder. "No. Complete deniability. Take your car, Jon. I'll see you on board." He started to turn away, then looked back at the colonel. "Jon, I'm pulling your chain. I'm actually going over to Arlington National to pay my respects to an old friend I lost long ago."

"Understood, sir. I'm sorry I pressed."

Mac watched his aide disappear in the right direction before walking to an interior courtyard driveway, where his driver was waiting. The unmarked car moved immediately into the throng of traffic around the Pentagon and smoothly accelerated to the north, pulling up to a back gate into Arlington National Cemetery a few minutes later. The guard verified the credentials the driver held up and waved them through.

Mac had visited Arlington many times during his career. Robert E. Lee's home, the Custis-Lee Mansion, was his favorite spot, but the revered anonymity and peace that permeated Arlington was something he'd always sought.

"We're here, sir," the driver announced.

"Thank you. You know where to wait for pickup."

"Yes, sir."

Mac removed his hat and put on a light, non-uniform raincoat to hide all vestiges of a uniform.

The day was cloudy and cool, but invigorating nonetheless, and he made his way down a familiar path, stopping for a second near the Coast Guard Memorial, then proceeding to a grove of trees near the end of Dewey Drive, where a tall, blond woman in a long black coat was standing, reading the inscription of a large headstone.

Mac came up beside her quietly, reading the same headstone.

"He died the day before the Normandy landing," Mac said quietly.

"So I see," she replied, not looking at him.

"How are you, Lucy?"

"On a four-year-long, exhilarating, exhausting high. How about you?"

"The atmosphere isn't as rarified as where you've been living, but . . . it's been an interesting couple of years."

"Is the program ready?"

Mac sighed, a thousand worries tied into one moment of decision.

"Yeah. We're ready if we have to be. The list still the same?"

She nodded. "It is. Discovery would destroy us, Mac. We need to get it right the first time. You realize how important this is to the President personally, don't you?"

"I believe so."

"Maybe, but I'm not sure you fully understand the depth of his resolve."

"The timetable?" he asked.

"It's concurrent with the Pentagon's schedule. I assume the plan is the same for the containers?"

"Yes. Two per crate, manifested as one, and handled the way we agreed."

"And no problems as yet?"

"I've . . . had a few anxious moments, including this morning in Cassidy's office, but they've all been containable questions, no pun intended."

She chuckled. "Right. Good luck, Mac," she said, turning away and strolling casually toward the adjacent roadway. Mac forced himself to stay focused on the gravesite before him, even kneeling down and putting on his reading glasses before standing and stealing a look around.

She was nowhere to be seen.

Mac checked his watch and turned to the south. He could see the car waiting at the appointed spot through the trees. With luck, they could lift off from Andrews by 11:30 A.M. local for the nearly seven-hour flight, putting them into Elmendorf at 2:30 P.M. He caught himself sighing and longing for sleep. There was a comfortable couch on the Air Force Gulfstream, and he'd have to take advantage of it, since the evening would involve some very long hours aboard an AWACS.

TWENTY-SIX

FRIDAY MORNING, DAY 5

ASPEN HOTEL

VALDEZ, ALASKA

A telephone rang somewhere in the darkened hotel room, jangling April back to consciousness. She rolled to the left to reach for it before remembering that she wasn't in her apartment. She sat up in the pitch darkness, feeling for the edge of the bed, unable to dredge up a memory of the previous evening, or where she was now.

Okay, wait . . . I was in Sequim, then . . .

As if flipping a switch, her memory flooded back, bringing with it a depressing recollection of the previous night.

Valdez! I'm in a hotel in Valdez.

The phone was still ringing somewhere to the left and she flailed around in search of it, knocking something off the nightstand as her hand found the receiver.

"Hello?"

"April? Gracie. I'm sorry to wake you."

"S'okay," she said, rubbing her eyes, then trying to find the lamp. "I had to get up anyway to answer the phone."

She could hear Gracie sigh in response. "You awake enough to talk to me about last night?"

"You got my message, then," April said.

"Yes, but . . . I can't figure out why you couldn't get hold of me last night."

"Maybe . . . 'cause someone else had hold of you last night?"

April smiled to herself as Gracie squirmed on the other end and cleared her throat. "I was on my boat, alone."

" 'Kay. I'm awake now, and we've got a big problem. We found Dad's plane, I got pictures of it on an underwater video, and the Coast Guard took it."

"Wait!" Gracie interrupted. "Slow down. Tell me everything that happened, in order. You say you found the Albatross and had a tape of it, and the Coast Guard *took* it?"

April related the entire sequence of events, including the embarrassing experience of being hauled into the state police office with Jim and Scott and being searched.

"They searched for the tape, then?" Gracie asked.

"He."

"Okay, he. But he found it? You didn't volunteer it?"

"The salvage guy—Jim—told him he had several tapes, and he produced, I think, four, but it was obvious the trooper wasn't going to stop until he found the one the Coast Guard wanted, which was in my pocket."

"So, you volunteered it?"

"Well, I told him I didn't believe that the State Patrol or the Coast Guard had a legal right to claim that tape, and that I'd turn it over only if we watched it first, and then under protest."

"And he, of course, tried to convince you that he didn't need a warrant."

"Yes. Did he need one? I mean, he was nice, but he was threatening arrest."

"I'm not sure whether he needed one or not. I don't even know under what coloration of law he was claiming to act as an agent for the Coast Guard. I'm going to have to think this through and research it quickly."

"It was pretty confusing."

"I'll bet. Did he let you watch the tape?"

April shook her head, her eyes closed, her head full of cotton. "No. He wouldn't let us look at it. Even when I explained how incredibly important it was."

"Well, the other two guys saw it, though, right? As you filmed the wreck?"

"No. *I* saw it. They never did."

"Are you sure? Where were the other two?"

"Jim Dobler, the fellow with the salvage company, was up front in the Widgeon with his back to the screen at the moment I saw the aircraft come into view, and Scott—the pilot you hired for me—was in the back."

"I see," Gracie replied, her professional and personal concern painfully apparent.

"Gracie," April said, "don't worry. *I* can testify that I saw it clearly. The plane's a mess, of course, but that engine was an indelible image. Frankly, it scares me to say this, but I'm surprised Mom and Dad survived." She related the details: the right engine hanging off its mountings and cocked to one side, the heavily damaged right wing, the bent propeller blades. "So we can blow the FAA out of the tub on this one. I mean, we need to get those unopened liquor bottles, too, but as for the reckless flying thing, no way could that engine have been knocked off just by impact with the water and still chew up the wing. The props would have stopped instantly."

"And . . . they didn't?"

"Gracie, the right wing was shredded metal. It could have collapsed."

"Of course, we can expect the FAA to look at it differently."

"I don't give a damn what the FAA says. You can't argue with facts. I know what I saw. That wreckage is down there right now giving mute testimony to the fact that their charges are ridiculous."

"How many blades did you see, April? Two or three?"

"I don't know. That I couldn't make out. I was hoping that once we got back here, the tape would have enough detail to tell us for certain. But we should have enough now, right? I told Dad last night by phone we did."

"Enough to exonerate him?"

"Yes. Not the drinking charge, or at least not yet. But the reckless charge."

"Not without that tape, April. I mean, we need to get Ted Greene, the D.C. lawyer, on this immediately. Did the state trooper say why the Coast Guard wanted it?"

"No. Gracie?"

"Yeah?"

"You're scaring me. Why are you so negative? What am I missing here? I told you I can clearly testify to what I saw even without the taped evidence."

"I know, kiddo, but think about it from the point of view of a neutral third party. You're the loving daughter of the accused, presumably ready to do anything for your dad. Same problem Rachel has testifying he wasn't drinking. You're smart, you're a pilot who knows the ropes, and you're the one who's going to swear you saw evidence that would magically clear his record. Unfortunately, it's evidence that virtually no one else saw, that's no longer available, and that's recorded on a tape that may not exist."

"Okay. I can understand that kind of prejudice, but the tape *does* exist and the Coast Guard has it. Can't we get a court order to force them to hand it over?"

"If they don't have a magnetic accident and erase it, or make some claim of national security, which might or might not block us, then probably so. But if there's something down there on the ocean floor they don't want anyone to see, and they want to claim that the tapes show whatever that is, then we may never get it back intact. And, April, the more time that elapses between when you shot the tape and when it's finally sealed as evidence, the more opportunity the FAA has to say that it was electronically altered or even staged."

"That's ridiculous!"

"No, it's not. Remember what you showed me on your computer? Even you carry around a computer program that can completely alter a photo."

"Well, yeah. A still photo."

"Videotapes are just a series of stills, April. And you're Ms. Electronics. They'd have a field day."

April was rubbing her forehead, her attempts to find the lamp switch unsuccessful. She felt like bawling. "Why, Gracie, are we now fighting both the FAA and the Coast Guard? What is this, some sort of bizarre conspiracy to get Dad?"

"I haven't a clue why the Coast Guard would come out and harass you and seize the videotape," Gracie replied. "But suppose they're testing some new submarine or laying an underwater cable or who knows what?"

"But these guys are supposed to be on our side, aren't they?"

"Sure. 'We're from the government. We're here to help you.'"

"I mean, just Wednesday I talked to a very helpful Coast Guard officer in Anchorage. Oh, God!"

"What?"

"Things have been moving so fast, I completely forgot."

"What are you talking about?"

"Remember I told you about the somewhat clandestine meeting with Lieutenant Hobbs—Jim Hobbs of the Coast Guard in Anchorage?"

"Yes. At Starbucks. I figured he was hitting on you."

"No, he was trying to warn me, and I didn't take it to heart. He said there were other agencies interested in Dad's situation. I asked him for the radar tapes, and he said he was told there was nothing there that would help. I handed him the exact coordinates from the on-board GPS, and then blundered into the area without ever thinking that they might be waiting and watching. That's what Jim Hobbs was trying to warn me about."

"Hey, I would have done the same thing, April."

"It's funny you'd mention submarines, Gracie. Scott McDermott is an ex-Navy pilot, and he was saying exactly the same thing last night—that they may be protecting some Navy operation."

"All the more reason to raise that aircraft as soon as possible."

"That's the other problem," April sighed, relating Jim's reluctance even to apply for permits, now that the area was supposedly restricted.

"April, push those two guys hard to help you. I'll . . . Wait a minute. I know someone down here in the Coast Guard. Let me see if I can find out what claim of legality they're using to rope off that area and confiscate tapes. In fact, I'll recommend to Ted Greene that we just charge into this immediately and file for an emergency restraining order to locate and protect that tape."

"My head is so fuzzed up right now, Gracie, I can't think."

"You need coffee."

"Yeah. But more importantly, I need something encouraging to tell Dad."

They ended the call, leaving April feeling overwhelmed.

There was no way she should be wide awake at five-thirty in the morning after less than five hours' sleep, April thought, but she was. The burning desire to finish the mission she'd come to Alaska to accomplish drove her into the shower and out of the room around six, looking for a coffee shop open for breakfast at that hour.

"Totem Inn's the only one, ma'am," the desk clerk said, pointing the way. She zipped up her parka and trudged the relatively short distance through the quiet, darkened streets of the small town. The temperature was in the mid-thirties, and while winter was officially over, the frigid air cascading down the mountain slopes from the surrounding glaciers kept the town in a constant state of refrigeration.

April snuggled into a booth and ordered. The coffee tasted far better than it actually was, but the eggs were perfect, and she finished the meal and sat quietly for a few minutes, her eyes on a distant light across the bay, her mind working through the central question of what to do next.

Scott McDermott was bunking, as he put it, with Jim, and they had agreed to meet in the morning with no clear idea of why. Gracie was right, April thought. She needed their help.

Okay, she told herself. *Focus. What do I want them to do? They can't steal the tape back.*

It had been a mild torture to lie in the hotel bed earlier with the knowledge that the state trooper who'd waylaid them wasn't leaving Valdez with her tape until morning. That little cartridge might mean her father's livelihood and happiness, and it was physically less than two hundred yards distant at the tiny state police office. The thought of breaking in had crossed her mind. There were no steel doors or bars on the windows. It was little more than a portable building, and she could probably gain access with a screwdriver.

At 1 A.M. April had slipped from beneath the covers, shivering in the cold of the hotel room, and peeked out the window, staring at the nearby building as a Valdez police car motored by.

Am I crazy? I'm not going to burgle a police station. Like they wouldn't know who took their tape.

She'd gone back to bed and fallen into a deep sleep replete with odd dreams of a beautiful mountain field and saddled horses that couldn't be ridden. She'd chased the unattainable mounts for endless hours in the dream before Gracie's phone call had shattered it.

April thanked the waitress for the latest coffee refill and refocused on the present. She couldn't steal the tape, and she couldn't even talk the officer into letting the other two guys see it, and Gracie obviously thought that was a fatal problem. Yet the key to Arlie Rosen's exoneration was sitting under 250 feet of water just sixty miles south, and even Gracie was afraid something might happen to the wreckage. Full, unopened bottles in the cabin of the Albatross would destroy Harrison's theory.

We've got to go back out, regardless of the risk, April concluded. She had Jim's address. She should probably walk there and knock on his door about seven. McDermott might be grumpy, but Jim would be gracious, and she could plead with him shamelessly, the damsel in distress, as Lieutenant Hobbs had characterized her. She hated manipulating, but this was different.

April paid the check and studied the local map in the tiny Valdez phone book at the café before pushing through the door into the cold. The glow of dawn was already on the eastern horizon as she reached Jim Dobler's door, surprised to find a light on in what must be the kitchen or dining area. She could see through the window by the front porch that it was Scott McDermott sitting alone over a cup of coffee. She tapped lightly on the glass, surprised when Scott jumped, startled, then smiled when he saw her face through the glass door. He got to his feet to let her in.

"April! You're up early."

"Yeah. Good morning. So are you."

He closed the door quietly behind her. "Jim's still snoring in his room, and I was just trying to get a handle on the day."

"Me too." She smiled.

"Would you like some coffee? It's kind of cold out there."

"Love some," she said, deciding there was no point in discussing her breakfast.

She sat at the small kitchen table as he handed her a fresh cup.

"Jim's got good taste. Starbucks, Seattle's Best, Millstone . . . the good brands."

"Scott, I need to go back out there and try again."

He stopped rummaging through Jim's pantry and turned toward her, his eyes narrowing slightly as he studied the determination on her face. She saw him sigh and close the cabinet before sitting down, folding his hands, and looking her in the eye.

"April . . ."

"I have no choice. My dad's career, his financial survival, maybe even his life, are on the line, and the proof that he wasn't negligent—the proof that can partially end the problem—is right out there." She pointed to the west and he corrected her, his finger roughly describing the magnetic course to the crash site.

"Look, I really want to help you with this," Scott began. "Hell, I could use the money, and so could Jim. But, April, you've got to be practical. The Coast Guard will more than likely give you that tape back, so you really don't need us. I'd have to charge you a small fortune anyway for the risk."

She nodded, her face hardening. "I see. We need to set a price, then."

"A price?"

"You, know," she said, a sharpness creeping into her voice. "How many pieces of silver will it take to get you to help me?"

"Pieces of silver? What, as in a biblical reference?"

"Of course. I mean, you're obviously concerned with money."

"Well, hell, lady, I'm not in this for love!" he snapped, instantly regretting it. "Sorry. I'm just trying to run a flying service, and the winters get pretty sparse."

"I'm not asking for charity, you know. I'll certainly pay your tab without fail."

"I'm not worried about . . . Look, I apologize if that seemed mercenary."

"It did."

He glanced away for a few seconds before meeting her gaze again. "Look, April, if we try to bust through their prohibited zone, either or both of us could end up out of business. They could take Jim's permits and financially strangle him! And they could cashier my pilot's license like . . . like . . ." He was gesturing uselessly and unable to back out of the reference he now wanted to avoid.

"Like what they've done with my dad's license?"

"Well . . . yeah."

"Who the hell is 'they,' Scott? Who am I fighting?"

He shook his head. "I don't know, but—and I thought about this last night a lot—it really does have to be something to do with the Navy. I mean, it's water, it's military . . ."

"What do you mean, military? The Coast Guard is primarily government."

"Yeah, but you remember that so-called fishing boat Jim said was faking fishing? Just before the cutter showed up?"

"I forgot."

"I finally remembered where I'd seen that hull before. Adak. I've had a few contracts to run in and out of there, and I remember seeing him. That's a Navy tender based at Adak Naval Air Station. April, we've stumbled into a Navy operation and . . . and it probably is legitimately associated with national security. It's just unfortunate your dad happened to go down in the wrong place."

"I'll be sure to warn him to do a better job of crashing the next time," she said, her voice sharp and sarcastic.

Scott raised his hand, palm up. "I'm sorry—that wasn't meant to be offensive."

April nodded, her eyes on the window as she watched the growing light in the eastern sky, a backdrop glow over a glacier-encrusted mountain bordering the western end of the Valdez inlet. She turned back to him, her jaw set. "Scott, I need help. Name your price. I'm going back out there even if I have to buy the equipment and rent an outboard. If neither you nor Jim will help me, then I'll go alone."

He was shaking his head. "I'm sorry, April. Unless I can get clearance to legally go there, I'm out of this. I'm not nuts."

"You're quitting? Just like that? I said I'd meet your price."

"So I get paid and lose my license. What's wrong with this picture?"

"You're the big macho ex-Navy go-get-'em damn-the-torpedoes guy I was told could do almost anything, and you're running from this? Apparently they were wrong."

He was getting agitated, his gestures becoming broader, his face darker.

"Who is 'they,' huh? Who the hell told you I was some sort of testosterone-soaked risk taker?"

"Synonymous with fighter jock, right? Or was that only the previous generations in 'Nam and Desert Storm?"

"Hey! I served in Afghanistan before hanging it up!"

"But this scares you?"

His voice rose another notch. "Damn, woman, what is it about professional suicide you don't understand?"

"I understand that . . . that . . . I'm begging for your help, Scott."

"Oh? What, now you're the helpless female begging the macho male to go slay her dragon?" He snorted derisively as he got up from the table and paced to the end of the kitchen, turning, his voice raised. "I've been jerked around by some of the best manipulating bitches in the world, and you're no match."

"Fine."

"How dare you try to goad me."

"Forget it," she said, looking away, genuinely trying not to cry. She started pawing at her purse, trying to get the latch open to pull out her checkbook, anger mixing in a confusing mélange with a wave of despair. "I'll write you a check so you can get the hell out of Dodge."

Jim Dobler had been leaning against the far entrance to the room in the shadows, listening. He moved toward the table, watching April flipping through her checkbook, pen in hand.

"Sit down, Scott," Jim said.

"Hey, don't—"

"*Sit,* son! For God's sake, respect your elders."

Scott snorted and sank back into his chair.

"And, April? May I have your attention, please?"

She stopped writing the check and looked up, then set the pen down. "Certainly, Jim."

"Thank you."

"How long were you standing there?" she asked.

"Long enough," he said, settling into a kitchen chair backward. "Long enough."

TWENTY-SEVEN

FRIDAY MORNING, DAY 5

USAF SAM 3994 SPECIAL AIR MISSION,

EN ROUTE ANDREWS AFB TO ELMENDORF AFB

Lieutenant Colonel Jon Anderson placed the small laptop computer on the polished tabletop in front of Major General Mac MacAdams and opened the screen.

"I just downloaded the shots the Navy took for you, sir."

"They got them this fast? Great."

Anderson sat down in an adjacent seat. "According to the message, they had an unmanned remote submersible available, and they located the wreck quickly—thanks to having the coordinates transmitted by the Albatross itself right before it went in."

"I heard about that on-board GPS system."

"One more thing I need to tell you. When the Navy ship carrying the submersible was approaching the area yesterday, they found a small civilian amphibian aircraft sitting over the site and dangling a private submersible camera over the wreckage. In the aircraft was the daughter, April Rosen, and two men."

"Did they succeed?"

"Yes, sir. Apparently she hired the pilot and his little Grumman amphib—a Widgeon—out of Anchorage, and they got the video equipment from a company in Valdez."

"So . . . they've now got footage of the wreck. That's good if it ends her search for a way to get her father off the hook."

"Well, we've kind of intervened. Through the Coast Guard."

"Meaning?"

Anderson related the boarding and confiscation of the first tape. "When they got the tape aboard the cutter, one of the crewmen had a camcorder with the same format and they played it, but the tape had only a few frames recorded, and they figured—correctly, it turned out—that Rosen had kept the real tape. They had the police catch up with her when her airplane landed in Valdez, and they confiscated the tape there."

"Confiscated?" Mac sighed. "I'm not a lawyer, but that worries me. I'm not sure we have the legal right to snatch a civilian tape. Do we know what it showed?"

"An oblique view of the wreckage, showing the right engine hanging off its mounts and a badly damaged wing where the right prop tore into it."

Mac was nodding. "So, Ms. Rosen knows for certain that something happened in the air that probably caused the crash. If I recall correctly, you told me before that she was trying to prove the propeller threw a blade. Was there evidence on that tape of a thrown blade?"

Jon shook his head. "On the tape she got it's inconclusive, but the Navy's pictures tell the tale clearly, and there's no doubt. It threw a blade in flight."

He punched the keyboard and the image of the Albatross's right engine filled the screen, one prop blade clearly missing, the other two severely deformed from slicing repeatedly into the right wing.

"So, Ms. Rosen was right."

"This is the broader view taken by the submersible sitting right in front of the nose," Anderson said.

"Good lord, look at that wing!" Mac's eyes traced the damage in the clarity of the picture as he drummed his fingers on the airborne table. "All right. Jon, remember I didn't want Ms. Rosen or her father pushing for exonerating evidence and accidentally uncovering our project in the process? Well, now that she's found the wreckage and photographed it, she *knows* he had a real airborne emergency. But we've just snatched that proof away."

"Yes, sir. Apparently. And it's far more critical now for them because, based on that FAA inspector's recommendations, FAA headquarters revoked the father's pilot license, and the man's an active airline captain."

"On what grounds?"

"Reckless operation of an aircraft and violation of visual flight rules, and I understand there's a charge of flying while intoxicated."

"Intoxicated? Really? That's disturbing. Of course, what the wreckage shows is that the reckless operation charge is wrong. What is his name?"

"Captain Arlie Rosen. A senior 747 captain for United."

"Captain Rosen has to be able to prove that reckless charge false, and without the physical evidence or video evidence, it's going to be difficult. So what do you think a determined young woman like Ms. Rosen is going to do, Jon?"

"I think she'll keep on trying."

"You can bank on it. But how? What can we expect her to do next?"

"Agitate to get her tape back?"

"Correct. From your briefing we know she's smart. She's worldly. She knows the Coast Guard has snatched her tape and that there has to be more to it than just flying into the wrong place. She's probably thinking anything from government cover-ups to conspiracy thoughts right now, and I'll bet you she has enough experience with the government to know that getting that tape back may take a lot of time. All of which means what?"

"General, you're sounding more like a professor every day. I don't know where you're going with these questions."

"Well, what I'm getting at, Jon, is that she's sure to find a way to go out there again, Coast Guard–restricted areas or not. She'll try to get the same video shots or better. And for us the question then becomes, is there any reason we should stop her?"

"Yes, sir, I'd say there is, if there's anything on that wreckage that might suggest our Gulfstream and their Albatross traded paint."

"But, Jon, we looked the Gulfstream over in the hangar, and we couldn't find any evidence of an impact. Right?"

"Yes, sir, but . . . I just get the creepy feeling we're missing something that could badly hurt us."

Mac sighed and sat forward, his hand out, palm up. "What would it take to raise that plane ourselves?"

"The Navy's ready to go for it, sir. Wouldn't take much. They could put it on a small barge and cover it until we get the chance to inspect it."

Mac sat in thought for a few minutes. "Well, instead, suppose I just pull enough horsepower together to get to the FAA administrator and have her reinstate Captain Rosen's pilot's license?"

Jon Anderson winced. "Sir, with all due respect to your ability to make that happen, it would open a lot of doors to a lot of questions and explanations, including the basic one of who you are and why you're involved and interested. Even pleading national security doesn't stop the widening of the circle."

"Well, hell," Mac said with a snort, "maybe the Navy just happened by with a camera, and here's the photo. Doesn't have to involve us."

"It would take more than that photo, General. I know the FAA very well. To counter an angry FAA inspector who's managed to convince headquarters to take away an airline captain's ticket on three different charges, you'd have to give the FAA administrator a very forceful, very direct explanation, and that means pretty much blowing our cover. We're keeping the majority of the Pentagon in the dark on this project anyway, and we've spent a heck of a lot to make sure it doesn't leak, so . . . do you really want to involve the FAA's key people?"

"In other words, you don't think we can help the Rosens without a potential security breach, even though solving their problem would keep them off our trail?"

Jon nodded. "Yes, sir. In a nutshell."

Mac sighed and turned away in thought. He turned back suddenly, swiveling the chair around to face Anderson. "Dammit, I know you're right, Jon. This is just so frustrating. I'm a pilot, and here's a fellow pilot getting screwed, we're holding his get-out-of-jail ticket, and we can't give it to him without revealing we're here."

"General, one of the best memos you've written in this whole project was the one that asked us to place security considerations above all others. It was eloquent and convincing."

Mac shook his head, smiling ruefully. "What? You framed it?"

"Well, it wasn't *that* timeless, but it was right on point."

"That leaves poor Captain Rosen and his daughter as unwitting victims."

"Sir, don't forget there are two other serious charges against Captain Rosen, and we don't have a clue whether they're valid or not."

Mac sighed. "That point is valid, though it may not be enough to use in good conscience as justification." He looked at his watch. "Okay. Another two hours and we'll be there. Everything on time for tonight's test flight?"

Jon Anderson nodded. "The AWACS is set to launch at six-thirty local with us aboard, and the Gulfstream should be airborne about ten minutes later."

"This better work," Mac said, getting to his feet.

VALDEZ, ALASKA

High clouds were moving over Prince William Sound to the west as April left the warmth of Jim Dobler's office for a few minutes to peer over the edge of the dock, feeling the bracing cold of the zephyrs whipping down the channel and churning the waters in the protected breakwater below. There was a distant noise behind her, and she glanced around at the office window to watch Jim still on the phone, trying hard to clear the way to salvage the wreckage of the Albatross without running afoul of the law or the Coast Guard.

She sighed and shook her head as the image of Scott McDermott floated across her mind again, wondering what had happened in his background to make him back away so quickly from a challenge.

He's probably back in Anchorage by now, she thought. He'd left hours ago, after Jim had intervened in the heated early morning exchange. She'd pressed a check in his hand, but he refused it at first, accepting it only after she insisted that it was only for the originally contracted charter fee and not his additional efforts on her behalf. For some reason, the distinction had become terribly important to him.

She felt her cell phone vibrating in one of the pockets of her parka and fished it out to find Gracie on the other end.

"April, I've just been down to the Federal Building here in Seattle and filed for a temporary restraining order against the Coast Guard and the Alaska State Police to forbid them from monkeying with that tape, and I've asked for an expedited hearing for tomorrow morning to demand its immediate return."

"I thought the D.C. lawyer was going to do that," April said.

"Yeah, well, I did, too, but I couldn't reach him, and I was closer to the facts and better equipped to handle it here."

"You think we'll get it? That injunction, I mean?"

"Yes, provided they don't claim that they've already lost it or that it was blank. Since we have no idea what's going on and who's involved, we really can't know what to expect. What's happening there?"

April briefed her on Jim Dobler's efforts to get permission for a salvage operation. "I'm not optimistic, Gracie. He's a really nice guy and he's trying hard, but even before the Coast Guard tackled us, he warned me how difficult it was in these waters to do anything."

"And you can't fly out there again?"

"Yeah, well, our flyboy cut and ran. I mean, I shouldn't be unap-
preciative of what he did, but . . . as soon as officialdom moved in,
he got spooked."

"He *left?*"

"Yep."

"Damn. Well, if Dobler can't make it work, I'll call my client back
and see if he has any other ideas. Aside from that, could you, maybe,
rent that video equipment and take a boat out there?"

"What if the Coast Guard is watching? They'd see any boat I
could use."

"Not a wooden boat, I'll bet."

"Like a rowboat?"

"Yeah."

"Gracie, this place is out to sea. Even in an outboard I'd run a real
risk of capsizing. The waves can get huge and it's very, very cold water. After all, that's what almost killed my parents."

There was silence from Seattle.

"Gracie?"

"Yeah, I'm here. I'm . . . just thinking through this to see how we
can get this resolved quickly."

"Is there a greater need for speed than I'm already aware of?"

April could feel her hesitation.

"Gracie? Level with me."

Gracie sighed. "Okay. Look, the captain's not taking any of
this well."

"I know. I told you that."

"No, it's . . . worse. Your mom called me and she's really spooked.
She says she's never seen him this despondent, and . . . I have to tell
you this . . . the airline's chief pilot called him up and instead of being supportive, basically threatened him."

"What?"

"It's about the alcoholism. He told your dad that if he couldn't
prove there was no alcohol involved, he'd be terminated regardless
of the FAA's ultimate decision on his license. The FAA appar-

ently made sure the airline knows about the liquor purchase in Anchorage."

"Oh, no!"

"I'm sorry to have to tell you, April, but you need to know. We
really have to get this solved rapidly. Especially the drinking charge."

"Dad's union won't tolerate that, will they? I mean, everything's
governed by union contract, isn't it?"

"Yes, but I'm still going to rattle the airline's cage. Don't worry,
I'm including the Air Line Pilots Association, and I've already
warned the head of his union that a life hangs in the balance here."

"A life?"

"Well, you know. The psychological impact on the captain."

"Gracie, you're . . . not suggesting Dad is suicidal, are you?"

"*No!* No, I . . . don't think so. I'm just . . . I can't imagine your dad
even despondent. I've never seen him like that, and it scares me, too."

"I've never seen him really down, either, " April said quietly.

"Look, I'll do everything I can on this end, but . . . you may need
to pull a really large rabbit out of a hat there to get that broken prop.
Somehow."

"I hear you."

ELMENDORF AFB, ALASKA

Ben Cole presented his identification documents to the security gate
bordering the hangar at 1 P.M., and by 4 P.M. had all but convinced
himself that whoever had loaded the renegade computer code on
the Gulfstream's computers before had failed this time.

Okay, that's it. There's simply nowhere else to look.

There were footsteps in the cavernous hangar and Ben got up to
stretch and looked out the front entry, waving to the flight crew as
they approached the Gulfstream.

"Hey, Ben!" the chief test pilot said with a smile as he started up
the built-in airstairs. "Winky ready to go at long last?"

Ben winced at the nickname as the pilot chuckled. "You just hate that, don't you?"

"Yep."

They shook hands at the top of the steps.

"Seriously, Ben, are you satisfied that we're ready?"

"I . . . yes, in one respect."

"What's that?"

"I know the—for want of a better word—*virus* that was infecting us is not aboard."

"Thank God."

"But . . . are you aware of the new T-handle on the flight deck?"

Ben watched the pilot's face closely, but the expression never changed. "Yes. It's supposed to physically pull Winky's claws off the flight controls if nothing else works. I've been warned it will really damage the computer servos if we use it, but not the flight controls."

"You're sure it's operational?" Ben said, his voice steady.

The pilot leaned around the edge of the cockpit door to verify the new handle was still there. "Well, let me grab the maintenance log." He swung back out with the metal-bound logbook and opened it, flipping through several pages of maintenance write-ups and repairs. "Here we go. Installation begun . . . installation canceled."

Ben was nodding. "That's what I thought. I—"

"Installation restarted. Modification complete, and here's the sign-off," the pilot said, holding up the log for Ben, who studied it for several seconds. "Problem, Ben? You look unconvinced."

"It's just that . . . I was out here on Wednesday and the T-handle was installed but connected to nothing, and the plans were on the seat with a 'canceled' stamp."

"Well, that's what it says. They stopped the job, then they restarted it and signed it off."

"I guess there's no way to easily test it?"

The pilot was shaking his head. "I've been warned. We pull that handle, we'd better be prepared to terminate the test for several days.

It'll disconnect, but it will break things in the process. It's an extreme emergency backup."

"Well, good," Ben said, feeling confusion whirling around his head. "I wish I'd known that they'd finished it," he added, deciding to avoid mentioning how scared he'd been that the impending flight would end in a fatal crash despite their best efforts.

"What are you planning to do after this, Ben?" the pilot asked.

"After the flight?"

"No, after the project. We get signed off tonight, they start building and deploying the Boomerang devices immediately, and we're out of a job."

"I guess I really haven't thought about it. What do you mean they'll deploy them immediately?"

The chief test pilot raised his hand and smiled. "Hey, you didn't hear that from me, okay?"

"But . . . that's true?"

The pilot was backing away with a broad smile, his head nodding in the affirmative. "Let the record read the defendant properly refused to answer Dr. Cole's question because he had no need to know."

Ben smiled in return and waved him off, returning to his computer console in the cabin in mild alarm.

What does he mean, "immediately"? I thought we'd have several weeks to clean up any remaining problems with the program. The mere thought of a software problem suddenly activating a Boomerang black box in an Air Force bomber during a routine flight was beginning to haunt him almost as much as the presence of the commercial airline data he'd discovered.

UNIWAVE HEADQUARTERS

A half mile from the Uniwave hangar, General Mac MacAdams's arrival back on the Elmendorf flight line had been carefully coordinated with a staff car to whisk him back to his office in the project headquarters building for several urgent meetings, the last of which had been postponed until nearly 5:30 P.M.

"General, a Sergeant Jacobs dropped a package by for you," his secretary announced as he came in the door. Mac nodded to a man in a gray business suit and gestured for him to wait a minute as he took the small rectangular box from her and leaned over her desk to scribble a note:

> Please erase from your memory and any logs the fact that Jacobs brought this. And shred this note.

She read it quickly and nodded as he turned to the seated man. "Come on in, Dan," MacAdams said as the security chief moved into the office and closed the door behind him before picking up a small portable control device.

"May I turn on the bug neutralizer, General?"

Mac nodded, and Dan Jerrod punched the appropriate button, inundating the office with a wild array of silent radio signals designed to foil any clandestine listening device.

"Jon passed on your cryptic message, Dan. Our Dr. Cole is becoming a problem?"

"He's a smart man, General, and a loyal one. He not only found renegade computer code and commercial airline information embedded within, he figured out what the code was, and I have no doubt his mind is working away right now on the question of what possible explanations there are."

"And what are the possible explanations?"

"Dangerous. Some of them. If he goes down the wrong track, he could conclude all sorts of things that could cause us real security problems; and if he panics and goes outside the fold, the damage could be monstrous."

Mac sank into one of the chairs arrayed around a coffee table and sighed. "We're going to be airborne for the last run-through here in two hours or less. Any worries about Dr. Cole holding up?"

"No," Dan Jerrod said. "I'm far more worried about how he works this out in his head later on. He's not the type of guy to sit back and shut up, General. He's the careful type of whistle-blower who makes sure he's got the case nailed down first, then will not be silenced—except physically."

"Our best, worst nightmare always in military and government. Precisely what we fear, and precisely what keeps us free as a people."

"Yeah, weird, isn't it? And they say the Chinese have a ying and yang ability to tolerate dissimilar realities."

"How loose a cannon is he? And, with this information he has, precisely what kind of threat are we looking at?"

"I, unfortunately, didn't help much when I told him to talk only to me because there could even be moles in the organization."

"Nothing like planting ideas, Dan."

"I know it. I'll consider myself spanked for bad judgment."

"You're aware of the Rosen situation, by the way?"

"The lost Albatross, the daughter, and the angry FAA? Oh yeah. That's another volatile mix I'm watching, although I think we've got it contained—thanks to your help with those radar tapes."

"He found civilian airline data embedded in that so-called renegade code, Dan," Mac was saying as he watched the security chief's eyes for a reaction. "That *really* has me worried."

"Me, too."

"And, you're working on it?"

"As best I can."

"I don't have to tell you, I'm sure, that the project is paramount, or that the urgency comes all the way from the White House."

"Sir?"

Mac shifted uncomfortably in his chair, very glad the anti-bug device was busily blocking any possibility of his words being emblazoned on what could otherwise end up being the tombstone of his career.

"If we should be unfortunate enough to end up in a contest between Dr. Cole and what we're trying to accomplish . . ."

"Yes, sir. I understand. The project comes first."

TWENTY EIGHT

April could read the defeat on Jim Dobler's face before he hung up the phone. He sighed and turned to her, shaking his head.

"April, I'm truly sorry, but the only way I can take you back there on the surface is through a line of Coast Guard pickets, and they won't be amused."

"The area's still restricted, then?"

He nodded, sitting back in the faded cocoon of his time-worn desk chair to the sound of creaking springs and squawking imitation leather. A pleasant aroma of wood smoke hung in the thick air of the office, giving it more the feel of a tiny rural country store than a dockside office, but the trappings of a waterfront operation were all around, including a large aluminum fishnet hanging on the wall.

A burst of static filled the room suddenly, coming from one of the active two-way base station radios he kept on the side of the desk, but Jim ignored it as he continued the explanation he needed to give her.

"I know where we could get a miniature submarine with a couple of grappling devices on the front, but they'd charge a fortune, and it would take weeks to get it here."

"Frankly, I don't have either the fortune or the time."

"Well, the other problem is . . . whatever they're doing out there, they don't want any of us watching, and even if we could get the sub, they'd probably detect it and go nuts."

" 'They' meaning . . . ?"

"The Navy. I'll bet Scott was right about that."

Another burst of static, irritating in its intensity, filled the overheated room again. Jim reached for the volume control and cranked it down slightly.

"What's the radio for?" April asked.

"One's a standard marine band, for anyone inbound who needs fuel or the other services we can provide. The other's an aviation radio tuned to the common channel out here."

She looked at him with a puzzled expression, prompting more.

"Seaplanes land here, too, just like you and Scott did the other day, and they can call me on that to—"

An irritated voice cut through the channel at the same moment. "Dobler, will you please come out here and tie me up!"

Jim smiled as he got to his feet and grabbed his parka.

"I don't see anyone out there," April said.

"When it's low tide, this part of the dock isn't floating, so the fuel dock sinks out of sight."

April pulled on her parka and followed Jim out the door and onto the ramp down to the floating dock, where a Grumman Widgeon was floating motionless, the engines already stopped. She watched the nose hatch open and Scott McDermott appear, nodding to April as he focused on Jim and held up his hand to catch the mooring line. The two men secured the Widgeon before Scott stepped onto the dock. She could see he was working hard to make the arrival seem routine, but the way he began fumbling for words as he saw her waiting with folded arms told the tale.

"Hello, again," Scott said.

"Hello. Forget something?" she said, keeping her expression carefully neutral. There was no point in reigniting the morning's unhappy exchange.

He snorted and looked skyward, as if checking an inbound storm.

"Naw . . . well, yes." Scott turned back to her, glancing at Jim, who was also standing with folded arms and a knowing expression. "I stumbled across something I thought was interesting."

"You talking about Ms. Rosen, here?" Jim quipped.

Scott began blushing, his entire face shifting toward red as he pretended not to understand. "I . . . ah, thought she might be interested in this," he said, turning to meet April's eyes. "I was on the way back when I checked with Anchorage Radio, which is the . . . ah, a service they provide . . ."

April was nodding. "Anchorage Radio is an FAA Flight Service Station. I know. I'm a pilot, too. Remember?"

"Oh. Right. Well, I was getting an inbound briefing—"

"In the air? I thought you were supposed to do that before departure."

The jibe stopped him cold for a few seconds.

"Ah . . . usually that's the way it's done . . . before leaving. But . . . anyway . . . I happened to hear about a temporary military operations area newly created not far from here, and . . . I just got curious, because I've never heard of one right along there."

"Where is 'there'?"

"Well, the eastern end of it is a bit southwest of where we found the Albatross, and the western end runs west of Seward."

"They've got the surface all restricted to boat traffic now, Scott," Jim said. "I've been on the phone all afternoon."

"Well," April said, "Mr. McDermott, thank you for coming back to tell us this."

Scott hesitated, looking sufficiently off-balance to trigger a tiny spark of sympathy in April, especially when he began studying his shoes and tapping some incoherent code on the wooden dock with his sole before looking her in the eye.

"Look, April, I apologize for leaving you in the lurch."

There was a guttural sound from Jim Dobler. "Don't think my house was ever called a 'lurch' before," he said. "Is that like a yurt?"

Scott ignored him. "We both agree something strange is going on out there but . . . hear me out a second. When I got into Anchorage, I went over to the FSS and did a little personal research on what was going on last Monday night when the accident happened, and guess what? The very same military operations area was created for that night, too."

April uncrossed her arms, remembering the F-15s she'd seen landing at Elmendorf days before. "There's an awful lot of Air Force fighter activity around here, and I'm sure there's a lot of training going on. Why would that restricted area be connected with what happened to my father?"

Scott shrugged. "I don't know that it is. But it's unusual. I know the restricted airspace around Alaska—this part, at least—and this kind of sudden military-operations-area creation is very odd."

"What are you thinking, Scott?" Jim asked.

"I'm thinking there's a special operation of some sort going on tonight, and I'm thinking there was one on Monday night, and even if it has nothing to do, April, with what happened to your folks, it's too coincidental to ignore."

She was shaking her head. "Dad lost a prop blade. Either it came off by itself, which is possible, or he clipped some metallic structure below, like a ship mast. The zone you're talking about—this new MOA—has to do with airplanes and airspace."

"Didn't you say you asked the Coast Guard to see a tape of their vessel traffic system for that night?" Scott asked.

"Well, sure . . . to see if the Albatross showed up on-screen and to check on what ships might have been coming through the area, but they haven't performed. I figure we'll have to sue them to get that information."

"April, stop and think about this. The Coast Guard charged in and took those tapes. That sort of thing just doesn't happen unless there's a military operation of some sort going on, and it may well be connected with these restricted areas."

"But, I don't understand how they could connect."

"Maybe your dad *did* hit a ship on the surface that was taking part in some airborne exercise. Hell, I don't know, but I tell you, my instincts are telling me there's a connection, and I think we should go take a look."

"We?" April said.

"Yeah. Unless you, you know, don't want to. There's no charge, April. This one's on me."

"Either way, yes, I want to. Just sitting here doing nothing is tearing me up," she said, suddenly realizing the import of her words and glancing at Jim, who was reflecting ever so slightly their impact. "Jim, I'm sorry for how that sounded. That was not a reference to you and all your tremendous efforts on my behalf."

"I know."

"It's just the fact that together we've been unable to move things forward."

He shrugged, a shy smile registering appreciation. "Glad to help, April. So, you want the generator and the camera stuff again?"

"No, Jim," Scott answered for her. "I'm just low on gas."

"Well, that I can change." He started to turn to get the fuel hose.

"Jim, you want to come along?" Scott asked.

Jim shook his head. "No. I'd just be ballast."

"Well, we've got about an hour of daylight left. I'll have to land back at the airport. Would you mind picking us up in a few hours?"

"Naw, I wouldn't mind."

With the waters of the bay a bit more choppy than the previous afternoon, the takeoff was a series of heavy shudders through the wave tops before Scott could yank the Widgeon free of the surface, barely skimming the next swell. They climbed to the west, turning then to the south down the channel toward Bligh Reef.

"We're going to stay low?" April asked when she finally got the David Clark headset adjusted and the boom microphone in position, barely touching her lips.

He nodded, his head on a swivel for other traffic, before looking at her. "I thought we'd stay a bit ~~higher~~ be below most of the air traffic radars. We could be seen by anything airborne, of course."

"Like an AWACS?"

"Yeah, or those F-15s you were mentioning. I've got the restricted area figured out on my GPS screen. I thought we'd drag the eastern side of it before the light fades and see if there's any surface traffic."

"How close can we get to the crash site?"

"Within two miles. It's strange, April. The surface area the Coast Guard has declared restricted to boat traffic does not correspond with the military operations area for air traffic, except over the crash site. But there's something else I didn't tell you. Tonight, that military airspace is from the surface up to thirty thousand feet."

"Okay."

"On Monday evening, when your folks were coming through, it was from five thousand to thirty thousand feet, and if I'm calculating correctly, they flew right under it. You know what that suggests to me?"

"I think so," April answered. "It means that between Monday and now, something has changed and they now want all the airspace."

"And what may have caused that change is your folks flying legally right underneath their Monday-night block. The change suggests that something happened, and since we know the Albatross crashed in that airspace, it's a pretty good bet that that's it."

"The connection, in other words?"

"Yes. I don't know how. I mean, did they clip something, or did they have a mechanical failure? Either way it's coincidental, but provocative."

They flew in silence for nearly ten minutes as April let herself marvel at the verdant beauty of the forests lining the inlet on either side almost down to the water. The beaches were rocky and narrow here, with occasional sandy patches, but just as often a small slope or cliff marked the point where land and sea met.

"Scott, look out there at eleven o'clock." She pointed to the looming shape of a large surface vessel on the horizon ahead.

He nodded. "It's an inbound supertanker. See how high he's riding? He's empty, coming in from California."

The sun was riding low on the southwestern horizon as Scott studied the GPS screen. "The crash coordinates are just ahead, April, about five miles. The MOA starts three miles ahead. I'm going to turn and parallel it by a mile to make sure anyone watching doesn't misinterpret what we're doing."

"So what *are* we doing?" she asked.

He shrugged. "Beats me. I . . . let's just loiter out here and see if we can see anything unusual."

"Scott, do you have a raft aboard?"

"You mean a survival raft? No."

"Could you carry one?"

"Yeah, but, April, this is a flying boat, remember?"

"I'm not talking about safety. I'm talking about landing, inflating a radar-invisible rubber raft, maybe with a small motor, and putting over to the site with the camera, recorder, and battery and stuff."

Scott was silent for a few seconds. "We could do that. I don't see why not, but it would have to be at night, and I can't risk landing us out here in open water at night."

"How about landing at dusk safely out of the restricted area, tying up somewhere, and going in after dark?"

"We'd need exposure suits."

"Jim has those. He told me."

"Okay. We might just have time—"

"Not tonight. I'm thinking tomorrow. I want to be completely prepared."

"Okay."

She turned and looked at him until he met her gaze. "Everything rides on getting those shots on tape, and I think my friend Gracie, the lawyer, would tell you that I'll need your testimony to validate what I see, what's on the tape, and the fact that whatever we get will not have been electronically altered. That okay?"

"You mean, in court?"

"Yeah. Problem?"

He shook his head. "Oh, no."

She grabbed his arm suddenly, her right hand pointing ahead. "What's that, Scott? That ship."

"More of a boat. Hold on." He altered course to the north slightly to get a better viewing angle.

"What is it?"

"That's a Navy ship. I don't recognize her, but she's a fleet support or supply vessel of some sort. Don't often see one like that up here. See the odd angles on the superstructure on the stern? I'm not sure what that's for."

"She's westbound."

He nodded. "Yes. And on a course that, if I'm reading this right, had to have passed directly over the crash site."

TWENTY-NINE

This is the test director. We're go for engaging, Sage Ten. Systems report?"

"Sage Ten flight deck is a go," the chief test pilot's voice replied from the Gulfstream.

"Sage Ten, Test One is go as well," Ben Cole answered.

"Very well," the test director continued, "then Test One is cleared to engage."

Ben acknowledged the clearance and placed his index finger over the appropriate button, hesitating for a few seconds as he ran back through all the parameters. They were at twenty-two thousand feet, steady on a heading of 135 degrees magnetic in reasonably smooth air. Pressing the button should cause no sensation at all, just the display of streaming data from the AWACS as the pilot in the remote cockpit aboard the AWACS took over the controls.

"Engaging," Ben said, feeling the tiny feedback click of the button as the computer screen changed to reflect the remote engagement. "System engaged and locked," he continued.

"Crown is affirmative on the lock. We have control."

Ben realized he'd been holding his breath and permitted himself to exhale and sit back slightly in his seat in the familiar environment of the Gulfstream's otherwise deserted cabin.

Straight and level. Good!

On an intellectual level, he'd expected nothing less after hours of checking and rechecking to make sure no strange commands had been embedded in the Boomerang master code.

"So far, so good," Ben said into the headset, aware that the comment would be considered nonprofessional by the hardcore test engineers.

The screen was changing suddenly, the list of streaming data locks staying the same, but the control inputs moving as the Gulfstream began banking left.

"Are you commanding a bank to the left?" Ben asked, the immediate anxiety in his voice all too apparent.

There was a small chuckle embedded in the rapid reply from the AWACS remote pilot. "Roger. That's just me playing with the controls. Coming left twenty degrees and a thirty-degree bank, then I'll come back to the right before getting into the systems checks."

Ben willed himself to relax and look around. He massaged his neck muscles and realized they were as tight as steel bands, a direct reflection of the tension. He wondered if the Gulfstream pilots were feeling the same anxiety. If so, they'd never admit it, Ben knew. It was against the pilot code, and especially true of test pilots, though he'd observed the inherent discomfort of the pilots in giving up control to a mechanism or a remote pilot not under their command.

"Coming back to the right now," the remote pilot was saying, his voice cheerful as he watched his "instruments" on the mock control panel with heading, altitude, and airspeed readings coming back up live from the Gulfstream.

The thought that this test flight was unfolding correctly and safely had been merely a wish a few minutes back. They had already passed the critical point in time when the computer had suddenly started diving them in the Monday night test flight. All systems seemed to be operating normally, which meant perhaps thirty minutes of flight maneuvers before they could go home and Uniwave could collect its life-giving green government check.

The problem of who sabotaged the program Monday night was still with them, of course.

"Okay, starting down the flight control list now with the speed brakes."

A wave of warm feelings for Schroedinger and innate happiness that he would, in fact, be seeing him again filled Ben at the same moment another more sinister connection came together in his memory. He ripped his attention back to the moment, searching for whatever that connection had been.

Wait . . . something the AWACS pilot just said . . .

His seat began falling gently out from under him as his stomach got lighter, and Ben diverted his eyes to the altitude readout.

"Whoa! Gentle on the sudden descent there, Crown," the Gulfstream pilot said.

"What descent . . . wait. Sage Ten, have you seized control?"

"Negative, Crown. We're showing you still locked. Don't tell me this is happening *again?*"

The figures on Ben's computer screen confirmed the sequence, the converted business jet now moving vertically toward the terrain below and out of twenty-three thousand at a rate of first two thousand, then three thousand feet per minute downward.

"Oh, shit!" the remote pilot said. "Yes, Sage, it does appear to be happening again. I'm commanding a climb and you're not following."

"Are you showing the telemetry link still locked?" the Gulfstream pilot asked.

"Yes."

"We're descending now through flight level two-zero-zero, and I'm not going to wait very long this time before I pull the plug. Ben? Are you on?"

"Yes. All indications are contrary to what's happening, except that

I see the altitude loss. How low should we let her go before we disconnect?"

"This is the test director. We're disconnecting all the telemetry links now."

The descent was continuing. Ben watched the figures, hoping for a flattening, but they were falling through seventeen thousand now, with no change in deck angle.

"This is Ben . . . ah, Test One. You guys up there physically locked out again?"

"Yes. Should we use the new T-handle?'

"Stand by on that. Crown? Test One. Have you disconnected?"

"Affirmative, Sage Ten. We physically shut off the transmitters."

"Problem is here again. Okay. I'm beginning electronic disconnect now."

"No change, Ben," the pilot announced.

"Roger . . . going to secondary method."

"Still nothing. We're coming through fifteen thousand."

"I'm shutting down the computer like last time," Ben said, reaching for the power switches and watching the information on his screen collapse to a point of light, then nothing.

But they were still descending.

"Pilot, Test One. Are you free?"

"No. Have you shut down?"

"Yes. Pull the T-handle."

A long silence followed as the descent continued. Through the windows, Ben could see the last vestige of daylight on the western horizon lighting up the exposed sides of the Alaskan terrain to the left, painting a warm reddish light on the mountains and ridges that were simultaneously coming up toward them.

"Go ahead with the T-handle," Ben said again.

"The damn thing didn't work!" the pilot said, more tension in his voice now than five days before. "Ben? I can't believe we're here again and out of options. How about you?"

The same wave of confusion and uncertainty that had overwhelmed him Monday evening washed over him again, but this time he pushed through it immediately and mashed the interphone button.

"The computer's completely off. I do not understand this! There's no telemetry, there's no computer, the T-handle doesn't work, and you can't override the controls, right?"

"That's right. We're fighting several hundred pounds of force in either direction, and the trim won't budge. We're coming through eight thousand feet. Let's just hope this thing wants to level at fifty feet again."

"What happened when you pulled the T-handle?" Ben replied.

"It came out about three inches, I felt it tugging on something, then nothing else changed."

"I'm turning the computer back on."

"Just do something, Ben!" the pilot said. "This is ridiculous! Passing four thousand feet."

They've succeeded after all! Ben thought, taking a split second to be angry with himself for not seeing that any test flight would be suicidal until they caught whoever was responsible.

"Through two thousand!" the pilot was saying, his voice tense.

The computer was just beginning the reboot process, and it was clear it wouldn't be on-line fast enough, even if he could think what to do.

"Two thousand nine hundred, Ben! It's now or never!"

"I'm . . . rebooting . . . but somehow I don't think that's the problem."

What was the atmospheric pressure setting on Monday? Oh, yeah. Two-nine-four-two. What is it tonight?

He pulled a notepad to him, the figures leaping off the page: 30.10!

He jabbed at the interphone button. "RESET ALL ALTI-METERS TO THREE-ZERO-FIVE-ZERO IMMEDIATELY! DON'T ASK WHY! DO IT!"

ABOARD WIDGEON N8771B
IN FLIGHT, OVER THE GULF OF ALASKA

Scott had given a wide berth of at least a mile to the Navy support ship April had spotted as they climbed to two thousand feet to remain well clear of the restricted area. The ship was miles behind them now, and the sun was just about to drop below the horizon, making forward visibility difficult. Scott spotted the reflection of a high-flying aircraft ahead and pointed it out.

"Probably a big military jet like a KC-135 or a KC-10, and probably above twenty-five thousand."

"He's in the restricted area? The MOA?"

Scott nodded, his eyes on the metal underbelly of the distant aircraft as it caught the long-wave rays of sunlight and glowed bright for a moment in the purplish sky.

"Wow," April exclaimed. "That's beautiful!"

"Sure is. Amazing what you see from cockpits, especially at night. I've got a friend who flies for Alaska Airlines who made two circles one night in a 737 on the way to Fairbanks from Anchorage because the northern lights were so incredibly bright and beautiful. All the passengers were gasping! He even got video, and the passengers gave him a standing ovation when they parked."

"How'd the airline respond?"

"They loved it," Scott chuckled.

Another airborne metallic body caught the sunlight, blinking on and off again just as April looked in that direction.

ABOARD CROWN

"Sage Ten, Crown. Traffic twelve o'clock, southwest-bound, altitude showing as two thousand feet."

Mac MacAdams had remained silent through the entire sequence of events, but with the onboard controller's words in his ears, he turned, spotting Sergeant Jacobs at a console two rows back, motioning him to come quickly to his console.

Mac nodded and moved back, taking the offered headset as Jacobs filled him in.

"The intruder is just outside the MOA, sir." He punched his microphone button again.

"Sage Ten, Crown, I say again, traffic twelve o'clock, fifteen miles, southwest-bound, reported at two thousand level. Can you change course left or right?"

"Negative, Crown! No control . . ."

Jacobs turned back to Mac. "Range is thirteen miles."

"Where are the eagles?" Mac asked, referring to a flight of four F-15s doing the shadow duties for the test flight.

"Flying high combat patrol."

"Open the channel," Mac directed, and Jacob's hands deftly clicked the appropriate switch and held down the push-to-talk as Mac immediately ordered two of the F-15s to intercept the low-flying civilian aircraft.

"You're going to shoot him, sir?" Jacobs asked.

"Of course not!"

"They can't reach him in time," Jacobs said. "They're closing too fast."

The lead eagle driver asked for more instructions and Mac issued them quickly. "Force him to land at Elmendorf. If compliance is refused, destruction unauthorized."

Mac looked at Jacobs and pointed to the radar display. "What's the range?"

"Five miles left. It's gonna be close, sir."

ABOARD WIDGEON N8771B

"More traffic at almost twelve o'clock," April said.

"Didn't see him."

"Much lower I'd say, by the angle." April strained to see the speck again through the slightly scarred Plexiglas of the Widgeon's windscreen. There was a faint hint of a light, different this time, more white and self-generated, and she relayed what she'd seen.

"If he's got landing lights on, it's someone under ten thou . . ."

Scott's eyes had been searching the same spot of sky. He stopped speaking, leaned forward, focusing on . . . *something* . . . getting larger ahead of them.

"Oh SHIT!" he yelped as he jammed the control column forward, lifting April out of the seat with negative G forces.

The onrushing dot had been growing at an alarming rate and not moving in the windscreen when Scott latched onto it visually, realizing almost too late that it was an aircraft closing on them at jet speeds. The calculation of relative flight paths led to the emergency dive, but as soon as he had the Widgeon standing on her nose, it was sickeningly obvious he'd gone the wrong way! The oncoming jet was diving too fast for Scott to get under him. He yanked back on the Widgeon's yoke and firewalled the throttles. Gravity jammed both of them into their seats. A large metallic T-tail loomed at them from the twilight sky just ahead as time dilated, inducing a feeling of slow motion, the huge structure passing almost laconically beneath them with a horrendous "whoosh" and a mighty roar. The Widgeon's stall warning horn sounded at the same moment, and Scott fought to roll off to the right and let the nose drop, regaining speed and finally righting the aircraft.

He glanced at April, who was drained of color.

"What the hell was that?" she stammered.

"A near-midair!" he said. "Some sort of bizjet . . . I couldn't tell."

Scott could feel his heart racing and his breathing trying to catch up, but his voice sounded funny.

"You all right?"

She nodded, unable to speak.

ABOARD SAGE TEN

"Below two thousand now, and thirty-fifty is set!"

The Gulfstream pilot's words were clipped and urgent. The descent was continuing with only seconds left until they hit the water, when once again Ben felt the nose starting to come up as the descent rate slowed. He could see enough through the windows to know they were very low, but the horizon line—or what there was of it in the gathering darkness—was now nearly horizontal.

"Jeez, Ben! What was that?" the pilot demanded.

"Are we level?"

"Yes . . . at sixty feet this time. What on earth . . . ?"

"Do you have control back?"

"No. It's still locked, but we're level and the power's coming up."

"Try to disconnect the autothrottles."

More silence, then a yelp of triumph. "*THAT* worked! What's it doing, Ben?"

"I still don't know why, but it has to do with the altimeter setting. You reset them all?"

"Yes! Hell, you didn't give us a choice, thank God. But what's still holding on to this bird, if it's not the computer?"

It was Ben's turn to hesitate. His finger moved to the interphone button, but the pilot beat him to it.

"Wait! It's the damned autopilot, isn't it?"

An autopilot disconnect warning horn sounded through the interphone as the Gulfstream jumped and both pilots let out a war whoop.

"Got it!" the captain whooped. "By damn, that did it!"

"How?" Ben asked.

"The autopilot disconnect! Somehow the autopilot had seized control, and with all the modifications we've made, it couldn't be overridden."

"We're back under control?"

"Yes! And climbing. Crown, you copy?"

There was a sigh from the test director aboard the AWACS.

"Yes. Stand by while we finish performing CPR on each other."

THIRTY

Arlie had noticed the dark blue Chevy van earlier in the afternoon, a utility version with no windows motoring down the road leading past his property. The van stopped for several minutes before moving on. Addresses were hard to find among the widely spaced properties in the area, but it was the third appearance of the same van within three hours that snagged his attention as unusual. When it showed up several cars back in traffic as he drove into nearby Port Angeles, Arlie realized he was being followed. He turned suddenly near the center of the downtown area and turned again into a hotel parking lot, racing past the separate lobby structure and around the back, where his car would be hidden. He sat, waiting for several minutes, before deciding to investigate on foot.

He reached the main street and walked several blocks in each direction, but the blue van was nowhere to be seen, and he retraced his steps to the hotel parking lot feeling slightly foolish.

I must be getting paranoid, he thought, as he rounded the corner of the building and looked up to see the dark blue van parked right next to his car.

"Captain Rosen?" A male voice startled him from directly behind, and he turned abruptly to find himself facing a broad-shouldered man with a weathered face.

"Yes? Who are you?"

The man smiled and looked around before meeting his gaze. His hands were stuck in the pockets of a long black leather coat, and he held himself with easy confidence. Arlie glanced at the broad pockets of the coat and wondered if either contained a gun.

"Consider me a friend, Captain."

"Okay, but do you have a name?"

The man ignored the question and fixed Arlie with a cold stare. "I have a vital warning for you, and I did you the favor of coming a long distance to deliver it in person."

"What, you couldn't ring my doorbell?"

"I doubt you would want your wife to be as frightened as you're about to be."

"Excuse me?"

"Captain, you've blundered into something way over your head, and your daughter and her pretty friend, Gracie, are making some very powerful people very upset with their questions and lawsuits."

"What the hell are you—"

A large right hand came out of the jacket, motioning for silence, and the accompanying look on his face stopped Arlie cold. "I'm not here to answer questions. I'm here to warn you to call your girls off, withdraw your lawsuits, fire your lawyers, and just hunker down. You will withdraw those legal actions on Monday and bring your daughter back now. If you do, your license will be reinstated in a few weeks. If you don't, you'll never fly again, and someone's very likely to get hurt."

"Are you threatening me?"

"Rosen, the people you're challenging will stop at nothing to protect their interests. Do you understand what that means?"

"Yeah. You, or they, are threatening my family. If you're a government agent, I'll have your badge for this!"

Once more the man smiled and studied his feet before replying.

"Who I am is not important. What's involved is. Stop your little war and you'll get back in the cockpit. Keep it up, and lives will be changed drastically, jobs extinguished, and careers ruined. Especially your daughter and her friend. Do not tell them, or anyone else, about this conversation, or I'll be back to deal with you."

Arlie's jaw was set and his fists clenched as he stepped forward, but he was unprepared to see the man's left hand pull a silenced Glock 9mm from his coat in one unbroken motion. He raised the gun to Arlie's chest, and just as quickly jerked it to the right and pulled the trigger. A surprisingly loud, muffled noise caused Arlie to jump and whirl to his left in time to see shattered glass falling from his side-mounted rearview mirror, which now featured a bullet hole in the very center.

"What the hell . . ." he yelped.

The man shoved the gun back in his pocket. "Don't delude yourself into thinking this isn't just as serious as I said."

"Jesus Christ, man!" Arlie was backing up, his eyes wide with alarm as the man turned and walked past him to the blue van, turning at the rear bumper.

"We're not kidding, Rosen. Don't risk it."

ABOARD WIDGEON N8771B
OVER THE GULF OF ALASKA, SOUTHEAST OF ANCHORAGE

The voice in their headsets came from nowhere.

"Unidentified aircraft flying at two thousand feet five-zero miles east of Seward, come up on guard frequency, one-twenty-one-point-five, immediately."

"Who's that?" April demanded.

Scott looked to the left, then back to the panel, confirming that one of the radios was, indeed, tuned to the emergency "guard" frequency. He flipped a switch and pressed his microphone button.

"Who's this?"

"This is a U.S. Air Force fighter, Husky Eighteen. You have violated restricted military airspace and we are intercepting you. You are directed to comply with our orders and follow us back to Elmendorf Air Force Base to land."

"I haven't violated any airspace, Husky Eighteen. I've got two GPSs and they both confirm I've never been over the line."

"State your call sign."

"That's a negative. You don't need to know my call sign, and I will not follow you."

"State your call sign, unidentified aircraft. We are proceeding with the approved rules of interception. If you do not comply, you will be shot down."

"Scott? What does he mean?" April asked in alarm. The shock she'd seen on his face moments before was turning to anger, and she could see his jaw set.

"Hang on, April."

Scott reduced power and kicked the Widgeon into a sudden, tight right, descending turn, as he spotted the lights of the two fighters coming in from behind with a closing speed of several hundred knots.

"Scott! I do not want to get blown out of the sky."

"Those clowns are not going to get a firing solution on me . . . not to mention the fact that they don't have authorization to fire. It's a standard bluff."

The nose of the Widgeon was pointed down at a twenty-degree angle and April felt herself grasping the edges of her seat. Scott pulled the throttles all the way back to idle and extended the flaps as he continued the spiral to the right. The water was coming up, the land mass in partial shadow on her right, then her left, as she began calling out the altitude.

"Six hundred . . . five hundred . . . four hundred."

"I'm leveling. We're going up one of those fjords."

"Scott . . . two hundred . . . one-fifty . . . one hundred."

He worked the controls to level the wings and bring the nose up, flattening their trajectory just above wave height. There were more strident calls from Husky Eighteen.

"Unidentified amphibian, this is Husky Eighteen. We say again, you must obey the rules of interception and follow us, or you will be shot down."

"Sure I will," Scott snorted to April. "He's getting frustrated."

"Unidentified amphibian, be advised you can't get away from us even down in the weeds!"

Scott brought the Widgeon toward the northern bank of a fjord leading inward and began hugging the cliff, less than a hundred yards from the passing trees.

"Scott? Couldn't they get your license for evading them?"

"Prove I'm out here. They don't have my registration number and they're not going to get it."

"I really don't think this is a good idea," April said, trying to catch his eye, but worried about distracting him with the cliff mere yards away to the right. The daylight was fading fast as the jagged coastline they were shadowing wound its way toward a glacier she could see looming a mile or so ahead.

Scott craned his neck above the dash panel to spot the fighters. "There! Hah!"

"Define 'hah' please."

"They had to go halfway to Anchorage to turn around, and now they're trying to get in behind and lock us with their tactical radar down here in the so-called weeds. They've got 'look-down, shoot-down' capability, April, but they've got to have a stable target, and we're going to deny them the pleasure. I know a place to hide."

"You mean, they could shoot us with guns?"

"Missiles. Technically yeah. It's really hard to do . . . but not impossible."

"Oh, that's a comfort!"

There was a gentle upslope over the top of the cliff leading to a clearing on the right and they saw it simultaneously. Scott banked right and brought the Widgeon less than thirty feet over the top of the ridgeline, flying between the trees as he flew up the meadow and turned with the meandering terrain. He added power to climb with the slope as he extended the flaps to the fully deployed position.

"This'll keep us as slow as possible. The air farce up there can't get much below two hundred and we can fly at seventy."

"Scott?"

"Yeah."

"Why, exactly, are we doing this?" she asked.

"No time to explain. I have a plan."

"Really?"

"Yeah."

"Care to share it?"

"No. Whoa!" He pulled up and over a row of trees that hadn't appeared to be as high as they were, and followed a small draw to the left where the terrain ended at the edge of a thousand-foot-high promontory. April watched spruce and lodgepole pines zip by on either side, their tops soaring considerably above the small aircraft's altitude.

The vertical face of a giant valley glacier lay beyond, its base sitting in an inlet of milky blue-green water filled with newly carved icebergs.

"What are you planning, Scott?" April asked, tensing as he descended the Widgeon to less than ten feet over the meadow leading to the drop-off. The terrain and alpine grasses were flashing by at a dizzying speed, and a startled pair of Dall sheep jerked their heads up in alarm and took off to the right. The edge of the drop-off leading to the glacier and the inlet was coming up quickly, the illusion of speed intensified by the low altitude as they traversed the last thirty feet before the cliff.

And suddenly the feeling of speed disappeared in an instant as the rushing ground gave way to a thousand feet of air over the choppy, frozen waters below. April felt as if she were hanging motionless over the glacial waters, the illusion of instant deceleration a physical shock, the sheer rock face disappearing unseen behind them.

"Wow!" she said, involuntarily.

"I love this stuff! Although I don't usually get chased into it by fighters."

The F-15 lead pilot was back on the radio, his voice betraying a touch of upset. "Unidentified amphibian, we observe your progress and have you locked up on radar. You will immediately climb and pick up a heading of one-nine-zero degrees, or we will fire. This is your last warning."

"You're sure they're bluffing, Scott?" April asked.

"Yeah, I'm pretty sure."

She looked at him wide-eyed. "*Pretty* sure? What do you mean, 'pretty sure'? We need to be absolutely sure!"

He pointed to the right, to a gap in the glacial ice field at least a hundred yards wide. It was a giant crevasse, or valley, slicing the glacier in half and leading inland and upward, and she realized in a flash of fear that he intended to fly into it.

"No, Scott!"

"Yeah."

"No, really! Let's not do that, please?"

He turned and grinned. "I know where this leads."

"Yeah, so do I, and if it's all the same to you, I'd rather not die with you until I get to know you better."

"Is that an invitation?"

"If it'll get you to stop this, yes!"

He chuckled as he worked the throttles and controls to slide the Widgeon around a sudden turn to the right.

"Well, if I was *sure* I could take you to dinner sometime . . ."

"That's blackmail!" she said almost absently.

He nodded as the towering ice walls enfolded them on either side and the Widgeon entered the ice canyon, the unique deep blue of glacial ice soaring above them for at least a hundred feet.

A shuddering explosion suddenly burst somewhere to their left, and the image of an orange fireball reflected off the icy canyon walls.

April jerked her head around in time to see the leading edge of a massive cascade of fragmented glacial ice barely missing them.

"What was that?" she gasped.

"Oh, shit!" Scott muttered.

"What? *WHAT?*"

"I didn't expect *that!*" He looked at her, real apprehension reflected in his eyes. "The bastard actually fired a missile at us!"

ABOARD CROWN

"Husky Eighteen, Crown. What's your status?" Mac MacAdams asked as he watched the maneuvering F-15s on the computer-generated scope chase a target now too low to be visible to the AWACS's radar.

"He's hugging the terrain, Crown, and literally flying up a glacier. We've launched fox one unsuccessfully and are maneuvering for another shot."

"You WHAT? Cease fire! You were ordered to proceed *without* deadly force."

There was a prolonged silence.

"Crown, we heard the order as 'Force him to land at Elmendorf. If compliance is refused, destruction authorized.'"

"Unauthorized, dammit! The order was destruction *UN*-authorized."

There was a long pause before the F-15 lead pilot pressed his transmit button again. Mac could imagine him thinking fast to use the right words.

"Sorry, Crown. We did not copy the 'un' part."

Mac shook his head and sighed as he punched the transmit button. "Well, thank God you didn't hit him, Husky."

"Scott, this canyon has to end somewhere," April said through gritted teeth, her eyes riveted on the unfolding chasm of ice. "Now
would be a very good time to climb!"

"In a minute."

"I don't think we have a minute."

"See the cloud cover ahead?"

"Yes."

"That's what I'm aiming for."

"You want to go on instruments playing *Star Wars* down the middle of a giant crevasse? Are all Navy pilots insane *and* suicidal, or did
I just luck out with you?"

"You're just a lucky gal, I guess. Stand by to climb. We've got to
get under that layer of clouds ahead."

There was another sharp bend in the ice canyon some thirty degrees to the left and Scott guided the Widgeon around the turn as
April realized that the vanishing point she was seeing ahead was actually the end of the canyon.

"CLIMB! NOW, SCOTT!"

"I see it," he said, firewalling the throttles and pulling back sharply
on the yoke, trading his small surplus of airspeed for altitude as they
slid beneath the cloud cover overhead. The Widgeon popped above
the top of the walls on each side and Scott guided them to the right,
over the broken and deeply crevassed surface of the glacier beneath
an overcast hanging no more than two hundred feet above them.

"See?" He grinned.

"See what? Aren't there cliffs in these clouds?"

"Yeah . . . but there's a little place I know over to the right . . ."

"Not another one?"

"Hang on."

"I really hate it when you say that!" April replied, her hands still
in a death grip on the armrests of her copilot's seat.

ABOARD HUSKY 18 LEAD

The Air Force F-15 pilot pulled his ship around sharply to the right, racking up nearly eight Gs in the turn to get another look at the amphibian. His wingman was working hard against the G forces to hang in position on his left wing and barely succeeded as they rolled out of the turn together.

"You have him, Two?" Lead asked.

"Negative. I think he ducked under that cloud cover."

"He's crazy if he did."

"Well, I rest my case," the wingman said. "What now?"

"Let's orbit and see if he comes back out," Lead replied, his concentration still divided by the fact that they'd apparently misunderstood a rules-of-engagement order and almost succeeded in accidentally destroying a civilian aircraft. The prospect had made him queasy, something no amount of G force or maneuvering had ever done.

"I'm ten minutes to bingo fuel, Lead," his wingman announced.

"Yeah?" Lead replied, looking at his own fuel gauges and feeling further embarrassed that his wingman had to be the one to remind him. "Roger. Crown, Husky Eighteen. Thanks to the dash in burner and the maneuvering, we're almost at bingo fuel and we've lost him now beneath cloud cover over the glacier."

The voice from the AWACS belonged to a general officer, the lead pilot knew, which made the previous mistake all the more worrisome. He could hear the general key his microphone now and give a subdued sigh before he spoke.

"Very well, Husky. Head back. We'll try to track him from here. Where do you think he's headed?"

"I'll be surprised if he doesn't crash, Crown. He's under cloud cover over a glacier in a high mountain valley. The guy's nuts. I'd recommend you launch a search-and-rescue op immediately. But I think you're only going to find spare parts."

THIRTY ONE

Once again the terrain was rushing by mere feet beneath the thin metallic skin of the Widgeon's fuselage. This time, however, a lethal mixture of ice and boulders replaced the meadow, their jagged surfaces clawing toward the small amphibian.

Scott McDermott was working to keep the aircraft just above stall speed, the engines straining at full power to keep up with the rising terrain as the ceiling above hung lower and lower toward the surface of the glacier. There had been nothing but murky gray ahead of them, but a hint of something else began to emerge where the overcast melded with the ice.

April's knowledge as a pilot was fully engaged as she monitored Scott's physical flying of the airplane. Airspeed, altitude, power, rate of climb, and the constant movements of the controls were familiar and almost comforting as they somehow remained airborne, but the alien landscape below them was simply too bizarre to register. She expected impact at any moment, followed by a blinding and painful plunge into snow and ice, accompanied by the sound of ripping metal.

But for some reason, in defiance of logic, it wasn't happening. They were still aloft, still flying.

She thought several times of grabbing the controls and taking over, but they were committed. It was too late to turn back. There was no room to turn the aircraft around and no place to land safely. The only choice was continued flight over the vast upslope of a massive valley glacier to an uncertain destination.

"There!" Scott said in more of a shout than a statement.

April peered ahead, seeing nothing new.

"What?" she managed, her voice little more than a high-pitched squeak. She quickly cleared her throat and tried it again. "What do you see?"

"What I've been aiming for. Right where I figured. Stand by . . ."

There was something ahead now. She could almost make it out. It was a horizon line of some sort. Not well defined, but definitely a darker line between sky and ice than an illusion would be. They were still airborne, and Scott was actually throttling *back* now as the ice field below them flattened.

"There's a lake up there," Scott said, nodding in the direction of the nose.

The line ahead was coalescing steadily, and it became a small ridge now with a hanging mountain lake beyond, the surface of the water just a shade darker than the gray clouds almost enfolding their wings. April knew there had to be sheer rock walls of the mountain on the far side, but she couldn't make them out. The ridge bordering the lake's downsloped shoreline was drawing closer by the second, the lake beyond anything but a welcoming sight. It was a small body of water filled with huge chunks of floating ice, each of them jagged white ships afloat in a sea of milky blue-green water.

"You're not planning . . ." she began, noticing in her peripheral vision that he was already nodding. She stole just a quick glance at him, as if her looking away would destabilize their flight path.

The sight of Scott McDermott grinning maniacally profoundly scared her.

"Stand by, April!"

"Those are icebergs!"

"Yep."

"We can't land in that! There's no room!"

He chopped the power to idle just as they topped the ridge, shoving the yoke forward to drop the Widgeon toward the surface, then throttled up and flared as he walked the rudder to the right, clearing the largest ice floe and looking for enough clear water to allow a landing.

There were huge icebergs everywhere.

"Damn," he said. "More than I figured for this time of year."

She felt the Widgeon respond again as he shoved in more power and slipped safely over the back of an iceberg as big as a two-story house, then banked sharply left, right around another equally huge one, holding the fragile amphibian five to six feet above the icy surface at sixty knots.

Another large line of ice floes was just ahead, coming fast, and he popped up a few feet to see over the top. With the opposite end of the glacial lake approaching less than a quarter of a mile away and no room to turn around, Scott chopped the power once again and pushed the Widgeon over the top of another large chunk of ice, dropping the hull into the lake. He yanked back on the yoke, creating an impressive flare of water on both sides as the aircraft decelerated toward another large iceberg that sat just ahead and much too close.

April could see the angular facets of the iceberg in great detail now as it loomed in front of them. She could see the needle of the airspeed indicator still hovering above fifty miles per hour. There were no anchors to throw out or brakes to push, only the suction of the water as the aeronautical hull of the Widgeon slowly sank into the water and became hydrodynamic, killing the forward speed. It wasn't happening fast enough.

We're going to hit, April thought, the realization merely a fact to be stated. She leaned forward instinctively and buried her head on her knees, bringing her arms around her head, aware of a vague thought that maybe they would be slow enough to survive an inevitable impact with the ice wall ahead.

Time dilation took over, the feeling of time slowing down in the midst of a crisis reaching new heights. The seconds ticked by with agonizing sloth as she waited for impact, tensing her body, listening to the diminishing sound of the water pounding on the hull until it, too, had subsided.

A sudden quiet replaced the cacophonous sounds of seconds before, and still she waited as the Widgeon's forward speed through the ice-laden lake all but exhausted itself, the kinetic energy ending with an anticlimactic *thunk* and a slight shudder as the nose bumped gently, harmlessly, into the ice.

April heard Scott exhale. A nervous burst of laughter followed, causing her to unfold quickly from her brace position and take stock of the reality that they'd survived.

"Wow!" he exclaimed.

"Wow, what?" she managed.

"I wasn't sure we were going to stop in time. Whew!"

April looked at the twenty-five-foot-high iceberg soaring above their nose, words failing her for a few seconds.

"You okay?" Scott asked.

She turned to him, emotionally exhausted, and weakly flailed her right hand in the general direction of the iceberg. "Other than the fact that I think both the Air Force and you were just trying to kill me, yeah. Other than the fact that we're sitting God knows where in the middle of an icy lake in which no sane pilot would have tried to land, and from which we won't be able to take off. Yeah. Sure, Scott. I'm fine."

"Good." He grinned. "Quite a show, huh?"

She looked around again, out the windscreen and the windows on each side. The overcast above them was darkening.

"Scott, we'll never get your airplane out of here, and if you haven't noticed, it's already nightfall."

"Yeah."

"We're stuck! I mean, what do we do? It's cold out there!"

He was nodding, a more appropriate look of seriousness crossing his face as he looked around. "Yeah, takeoff will be a challenge."

"A *challenge?* How . . . ? Where . . . ?"

He was grinning again, and the expression fed her growing anger.

"Damn you! How are we going to get out of here? Huh? It's nightfall, there are armed fighters trying to shoot us down, my family will think *I've* been killed, and . . ."

Scott reached out and tried to put a hand on her shoulder but she shrugged it off.

"Don't touch me!"

He withdrew his hand. "Yes, ma'am."

"I'm serious, McDermott. What do you propose we do to survive, let alone get back? I was out here trying to help my dad, not give him a heart attack when he hears I'm missing."

"April, calm down."

"Calm down? I'm very calm. Considering what you just put us through, I'm incredibly, awesomely calm."

"Then listen to me, okay?"

"Do I have a frigging choice?"

"Not really."

She folded her arms, trying to retain some professional control. She was the client, after all. And for all his on-again, off-again help, she had apparently retained a maniac. "Go ahead."

"I had a good reason for not complying with that fighter pilot's orders, April."

"I'd love to hear it," she said, shaking her head.

"Whatever's going on out here is very clearly a military project, and classified. Probably top secret classified."

"So?"

"I've already told you I think whatever they're doing is tied in to what happened to your dad. Remember?"

She nodded.

"Okay. If I had followed them back to Elmendorf like a good little pilot, not only would *I* be out of the ball game and unable to help you get a camera back on your old man's plane, *you'd* be out of the game as well. Hell, they might even lock us both up for awhile."

"You're trying to tell me you almost got us killed to protect *me?*"

"And your mission, yes."

She turned to him, nursing the scowl on her face. "You know, you're so full of it, McDermott. You must think I'm a brainless bimbo."

"No, I don't think you're brainless," he said, almost under his breath.

"Oh. Just a bimbo, huh?"

"No, no, no! I misspoke. I don't think you're either a bimbo or brainless."

"Right."

"A real babe, perhaps," he said with a smile.

April shot him a scathing look. "Enough of that!"

Both palms went in the air. "Okay, okay. I'm sorry."

She leveled an index finger at him, sighting along it as if it were a gun. "No, the *real* reason you ran from those fighters up there is very simple. No one tells Scott McDermott what to do. Right?"

"Now, wait . . ."

"Am I right?"

He sighed. "Okay, maybe a little of that is true, but, honestly—"

"Honestly? I'm not sure you know the meaning of that word."

"Hey. Let me finish, okay?"

She paused, staring him down, before responding. "Go ahead."

"The truth is, I was very irritated at their trying to ensnare me illicitly when I'd been surgically careful to stay out of their restricted area, and . . . just as I said . . . I knew if they'd grounded us, you'd never get the wreck videotaped. Besides, tonight told us a lot."

"Oh? Such as?"

"April, that aircraft that almost hit us was coming out of their restricted area."

"Were the fighters chasing us by mistake, then? You're saying they should have been chasing the jet?"

He was shaking his head as her eyes flared in sudden understanding and her arms came unfolded. "Oh my God! You're saying that jet
was coming out of the restricted area because it was part of whatever
they're doing!"

"Exactly. He came out at an angle, but that's where he came *from.*"

April sat back heavily. "And the same restricted zone was created
on Monday night when my folks were there, but then it didn't extend to the surface."

He was nodding more forcefully now. "Right. So now they rein-
stitute the same restricted area with one significant change. Now it
extends all the way down to the surface. Why the change?"

"Because," she finished the thought, "the change was an incorpo-
ration of a lesson they learned Monday night."

"Yes! Dammit, yes! That's what I was trying to tell you before,
April. Something happened to them Monday night that prompted
them to restrict the airspace all the way to the water tonight, and that
something was your old man."

"I hate that reference."

"Okay, your dad."

She nodded, her eyes on the rapidly darkening field of icebergs
floating around them, her ears picking up the gentle sounds of the
water lapping at the Widgeon's hull. "So, do you think the same aircraft or something like it came streaking out of the blue Monday the
same way and hit my dad's Albatross?"

He shrugged. "I wish I knew. I do know they're testing an aircraft
at low altitude and high speed, as we saw. Maybe that same aircraft
we saw traded paint with your dad."

"But how, Scott? He lost a prop, and that's most likely the cause
of the right engine rotating off its mount and the prop blades chop-
ping into the right wing."

"Some of that damage could have been from a collision," he said.

April was nibbling her lower lip in thought. "Yes . . . or maybe . . .
one small spot on the jet contacted one single prop blade, causing it
to fail."

"Did your father report another aircraft in the area?"

She was shaking her head no, then stopped. "Wait a minute. I seem to recall Dad mentioning some sort of rushing or whooshing noise just as the prop broke."

The sound of Scott snapping his fingers caused her to jump slightly.

"That's it, April! He heard a jet go by as one of the blades hit it and broke off!"

She thought for a second. "Could be."

"No, that has to be it. Whoever's doing these tests—Air Force, Navy, Army—they had to know they clipped a civilian aircraft. April, you want to know what all this is about? Why they had the Coast Guard jump us and take the tape? Why the FAA seems to be on a vendetta against your old . . . your father? Because they're covering up a midair collision."

"Why would they try to cover it up?"

"Because they were doing a high-speed, low-altitude test run of some sort without making sure the restricted area was completely empty of all aircraft at all altitudes. They screwed up and failed to extend the prohibited area all the way to the surface."

"You think the FAA's in on this, too?"

"Oh, yeah. Doesn't it make sense, April? If our government can prevent any photos of the wreckage, or any other examination of it, then they won't have to admit to making a big mistake."

"A government cover-up is hard to pull off, Scott. That sounds like a conspiracy theory."

"No, look. What's the first thing frightened people try to do when they've made a huge mistake that no one's caught as yet? They cover it up. They try to pretend it didn't happen. Make it go away. Sometimes repairing a problem and then pretending there never was any damage to begin with is part of the syndrome, but the tendency is always to pretend it didn't exist."

"This is so hard to believe," she said.

"Yes, but trust me. We're just as good at it in the military as the civilian world."

She sat in thought for a few seconds. "If your theory is right, Scott, they won't just stop with preventing me from taking pictures or video. They'll come in there and raise the wreckage themselves and steal it."

"You could be right."

"Which they could be doing right now while we float around on some nameless lake," she added, turning to him. "Seriously. How do we get out of here? And when?"

Scott was smiling and nodding as he looked around, then met her eyes. "We're okay until morning. I've got sleeping bags in the back, emergency food, a small stove that's carbon monoxide–safe to keep us warm, coffee, and even a satellite phone to let your parents know you're okay."

"We . . . don't need to call for help?"

"Last thing we need to do. That would bring the Navy and Air Force and whoever else is involved right down on our heads. No. Just pray the cloud cover remains until morning."

"And then what? We swim out?"

"No, we fly out."

"Using what for a runway? There are enough icebergs floating around in this lake to sink an aircraft carrier!"

"We'll take off between the icebergs."

"Between the . . . *How?*"

He had a finger in the air. "Trust me."

April sighed and shook her head. "I was truly afraid you were going to say that."

THIRTY-TWO

rlie had grabbed for his cell phone as soon as the blue van disappeared around the corner. He punched in 911 with the words forming in his head to report an armed assailant in a utility van with no license plate. Port Angeles was fairly small, with limited roads in and out. The State Patrol could find him.

But an inner voice stayed the call, and he replaced the phone on the seat. If the warning was genuine, a manhunt for the messenger wasn't the best solution.

Arlie drove home in a fog of agitation, each automatic glance at the now-shattered side mirror a slap in the face, a stark reminder that the bullet had been momentarily aimed at his heart. The gun was real, the silencer was real, and the warning had to be considered real.

And if so, Arlie thought, April and Gracie were sailing in harm's way. It could be a bluff, but he couldn't take the chance. A growing sense of dread was seeping into the cracks of his resolve, propelled by the promise that heeding the man's warning would bring his license back.

By the time he wheeled into his driveway, the urge to call both

April and Gracie was growing exponentially. Maybe he could keep from alarming Rachel. The man was right. He didn't want her anywhere near as frightened as he was.

UNIWAVE HANGAR,

ELMENDORF AFB, ALASKA

EVENING

The Gulfstream had already been moved inside the large Uniwave project hangar and the doors motored closed behind it when General MacAdams arrived with three of the test crew from the AWACS. A small ready room full of folding chairs and a long, government-issued table was already filled with the Gulfstream pilots, Ben Cole, and Joe Davis, who had been rousted from his home by a phone call from the general on the return flight.

Mac ushered Master Sergeant Bill Jacobs, the test director, and the remote pilot into the room and closed the door behind them, waiting for them to pull up chairs before speaking.

"All right, gentlemen," he began. "The contents of this briefing are top secret, just like every other aspect of this project. I know you're all tired and want to go home, but I need this immediate postmortem for two reasons. First, this system is either operable or it isn't, and as we all know, Uniwave hangs in the balance. Second, I want to know what the hell happened tonight." He looked at Ben Cole, who was still a bit pasty. "You first, Dr. Cole."

"Where do you want me to start, General?"

"Question one. Is Boomerang viable and ready for deployment, or not?"

"Yes, sir. It is viable and operable and ready to go. The repeat performance tonight of our unscheduled dive had virtually nothing to do with the Boomerang master code or system."

"Very well, Dr. Cole. Why not?"

Ben took a deep breath and gulped a bit of his soft drink before beginning. "In customizing the Gulfstream's autopilot to work with our remote control Boomerang system, we apparently overlooked something very small, and very significant, General." Ben reached for a thick technical manual and flipped it open. "We failed to catch the existence of a particular added function of this autoflight system. It's a smart little feature designed to save the lives of an aircrew who can't get their oxygen masks working in time during a rapid depressurization emergency."

"What do you mean, 'feature,' Ben?" Joe Davis asked.

"You might call it a 'mode,' too. It's called an EDM, an Emergency Descent Module. It only activates within the autopilot computer's logic circuits when it senses a rapid depressurization coupled with an indication that the pilots aren't functioning. In other words, no control inputs for a certain number of seconds. If that happens above twenty-seven thousand feet, the autopilot begins a steep, controlled descent and automatically levels itself off at whatever altitude is safe for that area as dictated by the GPS system. That gives the pilots and passengers time to regain consciousness if they've passed out. We didn't realize the feature was in this autopilot, so when we were modifying the autopilot's logic circuits, we didn't take this out. Instead, we confused it."

"How do you mean 'confused it'?" Mac asked.

"Well, because when we disconnected its prime altitude reference, we not only left the emergency descent system activated, we inadvertently, electronically led it to think that sea level was where it ought to descend to if it ever had to take over. Now, what we call a 'standard day' at sea level is when the altimeter setting is two-nine-nine-two, or twenty-nine point ninety-two inches of mercury. On Monday, the actual outside atmospheric pressure was a bit higher at sea level than two-nine-nine-two, so when it leveled the airplane at what it thought was precisely sea level, that was actually fifty feet above the water, thank God."

"And tonight?"

"Tonight, General, the atmospheric pressure out there was no longer lower, it was higher than two-nine-nine-two, and if we hadn't reset the altimeter it was watching to fool it, our little automation circuit would have tried to fly us sixty feet under sea level."

"So, Boomerang's program was not the problem?"

Ben shook his head as he glanced at the two Gulfstream pilots, who were both nodding. "No, sir. On Monday night, Gene—Captain Hammond here—happened to hit the autopilot disconnect button instinctively just as I hit the reset button on my computer. We assumed at first that my computer had ordered the dive and the hair-raising level-off at fifty feet, because Gene didn't recall hitting the autopilot disconnect. But after we got back a while ago and were waiting for you, we rechecked the flight data tape printouts from Monday, and there it is, big as life. It was the autopilot disconnect that restored control, not my computer reset."

"Yes, but the dive began while we were still remotely controlling the aircraft," Mac added.

"True, but remember that our Boomerang system required a major upgrade in the way the autopilot system holds onto the flight controls, making it all but impossible to disconnect it once you connect it. We did that so a hostile force, such as a hijacker in the cockpit, couldn't override the remote inputs from the AWACS. But the EDM circuit used the same equipment, and we couldn't knock it loose with the computers."

"All you needed was the autopilot disconnect?" Mac asked.

"That's right. As simple as that," Ben remarked. "We just didn't realize the autopilot was even involved."

"Okay, but what initiated it? What made the autopilot think there was a rapid depressurization?"

"The speed brakes. Whenever the speed brakes were deployed, a mis-wired circuit sent a completely false message to the flight data recorder and the autopilot telling them a rapid depressurization had occurred. Each time we were in full test mode and Captain Hammond pulled the speed brake lever, he was inadvertently telling the autopilot that we'd had a rapid depressurization, and off it went." Ben got to his feet before glancing over at Joe Davis. "So, bottom line? Boomerang is ready. I have no reason to conclude that there's anything in that program code that needs changing. In fact, I think we've gone substantially beyond the minimums."

*B*en held back as the rest of the assembled team headed for the doors, and Mac MacAdams noticed. A very nervous Joe Davis was pumping Mac's hand in an obsequious display of appreciation, but the general finally sent him on his way. Once the room was empty of everyone else, Mac moved to where Ben was sitting and straddled a chair backward, his arms folded along the back as he studied the chief software engineer.

"Anything wrong, General?" Ben asked, squirming under the un-spoken scrutiny.

"No." Mac smiled. "But I have an important question for you."

"Yes, sir. Go ahead."

Mac glanced around to verify the room was empty of other ears. "Ben, you know we'll have a lot of lives at stake, both in Air Force aircraft and on the ground, when this system gets installed and turned on."

"Yes, sir. I'm well aware of that."

"You're also aware, are you not, that once Boomerang is deployed, any mistakes in the basic program will be much more difficult to fix without compromising safety."

"Of course."

"I know you've been working your tail off in the last few days to fix the program, even though we now know it didn't need fixing. I want you to know that I'm very appreciative of your efforts and your dedication."

"Thank you, General, I . . ."

Mac waved him down. "This isn't an awards presentation, Ben."

He sighed, his eyes darting around the room once more, well aware he should wait until Dan Jerrod could be located and brought in with his anti-bugging equipment.

Never enough time, he thought.

"Ben, I know all about your visit to Dan Jerrod's office. I know precisely what you told him and what he told you. You probably didn't realize that he only pretends to work for Uniwave. In fact, he reports directly to me and no one else."

"I . . . didn't know that, sir."

"And you still don't. Understand?"

"Yes, sir."

"And we will not speak of details discussed in that meeting. But here's what I need to know, and bear with me because I'm shooting from the hip right now and thinking out loud. I know the system tested okay, and I accept that. But I know what you were worried about. Did any portion of that problem—that extra stuff that you found that worried you—show itself tonight?"

"No, sir."

"But you're still worried?"

"Of course, General. I can't explain what it was . . . why it was there, you know? It's eating at me. There's no way that extraneous code should have been inside the program at any time. I have to view it as potentially hostile."

Mac was nodding, his mind racing to choose the right words.

"Very well. Ben, there are many things that you have no need to know, and therefore I cannot discuss with you. I *can* assure you, though, that thanks to your speaking up and coming to Dan, we've solved the riddle and uncovered and neutralized the source. In other words, we've terminated the problem. The unfortunate part is, I simply can't tell you the details."

"It was . . . I mean, it's all taken care of?"

"Yes, Ben."

"There was a threat, but it's completely defused? I was afraid that

I'd merely interfered with them, and they'd try something else. Whoever 'they' is."

"I understand. I wish to hell I could give you the details, but I can't."

"That's okay. I understand, sir. I'm very relieved to hear this."

"You're a very diligent fellow, Ben. I knew you wouldn't stop thinking this problem through and searching for a conclusion unless I told you personally it wasn't necessary."

Ben smiled. "Yes sir, you're right. It's been eating at me very actively, to the point that I'd begun to suspect everyone."

"That includes me as well, I assume?"

Ben smiled sheepishly. "Really hadn't gotten around to you yet, General. But I was becoming suspicious of friends and even my cat. Or his collar, at least."

"I'm sorry?"

Ben laughed and waved it off. "Not important. Just something Dan Jerrod said."

"Okay. Well, you can cut out the worry now. The responsible parties are contained."

"Great."

Mac got to his feet carefully and pushed the flimsy gray chair out of the way.

"Go on home, Ben. Get some well-deserved rest. Oh, and if no one's told you, the start of the post-development program for Boomerang to maintain the system will be announced next week, and we very much want you to stay on for at least another year."

"That's good to hear, sir."

Mac shook Ben Cole's hand and walked him to the door of the hangar office, holding it open. He watched him go, before turning back into the room to get his coat. He would need to call Jerrod immediately to let him know what had been said. The security chief would be nervous, of course. Saying anything to Cole and keeping him on was a calculated risk, but it had apparently worked. Ben Cole was more than likely neutralized.

At least, for his sake, Mac thought, *I certainly hope so.*

He tried Dan Jerrod's cell phone and home numbers with no luck. The office extension rang uselessly as well. Mac sighed and punched in another number, assigning to Jon Anderson the task of tracking Jerrod down.

Mac focused on the door, well aware there was work to do, but the lure of the beautifully designed Gulfstream sitting like a crouching tiger on the hangar floor a few dozen yards away was too powerful for a lifelong pilot to ignore. He turned away from the outside door and entered the hangar, intent on strolling around the Gulfstream for a few minutes, contemplating her sleek shape and how she looked suspended in flight.

There was no one else in sight as Mac shoved his hands in his pockets and forced himself to relax, breathing deeply, his nose catching a hint of kerosene and other aviation solvents, aromas that painted an olfactory picture of the hangar's interior.

The absence of anyone else in the hangar was comforting. A general officer poking around was, by definition, suspicious, his mere presence threatening to spark an alert among subordinates, who would instantly assume that the big man was searching for something to criticize. It helped to be anonymous every now and then, escaping the inevitable bow wave of recognition that the stars on his shoulders brought.

Mac stopped thirty feet in front of the nose of the Gulfstream, admiring its lithe appearance. Gulfstreams were the gold standard for executive jets, a $43-million luxury liner. He chuckled at having the audacity even to daydream what it would be like to own one on a general's salary.

Not yet, at least, Mac thought, his mind poking into fantasy images of his post-military life to come.

He began at the nose and walked beneath the fuselage to the tail, reaching up to touch the aircraft every twenty feet or so, letting his fingertips merely brush the cool metal as he passed. There was something mystical about an aircraft in a quiet hangar at night, Mac thought. Air museums had always intrigued him as a result. Walking around a silent, powerful airplane inside a huge building always inspired feelings of awe, which contrasted with his technical knowledge the way that logic and emotion always clash. "I could put you to sleep explaining how a 747 flies," he'd told a high-school class as a career-day speaker once, many years back, "but I will be forever emotionally mystified at the fact that so much metal can be supported by the wind and actually fly as a thing of beauty." Airplanes were merely collections of man-made parts capable of using wing shape and power to suck themselves into the air, and yet they could stir the heart of even the most jaded pilot. Every time he'd visited the Air Force Museum in Dayton, Ohio, or the Air and Space Museum in Washington, a planned hour had become an afternoon with the doors closing behind him.

He stopped for a second beneath the Gulfstream's tail and then walked to the right wingtip, enjoying the changing perspective of the jet as he moved. The wings were turned up at the end in an appendage known as a winglet. He stopped for a second to admire the right one, the bold rake of its shape shifting the horizontal wing to a vertical fin, a design that lessened the aerodynamic drag of the aircraft and made it more fuel efficient. The winglet was painted blue to match part of the body paint, but there was a patch at the very front of the winglet, on its leading edge, that seemed darker.

Why is it that way?

Aircraft as big and expensive as a Gulfstream were painted or repainted all at once in special facilities. Yet, in the orangish light of the hangar's sodium-vapor lamps, a foot-long expanse of the winglet's leading edge appeared darker.

Must have been a bird strike or some other repair, Mac thought casually as he began walking away. But he stopped suddenly and walked back under the winglet, studying it intently, though unable to touch it because of the height.

There was a stepladder in one recess of the hangar and Mac retrieved it to climb up for a closer look. The difference in the paint shade was very subtle. It was no wonder they'd missed it when they'd looked at the aircraft for damage a few days earlier. But whether it was the telltale aftereffects of a repair, or just an inconsistency in the original paint, he couldn't be sure.

Mac ran his fingertips lightly over the area, feeling for a sharp edge where someone might have masked off a section before re-painting. He could feel nothing unusual, but his eyes detected a small irregularity, as if a dent had been repaired imperfectly.

He looked around, relieved that apparently no one had been watching him, and returned the ladder to the spot it had occupied.

Suppose they'd come back Monday evening with damage from hitting that Albatross. Is it possible they could have repaired it secretly and said nothing? Our contract requires a report. Mac climbed inside the Gulfstream and searched the maintenance log, but there were no indications of a wingtip repair.

He thought about the Uniwave manager who ran the test aircraft program. He was, Mac concluded, perfectly capable of trying to cover up something that would have seemed insignificant, in order to avoid the paperwork that even a bird strike would trigger, espe-cially if the discovery had been made after news of the Albatross crash reached his ears.

But we didn't even suspect the possibility of a collision ourselves until we looked at the radar tapes, Mac reminded himself. *Why would he?* No, he concluded. If a damaged winglet had been discovered, they might or might not have asked the pilots about it, but afterward the aircraft would have been quietly repaired and the damage marked off to im-pact with an unseen object.

Mac left the Gulfstream cockpit and stood again on the hangar floor, studying the aircraft. He winced at the memories of his own involvement as a young officer in helping commanders minimize and hide major aircraft damage. It didn't matter that cover-ups were a widespread practice carried out in order to avoid hurting the Air Force safety record or embarrassing a particular command; he'd al-ways known it was wrong—if not criminal. Sometimes it was nothing more sinister than the maintenance staff working a few nights to repair a small dent in a wingtip rather than formally reporting it, but at other times an entire squadron would labor in secret for months to keep the cost of an accident from exceeding a million dollars and becoming a so-called "Class A," which was the most embarrassing level. The possibility that Uniwave might have done the same thing to avoid contract problems chilled him. Even worse was the thought that the beautiful twin jet sitting before him might have caused the loss of a civilian amphibian, and not even he was being told the truth.

Two miles away Ben Cole parked his car in front of his favorite Mexican restaurant on Spenard and got out, locking the door as a black van he'd noticed before pulled into the same lot and parked several stalls down. He felt a small chill as he realized he'd seen the same vehicle in his rearview mirror since leaving the base.

The doors were still closed, the windows darkened.

Ben began walking toward the front door of the restaurant, his mind searching for another explanation. He stopped in the doorway and looked back, waiting to see movement around the van.

A young couple pushed through the doors to the street, almost knocking him down, the woman sidestepping in her high heels to miss him.

"Whoa! Sorry, fella," she said. A small cloud of Giorgio's Red wafted by, a fragrance he loved, but neither that nor the black leather pants she was wearing distracted him. Ben nodded absently as he caught the door and held it open, his eyes focused on nothing.

No one's getting out. Why?

"You coming in, sir, or just practicing?" a woman asked from just inside.

"Sorry?"

"Welcome to La Mex, sir, where we actually have the ability to close the front door and keep the cold out."

"Oh. Sorry," Ben said, moving inside.

"Table for one?"

"Yes."

"Right this way."

He followed, forcing enough cognitive brainpower to the task of walking behind her without stumbling.

I was followed. Oh my God, that means I'm under surveillance. Could it be Dan Jerrod's people? Or MacAdams's? After all, I just came from MacAdams.

A memory of himself in the lab transmitting classified data over a non-secure cell phone flashed in his mind. Had they seen that, too?

An extremely deep male voice coming from one of the television monitors was echoing through the bar as he walked by.

. . . This . . . is CNN!

"Here you are, sir. Your waitress will be with you in a minute."

"Thanks," he replied, barely acknowledging her as he took the menu, ignoring the teaser for the Larry King show in the background, which faded to the voice of Aaron Brown in his New York studio.

"Would you like something from the bar first, sir?" the waitress asked. He looked up at her: large brown eyes framed by short blonde hair, as she poised to write. He tried to smile but his face was frozen, and the thought of drinking anything suddenly became nauseating.

She stepped back as Ben got clumsily to his feet.

"I . . . ah, I'm sorry . . . I suddenly realized I've got to, you know, be somewhere."

"You're leaving, sir?"

"Yes. I'm sorry." He yanked a small wad of bills from his pants pocket and laid one on the table.

Ben made his way back to the parking lot and climbed in his car. The black van was still there, still unopened. Ben pulled Jerrod's business card from his shirt pocket and punched in the cell phone number. He pressed the transmit button, then canceled the call, then pressed it again, only to cancel it once more before the number could ring. His mind was a whirl of horrific possibilities.

Gotta think straight, here, Ben lectured himself.

There was a gentle buzz from the phone and he jumped slightly before reading the screen to find a message waiting. He punched in the appropriate codes and Nelson's voice coursed from the earpiece.

"Ben, I've been looking for you. You're not at home, of course, and all I can do is leave one of the messages, which you know I hate. But here goes. I'm at Chilkoot's again and wish you'd come down here and drink with me. You've been acting really strange lately. Call me. This is Nelson. Bye."

Ben's eyes shifted toward the big, rustic sign over the entrance to Chilkoot Charlie's right across the street. He'd forgotten Chilkoot's was located across from La Mex. The fact hung there like the hint of a distant image through fog.

Suddenly the reason for trying to call Dan Jerrod seemed obscure and silly, and yet compulsive. He needed the reassurance that he wasn't in trouble, and that was the fastest way. Talk to the source.

He saw the doors of the bar across the street open and Nelson himself pushed through onto the sidewalk, looking around and stretching, his big smile flashing at no one in particular. Ben felt a flash of pleasurable recognition as he fought the urge to get out of the car and yell to him. It was far more comfortable to think of sharing a beer with the jovial Alaskan than to sit there worrying himself silly about his career and his freedom, and whether he was already in serious trouble. If he was being watched right there right then, going across the street to share a few drinks with his friend could raise alarm bells. After all, it was Nelson he'd said too much to in the boat, and that entire conversation could have been monitored from the shore.

Ben felt a wave of loneliness. Nelson was always so much fun to be around, his outlook on life always positive, his sense of humor ranging from rollicking to subtle.

But tonight wasn't the right time.

He hunkered down behind the wheel and put the car in gear, turning away quickly into traffic with the odd sense that he was betraying a friend.

There was something else MacAdams had said that had been scratching at his mind and triggering alarm bells. A half mile from downtown, Ben pulled to the right lane and stopped long enough to reach into his briefcase and pull out a copy of *The New York Times*. The article he'd remembered seeing was on page one but below the fold, a small item quoting an unnamed source in the Transportation Department warning of a new threat to civil aviation from sophisticated terrorists trying to find ways of manipulating the largely unguarded electronic control systems on modern jetliners. There were references to engine control computers and autopilots and refusals by industry spokesmen to comment, the words sounding too familiar.

Ben placed the paper on the right seat and accelerated back into traffic, pulling off the main road several blocks away and parking at the curb to think. General MacAdams's reassurance that the airline-related listings he'd found embedded in the renegade code were no longer a threat replayed. "You can cut out the worry now," MacAdams had said. "The responsible parties are contained."

What does "contained" mean? Ben asked himself, remembering as well that MacAdams had asked if Ben suspected even *him*. The two-star general's words had seemed totally reassuring and even fatherly, and after all, how could a United States Air Force flag officer not be trusted?

MacAdams can't be mixed up in anything. I can trust him.

But Dan Jerrod had told him specifically to discuss his findings and worries with no one at Uniwave and no one in the Air Force, and Jerrod had even mentioned the possibility of a mole. Surely that wouldn't include MacAdams.

How do I know I can trust Jerrod? Ben asked himself, remembering that his survival of the final flight and the absence of any new sabotage argued well for Dan Jerrod's veracity. Maybe MacAdams was right, but the way to find out, he concluded, was to ask Dan Jerrod himself.

He pulled Jerrod's card from his pocket again and punched in the number, with no success. There were probably other numbers, Ben thought in frustration, and the guards at Uniwave would surely know how to reach him in an emergency.

Ben put the car back in gear and headed toward Elmendorf.

THIRTY-THREE

April pressed the satellite phone to her right ear and glanced at Scott McDermott, who was trying to look disinterested as he sat in the Widgeon's left seat and nursed a cup of coffee in the dim light.

"Gracie, can you hear me?"

"Who's asking? *April?* Is that you?"

"Of course it's me."

"Your voice sounds weird."

"And you sound like you're next door. I'm on a satellite phone."

"Gad! I was about to launch the Coast Guard again, this time to find *you.*" Gracie's voice was tense, April noted, her words coming rapidly.

"I called that guy Jim, in Valdez, and he said you and that jerk of a pilot who abandoned you flew off in late afternoon and he hadn't seen you since."

"It's a long story," April said, glancing at Scott as she tried to reduce the volume on the phone's earpiece, "but we're okay."

"Yeah? We? But where are you, Rosencrantz?"

"We're in Scott McDermott's airplane right now, floating in a half-frozen lake and waiting for daylight."

There was a short chuckle from Seattle. "Only my buddy April Rosen would get herself into a frozen lake at midnight and be telling me about it on a satellite phone. What lake, exactly? And what's been going on? Were you able to replace the video of the Albatross?"

April filled in a brief chronicle of the flight, leaving out the harrowing parts over and through the glacier. "We're going to fly out of here at daylight and try once more to get to the crash site."

"How, April? You said the crash site was a secured, patrolled area."

"Scott's friend Jim, the one you talked to, is gearing up to help us. We'll meet him . . . at a location I don't want to mention . . . and give it another try. What's up there?"

"Well, nothing amorous, I can assure you. I'm in my cloistered bedroom on the boat." There was a long pause and April could hear her sigh. "Your dad called me last night and wanted me to put everything on hold."

"WHAT?"

"That was roughly my reaction, April. I do not understand what's gotten into him. I've never known the captain to be afraid of anything, but he sounded almost panicked. I must have asked him why a dozen times, but all he'd tell me is that he feared for my career and wanted me to stand down."

"Have you talked to Mom?"

"Yes. He came in yesterday afternoon agitated about something, but won't tell her what."

"Gracie, we can't quit now . . . can we? Is there any reason to?"

"No! And I forgot to tell you that I got the TRO, the temporary restraining order, and we served it almost immediately on the Coast Guard in their offices in the same building. They were very surprised."

"I'll bet, but does that mean we'll get the tapes back now?"

"Well, it only means they're ordered not to destroy them or lose them. We've got a show-cause hearing Monday. I tried for Saturday but the judge laughed at me."

"Damn."

"Yeah, I know. Trust me, it's not fun to have a federal district judge laugh at you from the bench."

"What are our chances of getting the tapes on Monday?"

"I don't know, but we'd better try everything else possible, and I've got other things working, but since you're worried about this line, maybe I'd better not say."

"Okay. Is it good?"

"If it works, yes. I called our client back and kind of asked another favor."

"Thank you, Gracie. Will it cost much?"

"Not in dollars, but maybe you can visit me on the Arabian Peninsula, 'cause he said I'll have to be his mistress for at least a decade."

"Gracie, just like Dad said, I don't want you endangering your position with the firm."

"Oh, it's okay. So far, all I've promised the man is dinner."

"Good."

"In Kuwait."

"What?"

"Just kidding."

"You worry me, O'Brien," April said, smiling to herself in spite of the intense worry over her father's sudden change of heart. She wished there was time to relate the details of the wild flight and roller-coaster emotions of the previous day.

"April, the captain wants you to come home and give up as well."

"Not only no, but hell no."

"You should call him. You have a number on that satellite phone I can call until you return to civilization?" Gracie asked.

She asked Scott for the number and then relayed it.

"April, you're sure you two are okay out there? Floating around on an Alaskan lake in the middle of the night sounds a bit dangerous, not to mention cold."

"We've got a heater. It's actually toasty in here."

"And food?"

"Yep. Even Starbucks coffee."

"Okay. Call me as soon as you can from a safe phone, okay? And be careful. And if you get any more insight into what's spooking your dad . . ."

"Yeah, I'll call," April said. "In the morning. I know he'll ask where I am and I don't want him worrying."

"He's already worried, but I'll relay to Rachel that you're okay. Be careful, please, getting out of there. I don't want to have to break in a new best friend. The darn process takes decades, you know, having to go back through kindergarten and high school, and double-dating, training bras, guys . . ."

"Say good night, Gracie."

There was an uncharacteristic moment of silence from the other end, followed by a sigh. "April, I swear, if I hear that line one more time from you . . ."

"Sorry. I'm just trying to find some humor in things, you know? But seriously, thanks for . . . well, what I'm trying to say, Gracie, is thank you for keeping tabs on my folks. I really appreciate . . ." Her voice trailed off as she found herself suddenly choking back tears that had come from nowhere.

"It's okay, April. That's a given. I love them, too."

"Thanks."

April punched off the phone and shifted her gaze to the front windscreen, aware that Scott had heard almost all of the exchange.

"As you've no doubt figured out, Gracie and I have been best friends since we were knee high to a duck."

He nodded, his eyes on the ghostly shapes of ice barely visible in the darkness of the lake. "Not a problem. I like her sense of humor. And yours."

The flickering light from a kerosene lantern he'd set up in the aft cabin of the Widgeon reflected off the nearest iceberg, creating dancing images of shadows and silvery white reflecting off the water. The gentle slosh and slap of small wind-driven waves could be heard against the aluminum hull of the Widgeon, but aside from the hiss of the lantern, the quiet was all but overwhelming, and April felt the silence demanding to be broken.

"Have you ever overnighted in here before?" April asked, pulling her jacket tighter around her, glad Gracie couldn't see how chilly it really was with the only heat coming from the puny catalytic heater he'd set up under the open nose hatch.

Scott nodded, the movement almost synchronizing with the flickering light from behind him.

"Yeah. Many times. Sometimes to save hotel money. Sometimes just to hear the quiet."

"Nice oxymoron."

"Hmm?"

" 'Hear the quiet.' Beautiful image. In fact, if I wasn't so wrought up over my dad, as well as completely unable to see how we'll get out of here without killing ourselves, this would be one of the most beautiful nights I've ever spent."

"I take that as a compliment."

She looked at him and smiled before letting her eyes drift back to the icebergs. "Actually, I was talking about the setting."

"Thanks anyway."

"I do appreciate your coming back."

He laughed. "If you're afraid I'm going to take offense at the 'jerk pilot' thing, don't. That was a jerky thing to do, leaving you this morning."

"Well, you came back."

"Yeah," he said.

She turned to him, catching his eyes. "You came back to help me, right? Not just to take me to dinner?"

"You're very direct, aren't you, April?"

"When I'm floating around at midnight in the middle of nowhere in the effective physical control of a male I barely know, darn tootin' I'm direct."

"The answer is, yes, I have no bad intentions. I came back to help you, not chase you."

"Good. Because nothing's going to happen tonight. Understood?"

"Of course."

"Just, you know, so there are no expectations."

"Uh-huh."

"I mean, this beautiful setting and all could lead some guys to . . ."

"April," he said suddenly, smiling at her.

"Yes?"

"It's okay. Calm down."

"All right."

They sat in silence for several minutes before she heard him stretch. "Tell you what. Why don't we sleep in shifts? That way you can pull one of the sleeping bags inside the other back there while I make sure we don't drift between two of these bergs."

"What if we do? You can't physically push something that big away, can you?"

He was nodding. "Actually, I can push us out of harm's way. This little bird only weighs four thousand pounds."

"Will you wake me up in, what, three hours?"

He smiled as he pulled himself out of the left seat to retrieve the lantern and put it in the nose section. "Okay. Three hours."

There was light in her eyes when April returned to consciousness. She sat up suddenly, recognizing the filtered daylight through an overcast above the lake.

"Scott?"

"Good morning."

"You didn't wake me?"

He shrugged. "No need. I was doing fine up here."

She unzipped the bag, feeling the sting of the cold air in the frigid cabin and seeing the extra parka he'd wrapped around himself.

"That wasn't the deal, Mr. Macho."

"So sue me," he said, his smile somewhat strained. The remark puzzled her.

She stowed the sleeping bags as he moved forward to the nose section to fire up a small camp stove, and they sat for awhile when he was done, nursing steaming mugs of coffee and munching on cereal bars. She watched him survey the floating ice around them.

"So how are we going to do this?"

"Just watch," he said evenly. He finished his makeshift breakfast and they began stowing the lantern, stove, and heater to secure the cabin. When everything was back in place, he eased himself into the left seat and handed her the checklist. April began reading the items, checking his fluid responses as he positioned the switches and reached at last for the starter.

"Cranking number one."

The whine of the electric starter struggling with limited power against the engine's cylinders warbled for a few seconds, then began to fade. He switched off the starter and worked the primer, squeezing raw fuel into the carburetor before trying it again, his face hardening with worry.

"Starting one," he said, the words clipped as the propeller began rotating in jerky fashion, its motion slowing until one cylinder fired, then another, followed by silence.

"Oh, Lord, don't tell me we're out of battery power?" April said. She could see him biting his lip. "Scott?"

"God*dammit!*" He peered carefully at the DC voltage meter.

"We're screwed, aren't we?" she asked.

He got out of the seat without answering, and she turned to watch him rummage around in the back of the cabin and pull out what looked like a tool kit. He lifted out two yellow rectangular devices and came forward, plugging them into the empty cigarette lighter in the lower forward panel.

"May I ask what you're doing?"

"Yes."

More silence as he checked the meter.

"So . . . what are you doing?"

"Starting number one," he said as he worked the primer before turning the starter switch.

Once more the left propeller began jerking into motion, but this time the cylinders fired with authority and the engine roared to life with a comforting rumble.

Scott sat back in the seat and exhaled, his eyes on the oil-pressure gauges as they came up smartly to operating pressure. He turned to her finally and shook his head.

"I'm sorry, April. We almost . . ."

"Those things are portable battery boosters?"

"Yeah. Automotive. I've never needed them before. I wasn't sure they'd work."

"We used too much battery last night?"

He looked chagrined. "I left the master switch on too long while you were sleeping. I was checking weather on the radio."

He turned back to the task of starting the right engine. Bolstered by the current from the left generator, the right engine started immediately, and they ran through the checklist before Scott brought the props out of the feathered position.

The Widgeon began moving through the water immediately, and he guided it toward one of the largest icebergs, turning at the last second to let the nose bump into the ice at the angle he wanted. When the prow of the Widgeon had nudged itself firmly onto the iceberg, Scott brought the engine power up, watching the shoreline carefully until he was satisfied the huge iceberg was in motion.

"So that's it! You're going to shove them out of the way."

He nodded.

"And create a runway, right?"

"It's worked before," Scott said. "But it'll take an hour or so to push enough of them to each side to form a runway, and I'm going to need you up in the nose hatch with that oar to push us away from each one when I'm finished with it."

"How much open water do we need?"

"About twenty-eight hundred feet."

"How long is this lake?"

Scott chuckled. "About twenty-five hundred feet."

"What?"

"But it's all downhill."

Schroedinger had been trying fruitlessly to awaken Ben for at least fifteen minutes when the telephone rang.

"Dr. Cole?"

"Yes?"

"Sorry if I called too early, sir. This is Jim Lucavitch in security at Uniwave."

Ben pulled himself upright on the bed, forcing his mind to accelerate to full consciousness.

"Yes, Jim."

"You were by here last night trying to locate Mr. Jerrod, I understand, and I've been following up on that."

"Good. Is he in this morning?"

"No, sir. Mr. Jerrod is out of the country. That's all I'm at liberty to tell you."

"Do you . . . have any idea when he'll be back?"

"No, Dr. Cole, I don't."

"Well, it's really urgent that I at least speak with him. Can we arrange that this morning? I can come in for security purposes."

"No, sir, that won't be possible."

Ben felt himself pass the fully awake point, a slight warning buzzer going off in his head announcing the need for immediate caution. Something was very wrong with this response.

"Okay, Jim. Let me put this to you as clearly as I can without breaching any security rules or regulations. It is imperative that I speak personally on a secure line with Mr. Jerrod today, and it involves a matter of national security of the highest interest to Uniwave. Understood?"

"Dr. Cole, I understand, but I'm not a magician. I quite frankly have no idea how to reach Mr. Jerrod at the moment, and all I can say is that we'll keep trying. If you need some emergency protection, we can come get you in fifteen minutes."

"That's not necessary. It's not a protection matter. At least, not about protecting me."

It was going to be futile to pressure the man further, Ben realized. He terminated the call and sat rubbing his eyes for a minute, working to bat down the hopefully fictional scenarios that could explain Dan Jerrod's sudden disappearance.

Schroedinger was making it very clear that a formal charge of feline abuse was in the offing if his breakfast was not served within the next few minutes. Ben gave him a conciliatory head scratching before following the aggravated cat to the kitchen. He made coffee and reached out the front door to retrieve the *Anchorage Times,* opening it on the center island in the kitchen as he settled onto a stool to catch up with the world. He was into the third section before a small article about a recent plane crash caught his attention.

FAA ACCUSED OF OVERREACTION IN
MONDAY'S SEAPLANE ACCIDENT

Midair Collision Possible

The Monday night loss of a private twin-engine seaplane some sixty miles south of Valdez has led to cancelation of a senior pilot's license to fly and resulted in countercharges that local Federal Aviation Administration officials are persecuting the pilot.

The aircraft, a World War II–vintage Grumman Albatross, crashed south of Prince William Sound late Monday on a flight from Anchorage to Sitka. The owner-pilot—a senior airline captain for a major U.S. airline—reported a sudden fog bank at low altitude at the same moment his right engine mysteriously lost a propeller blade and broke loose, causing a loss of control. Captain Arlie Rosen of Sequim, Washington, and his wife, Rachel, were the only occupants of the aircraft, which was featured last year in the Living Section of the *Anchorage Times* for its motor home–like interior. The couple survived the crash without serious injury and were rescued late Tuesday morning by the Coast Guard. They were taken to Providence Hospital with mild hypothermia and released the following day.

The wreckage, which sank in some three hundred feet of water, has not yet been examined and may be very difficult to raise. The Coast Guard confirms that they have no current plans to raise the wreckage. Meanwhile, the FAA has already taken the highly unusual step of revoking Captain Rosen's pilot license and charging him with flying while intoxicated, operating an aircraft recklessly, and violating several FAA regulations regarding flight into marginal weather conditions, charges Rosen vehemently denies through his attorney. Sources close to the case say the FAA does not believe the aircraft lost a propeller blade, but that instead, the pilot simply flew too low and drove the aircraft into the water.

The revocation, which came from FAA headquarters in Washington, D.C., effectively grounds Captain Rosen from his airline job as well as from private flying. Rosen's attorney, Seattle lawyer Gracie O'Brien, told the *Times,* "There is no justification for the FAA's actions. They've gone off half-cocked, without even the most cursory evidence, and have egregiously damaged the reputation of one of the finest senior pilots in the nation."

Ms. O'Brien added that "thirty-thousand-hour airline captains do not just negligently fly airplanes into the water." Ms. O'Brien accused the FAA of staging an unexplained vendetta from the very first interview, citing a hostile hospital room exchange on Tuesday between Rosen and an FAA investigator. "The FAA is refusing to investigate any of several other very possible scenarios, such as the possibility that the propeller clipped another aircraft that perhaps didn't have the authority to be where it was."

Local FAA officials have refused to comment on the case, referring all inquiries to officials in Washington, who are also refusing to comment.

That's a shame, Ben thought, feeling an uncharacteristic bridge of camaraderie to anyone alleging government overreaction. He reread the next-to-the-last paragraph, his mind latching onto the mention of a possible midair collision, as the subtitle had bannered.

Monday night. Where was this?

He searched out the part that mentioned the location, some sixty miles south of Valdez, and moved to his laptop to call up a detailed Alaska map program. He pinpointed the area and sat back, his thoughts accelerating.

Where were we? And when did this occur?

The article hadn't mentioned the exact time of the crash, he discovered, but a quick check of his own test notes pinpointed the time of the Gulfstream's harrowing dive to fifty feet, and its deadeye aim at the oil tanker miles ahead.

The tanker was coming out of Valdez. That would put him about here, which means we were about here.

Ben shook his head to expunge the unwanted conclusions. He had been there, after all. If they'd hit anything, including some lumbering warbird's propeller, he would have heard it and probably felt it. Besides, the fact they were in the same area on the same evening was hardly evidence they'd come close to each other. There were probably dozens of airplanes out that night, and who knew how many might have been nearby?

Just a tantalizing coincidence, he told himself.

But, just in case, he decided to clip and save the article.

ELMENDORF AFB, ALASKA

Mac MacAdams was in a grumpy mood from waking up over and over during the night, and his wife, Linda, knew the warning signs. The fact that her sleep had been all but sabotaged by his insomnia was best suppressed for the moment, she figured. Mac was a compassionate and caring husband, but she knew the energy it took for him to be reasonable when the storm warnings went up from lack of sleep. Something was troubling the general, and the general's wife was smart enough to know how to quietly fix his breakfast, serve it with the morning paper, and judiciously withdraw.

He would, she knew, be contrite later, and that was always useful.

Mac knew very well what was bugging him, and it made him even more irritated that such a small, potentially useless suspicion was leaching away so much of his attention. So what if they might have covered up a small ding on the right winglet of the Gulfstream? No way could that be evidence of some midair collision.

But the issue wouldn't leave him alone, and the toll it was taking on his concentration reached a new level when he opened the *Anchorage Times* and came across the same article Ben had read about the FAA's alleged overreaction.

Goddammit! Mac raced through the article, fixating on the subtitle and the ending reference to the possibility of a midair. He put his coffee mug on the counter with a thud and launched himself toward the secure Air Force official phone in the living room of the large, comfortable base house.

"Yes, sir?" a captain at the command post answered.

Mac checked a small notebook for the name. "The test flight manager for Uniwave, Richard Wilcox. Get him on the phone, tell him someone from the command post will pick him up in a staff car in ten minutes. Send someone to do exactly that, get him on a secure line there and call me."

"Yes, sir."

"Sometime yesterday. Understood?"

"Yes, General. Immediately, sir."

He replaced the receiver and began pacing in a predictable pattern around the living room. His oldest son, who had already graduated from Air Force pilot training, loved to kid him about his pacing, which always aided his thinking.

"Mom? Dad's flying a holding pattern around the living room again," Jerry would announce. "Standard right-hand turns, one-minute legs."

Mac stopped and took a deep breath as he planned the conversation he was about to have, wondering if it would be more effective to face Wilcox down in person.

No. I can terrify him on the phone better, he concluded.

He'd had a few contacts with Dick Wilcox and none of them had been a confidence builder. Wilcox was a glib and slightly arrogant man Mac neither trusted nor liked, and the fact that he was a non-pilot running a flight test unit exacerbated the impression.

The secure line rang again in twenty minutes and Mac yanked it to his ear.

"General MacAdams."

Judging by his voice, Mac figured, the civilian on the other end had been appropriately chastened by the summons and the quick trip to the command post.

"Ah, this is Dick Wilcox, General. I . . . is there an emergency?"

"You're the one who's going to answer that question, Mr. Wilcox."

"I'm sorry?"

"I had you brought in to use a secure line for a reason. What I'm about to discuss with you is classified, but I also want to warn you very sternly that if the answers you give me are anything but the complete truth, losing your job will be just the start. Understood?"

"I don't understand what you're talking about, General. I can assure you that threats aren't necessary to get me to tell you the truth."

"Okay, here's the problem." Mac related the inconsistency in the paint on the Gulfstream's right winglet and the roughness in the leading edge. "The question is this, Wilcox. Did your maintenance team, or anyone on it, conduct a repair of any sort to that aircraft following Monday's test flight?"

"Repair?"

"I think you understand the word and the concept, and asking a one-word question like that is a stalling tactic."

"No, it isn't! Sir, you really have no cause to be this hostile with me."

"Answer the question, Mr. Wilcox."

"No, we didn't repair anything! At least . . . I'm not aware of any damage, any repair, or anything in the maintenance log following Monday's flight that would indicate such. Did you look in the log?"

"Yes, and as we both know, logs can lie."

"Not on my shift, General. And I professionally resent that implication."

"Mr. Wilcox, a repair of some sort exists in the history of that aircraft. I need the absolute truth of when and where and by whom it was made."

"Today, sir? Well . . . of course today." There was a tired sigh on the command-post side of the connection. "Okay. I'll go over there and get right on it. We've owned that airplane for four years, but I may have to delve into the history before we acquired it."

"Be careful and precise about this, Mr. Wilcox. There is always a possibility something was done without your knowledge, and there is also a possibility that this is a case of planned, plausible deniability. In either case, I will hold you personally responsible for the accuracy of the answer."

"General, may I ask what this is all about?"

"No. Get to work. I'll expect a call back by this afternoon."

Mac replaced the receiver and resumed pacing for a few minutes, deciding instead to go for a walk. The day was overcast and cool, the temperature in the mid-thirties, and he pulled on his parka before telling Linda he would be out walking for a while. He didn't have to announce he would be taking his cell phone. He was well known for being all but surgically attached to it.

Should have a damn dog to walk! he thought, regretting once again his long-standing promise to buy a dog for the kids when they had a place big enough to accommodate one. Over an entire career the right place had never happened, and the kids had grown up with cats, ferrets, canaries, assorted rodents, and the eternal hope of a dog at the next base.

Elmendorf Air Force Base was a beautiful place for walking and jogging. Not as beautiful as the tree-lined streets of McChord Air Force Base in Tacoma, Washington, or the old-world elegance of Langley Air Force Base just north of Norfolk, Virginia, but one of his favorites, nonetheless. He stuffed his hands in his pockets and started out in a brisk stride to the south, toward Fort Richardson, letting his thoughts circle around the true nature of the threat presented by the article he'd just read.

With a newspaper interested in the story and an aggrieved pilot and his daughter fighting for justice, the possibility of exposing the project by nosing their way to the existence of Monday's test flight had grown another notch, and it was his responsibility to make sure the project stayed black and invisible. Certainly thousands of Alaskan residents and Air Force personnel knew there was a Gulfstream on the base, and many knew Uniwave had offices there. Uniwave even had a listing in the local phone book. But the cover story had always involved Uniwave's development of electronic systems for the AWACS aircraft on the base, and there had been very few anxious moments in keeping the cork in the real bottle.

The radar tapes were taken care of, Mac reminded himself. No matter how enterprising any local reporters might be, there was nothing to find, other than a radar target with an innocuous call sign flying with an AWACS, which was wholly consistent with the cover story.

So why am I worried enough to beat up Wilcox? he asked himself as his cell phone began ringing.

Mac stopped and pulled the instrument from a pocket in his parka, barely punching the answer button in time.

"Mac? That you?"

"Yes. Who's . . ."

"This is Lou Cassidy."

The voice of the four-star general he reported to was a mild shock. "Yes, Lou."

"What the hell are you doing up there?"

"Excuse me?"

"Mac, we've got to maintain reasonably good relations with Uniwave's people, and I've just been gnawed on by their chairman, with whom I play golf. His damn call was inappropriate as hell, but I don't like what he was complaining about either."

"What was he chewing on you for, General?"

"About you insulting his man up there a little while ago. I'm told you accused him of performing some illegal maintenance and then lying about it, and that you were pulling rank and being extremely abusive to the man."

"Lou, that is completely inaccurate—"

"Look, dammit, it's Saturday. Let's make this brief. Make it go away, Mac. Uniwave's chief assured me there was no damage to their airplane, no repairs, no cover-ups, and no grounds for upsetting their people."

Mac took a deep breath, his mind racing over the elements of the situation.

"Lou, you've never questioned my judgment before based on a civilian contractor's complaint."

"Doesn't sound like you used much judgment, Mac. Or am I missing something. Did you call the man?"

"Yes, I called him, and yes, I'm suspicious, and yes, I'm using the power of my position to hopefully force an honest answer, which I think is critical."

"About what? Something you haven't told me?"

"No . . . at least, right now it's just a worry. Remember when I was there I told you we had a small glitch on the next-to-last flight test?" He detailed what had happened and his caution about any possible interaction with the lost Albatross.

"Well, hell, Mac. I've seen bug strikes that could mess up paint."

"This wasn't a bug strike, Lou, nor a bird strike. Something dented metal and was repaired. I think I'm being lied to, but I've got to be sure, and I'll tell you, the fact that Wilcox would call his chief and the president of the company—"

"Chairman."

"Okay, the chairman. The fact that the chairman would risk calling you on a Saturday to get you to chew me out makes this even more suspicious."

"Give it up, Mac. Nothing happened, except that we're stupidly saying too much on a non-secure line. Fix it."

"Sir . . ."

"Goddammit, Mac, fix it! I don't want calls like that."

"Yes, sir."

He heard the Washington end of the call go silent and folded the phone, fighting a flash of anger and struggling to concentrate on any deeper meaning. Whichever way he looked at it, the implications were disturbing.

This has nothing to do with personal insult. I touched an exposed nerve, and this was the reaction.

He turned and looked back, startled to see his house less than a hundred yards behind him. An AWACS was lifting off from Runway 05 and clawing for altitude, the throaty roar of its engines trying unsuccessfully to distract him.

Mac resumed walking, calculating a path to the jogging trails around the base. He'd been given a direct order to "fix" the upset, which meant apologize and withdraw his demand for information. He could do that on the cell phone in a few minutes, but first there was something more important to figure out. The front-door approach had backfired. The information he needed would now have to be obtained clandestinely and fast, and that meant he needed unofficial help.

He closed his eyes for a few strides, then opened them and picked up his pace as he remembered the presence of a pay phone just ahead.

A pay phone would be a lot safer. He picked up the receiver and dialed a carefully memorized number.

THIRTY FIVE

*I*n the master bedroom of her yacht, Gracie O'Brien swam slowly back to consciousness from a deliciously sensuous dream and stretched luxuriously in the king-size bed, letting the feel of the satin sheets she loved extend the fantasy a few more seconds.

The ceiling was arched with rich, oaken beams, giving the central below-decks room an appropriately nautical feel. She'd visited the factory, studied the plans, and knew the beams were fake, but the effect was perfect. She loved waking up to the gentle motion of the yacht in her owner's stateroom, and loved even more the fun of climbing up to the open flying bridge in the morning with a cup of coffee and the breeze in her face.

For no particular reason, Gracie looked at the phone to the left of the bed, her eyes fixating on it just before it rang.

She reached for it, loving the feeling of sliding her trim body across the sheets again as she caught sight of the time and felt a burst of guilt.

Omigod! Nine already!

The plan had been to get up at seven, exercise, and get back to work for the Rosens. The possibility that April or Rachel might be on the other end of the ringing phone crossed her mind as she pulled the receiver to her ear and rolled to a sitting position.

"Hello?"

"Gracie?" The voice was deep, somewhat gruff, and the owner clearly unhappy, all of the conclusions conveyed in a single word.

"Yes?"

"This is Ben Janssen, your managing partner."

"Yes, sir, Mr. Janssen. Good morning."

"Well, not so good as all that, Gracie. I'll be frank. I'm pretty pissed off at you right now."

She felt a wave of adrenaline course through her bloodstream, mental cautions mixing with conflicting loyalties underlaid with an intense desire not to be in trouble with her firm.

"Why, Mr. Janssen? I mean, I'll apologize in advance for anything I've done wrong, but—"

"Look, there are protocols in a major law firm, young lady, especially when it comes to asking big clients for favors, and you didn't just cross the line, you blew across it."

Gracie fought to keep her voice even and friendly, but she could feel her stomach fluttering, the vibrations threatening to rattle her diaphragm and progress to a shaky voice. "You mean Bernie Ashad, sir?"

"Of course I mean Ashad, for God's sake. Who the hell told you it was okay to go shaking your cute little tail at one of our most important clients to get him to help you on a completely personal matter? Hell, I ought to can your ass right here, right now."

"Mr. Janssen, in no way did I—as you put it—shake my tail at anyone, least of all Mr. Ashad. I—"

"I don't care what the hell you told him."

"Sir? Please! You've launched a full-scale attack on my actions, along with some rather raw sexual innuendos, and I believe I should have the opportunity to defend myself."

There was momentary silence on the other end and she could hear the receiver being shifted to his other ear.

"All right. Go ahead."

"Thank you. The facts are, sir, that I had a call from Mr. Ashad on Tuesday wanting to set a time for a conference call between us on the lease for the commercial property in Lancaster, Pennsylvania, I've been working on, and one of the times he suggested conflicted with the personal matter you referred to. I had requested and received approval from Dick Walsh to be gone that afternoon, and I requested we set the conference time two days hence. He said that was fine, remarked that I sounded worried, and asked why. We've met and had dinner as lawyer and client, and I believe he respects me. I told him in very brief detail about my best friend's problem—her father's problem in Alaska—and he kept pressing me for details. I provided those details. I volunteered one thing and one thing only in that call, and that was the fact that I was in need of finding a salvage firm that could raise a sunken aircraft. He said his equipment was too big and far away, but he knew just the man to call in Valdez, and I later acted on that recommendation."

"Yeah, well, then you apparently asked him to go fish out some airplane for free."

Gracie could feel her insides vibrating with tension and fear, but she fought hard to control her voice, barely succeeding.

He is not going to make me come apart!

"Mr. Janssen, that is entirely incorrect. I would never do such a thing, and I can't believe Mr. Ashad would say I did."

Janssen was silent, practicing his well-honed ability to draw out statements people didn't want to make. April cautioned herself not to fall for it.

"What happened," she continued, "is that Mr. Ashad called me on Wednesday and asked how things were going with the Alaska dilemma affecting the Rosens. I appreciated the call and I told him about it briefly, and I also discussed his business and the progress of the lease negotiations. When we finished with the subject of the lease, he asked me to call him if I needed any more help or advice for the Rosens. On Friday, having been given leave again by Dick

Walsh to go file for a TRO against the government for Captain Rosen, I took Mr. Ashad up on the offer, and called and asked him if the Rosens could hire his people for a salvage operation. That's 'hire,' Mr. Janssen, not 'donate.' He wouldn't hear of it. He said he'd been surprised to find one of his ships was sailing through the area, and if I'd give him the coordinates of the wreckage, they'd see what could be done. I again promised normal compensation by the Rosens and he told me their money was, as he put it, 'no good,' and that all he expected was my letting him take me to dinner the next time he's in Seattle. When I had dinner with him before, he was a perfect gentleman and there was no hint of sexual interest or intent, nor is there now, so I agreed."

"Are you through?" he asked in a sarcastic tone.

"I'm . . . finished relating to you precisely what happened, sir. And may I ask you a question?"

"Go ahead."

"Does any of what I just told you vary in any particular to what Mr. Ashad has told you?"

Another long pause hung on the line between them as Gracie listened to her heart pound in her ears. She'd fought so hard for the position at Janssen and Pruzan, the last thing she wanted was to lose it, especially with the onus of being indirectly called a tail-wagging slut.

There was a long sigh on the other end. "No. He didn't say anything different. He just didn't tell me enough, as usual."

"Sir, I'm extremely sorry if I did cross a line. You've given us excellent advice on how to nurture and develop a working relationship with our clients, and I was only trying to follow that advice."

"Look, you're young and somewhat naive, Gracie. Bernie is a . . . a . . . for want of a better phrase, a serial cad, okay? That's an old term meaning a guy who uses women sexually and shamelessly. Anything female and attractive and he turns on the charm and starts the chase. To him a female attorney is simply a sexual challenge, not his counselor."

"Why was I assigned to him, then, sir?"

"Good question. I hadn't realized you were. Who paired you up?"

"I don't know. I remember Dick Walsh being somewhat surprised."

There was a rude laugh on the other end. "Yeah, I bet Dick was shocked. Dick's a decent guy. I'm going to find out and fry whoever did this because—and I'm going to say something here I'll deny if you ever try to rub my nose in it—whoever assigned you to Ashad is a sexist comedian who wanted to see how fast Bernie could nail you."

"Well, I can assure you that no such thing has, or will happen."

"You ever received a five-hundred-thousand-dollar bracelet as a thank-you-for-dinner gift?"

"Wha . . . what? No!"

"Would it turn your head? Make you just a little inclined to stay the night?"

"I . . . honestly have no idea what I'd do, besides report it to the firm, if he was a client."

"Ever had some handsome, incredibly rich guy offer to buy you a million-dollar villa somewhere if you'll just take a six-month sabbatical and travel with him?"

"Of course not."

"Well, those are just two of the ploys he's used on women at our firm in the past. I lost my secretary—who later bore him a child in absentia—to the bracelet scam. Oh, he took the bracelet back, by the way. And then there was our young female attorney associate who got stars in her eyes and ran off with him for six months, lost her job, and was literally left penniless in Maracaibo, Venezuela. She woke up alone in a seedy hotel room one morning with no passport, no clothes, and no money, next to some local laborer who hadn't had his annual bath that year. Bernie thought it was hilarious, the sick bastard. He'd drugged her, effectively sold her to the guy, and flew off to Europe in his jet. It was his twisted way of saying goodbye."

"My God."

"Look, Gracie, you've got great promise as a lawyer, and I'm sorry if I've broadsided you here, but I'm warning you, stay strictly away from this guy except as an attorney, and under no circumstances get yourself in his debt. Understood?"

"What do I do if he's already helped my friends and calls back?"

"Call me as soon as he trots out the kicker—what he wants in return. It'll sound innocent. Don't fall for it, or I'll fire your ass. Understood?"

"Yes, sir."

"And regardless of who the client is, if you're going to ask for anything from one of our big payers in the future, ask Dick or me first. That's an order."

"Yes, sir."

"Good. See you Monday."

The line went dead.

Gracie sat in shock for several minutes, her mind replaying every nuance of the conversation, her faith in her previous impression and judgment of Ashad thoroughly shaken. She started to go up the companionway to the galley before realizing she was wearing nothing. She grabbed a terrycloth robe and pulled it around her, still feeling the hole in the pit of her stomach. She'd been getting nothing but praise from Walsh and all the other established members of the firm, and in one fell swoop she'd angered and dismayed the number-one senior lawyer in the whole place.

He thinks I'm a brainless slut! she thought, feeling her face flush at the embarrassment of being naive enough to believe Ashad's sincerity. She could always spot phonies. April was the one who got sucked in all the time. How could she have stumbled with Ashad?

The phone was ringing again and the sound sent a flash of apprehension through her. Was Janssen calling back?

She pulled the galley extension to her ear, keeping her voice as normal as possible.

"This is Gracie."

"Gracie, thank God! This is Rachel. You have a minute?"

"Of course, Rachel. You sound stressed."

"Oh, Gracie! Arlie's *gone!*"

She almost howled the last word, stabbing more adrenaline into Gracie as she tried to decipher what the word "gone" meant and shuddered at the possibilities.

"He just took off this morning with no word on where he was going."

"Took off? Oh my God, he's not *flying,* is he?"

"No . . . at least I don't think so. He took the car, one of the cars, and . . . I just thought he was getting up to go to the bathroom, you know?"

"Yeah."

"Before dawn, and I rolled over and snoozed a few minutes, until I heard a car leaving."

"No notes or messages left in the kitchen?"

"No! That's what scares me! Gracie, what should we do?"

"He take the jeep?"

"No. The Infiniti."

"Does it have a phone?"

"No."

"Have you called around?"

"Yes. All our neighbors. The airport. His favorite places in Port Angeles."

"What's that great little bookstore all the pilots love?"

"Port Book and News. I called. They haven't seen him!"

"Okay, look, don't panic, Rachel. The captain's just upset. He's probably just gone off to think."

"Not in all our years together, Gracie, has he ever turned away from me when he was upset or scared. I'm terrified!"

"Stay by the phone, okay? Keep your cell phone on, too. Or did he take it?"

"No. It's here."

"Keep it on. Give me a few minutes to think and I'll call you back."

"Okay."

Gracie replaced the receiver and stepped back to lean against the rear of the wheelhouse couch between the galley and the yacht's bridge, trying to control the spinning in her head. She had never known Arlie Rosen to leave Rachel out of anything except his time on duty in a 747, but the dark, unspoken worry that he might be planning something as extreme as suicide simply didn't make sense. The captain had always been the ranking optimist, a man in love with life. She could imagine him catastrophically despondent, but not to the point of hurting himself, and never to the point of committing what Gracie had always considered the ultimate act of selfishness, which would be to leave Rachel behind.

Thank God it's Saturday! she thought, struggling to decide what, if anything, she could and should do. The Rosens' Cherokee was still at Boeing Field, and although the morning was cloudy, there was a high overcast. She could fly it over and be in Sequim within an hour and a half, but what then?

Think, girl! Gracie commanded herself. She shut her eyes, trying to grab a fleeting memory hanging just out of reach, a peaceful place Arlie Rosen had talked about once. Or was she imagining it?

Dammit! The thought wouldn't come, no matter how much she struggled.

Okay, what's that technique April uses? Think of the question and let it go like a search engine. She let the essence of the question roll around in her mind for a few seconds, then purposely shifted her thoughts away.

I can't sit here on the boat. She turned and moved back down to the lower deck to fix her hair and get dressed as fast as possible, calculating the route to the airport. She would call Rachel back on the way, as well as call the corporate terminal to have the plane fueled. April had left the key at their service desk.

Hurricane Ridge!

The name popped into her mind without warning. A road leading south into the Olympic Mountains from Port Angeles wound its way to the top of a windswept promontory called Hurricane Ridge, and the place had fascinated him. What were his words? She recalled them suddenly, and they made the need to find him all the more urgent.

"It's a launching pad for the soul, Gracie," she recalled his saying. "It's windswept and beautiful. If there is a perfect point on this beautiful planet from which one could leave this life and just step into the clouds, that would be it."

THIRTY-SIX

Ready, April?"

Scott McDermott's voice sounded strong and confident, but April had seen his hand vibrating slightly as he held the yoke of the Widgeon and tried to pretend the impending takeoff was no big deal.

She nodded.

"Okay. Call out my airspeed."

His hand was already on the throttles that protruded from the ceiling of the cockpit, and he pushed them forward now to max power, holding the control yoke full to the right as both engines rose to a roar, and the amphibian began moving forward through the icy waters, a bow wave of water cascading over the nose and the windshield, obscuring everything.

They moved past the massive icebergs Scott had shoved out of the way with the Widgeon's nose, the effect one of a runway between a row of twenty-story buildings.

Quickly the bow wave diminished and they could see. Scott pulsed the yoke, and April felt the Widgeon jump higher in the water, the hull no longer floating but now planing along the surface "on the step" as they accelerated.

"There's forty," she called over the roar.

She could see the other end of the mountain lake coming at them, its lip only eight to ten feet above the water's surface, but the embankment from water to lip was catastrophically steep. If they weren't high enough out of the water to clear the berm, the impact would probably kill them.

"Fifty-five!" she said. "Sixty . . . sixty-five."

The end of the lake was looming close, and she felt herself mentally tensing.

"Seventy."

Without warning Scott yanked both throttles to idle and pulled the yoke as far back as it would go, letting the Widgeon sink back into the water in a cascade of spray, the hydrodynamic pressure rapidly slowing them as they floated over the remaining distance to the western end.

He kicked the left rudder at the last second, swinging the nose parallel to the embankment with several yards to spare.

"We can't make it?" April asked.

Scott nodded. "Not enough room that time."

"That time?"

He turned to her, his tone matter of fact. "Yeah. We need more distance."

Scott continued the turn to the left, aiming at the spot on the other end from where they'd started the takeoff attempt.

"Okay. How are we going to construct more distance? Avalanche? Earthquake? Tectonic event?"

Scott shook his head. "There's another method we can use, April. We almost had enough that time, but . . . I just needed another ten miles per hour."

"You're not seriously suggesting we try that again?"

"Yep. I'm not leaving this bird up here on this lake."

"We wait for more wind, then?" she asked.

"That's one way, but it's not likely to come."

"Then how? Come on, Scott, you're scaring me."

"I'll show you. It's an old trick."

"Does it work?"

"Sometimes."

"I'd rather not crash, you know. I'm allergic to disintegrating airplanes."

"Me, too. Crashing usually screws up my whole day."

"Usually? You mean you've crashed before?"

"Of course. Goes with the territory."

"Seriously?"

He grinned. "Been killed up here a bunch of times."

"Uh-huh."

She was gripping the sides of her seat again, wanting to be airborne, but rapidly losing faith in the technical possibility. "Well, I can promise that if you kill me trying to take off, I'll never go out with you."

He looked at her and laughed. "Then I'll assume the converse is true."

"Sorry?"

"If I *don't* kill you, you're committed to going out with me, and that's one hell of an incentive." He raised a finger for silence as they approached the end of the lake and swung the Widgeon to the right in an unexpected direction, moving nearly a hundred yards around the backside of one of the icebergs before spinning the amphibian around.

"Okay."

"Okay, what? We're aimed across the narrow part of the lake, if you haven't noticed. We're heading south. The so-called runway is due east. We can't take off like this."

"No, but if we use a sideways run to gain speed, then angle left around that berg to the middle of the channel we created, then head east, we'll get a better start."

"Oh."

"Besides, the Widgeon has a bad habit of trying to dig her left pontoon in the water, and this helps keep that from happening,"

"Okay."

"It'll work, April. We'll get up on the step before the turn."

"Don't you dare say 'trust me' again."

Once more Scott gripped the overhead throttles and moved them forward. The Widgeon began plowing through the water, moving past one of the massive icebergs as the aircraft rose on the step. He worked the left rudder, swinging the Widgeon back to the original easterly heading, the airspeed already at twenty-five knots by the time he steadied the course.

"Forty-five," April announced. She could see the end looming once more, but this time it seemed a bit more distant.

"Fifty-five."

The engines were roaring and the throttles firewalled.

"Sixty-five . . . rising slowly to seventy . . . there's seventy-five!"

They were at almost the same place as before, but this time the speed was obviously greater. Scott's hand held the throttles full forward, his left hand on the yoke, but not pulling.

"Scott, pull us up! Eighty. Scott?"

The end of the lake loomed ominously. Suddenly the yoke came back and the nose popped up to a frightening angle as the Widgeon obediently leaped free of the water, rising to what seemed insufficient altitude to make it over the embankment.

The sound of the metal hull brushing the upper crust of snow and ice on the edge of the embankment was unmistakable and gentle, the noise little more than that of a pine branch brushing the plane. A spray of white from the glancing blow showered the air to the right and was gone as the slope ahead dropped out from under them. Scott pulsed the yoke forward, dropping the Widgeon's nose as the stall warning horn shut off, and the aircraft traded altitude for airspeed and stabilized as a flying machine once again. He banked slightly to the left, following the downslope of the glacier as he built more airspeed, holding them under the overcast layer of clouds and heading for the massive face of the glacier several miles to the east.

When they'd gained more than a hundred feet over the ice, Scott looked at her with what was supposed to be a nonchalant grin, the effect betrayed by the twitching muscle in his jaw and the slight flutter in his right hand.

She smiled shakily and nodded.

When the face of the glacier was behind them, Scott dropped the Widgeon to less than fifty feet above the water and hugged the coastline as they headed northeast, crossing an open channel to stay equally close to another island. He checked his GPS display and wove an unpredictable course to the rendezvous point.

As arranged by phone during the night, Jim Dobler was waiting for them twenty minutes later in the appointed cove. Scott flew overhead, confirming the identification, before pulling up for a tight turn back into the wind. They touched down smoothly in the protected waters of the little inlet.

There had been no sign of any fighters out searching for them and no more radio calls on the guard frequency, but Scott had kept the radar and his transponder off just in case.

"You want me to get the bow line this time?" April asked as he reached to the overhead panel and brought the mixtures to full lean, killing both engines.

"Yeah, thanks."

She pulled the Velcro-ed curtain back from the small alcove in front of her copilot seat and released her seat belt, ducking under the instrument panel into the tiny passageway to the nose and popping open the hatch in time to catch the line Jim threw to them. Scott slid back the pilot's-side window as Jim waved.

"I brought the tarp, Scott."

"Tarp?" April asked as she stood up in the nose hatch.

"To cover the airplane. We'll tie 'er up to my tug."

"We're towing the airplane?" she asked.

"No. We're going in the small boat." Jim pointed over his shoulder to an eighteen-foot-long wooden whaling boat sitting suspended in a sling held by a deck crane. Compared to the tug or the Widgeon, which was thirty-nine feet long, the boat looked puny and dangerous. April recalled the discussion on the satellite phone, but somehow had expected a larger vessel for the open ocean.

"The Coasties can't see this one on radar."

It took twenty minutes to secure and cover the Widgeon. Jim and Scott cranked the wooden-hulled boat into the water, and Scott climbed aboard to load the gear and check the GPS and the satellite phone, as well as test the portable Honda generator. After several minutes of intensive effort he stood up and flashed Jim the thumbs-up sign.

The temperature was hovering around sixty and the winds were light, but with the boat pushing through the waves at fifteen knots, April had to zip her parka to stay warm, and Scott noticed.

"You'd be warmer back here, April," he called out. April turned from her position in the front of the open boat and shook her head.

"This most wonderfully clears the mind," she said, smiling at him.

"Ah, Samuel Johnson. Seventeen hundred something."

She nodded, her smile even larger. "An educated man. I'm impressed."

"Impressed, huh? Guess that's better than being surprised," Scott said out of the side of his mouth to Jim. He got up and moved forward with two paper cups and one of the Thermos bottles Jim had prepared. He sat down beside her and poured two steaming cups of coffee.

"As I recall," he said, handing her a cup, his eyes on the gray of the horizon as the boat pitched gently up and down. "Johnson's exact quote was, 'Depend upon it, sir, when a man knows he is to be hanged in a fortnight, it concentrates his mind wonderfully.' I don't know exactly what year that was spoken, but it came from a book about him called *Life of Johnson.*"

"It was written by a fellow named Boswell," she said. "I know. I was taking liberties with the quote."

"Shameful."

She sipped the fragrant liquid, wondering why coffee always tasted so much better in the open, even in a paper cup.

"Where did you go to college, Scott?"

"Oh, a little liberal arts school on the upper East Coast."

"Did it have a name?"

He nodded.

April chuckled. "Scott, there's nothing wrong with getting your degree from some unknown little liberal arts school. Sometimes they can be better than the big expensive schools."

"Okay." He turned away from the horizon to look at her all hunkered down over her coffee cup, her raven hair blowing in the steady breeze, her eyes sparkling. "Where'd *you* go to school, April?" he asked.

"University of Washington. But tell me yours."

"Is it important?"

"No. But now you've got me curious."

"It didn't affect me much. I managed to forget most everything I learned when I got my commission."

"Aha! Navy ROTC?"

"No."

"Annapolis?"

"Please! Do I impress you as Annapolis material?"

"You never know. You could be in rebellion."

"No. I barely made it through officer school. Emphasis on the 'barely.' I was in the I-hate-regimentation division. They'd order me to make my bed so they could bounce a quarter off it, and I would, and then sleep on the floor for six weeks so I wouldn't have to disturb my work."

"You were going to tell me the name of your alma mater," April prompted again, "even if it was small and obscure, I'm sure it was a very good school."

"It was."

"So, what was the name?"

"Princeton."

"*Princeton?*"

"Yeah."

"*The* Princeton?"

"I think probably there's just one." He smiled.

"And I was starting to feel sorry for you for being academically deprived."

Jim called from the stern and they turned to see him pointing to the left.

"Large vessel over there."

"What kind?" Scott called.

"Too small for a tanker. Not the right size for a Coast Guard cutter. Might be that same ship out of Adak you recognized Thursday."

"Can they see us?" April asked in some alarm.

Jim shook his head. "Not if we hold this course. But if they're patrolling, they'll spot us if we take too long over the wreck."

Scott had moved back to check the handheld GPS receiver Jim was watching. "Another three miles?"

Jim nodded. "Why don't you two get the generator going and make everything ready, then drop the camera and light bar over the side to about two hundred feet and start the video recorder. That way when we get there, we'll save a bunch of time."

April was looking up and pointing.

"What?" Scott asked.

"Blue sky."

He followed her gaze, noting the ragged end of the overcast rapidly blowing east and leaving a vista of higher cumulus clouds admitting a brilliant shaft of sunlight.

"Beautiful, isn't it?" she prompted, her eyes on the sky as his refocused on her.

"Sure is," he said, mostly under his breath.

The electrical generator was running and the color TV camera holding at a depth of two hundred feet as they closed on the point where the Albatross had sunk.

"Another thirty yards, Jim," Scott said, calling down the numbers. "Reverse her."

Jim slowed the outboard and shifted to reverse, throttling up until the GPS velocity readout hit zero.

"Perfect."

"We're there?" Jim asked.

"Dead over where we were before." He moved to April's side. "Why don't you watch the monitor now while I let the camera down to the same depth. When we spot the wreckage, we'll work it around to see that right engine and prop."

April seated herself in front of the color monitor and draped a small tarp over her head and the entire unit while Scott finished playing out the line. Jim began moving the boat at dead-slow speed, watching the GPS screen and crisscrossing the targeted coordinates.

"Anything, April?" Scott called.

Her disembodied voice came from beneath the tarp. "I see ocean floor, fish, and weeds, but no sign of the airplane."

Jim reversed course and came back fifty yards to the north, parallel to their first pass, reversing again on the other side. Still April could spot nothing resembling the Albatross wreckage.

"Scott, are you absolutely sure we have the right coordinates?" April asked thirty minutes later.

"If you recall, April, you wrote them down yourself and triple-checked them."

"Oh. Yeah. And you're sure the GPS is working, right?"

"It checks normal. Look, let's start running the pattern again at right angles. We were probably just lucky the first time."

Jim worked the boat back to the middle of the targeted coordinates and was lining up for a north-south search sequence when he once again pointed to the horizon.

"We've got company, boys and girls."

"Shit," Scott muttered, following his gaze.

"I think that one is Coast Guard," Jim replied. "Good news is, they're not aiming for us, at least not yet."

Scott turned his attention to the lump under the tarp. "April, you're not asleep under there, are you?" Scott asked.

"No."

"Just checking."

"I'm seeing zip, but I heard what you said. They're not coming toward us?"

"Not yet."

It was almost an hour later when April emerged from under the tarp, blinking and shaking her head. "Could a sunken airplane just drift away?"

"Well, you saw it before on the screen, April," Jim said. "Did it look like it was well seated in the sand on the bottom?"

She nodded.

"I don't know of any current around here strong enough to move it."

"Let's try the whole grid again, starting with a wider circle," she said, and once more Jim began piloting the wooden boat to the starting position and noting the coordinates on his log. They were crossing the precise middle of the coordinates when she yelped something inaudible from beneath the tarp.

"What?" Scott asked.

"I said, hold it! Hold your heading, stop the boat."

THIRTY-SEVEN

Mike Sanborn wheeled his jeep around the parking lot for the second time in an hour, looking for the man he'd spotted on the first circuit.

He's still there. Just sitting down the slope a bit.

He parked and pulled on the government jeep's parking brake, remembering to grab his ranger hat from the right front seat before getting out. The chief ranger was always riding him about the hat, which he more or less hated. It should be on the top shelf of his bookcase on display, he thought, not on his head. He was too barrel-chested and stocky to wear the damn thing. He had to agree with the innumerable kids who'd pointed to him and his full, black beard and turned excitedly to their parents to announce that there really was a Smokey the Bear. It was a part of the act he could do without.

Mike closed the door behind him and stuffed his hands in his pants pockets to foster a casual air.

Not that it seemed to matter. The man he was concerned about had his back to the parking area and was just staring off to the northeast, where Mount Baker could be seen rising majestically into an unusually blue sky.

Mike turned to look for Mount Rainier to the southeast, forgetting that the Pacific Northwest's preeminent volcano couldn't be seen from where he was standing.

The hat threatened to blow off as a twenty-knot gust of wind tugged at it from behind. *We did name it Hurricane Ridge, after all,* he laughed to himself.

Mike stepped over the guardrail and moved down the slope until he was standing alongside the seated figure, a man in his late fifties, he figured.

"Hello there," Mike said, keeping his eyes on the horizon, then turning to the fellow. "You ever see it so beautiful up here?"

The visitor looked up, recognizing the uniform and smiling thinly as he nodded. "Yeah. It's something."

"Mind if I join you?" Mike asked, sensing a deep sadness, his training as a counselor a decade earlier coming on-line.

The man was looking over at him again. "Am I not supposed to be here?"

"Oh, no," Mike said quickly. "You're just fine. The park's open."

"Then . . . if you'll forgive my being antisocial, I'd really like to be alone."

Mike felt himself nodding thoughtfully, but unwilling to turn away as he kicked at a small rock with the toe of his highly polished shoe. "Ah, you know, I realize I'm prying, but sometimes when someone is feeling really down, or . . . or when something's really wrong, it can help to talk with a complete stranger."

"Not today. Please. I appreciate your concern, but . . . not now."

Mike nodded again, his eyes on the ground. "Okay. I, ah, wish you well, sir."

The sound of an aircraft in the distance caught Mike's attention and he hesitated, watching the way the man instantly looked in that direction, his eyes tracking the single-engine aircraft as it approached the ridge at a slightly higher altitude. *He's a little low,* the ranger noted, recalling the rule that prohibited private pilots from flying closer than two thousand feet over a national park. But being a cop was the part of the job he never liked. So what if the pilot was a bit low, as long as he didn't scare or endanger anyone? He would be the last ranger interested in turning him in, though there were a few of his brethren who would leap at the chance.

Mike turned and began walking back up the slope toward the jeep, but the rising buzz of the private plane caused him to turn again to watch the approach.

The plane was a low-wing version, and the seated man had unfolded his arms now as he watched it approach, his interest obviously high. Mike unconsciously grabbed his hat once again as another heavy gust blew across the ridge. The little plane was bucking the strong winds as well. He could see its wings rocking, its speed diminished against the headwind, almost crawling toward them with at least a thousand feet to spare vertically. The pilot guided it to within a quarter mile and then banked sharply to the right and almost immediately turned back, as if he wanted to get a close view of the parking area and the ridge from the left seat. Mike squinted hard as he looked at the aircraft, almost imagining he could make out a face in the left window.

The man was on his feet now, shading his eyes against the sun and looking at the plane as if he might recognize it. Mike expected him to wave, but instead the man sat back down as the aircraft turned and disappeared off to the north, folding his arms around his legs again as before, his body rocking back and forth gently.

Mike made a mental note to cruise by again in an hour. There was a dangerous drop-off very close by, and suicidal visitors were not unknown to the park.

Gracie closed the Cherokee's throttle as she flared over the Sequim Valley runway, letting the main gear of the craft kiss its home landing strip again. She could see Rachel standing by the hangar. She ran the engine shutdown check as Rachel climbed up on the wing and opened the door.

"Gracie, thank you for coming, honey!"

"I think I spotted him on Hurricane Ridge. The color of the car seemed right. Only two in the parking area, and one was a ranger's jeep. Someone was standing down the way a bit. I think it was the captain, and we need to get up there."

Rachel backed away from the door as Gracie followed, closing the Cherokee's door behind her and locking it before sprinting across to the car and climbing in the passenger side, then jumping out again before Rachel could get behind the wheel.

"You mind if I drive?" Gracie asked.

Rachel hesitated in thought and looked down at the keys, before thrusting them toward Gracie.

"It would be smarter right now. I'm pretty wrought up."

Gracie waited until she heard the click of Rachel's seat belt, her feelings alternating between the heartache of what Rachel was going through—hurt and apprehension—and her own continuous embarrassment over being chewed out by Ben Janssen a few hours before. All of it, Gracie reminded herself, didn't compare to the nightmarish pain that had propelled the captain to Hurricane Ridge.

"Hurry, Gracie," Rachel said quietly, her hand massaging her forehead, her eyes closed. "Please."

SOUTHWEST OF PRINCE WILLIAM SOUND

With the wooden boat hauled onto Jim Dobler's tug, Scott McDermott looked at his watch and turned to April, who was helping stow the various ropes they'd used.

"You're sure the pieces you saw were from your dad's plane?"

"Yes. They had the same colors, and I saw the same piece of cowling before, when the plane was there. They took it. No question."

Scott fell silent for a few seconds. "I've got about four hours' fuel, and I'm going to use it to check out any ships that went through this area in the past six hours."

April sighed and wiped her forehead, her parka open in the cool breeze.

"You really think it could have happened this morning?"

"Yes. Yesterday, when we flew by, there were no ships in the area I could see, and whoever did this probably wouldn't have tried a night recovery."

Jim had joined them, wiping his hands on an oily rag that was making them even dirtier.

"Am I right, Jim?"

"About a night recovery? Not advisable but not impossible. I think you're probably wasting your time, Scott. Once someone hauls wreckage like that up on deck, they can take off at ten to fifteen knots and cover a lot of distance. Could be halfway to anywhere by now." He turned and left to take care of another pre-departure duty.

"I've got to try," Scott said.

"Okay," April replied, fatigue vying with disappointment. "Let's go."

"No. April, I think you ought to go back with Jim."

"Why? I'm paying you."

He smiled and nodded, glancing off to sea for a few moments.

"Yeah, well, there are times I like to fly alone, and this one's on me, okay?"

She cocked her head. "Straight up, Scott, why don't you want me along?"

"First, I think you'll be more productive and relaxed with Jim."

"That's a smokescreen. What else?"

"Because I may press a few limits and I don't necessarily want passengers or witnesses, okay?"

April nodded. "That I understand. You have the satellite phone. Can you call if you spot someone churning away with a wrecked Albatross on deck?"

"Immediately."

"Because, otherwise, I think we're screwed. Without that tape, or the wreckage, I've got zip to convince the FAA they're wrong about my dad."

Scott put his hands on April's shoulders and drew her closer. She looked up at him and started to speak.

"It's going to be okay, April. I know it."

"Well . . . I can hope," she said. He could see she was rapidly losing the battle to stay composed, the adrenaline and exertion and disbelief of finding the wreckage gone washing past her emotional limits and down her face. She closed her eyes and let him enfold her, her head on his chest. Scott tightened his arms around her and rocked her gently, patting her as she sobbed. There were disturbing feelings there competing for his attention. Knight-to-the-rescue feelings, and more. But they were far too confusing, and he forced himself to shove the deeper emotions aside and concentrate on the mission as he waited for her tears to subside.

ANCHORAGE, ALASKA

The tenor saxophone had been staring him down for weeks, sitting on its stand in the corner of his living room, but Ben had put off trying to play it until the crunch at work was over. That, as he reminded himself, had followed the year-long period of grief and agony over losing Lisa, a year in which all the music in his soul had gone silent.

He sat now on the black leather couch, staring back at the instrument he'd played so well for so long, recalling the times Lisa had pushed him to take it downtown to a restaurant that featured blues and jazz every Sunday where he'd join the paid musicians he knew for a few sets. He'd loved those sessions, all the more because of Lisa's smiling face looking up at him from the nearest table, her lips mouthing suggestive things only they understood until neither of them could stand it. A hurried trip back home and a trail of clothes from the garage to the bedroom made those wonderful nights so memorable. The saxophone had been the midwife to those evenings. "The joy of sax!" Lisa had dubbed it.

Sometimes, Ben recalled, they hadn't made it home before their passion for each other overwhelmed them. The memory of several risky sessions in the backseat of their car made him smile.

He knew what she would say now about the sax, if she could peek into his life for a moment: "Play it for *me!*" she would tell him. "Life goes on."

And now his last excuse for putting it off was apparently gone.

Ben sighed and got up, intending to pick up the sax and begin the long process of getting back his proficiency as a musician, but a glimpse of his computer screen flashing at his desk in the corner stole his attention.

Later, he mouthed to the sax, turning instead to his desk, where the screen was urgently reporting that new e-mail had arrived.

Ben triggered the appropriate keys, recognizing the communiqué as unwanted spam. He deleted it and began to turn away when an idea flitted across his mind. He triggered a web search engine and punched up his list of favorite websites, scrolling down until he found the one that provided a direct link to the FAA's command center in Herndon, Virginia, a program that let anyone track any airborne aircraft.

He found the right page and queried the database, pleased to see that he could effectively replay a particular point from the previous Monday evening, and entered the time they had begun plunging toward the Gulf of Alaska.

Seconds rolled by before the screen lit up with the response from the FAA's computers, and he worked to zoom in on the appropriate area.

He could find nothing with the Gulfstream's call sign, Sage 10, but there was one for the AWACS listed as Crown 12. He pushed the program forward in time, watching the blip designating the AWACS move steadily toward the east at the very time the Gulfstream, with him in it, would have been diving toward the water.

The article he'd seen in the *Anchorage Times* hadn't given a call sign for the lost amphibian, but it didn't seem to matter. Without a datablock, he couldn't tell where the Gulfstream was anyway.

I should have known. This is a time waster.

Ben exited the program and got up, then sat down again, wondering if there was a way to get raw air traffic control data from recent days.

There was a possibility, he decided, that an old friend and reformed hacker named Hank Boston might know a path. Hank, whose infamous screen name was Mastermouse, had quit breaking into computers about two steps ahead of the FBI in the late eighties, and had shifted instead to a lucrative business in protecting computers from people like himself. Ben chuckled at the thought that he'd learned more about computing from the University of Mastermouse than from Caltech. The best part was how much Hank loved airplanes. If there was a way to see what the FAA's radars had recorded, Hank would know how. Any contact, however, might be monitored, which meant he had to be very careful not to reveal too much.

It might as well be in writing, Ben concluded, pulling an e-mail form onto his computer screen and typing in a message. The effort was probably wasted, he told himself. Hank could be on vacation, in jail, or in some public arcade hunched over a computer game, oblivious to the rest of the world while he saved the earth from the fifty-thousandth alien attack he'd repulsed—for a half-dollar per game.

He sent the e-mail and sat in thought for a moment, wondering what was motivating him so urgently to find out whether the lost amphibian had been close to Sage 10 Monday night. The answer was ridiculously simple and naive and altruistic: revulsion at a senior pilot losing his livelihood to the unknown force of a passing aircraft whose interference might be cloaked in the secrecy of a black project. It was too much to bear, and too great a price to pay. It wasn't his problem, of course, but in some ways it seemed like it. It was as if the ultimate cause of the Gulfstream's dive had been *his* failure to spot the flaws in the program.

Hey! Don't forget the fatal flaw was the autopilot system. You had nothing to do with that.

But the expected relief from feelings of guilt wouldn't come.

A "new message waiting" notice was flashing on the screen. Ben clicked through the appropriate sequence to bring up the email, which was from Hank.

That was fast! he thought.

The message was vintage Hank:

Good to hear from you, Benji! Yes, I have a backdoor for what you need, though I wouldn't trust just anyone. They keep those tapes on computer in several places. I know the one they seldom guard. Give me 30 minutes and I'll send you a temporary web address that will interface for precisely 12 minutes. After that, it goes "poof" and can't be used again. Be ready with the right questions, among which are not "How did you do this?" Naturally, if you or any of those minions around you are caught or chastised, I will expect you to self-destruct. Goes for that damned cat of yours, too!
Mastermouse

As promised, within a half hour the follow-up e-mail arrived with a lengthy address and additional instructions, which Ben carefully entered. A long listing of database storage disks covering various dates and radar sites suddenly appeared under the FAA's logo, and he tried to ignore the reality that somehow he was almost instantly inside an FAA computer.

The names of the various air traffic radar sites were unfamiliar, but he called up an Alaska map and quickly scanned back and forth between the place names for the area south of Valdez and what was on the radar list. One name in particular stood out, and he selected it. The screen indicated a download of the requested clip, and Ben waited in apprehension, wondering if there was any way the altered identification codes his computer was sending could be discovered and the connection traced back to him.

The download complete, Ben broke the connection, collapsing the communications program and changing his computer's individual ID code back to normal. He called up the radar information for

Monday night then and worked to convert the format to something he could display, finally succeeding. A few more keystrokes and the picture enlarged to full size before him, each recorded sweep of the radar beam bringing a vastly clearer picture than what he'd seen from Herndon.

This was, after all, the raw data. He worked to refine it before identifying the Gulfstream, a task that proved simple once he'd located the AWACS on the screen.

Ben worked through the data, isolating the various blips as they appeared and disappeared, creating projections of their positions and moving them back and forth until the conclusion became obvious.

My God, if that's the amphibian coming from the southeast to the northwest, we crossed right over or under him at fifty feet! And immediately after that encounter with us, he disappeared for good.

The newspaper article he'd cut out earlier about the crash was sitting next to the keyboard. He reread it now, memorizing the name of the grounded pilot and querying an on-line phone book for his phone number.

Rosen, Arlie. Sequim, Washington. The phone number followed.

Ben copied down the number and punched it into the desk phone before thinking about the possibility that Uniwave—or someone else—might be bugging it. He hung up quickly. The cell phone would be safer, though even digital phones could be monitored by sophisticated agencies. Ben dialed the number and heard the line ring through to a voice mail message. "Ah, Captain Rosen, this is . . . Ben Cole in Alaska. I'm in Anchorage, and I noticed an article about the loss of your aircraft earlier this week, and there's something I think you need to know as soon as possible." He left his number and broke the connection, not entirely sure what he would have said had the pilot answered in person.

Schroedinger was sitting on the adjacent windowsill, watching him with intense disinterest, and Ben looked at him thoughtfully.

"So what do I say to him, boy, when he calls back? 'Hi, I'm with a government project I can tell you nothing about, but Monday a private jet registered somewhere else making a flight that officially never existed may have theoretically knocked you out of the sky? All you have to do is illegally hack into a government computer and risk ten years in prison and you'll find the evidence?' Not exactly a brilliant move." Ben shook his head in true confusion, acutely aware of the danger.

But the alternative of silence was even worse.

THIRTY EIGHT

SATURDAY, DAY 6

OLYMPIC NATIONAL PARK, WASHINGTON

Gracie's cell phone began ringing as she left the main road through Port Angeles and started up the mountainside toward Hurricane Ridge, twelve miles into the Olympic Mountain Range.

"Rachel, would you answer that for me?"

Rachel Rosen nodded and pulled the phone out of Gracie's purse, catching it on the fourth ring.

"*Mom?* Is that *you?*" the feminine voice on the other end asked as soon as she heard Rachel's "Hello."

"April! Oh, honey, where are you?"

"What's wrong? Where's Dad? I've been trying to reach him."

Rachel gave her a surprisingly cogent summary. "We're halfway up the ridge road right now."

"Gracie saw him?"

"Yes. Sitting, or standing—"

"Standing," Gracie filled in.

"She says standing by a parking area on the ridge. There was a ranger with him. Where are you?"

"On a small tug headed back to Valdez. Mom, let me talk to Gracie."

Rachel handed the phone over and Gracie shook her head. "Push the speakerphone feature, Rachel."

"Where?"

"Lower right-hand corner of the little window. The LED display. That one. Yes."

Rachel activated the button and held the phone out.

"April? Where are you?" Gracie asked.

"She's on a tug," Rachel said in a low voice as April repeated the same information.

"I just now got a good cellular signal," April added. "What's all that noise in the background?"

"We have you on speakerphone," Gracie replied, maneuvering the car around a hairpin turn to the right.

"Oh. Okay. Mom, you're still there?"

"Yes."

"All right. I . . . was only going to tell Gracie this, Mom, because I'm not sure it makes any difference, but the wreckage of the Albatross has apparently been, for want of a better word, stolen."

"*What?*" Gracie said, involuntarily looking at the cell phone speaker as if she could discern April's meaning.

April summarized what had happened. "We think the most likely culprit is the Coast Guard or the Navy. Scott has flown off to check on any ships still outbound, but if they snagged the wreckage two days ago, they could have it most anywhere by now."

"Dammit!" Gracie said, slamming on the brakes to slow for a turn she'd misjudged.

"I know it," April responded.

"No . . . I meant the road, here. But as to that news, yes, another dammit is in order."

"I'm more or less out of ideas," April said, amid the sound of wind roaring through the microphone as she stood on the tug's bow.

"Okay, let me think. I'm trying to drive, too."

"You want me to call you back, Gracie? After you find Dad?"

"Watch out, dear," Rachel said, pointing to a couple of bikers in the right lane ahead inching their way up the road. Gracie steered around them with squealing tires and accelerated up the next straight section.

"Okay, April, I think you're probably right," Gracie said. "The Coast Guard or the Navy. I'll have to go find the federal judge at home and file an amended complaint this afternoon . . . as soon as I can get back to Seattle."

"You're . . . we're going to sue them?" April asked.

"Kind of. I'm literally thinking out loud now, but . . . probably another temporary restraining order, and . . . best I can describe it without thinking this through . . . kind of a habeas corpus action for the Albatross. You know, demand they produce the actual body of the thing?"

"Gracie, I'm obviously not a lawyer, but even *I* know that a habeas corpus writ only applies to people, not things like wrecked airplanes."

"Yeah . . . I said kind of. I don't know, kiddo, but we'll figure it out. More important, we'll smoke them out and get to the bottom of who's doing this." Even with the tidal wave of bad news and driving demands crowding her brain, she ached to lean on April's shoulder and cry over the acidic tongue-lashing she'd received from Janssen a few hours before. But April and Rachel had enough to deal with. Her angst would have to wait.

"We're almost there, April. Let me call you back," Gracie announced. April clicked off on her end and Rachel folded the cell phone as Gracie negotiated the last curve to the parking area and slammed on the brakes, bringing the car to a stop in a cloud of gravel and dust. She jammed the gear shift into park and yanked the door handle, forgetting her seat belt and cursing the existence of the thing as she fought to untangle herself and find the release.

Rachel was already out of the car as Gracie alighted and motioned her in the direction of the slope where she'd seen Arlie. The incline down from the parking area was far steeper than she'd noticed from the cockpit of the Cherokee, and she slowed herself after vaulting over the guardrail.

He was thirty yards or so ahead, sitting on the ground and looking east, and she slowed to a fast walk as she approached, surprised his hair had become so thin.

"Captain?" she called.

There was no answer.

She closed to within fifteen feet before trying again, wondering why he looked so strange.

"Captain?"

He turned suddenly and looked at her with a blank expression on a face she didn't recognize.

"Sorry?" the man said.

Gracie came to halt in total confusion. "I . . . ah . . . thought you were someone else," she stammered. Rachel came up behind her and put a hand on Gracie's shoulder.

"That's not our car up there, Gracie."

She turned to Rachel. "No?" Then back to the man, whose curiosity had been piqued. "I . . . saw you from the air and thought you were . . . a friend."

He nodded. "I saw you fly over."

"You haven't seen another fellow out here in the last few hours, have you?" She described Arlie Rosen and he shook his head.

"Okay, thanks. Sorry."

The man resumed his contemplative position as Rachel put an arm around Gracie and headed them back to the car.

"I'm sorry, Rachel, I thought . . ."

"He's the same build as Arlie. He would look the same from the air."

"That explains why he didn't wave. I mean, here he was seeing his airplane and such."

They got the car in gear and started back as Rachel's cell phone rang, the three bars of Beethoven's Fifth symphony sending her hand into her purse in a lightning-fast movement. Gracie could hear the distraught male voice on the other end, despite the road noise, as Rachel held it to her ear.

"Rachel? Baby, where are you? Are you okay?"

The reply was a choked-back sob. "Arlie! Where are *you?*"

"Here at home. I just got back. What's happening?"

Rachel was crying openly now, waving her hand but having trouble forming words. She struggled back the tears and spoke, telling him how panicked they'd been.

"Honey, didn't you get my note?"

"No."

"On your laptop. I had it running like a banner to tell you I was going to go up to Elwha Dam and just think for a few hours."

"I didn't look at it, Arlie! I was too scared when I woke up and you weren't there. I didn't know what to think. I called Gracie and she flew over in the Cherokee."

"You've got to get back here. Something's come up. We've got to get out of here for a while."

"Why?"

"Just . . . just get back quickly."

After hanging up, Rachel fished out a tissue and wiped her eyes as Gracie negotiated the curves coming down the mountainside. Rachel's enormous relief was evident in the tears that wouldn't stop. She motioned toward a turnout just ahead.

"You okay now, Rachel?" Gracie asked, pulling in and stopping.

Rachel blew her nose hard, wiped her eyes again, then smiled and nodded. "Now I am," she replied in a steady voice, full control returning, "although he sounds really shaken up. I want to drive, Gracie, and let you get April back on the phone and tell her her dad's home."

"Agreed," Gracie said, as she set the parking brake for the transfer. "I should have known that wasn't the captain when I first caught sight of him back there. He didn't have enough hair."

Rachel began laughing as well. "I know. I remember thinking as we approached him, 'I know the last few days have been stressful, but . . .'"

"We should be ashamed of ourselves," Gracie said.

"Yeah, we should," Rachel replied as she glanced at Gracie and ignited a new round of laughter. "And then there was the matter of that paunch," Rachel continued. "I *knew* that wasn't Arlie when I saw that paunch."

"Well . . . now with all due respect, Rachel, the captain *does* have a belly on him."

"Not like that!" Rachel laughed as she opened the car door and winked at Gracie. "I happen to be an authority on his physiology."

"Okay, I'm not touching that."

*A*rlie could be seen in the kitchen window talking on the phone when Rachel and Gracie pulled into the drive. Gracie saw him turn and wave as he put the phone down and hurried out to scoop Rachel up and hold her tightly. He reached for Gracie as well.

"I've got a strange call I've got to get back to."

"What?" Rachel managed, but he'd already turned to Gracie. "You may want to get on the extension." He outlined the message left by Ben Cole in Anchorage.

Gracie entered the kitchen and picked up the phone as Arlie returned to the line.

"Okay Mr. Cole," Arlie was saying. "I'm sorry for the interruption."

"Actually, sir, it's Dr. . . . Ph.D.-type."

"Sorry, Doctor."

"Captain Rosen, this is delicate, and there are things I can't tell you—for reasons that I'm not at liberty to explain as I said a minute ago—but there is a substantial possibility that your aircraft actually had a midair collision—or your propeller did—with another aircraft Monday evening."

"Yeah, well, we're taking care of it."

"Captain, I can't discuss anything more over the phone. Maybe I could come down there and talk to you in Seattle or something, but I simply can't say more right now. I could be in desperate trouble for even calling you, but my conscience won't let me ignore this."

"Were you the other pilot?" Arlie asked, rubbing his eyes.

"No, sir. I'm not a pilot. I just know . . . there was another aircraft in the vicinity. I'm only assuming you touched."

Gracie was gesturing to him across the room and mouthing something.

"Hold . . . hold on, Dr. Cole," Arlie said, putting his hand over the mouthpiece as Gracie did the same.

"We could have April hook up with him up there!" Gracie said in a stage whisper.

Arlie shook his head vigorously. "No." He returned to the line. "Dr. Cole, let me have your number, and I'll call you if we need more. I appreciate your call."

There was a puzzled hesitation on the other end, and Arlie avoided Gracie's astounded look as they exchanged phone numbers and disconnected.

"Captain, what on earth are you doing? He could be vital to us."

"We're dropping it, Gracie."

"What?"

"I told you on the phone I want to drop it. You're going to get in trouble with your firm. You probably shouldn't even be over here right now."

Gracie walked to him, her eyes searching his.

"Captain, this isn't you. I know you care about my circumstances, but this isn't you to run from a fight."

Arlie was holding onto the center island of the kitchen with his left hand, and she could see him tighten his grip as he looked at the floor and licked his lips, tense seconds ticking by as Rachel watched in alarm from several feet away. At last he looked at Gracie, his eyes distant and hollow.

"There are . . . things I can't tell you, Gracie. But I want you to withdraw the things you've filed and just . . . just wait."

"But *why?* Your career hangs in the—"

"Because!" he snapped, instantly raising his left hand and shaking his head in apology. "Because," he continued, more softly, "I have good reason to believe that if we just hunker down and stop the frontal assault, the FAA will reverse their stance without all the efforts."

"Who told you that?" Gracie pressed.

He was shaking his head. "I can't tell you, Gracie."

She looked at him for the longest time, weighing the question she hadn't wanted to ask, but compelled to ask it anyway. He was the closest thing to a father she'd had, but she forced that reality aside as she looked at Rachel, amazed that she knew without a word. Rachel nodded and left the kitchen, leaving them alone.

"Captain, I have to ask you something. I . . . don't want to, but . . ."

His face hardened and she heard a disgusted sigh. "Was I drinking, right?"

She nodded in lieu of speaking the words, which wouldn't come.

"You, of all people, Gracie, doubt me?"

"I'm your lawyer now, and . . . and I . . ."

"I don't think I want to answer you. I'm very hurt that you'd have so little faith in me."

"Captain, please, I just have to be able to say that I've asked the question, you know?"

He stood shaking his head, his eyes on the floor, the tension and resentment killing them both.

"What if I was? You believe I was?"

"No. I mean, that's the last thing I want to believe, but when a guy who's had the struggle you've had with alcohol buys several fifths of vodka . . ."

"Everyone just naturally assumes he's fallen off the wagon. As do you. Stupid of me. Next time I plan to crash, I won't visit a liquor store."

She took a deep breath. "I love you, Captain. And I'm sorry. Do you want me to withdraw as your lawyer?"

There was another long, painful pause before he replied, his eyes on the other side of the room. "No," he said quietly.

"Okay."

"But by the end of the day Monday, Gracie," he said, "I'm formally directing you to withdraw whatever you've filed."

THIRTY NINE

The cell phone had barely succeeded in ringing when Mac MacAdams yanked it to his ear, momentarily puzzled that there was no one there.

"Oh, yeah," he mumbled to himself, realizing the electronic ringer that had gone off heralded incoming e-mail messages.

He maneuvered the screen around and grabbed for his reading glasses, spotting the series of numbers he'd expected, and launched himself out of the den chair he'd been in for the past half hour.

"I'm going out for a while, Linda," he called, aware that his wife had been judiciously steering clear of him all morning.

Mac slid behind the wheel of the restored 1963 Corvair Spyder he'd had since pilot training more than thirty-six years ago and headed off the base into the downtown area. He parked around the block from the Hilton and went inside, zeroing in on one of the pay phones. He dialed a number and waited for an interminable number of rings and clicks before a voice came on the other end.

"Hello?"

"This is . . . ah . . ." Mac fumbled with a piece of paper, looking for the code name he was supposed to use. "Ed."

"Of course it is! So, Ed, are you ready to receive some information?"

"Yeah, after I get an explanation of why you selected 'Ed' as my code name."

He heard a hearty chuckle on the other end. "You remember that old TV show about a talking horse, Mr. Ed? Well, you have a lot of horsepower. It fit."

"I never knew covert ops could be so much fun."

"Yes, you did. Anyway . . . bottom line? You were correct that there was damage to the right winglet. It was discovered late Monday night on a postflight walkaround in the hangar, and it was quietly repaired during the wee hours and the paint touched up the following night."

"Then, that sonofabitch flight test manager *was* lying."

"I don't think so. I doubt he knew a thing. I decided to target the maintenance lead who was on that night instead of him, and it was a good decision. The guy crumbled under the weight of my badge, so to speak."

"You have a badge?"

"You'd be surprised what I get to carry."

"You . . . didn't beat the man up or anything, did you?" Mac asked.

"Of course not. I merely made it clear what would happen to him if he ever discussed my visit, and he elected to retain the use and possession of his favorite body appendage."

"You're all heart. What did he tell you?"

"It was a towing accident, or so he thought. He'd been threatened with termination before because that very aircraft had been damaged by a poorly trained member of his night crew six months back when they shoved the tail into the back of the hangar. He reported that damage, he told me, but his boss made a huge deal out of it and tried to hang him. He said when he did the walkaround Monday night and saw the ding on the right winglet, he about expired right there."

"Figured they'd fire him, huh?"

"Exactly. Managers never learn how little it takes to drive people to lie."

"He didn't understand it was midair damage?"

"Still doesn't. He said two of his guys weren't paying close enough attention as they towed the plane back in and clipped the edge of a parked maintenance stand."

"Is he sure? Did he inspect the stand?"

"No. He said the stand was gone when he went back out to inspect it, and he spent the next two hours threatening to kill his tow team, then marshaled them all together to work the rest of the night hiding the evidence."

"And it worked? Well, of course it worked."

"You bet. No one noticed during the day Tuesday, and Tuesday night they repainted that section using some portable device to bake the paint on."

"And by Friday, when I inspected it, it looked fine."

"You got it."

"You think he's telling the truth?"

"Hell, I know he's telling what he thinks is the truth. That's why you called me, remember? To get the truth?"

"Yeah, okay. So it might have been the maintenance stand, and then again it might not have been."

"That's right. Clear as mud. Was there damage? Yes. Was it secretly repaired in a little hangar conspiracy? Yes. Did anyone see, hear, feel, observe, or inspect the results of the impact from the maintenance stand's point of view? No. Has any maintenance stand turned up with corresponding damage? Well, not yet. You only called me a few hours ago so I haven't surveyed the flight line, but you might want to do that. Or I'll do it."

"I would appreciate your doing it, Jerry."

"Oops! Name! Ouch!"

"Sorry! But that's just your alias, right?"

"Yes. Not to worry. Oh, by the way, two other things."

"Tell me."

"First, regarding the beautiful Miss Rosen. Following her was a distinct pleasure. And thanks to the cell phone calls she just made today, I've got some information you definitely need to know. Somehow, she returned to the crash site and is telling her family and a lawyer named Gracie O'Brien back in Seattle that the wreckage of her dad's aircraft has been stolen."

"What?"

"Not only that, the lawyer intends to file a new complaint this afternoon in federal court to include the FAA and the Navy, and she's demanding return of the wreckage. She said she intends to, and I quote, 'smoke out' whoever else is involved."

"Wonderful," Mac said. "That will eventually lead right back to our hangar."

"Judging from what she was broadcasting on that call, Miss Rosen's had a bit of an odyssey."

"I knew she wouldn't quit."

"Also, I have some really interesting insight into our FAA friend Harrison, and why he seems to want Miss Rosen's father on the ground."

"Good. Why?"

"You recall a major cargo airline crash in Anchorage quite a few years back in the seventies?"

"I think so. Remotely."

"Foreign airline and a contract American captain who was drunk as a skunk. Well, there was an FAA inspector who had tried to ground that very individual sometime before the accident because he suspected the man was flying under the influence. He tried to get his bosses to let him take action, but because there was supposed to be an FAA-approved alcohol rehabilitation program and this guy was supposed to have been a part of it, they refused and ordered him to sit down and shut up."

"And his name was Harrison, right?"

"None other. But it gets better. Mr. Harrison not only knew the contract captain, they were bitter rivals during their Air Force years. They both got out after Vietnam, the accident captain got a job with this airline and immediately blackballed Harrison, who was applying there, too. Harrison has been death on wheels to airline pilots since then whenever there's the slightest hint of a drinking problem, and he's been officially sanctioned twice by his bosses for trying to thwart airline alcohol program graduates' return to the cockpit."

"And our Ms. Rosen's father flew into his crosshairs?"

"Captain Rosen took the cure ten years back. Zero record of a repeat. Solid history as a pilot, but the moment Harrison saw that on his record this week, it was a foregone conclusion."

"Which, of course, Washington was never told."

"You got it."

"Can you get me hard copy of this report?"

"Yes, master. You ready for the last item? The one you really wanted?"

"You know I hate to do it this way."

"I know. But sometimes it's necessary. The answer is yes, I've got a file on the guy who rattled your cage. He's not terribly interesting and there's nothing felonious, but he's got some very embarrassing charges on his company credit card that, if you so desired, would be grounds for termination."

Mac sighed. "Okay. You have the documentation?"

"They'll be with the package. He'll be more than willing to apologize."

"I hate this sort of thing. You have a file on me, too?"

"No, see . . . you're one of the squeaky ones that spooks like me hate. I haven't seen you take so much as a paper clip or evince an extracurricular interest in the opposite sex yet. And before you're tempted to ask, same thing goes for your wife. You're both squeaky."

"Thank heavens. By the way, I counted six clicks on the line when I called you," Mac chuckled. "Somehow I got the impression that my call was being rerouted several different places."

"How clever of you to notice. Yeah, I have a lot of fun with false call-routing games. You may even be talking through a Pentagon line piped through the Anchorage police department switchboard and two drug dealers' headquarters before being routed through a local whorehouse into my phone."

"We have whorehouses in Anchorage?" Mac asked. "No, wait. I have no need to know."

"I would think not. Your wife really is a lovely woman."

"How would you . . . never mind. Of course you'd know."

"My job, Ed. Plus, you two had me over for dinner last year. Am I that forgettable? I even recited ancient Alaskan poetry for you."

"Bullshit. You recited Robert Service's *Shooting of Dan McGrew*. Hardly ancient. And no, you're not forgettable. Anything but."

"Thank you."

"Look, please let me know when you've surveyed all the maintenance stands at Elmendorf, will you?"

"I shall go and do that, oh great one with shoulder stars."

"Lord, what I have to put up with."

"Next time you and the missus feed me, I'll recite the poem of the perpetually perturbed polar bear. Provided there's a Guinness in it."

"You're on. And . . . if I haven't said so in the last few months, I just want you to know how much I appreciate having your help on this project."

"You're welcome, big guy. You remember what I told you. As long as I don't have to march or wear a uniform, I'm happy to help."

When the call ended, the man on other end began unplugging the communications equipment he'd used as he thought over what had to be done and how to best deliver the package MacAdams needed.

And then there's the matter of Dr. Benjamin Cole, he thought to himself. *I'm glad Mac didn't ask. Best to leave that subject completely undiscussed.*

BOEING FIELD

SEATTLE, WASHINGTON

3:20 P.M.

Gracie popped open the main cabin door of the Cessna 310 light twin before the propellers had stopped rotating. The man in the left seat finished the last few checklist items and killed the master switch as she reached around to shake his hand.

"Thank you very much, Captain Larson."

"Please call me Jimmy." He smiled, enfolding her hand in a huge paw and shaking it gently. "Anything to help out Arlie."

"Well, two hundred miles per hour really beats the Cherokee's hundred and fifteen. Please forgive my dashing off. You going back immediately?"

He was pulling his headset off. "After fueling and eating some of Galvin's popcorn," he said, gesturing to the main lobby of the flying service whose ramp they were on. "Or, I could stay over."

She climbed out on the right wing and stood up as he leaned over.

"Gracie, any chance you'd accompany an old retired airline birdman to dinner tonight?"

She put her hands on her hips. "Are you trying to date me, Captain?" she teased.

He looked startled. "Hey, now there's a concept. I could use a new trophy wife. I wore out the last one."

She began backing down the folding steps to the ground. "Okay, now I'm frightened. I'll take a rain check, if you don't mind. Besides, I'm going to be amazingly busy working on this thing."

"Gracie, you do know I'm only kidding, right?"

She looked hurt. "You *don't* want to date me?"

He waved and smiled. "In a few years, perhaps. When I grow up. Good luck with that judge."

She hurried back to her Corvette in the parking lot and moved into traffic, heading for the office.

The lure of diverting to a nearby Starbucks after parking her car was strong, but her office had a coffeepot and she had several hours of drafting and proofing to do before the amended complaint and the accompanying papers would be fit to present to a federal district judge on the doorstep of his home. She swung through the door of her office feeling strangely out of place, as if Ben Janssen might be waiting for her in abject disapproval.

There were several others at work in the sprawling offices, but she slipped inside unnoticed and closed the door. She pulled her laptop out of her briefcase and secured it in the docking cradle on her desk just as the urge to talk to April became overwhelming.

Sitting on the forty-sixth floor had an added advantage of a direct shot to the nearest cellular phone tower, so the signal was clear and steady as she punched in April's cell number, relieved when April answered on the third ring. The background sounds had diminished.

"Where are you, April?"

"About three hours out of Valdez."

Gracie reported Arlie's directive to withdraw on Monday whatever she'd filed.

"I don't want to do it, April, but ethically I don't have a choice if he won't relent."

"I'll talk to him. I tried after you called."

Gracie relayed the details of the call from Ben Cole. "I think you need to rendezvous with him as quickly as possible, before your dad orders you home, too."

"Ben who?"

"Cole. Ph.D. I think he's taking a big risk with his job, or something, so we'll need to arrange a very discreet meeting."

"Okay, go ahead. I'll be here until we reach Valdez, then I'll try to get a commercial flight or charter someone to get back to Anchorage." There was a pause on the Alaskan end and some words exchanged in the background.

"Sorry, Gracie. Just talking to Jim. What's the next step?"

"I'm going to sit here in my office and hammer out a new complaint, April. What I filed yesterday was a temporary restraining order to prevent the Coast Guard from destroying the tapes they took from you. Now we have missing wreckage. This may touch the laws of admiralty, so I've got some research to do very quickly, but what I need to accomplish is to have the judge order the government to disclose where the wreckage is, protect it, freeze it in one place, and give us the chance to inspect it."

"So . . . we're not suing them?"

"Well, it's a bit tricky. The FAA is the government, and essentially they're withholding evidence if any part of the government has something material. In this case they've gone out and snatched the prime evidence in open waters. I'm still working through the right theory, but they can't charge the captain with violative conduct and then affirmatively go obtain and hide evidence to the contrary."

"Can't we sue them for damages, too? I mean, as long as Dad will relent. After all, I've already spent several thousand dollars for the privilege of being accosted, looted, deceived, and frustrated by my own government."

Gracie was drumming her fingers on the desk in thought. "That's perfect, April!"

"What?"

"Obstruction of justice. That's essentially what they've been doing. First, there's a process in place in administrative law for violations against pilots, and the process enables the licensed airman to defend himself or herself and present evidence. But if the same government—read: ours—tries to get in the way and obstruct that process, it's arguable that they're committing a criminal act, and at the very least they're creating irreparable harm if the evidence is tampered with. And, civilly, let me see. I'll bet I can hang my hat on admiralty law, in that what they've done, regardless of which government agency did it, constitutes tortious interference with property rights."

"Admiralty law?"

"Yes. It governs things like this involving navigable international waters, and it's a separate and distinct form of what we call legal jurisdiction. There's common law, there's equity law, which is what I used to get that restraining order, and then there's admiralty, which goes way back to Great Britain."

"What's equity law?"

"In old England, as the common law developed, the regular courts could award money and property to injured or damaged people who sued other people and won. But the normal courts were powerless to act *until* an injury, or damage, had occurred. So another kind of jurisdiction developed we now call equity jurisdiction, handled by special courts that could *order* people to do something or not do something in order to prevent harm. In other words, if Lord Brighton threatened to come on Lord Smythe's land and cut down a favorite tree, Smythe could either wait for the damage to be done and then sue Brighton, or he could go to an equity court and get the court to order Brighton not to cut down the tree in the first place."

"Okay."

"Today, in our country as well as the UK, almost all courts have equity jurisdiction along with their normal duties. So judges can preside over damage trials as well as issue court orders, known as temporary restraining orders and injunctions."

"My head's spinning, Gracie."

"Yeah, well, here's what I think we'll do. You went out there with Jim Dobler to begin the process of salvaging the wreck of your dad's airplane as his appointed agent. There can be no question about abandoning the wreck, in other words. You never abandoned it."

"Of course not."

"But, you see, that's a big, big deal, April. If you don't abandon the wreck, no one can take the title away. A salvage operator can bring it up if you don't specifically tell him not to and at worst you might have to pay the fair value of those services, but no one can take the title to it. Not even our government, without due process of law."

"Which means?"

"The FAA or Navy or whoever would have to . . . I know this sounds silly, but . . . file suit against the Albatross."

"What?"

"I told you it sounded silly. It's called 'in rem' jurisdiction, where the title to property is being determined. I remember a case in law school that absolutely cracked me up. It was before the Supreme Court of the United States, and it was entitled: The United States of America versus One 1973 Rolls Royce."

"Who won?"

"Not the Rolls."

"So, unless we see the United States of America versus November Three Four Delta Delta . . ."

"That's it . . . they can't seize it, they can't hide it, and they can't interfere or claim you've abandoned it."

"Good. Don't listen to Dad. I don't know what's spooking him, but we carry on. Okay?"

"As long as I can do so ethically."

"We'll work it out. Don't withdraw anything."

"Call me when you get to Valdez, April. I've got to get this researched and written and find the judge before he goes fishing or something."

"You're hopeful, then, Gracie?"

"Heck, yes! They may just have saved your dad ten to twenty thousand dollars in salvage fees by illicitly interfering, as well as giving us the evidence we need to clear him."

"Wonderful!"

They ended the connection and Gracie began the task of pulling up the right cases on the computer, finishing an hour faster than she'd expected.

She checked the firm's carefully guarded listing of all the home addresses and phone numbers of the state and federal judges and found Judge Chasen's listing, her hand hesitating over the dial pad as she went over what she was going to say.

A woman answered the Chasen phone and Gracie introduced herself, giving the name of the firm.

"I apologize for bothering you, but I need to come to your home and file some court papers with the judge."

There was a sigh on the other end and a chuckle. "Let me get him. Hold on."

The receiver clanked on a table and several minutes went by before a gruff, familiar voice came on the line.

"This is Judge Chasen."

"Your Honor, Gracie O'Brien. I apologize for the necessity of this call, but there have been dramatic new developments in the case I'm handling regarding the crash of that private aircraft in Alaska last Monday."

"What, exactly, are 'dramatic developments,' Counselor?"

"The TRO you granted, Your Honor, concerned a confiscated private videotape of the aircraft wreckage. That tape was taken away. Now the wreckage has also been seized by the government without notice, without process, and without assurance that it will not be altered or tampered with."

"As I recall, this had to do with a Federal Aviation Administration license suspension, correct?"

"License revocation, Judge. Vastly more serious and damaging, but the evidence that will clear the plaintiff is in that wreckage, and this . . . unwarranted seizing of the evidence is, well, tantamount to obstruction of justice."

"Wait a second here. Are you alleging a criminal violation by some government entity?"

"At the moment, Your Honor, I need to come file a petition with you for a new TRO, restraining whichever branch of the U.S. government has damaged, moved, or otherwise imperiled the evidenciary value of that wreckage, and to request a court order essentially arresting the wreckage and requiring it to be delivered to the court's jurisdiction for inspection by us. I have a separate action against the FAA to file as well."

There was a chuckle on the other end, and a sigh. "So you want me to arrest the airplane and the FAA?"

"That would be a nice start, Your Honor."

"You have my address?"

"Yes, sir."

"Be here in one hour and I'll look at it."

"Thank you, sir."

"Thank me then, Counselor. Not now. I haven't seen your pleadings yet."

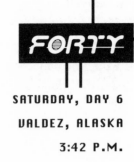

FORTY

im Dobler's coastal tug was closing on the Valdez dock when Scott McDermott's Widgeon appeared overhead, maneuvering for a landing. They tied up almost simultaneously, Scott shaking his head as he alighted from the nose hatch after securing the lines.

"No ships in any direction?"April asked.

"Quite a few, actually," he replied. "But none of them were candidates for carrying the wreckage. Whoever snatched it is probably already in port and the wreckage has been removed somewhere."

"Can you fly me to Anchorage?" April asked.

"When?"

"Now."

She explained the unexpected phone call from a man named Ben Cole, and the reservation she was holding on an evening flight back to Seattle.

"You're . . . heading back?"

"Yes, why?" she asked, momentarily puzzled at his startled reaction.

Scott recovered and shrugged. "No reason. Just a lot happening."

"Scott?" she probed, watching him carefully. "What are you thinking? Am I missing something?"

He laughed and tried to wave her away. "No! No, nothing."

"Okay."

"And yes, we can get started as soon as Jim puts some fuel in my aerospace vehicle."

"The Widgeon is an *aerospace* vehicle?"

"Well, a bit on the suborbital side. Real low orbit."

"I would think."

He turned away, then turned back. "You . . . planning on coming back up sometime soon?"

"To Anchorage, you mean?"

"Wherever. Alaska."

"Why?" April asked, suddenly understanding the uncharacteristic shyness she was misinterpreting.

"Well, you owe me a date, Miss Rosen."

"I do?"

"I got you off that lake alive. That was the deal. And I'd like you to wear a tiny black leather miniskirt."

"You don't get to pick what I wear, Scott. Good grief!"

"Well, at least you'll go out with me."

"We're here together right now. Can't we consider this the date?" she asked. "After all, I just kinda spent the night with you last night."

"Yeah, with me as your hired help. I wasn't the dater, so it doesn't count."

"Dater?"

"Yes. I'm the dater, and you're the datee."

"Now, *that's* romantic," she said.

Jim Dobler had turned with a fuel hose in his hand headed for the Widgeon. "Did I miss something, kids?"

April inclined her head toward Scott. "How long have you known this horn dog?"

"Too long."

"He always been like this?"

Jim chuckled. "We used to lock up our daughters and wives when he'd come to town."

"I thought so," April said, turning and putting a finger gently on Scott's chest. "Get me to Anchorage, please, and we'll arrange something next time I'm up here or you're down there."

"Great. By the way, a low-cut see-through blouse works really well with the miniskirt."

"Scott! Enough!"

He winked at Jim as he turned to help him with the fueling, leaving April to her cell phone and the task of arranging the meeting in Anchorage.

*T*he sun was on the horizon by the time the Widgeon soared over the top of the Regal Alaskan Hotel and settled smoothly onto Lake Spenard. Scott backtracked to the hotel dock and helped April out with her overnight bag and purse, then pulled himself up to the dock to stand awkwardly for a second trying to decide how to say goodbye. She suppressed a smile as she watched the process, and kept a neutral expression when he finally extended his hand to shake hers.

Instead she stepped forward and hugged him, pulling back with a smile and looking in his eyes.

"I really appreciate everything, Scott, and if that check doesn't cover your fees, I'll send you the difference."

"No, it's fine."

"But I thank you for going above and beyond."

She kissed him, quickly and suddenly, pulling away before he could reciprocate.

"And we'll go on that date."

She slung her bag onto her shoulder and waved as she found her way into the hotel and onto the front drive. April pulled the information out of her purse, matching the description of the car she was looking for with the one sitting near the entrance to the hotel and making sure the license number was the same. She walked quickly to the passenger side and got in, offering her hand to the driver, while she kept the door ajar.

"Hi. I'm April. And you're Ben Cole?"

"Ah . . . yes," Ben said with a startled expression. "I'm sorry . . . I didn't see you coming until the door opened."

"You wanted to be circumspect, and I want to be safe," she said, her right hand firmly on the door handle. "So please don't be insulted, but I'd like to see some identification."

He began fishing for his wallet.

"I'm . . . with a company called Uniwave Industries, Ms. Rosen." He pulled his ID badge from his shirt pocket, and then handed over his driver's license, waiting until she handed them back. April closed the door then and nodded.

"Okay. I think you probably are who you say you are."

He grinned. A good sign, she thought. He was in his mid to late thirties, nicely dressed and groomed, and altogether a good-looking man who would look even better with contact lenses. She was well aware that he'd been careful not to walk his eyes up and down her chest, and that restraint was appreciated. Instead, he met her gaze dead on.

"I assure you that I'm me, although quite often I'm also beside myself."

"Yes, me too," April chuckled. "You want to stay here, or . . ."

"If you don't mind, let's . . . just drive somewhere close."

"Fine."

He maneuvered the car out of the lot and turned northeast on Spenard.

"My dad briefed me on your call," she said.

"Good. I understand you have a flight to catch tonight, right?"

She nodded. "In about two hours. We don't have long."

"Okay." He pulled into the crowded parking lot of a restaurant called Gwennie's, letting the motor run. He turned to begin talking at the same moment her cell phone rang. April glanced at the screen, recognizing her father's number.

"Could you excuse me to answer this? It's my dad."

"Certainly. Should I step outside?"

She shook her head as she punched the button, her face hardening as she listened to Arlie's unexplained request that she come home immediately.

"Dad, I'll be on my way in an hour. What on earth is spooking you? Gracie said . . ."

She nodded in response several times before speaking again. "Look, let's . . . let's discuss this when I get home, okay? No . . . later, Dad. Just hang tight. Whatever's got you worried, we'll get past it. I love you, Dad."

She disconnected and tried in vain to turn her full attention back to Ben Cole, but a significant portion of her mind was churning over the panic she'd just heard in his voice.

"I'm sorry. Go ahead."

"Ms. Rosen, what I need to tell you has some big gaps in it because I am under severe legal constraints from my company because we do a lot of top secret defense work. If I cross a line and say too much, I could lose my job and go to jail, so I've got to be careful."

"Okay. You've got me very curious."

He looked around carefully and checked the rearview mirrors before continuing.

"You *are* concerned, aren't you?" April asked, immediately chiding herself for needling him, then feeling a flash of unfocused apprehension herself.

"I have a lot at stake," he replied. "Okay, this is what I can tell you. I've seen the raw radar data from the air traffic control radar station nearest to where your father went down. I have a copy of it on a CD, but it's only for you to see, because you can't use it in court or even admit you have it. If you can obtain the same thing directly from them, you'll see that your father's aircraft crossed the path of a jet Monday night just before his aircraft disappeared from radar and crashed. The jet aircraft can be seen clearly continuing on. He doesn't."

"Does the tape show the altitudes as well?" she asked.

He shook his head. "No. But I know for a fact that the jet was at precisely fifty feet above the water until just before its course change, and then he began climbing."

"My dad was flying under a hundred feet."

"I thought so."

"What was a jet doing that low?"

"It's . . . a long story, and one I absolutely cannot tell you."

"Was this a private aircraft?"

"Uh, yes and no. It's . . . a civilian aircraft, but it's involved in some, ah, government research."

"It's a modified business jet, right?"

She could see the color draining from his face. "What?"

"It has a T-tail, like a Beachjet, or a Gulfstream?"

"How . . . I mean . . . maybe."

"But I'm not supposed to know that?"

He nodded. "Look, what's been keeping me awake at night is your father's plight. I read the newspaper story. I know your dad said he didn't know why his propeller broke, but that the accident stemmed from that. And I know the FAA is trying to hang him and is discounting his version."

"They sure are. Among other things, they're saying he was reckless and just flew it into the water, which is absurd."

"That's why I called. That's why I had to call. The story I read indicated that they didn't believe the propeller broke. But, even though I can't prove it did, I can tell you a midair collision is a real possibility because there absolutely was another aircraft right there that night."

April shook her head and sighed. "I went to the FAA two days later, and they told me the tapes would show nothing because their radar wouldn't be able to see an aircraft that low. So I didn't push."

"Not being a pilot or a controller, Miss Rosen, I don't know whether that was a lie or an uninformed statement."

"April."

"Okay, April. Frankly, the FAA may not even know what they have."

"Tell me how you got to look at this information."

A trapped look clouded his face and he turned away.

"Are you protecting the FAA?" April challenged.

"No."

"Then who?"

"Me, primarily, since I can be . . . arrested if I say too much."

"Arrested? How could anyone arrest you?"

"Well . . . when your company works for the military, there are certain projects that require a higher level of secrecy."

"So, it's your company or whatever government agency they're working for that's hiding this computer record?"

"No, no, no. They're not hiding it. They don't even have possession of it. It's just that the computer record I looked at and copied for you is still in the FAA facility. I had a friend show me how to electronically sneak in the back door of their computer and get the file so I could look at it. Not change or damage it, but just . . . just view it, right from the database."

"And that's illegal, even though it's public record?"

"Probably."

She looked away and nibbled her lower lip for a moment. "All right, so what you've seen tends to establish that the planes crossed, number one, and number two, you know the jet was at my dad's altitude, as bizarre as that seems."

"I know that for a fact."

"At first, we thought he might have clipped the antennas of a passing ship," April said. "Now, I'm not so sure."

"Hitting a ship is possible, I suppose, but if the radar target on that computer record was your dad's plane, the most likely scenario is that he clipped the jet."

"That could certainly break a propeller blade."

"I would think so."

April turned sideways in the seat to look him in the eye. "I don't understand something, though, Ben. You say there was no data block or altitude information, and yet you know for a fact that the jet was fifty feet above the water. How?"

"I can't—"

"Yes you can! You've come this far, you've told me this much, and I need to know. My father's coming apart with worry down there in Washington state."

"Look, April, please listen. My purpose was to give you and your dad the best lead I could. You have to take it from here. I can't stand to see someone railroaded, but I'm also in serious jeopardy here if I say much more."

"But how can I use what you've told me?"

"Now you know what information you need to get from them. Maybe you need a lawyer."

"We have one, and we're filing actions. Can you come testify if we sue the FAA?"

"Good grief, no!"

"What if we sue your company? What was the name?"

"Uniwave. They'd deny everything, and the FAA would back them up."

"Why?"

"Well . . ."

"It's some sort of secret government test, isn't it?"

"I can't tell you! I've said all I can, and . . . I'm beginning to think this was a dumb Boy Scout mistake."

She reached out and touched his arm. "Okay, look. I'm sorry. I appreciate what you've done, and we're not going to get you in trouble. I promise you that. I'm just very frustrated."

"I can completely understand."

"But, Ben . . . I should tell you something as well. I should tell you why I know it was a Beechjet."

"Gulfstream," Ben said flatly.

"Okay. A Gulfstream."

"How can you know about the aircraft? I mean, I know it takes off in the clear from Elmendorf, but where it goes is not supposed to be public knowledge."

She watched him in silence for a few seconds as the tumblers fell into place. She inhaled sharply. "*You* were aboard Monday night, weren't you?"

"I'm sorry?"

"No, Ben, you heard me. That's how you know the airplane was at exactly fifty feet, because you were there, right?"

He licked his lips and looked down in thought, taking a ragged breath before meeting her eyes again and nodding. "You're spooky, lady. You know that? I've got a friend here who's just about as frightening with his insights."

"Oh?"

"Native Alaskan." His right hand went out, palm up. "Okay, yes. I was aboard. But don't ask! Do not ask me what I was doing on board that airplane, except my job."

"All right. What's important to me is that you know what you're talking about when you say the jet was at fifty feet. Did you hear a collision?"

"Absolutely not," he said. "I heard nothing. That does not mean we didn't hit the prop, but I just didn't hear anything or feel anything. In fact . . ."

"Sorry?"

He waved it away. "No, I can't get into that."

"I understand that I can't ask what you were doing, but I do happen to know it's some sort of low-altitude, high-speed test, and a secret government, or military, test of some sort."

"Well, you can speculate."

"Yes, I can. For instance, were you aboard last night's flight, too?"

She could see his eyes flare again in surprise as he started to speak, then closed his mouth and studied her.

"How do I know *that*, right?" April asked.

Ben nodded.

"Because that same Gulfstream almost collided with the airplane I was in last night at about two thousand feet out over the water when it came screaming out of the restricted area."

"I had no idea there was a near miss."

"There was. But what I want to know is, why are they covering this up? Is the FAA responsible for keeping all this secret? Is this somehow a vendetta to get my dad, or was he just in the wrong place at the wrong time?"

Ben shifted around in the seat to see her better. "The latter, as far as I know. April, secret flights that officially don't exist cannot be allowed to surface publicly. Therefore, if there really was an inter-action between a civilian aircraft and a secret flight, the incident itself has to be officially nonexistent. I think that's what you're up against."

April started to tell him about the missing wreckage, but decided to hold back for no reason she could discern.

Ben dropped her at Anchorage International's terminal a few min-utes later, bidding her goodbye with a short list of phone numbers she could use to reach him.

"You can call me anytime, but please don't expect anything more than I've already told you," he said.

April thanked him and melded into the crowd as she pulled out her cell phone and called Gracie, catching her on the way to the judge's house.

"So, this guy was aboard the plane Monday night?" Gracie asked.

"Yes," April replied, repeating what Cole had revealed. "But he was trying to point us to the telltale radar information. The copy he gave me is unusable as evidence."

"Damn. April, I'm still having a lot of trouble with this. We needed a picture of a broken prop, but when you got the shots, the Coast Guard took the tape. Then you found the wreck itself, but now they've snatched it away, taking our best evidence with them. You said we can't use this guy as a witness?"

"No, we'll kill him professionally if we try."

"Okay, but we know the FAA is withholding evidence, right?"

"Yes."

"Then that becomes the focus, and maybe a trade. They can keep their damn little secrets if they let the captain off the hook."

FORTY-ONE

SATURDAY, DAY 6
SEATTLE, WASHINGTON

$\mathcal{T}$he drive from downtown Seattle to the well-heeled neighborhoods of Mercer Island took less than fifteen minutes, and Gracie found the judge's waterfront home with ease. She left her Corvette in the upper driveway of the multistoried home, momentarily concerned what the judge might think.

There were few windows on the rear of the home, however, and his wife answered the door, showing her into a den with a sweeping view of Lake Washington.

"This is beautiful!" Gracie exclaimed, taking in the buildings of downtown Seattle rising above the ridge in the distance across the deep blue of the lake.

"Are you a native Washingtonian, dear?" Mrs. Chasen asked.

Gracie turned and smiled at her as a cascade of cautions clicked into place.

"I was born in Idaho, but . . . I've lived here all my life."

"I believe we knew an O'Brien family in Bellevue with a parcel of beautiful daughters like you. Would that be your family?"

"No, afraid not. But thank you for the compliment." She left it at that, as she usually did. There was no one who really needed to hear of the ravages an alcoholic mother could visit on the concept of family.

"Counselor?" a masculine voice asked from behind her, and she turned to find the second most senior federal district judge in Seattle standing with his hand outstretched. She smiled and took it.

"Your Honor. Again, I apologize for the intrusion."

"It does go with the job at times. Would you care to come into the dining room, where we can spread out the papers if necessary?"

She followed him in, expecting pleasantries in the wake of his wife's hospitality, but the judge sat down heavily at the head of the table and nodded to her.

"I've reviewed the brief from yesterday's filing. Why are we here today?"

"Your Honor, I offer the court two additional petitions. The first is a petition for a new temporary restraining order that combines an order to show cause and an order for production. The defendant is, in a broad stroke, the United States government, due to our inability to discover at this point which agency of the government— military or civil—has committed the act complained of, which specifically is the unauthorized tortious interference with the non-abandoned wreckage of Grumman Albatross November Thirty-four Delta Delta." She narrated the inability of the owner to find anything but a debris field where the wreckage had been forty-eight hours before. "We are seeking your order to force whichever agency has removed that wreckage to first and foremost safeguard it, to report to the court its location, and to make it available for our inspection and removal to the plaintiff's physical possession and control. We also petition the court for a show-cause hearing why the applicable agency should not be held in contempt for having removed the wreckage despite your order of Friday."

"That order, Ms. O'Brien, was against the Coast Guard."

"Yes sir, but I had also expanded the caption to include the entirety of the United States government."

He nodded. "Very well. I missed that."

"Your Honor, the problem here is that some agency of the government is attempting to cover up what may be perfectly legitimate military or civilian governmental tests of certain aircraft in the area, and they have apparently decided that the wreckage of my client's aircraft may somehow lead to exposure of whatever they're doing. In their pursuit of secrecy, they are causing great harm to the career, the reputation, the financial health, and the mental health of Captain Rosen, and if their actions have not already damaged or destroyed physical evidence that would vindicate him of the career-ending FAA charges against him, the actions they are about to take almost surely will. Specifically, I'm referring to the broken propeller and evidence that Captain Rosen had a monstrous mechanical problem that caused the crash, rather than the crash resulting from negligent operation. This is why I'm also filing a complaint against the FAA—"

"Hold it, Ms. O'Brien. Don't hand that to me yet."

"Sir?"

"I'll accept the first filing, and I'll issue the restraining order just as you've drawn it. But I don't think you want to file against the FAA here in Seattle."

The rarity of dealing with a federal judge without an opposing lawyer present was strange enough, but to get legal advice from such a man was all but scary. Gracie felt herself wobble off-center, as though a spinning gyro had suddenly become unbalanced. She fought herself back to center and cocked her head.

"Your Honor, I'm sorry, but I don't understand. This action necessitates a TRO as well against the FAA for essentially collusive activity with other federal agencies in attempting to suppress, secrete, or destroy exculpatory evidence that would clear Captain Rosen immediately, thus preventing massive continuing harm."

"Oh, I expected you were going to do that."

"Yes, sir—"

"But who in the FAA are you planning to serve these papers on, if I accept them?"

"Well, the FAA has a large presence here, sir, especially in Renton."

He nodded. "I know. The Northwestern Mountain Region." He sighed. "Let me suggest to you that a better forum would be Washington, D.C. All the major players are there, including the FAA administrator. Chasing the proper officials all over the local region can lead to heartfelt pleas to the court from government attorneys for schedule relief and reset hearings and other delays your client obviously does not need."

"So . . . I should, perhaps, go to a federal district court for the District of Columbia?"

"Doesn't that sound more reasonable? You've got the basic TRO, show-cause, and order for protection and production. I'll sign those, postpone the show-cause hearing set for Monday, and stand by to transfer it all to D.C. Now, I will accept your suit against the FAA if you insist, but if you elect to file that in D.C. and request consolidation with a D.C. court, the cases could be transferred immediately."

"Yes, sir. I see what you mean. I had not considered that. Okay, I'll hang onto the FAA action."

The judge began signing the various orders Gracie had prepared, checking the verbiage as he went and separating the small pile. She took back the pleadings against the FAA as he handed over the signed copies. "These will be stamped with the case number Monday morning," he said, getting to his feet and nodding toward the door. She thanked him and took her leave, slipping behind the wheel of her Corvette in a minor daze, the logistics of moving the fight to the nation's capital running roughshod over the need to reexamine the best way to proceed.

I really need to get Ted Greene on the phone!

Her irritation had built to the threshold of anger that the Beltway lawyer who was supposed to be so helpful had failed to return her calls for two days.

She reached in her purse for her PDA and found Ted Greene's home number in Alexandria, Virginia. She'd given up leaving messages on his beeper and voice mails on his office phone. Maybe, she thought, she'd catch him at home on a weekend.

Gracie entered the number but held off punching the send button, remembering she was still in the judge's driveway. She backed out and maneuvered a half block down the street before pulling to the side.

Greene answered on the third ring.

"Ted? Gracie O'Brien. Thank heavens."

"Yes."

"In Seattle? Remember, the Rosen case?"

"Yes, Ms. O'Brien. What can I do for you so . . . late on a Saturday evening?"

She caught the unfriendly edge in his voice and glanced at her watch, realizing it was past nine P.M. in Alexandria and she hadn't considered the time zones.

"I apologize for the hour, but I need to let you know what I am doing." She outlined the actions she had just filed, the one filed the day before, and the judge's recommendation regarding the FAA suit.

The voice from Alexandria was icy. "Oh, wonderful. Did you specifically name the Federal Aviation Administration in that TRO action, Ms. O'Brien?"

"Call me Gracie, please."

"Please answer the question."

"Well, yes," she said, much of her mind distracted by the obvious hostility in his voice. "I didn't name the FAA as the only party, but I included them as a named arm of government to incorporate the possibility that they might be involved as a volitional party to these acts. Now I need to have you file this new action that is directly against them. I've got it all drawn up."

"I see. So you retained me as a ranking expert on dealing with the FAA, but now you want to send me *your* work product and have me just accept your filing papers and find a court up here to file them in, or should I go do what you just did in Seattle and inconvenience a federal judge on a Saturday night so you can fire an ill-timed broad-side at a major federal agency and utterly destroy the work in progress?"

"What work in progress? And what do you mean, ill-*timed?*"

"Ill-timed. Ridiculously timed, in fact."

"Why? How?" She could feel herself flushing in potential embar-rassment at the possibility she could have made a major mistake.

"Well, let's see," he was saying, his voice just short of a sneer. "For starters, I have just begun the delicate dance with the FAA I was re-tained to conduct, an interaction involving the careful and profes-sional people I work with all the time at FAA headquarters, people whom I can deal with more often than not without litigation. But, if I follow your playbook, these same folks Monday morning would walk into eight hundred Independence Avenue only to discover that something that they thought was still very much in gentlemanly ne-gotiation had turned into a godforsaken war over the weekend. And with my name associated, I'd be in the position of essentially break-ing my implied word."

"Implied . . . ? Mr. Greene, I think we have more than a few ele-ments of misunderstanding here. First, I was under the impression that *I* hired *you,* yet you're speaking to me as if I'm some misbehav-ing junior associate."

"You retained me for the Rosens. I represent them. I allowed you to tag along as a baby lawyer playing cocounsel, especially after I read your curriculum vitae and discovered you had almost no experience. And here we are screwing up an otherwise lovely Saturday evening with the news that instead of consulting me, you've gone off half-cocked and sued the world."

Gracie felt the embarrassment metastasizing into anger, her breathing becoming more rapid as the need for caution competed with the desire for counterattack. But she also needed his counsel and his representation, no matter how obnoxious he was. And the captain, in particular, needed him.

"I take it, Mr. Greene," she said, "that you don't check your beeper or your office voice mail on the weekends. In fact, I left messages with your secretary all day yesterday and have been trying to reach you on the beeper since yesterday afternoon."

There was silence for a few seconds from Alexandria.

So, I hear the first hesitation in your smug replies, huh, Teddy? she thought.

"I . . . was in a deposition yesterday," he said, recovering. "I was unaware you were trying to reach me. I will apologize for that."

Interesting! Gracie thought. *Not, "I do apologize," but "I will." And when would that be?*

"Well, sir," she said, "the fact is, I did everything I could to reach you regarding developing matters of immense urgency on this case. I'm doubly sorry I was unable to get the benefit of your counsel, but I had an obligation to do what appeared to be the right thing given the circumstances."

"Ms. O'Brien, I'm not terribly concerned about your enjoining the Coast Guard, but naming the FAA is a huge mistake and a significant problem for me."

For you? she thought. *It's Arlie Rosen who's lost his license.*

"Why," Gracie asked, "is it a problem to join them on this issue? If they have no culpability, it's a nonissue."

She could hear his derisive chuckle on the other end, a caustic sound that echoed through her psyche into the dark recesses where she'd bottled up so many minor assaults over the years from those who thought the concept of a young, unpedigreed little girl taking on the real world in any way was simply contemptible. There he was, droning on, unconcerned with the plight of his client or the sincerity of her efforts, merely rising to the challenge of puffing out his manly chest and showing her how stupid she really was. And she was expected to instantly accept that conclusion based on his position, his experience, his gender, and the Ivy League law degree that was undoubtedly hanging on his wall.

"Gentlemanly negotiation," he'd said.

"Ms. O'Brien? Are you still there?"

Gracie shook herself back to the moment. "I'm sorry. I'm in a car."

"I was saying that the problem here is that you've gone, skipping with unwarranted innocence, into a real-world minefield. You obviously don't understand the FAA's hair-trigger sensitivity to being joined in any lawsuit. On top of that, Captain Rosen is extremely vulnerable, but as long as he didn't hit a ship or anything on the surface, which would prove he was too low, they really don't have much chance of making the reckless flying charge stick in the long run. The FAA just doesn't react well to challenge by lawsuit, and when threatened they tend to drop any deals or any reasonable treatment that might be pending and really attack."

"Mr. Greene, they could hardly attack more effectively than pulling a 747 captain's entire pilot's license, for crying out loud!"

Another derisive sneer, or was that a snort?

"You're whipping this into an artificial emergency, Ms. O'Brien. These things take many months at best. Other than the loss of license and the man's obvious desire to get it reinstated—which won't happen rapidly, I can assure you—I don't understand your panic."

"My panic, as you call it, probably was fanned to white-hot status when I discovered this morning that some arm of the United States government has now raised and stolen the wreckage of Captain Rosen's aircraft, although the condition of that aircraft is a key to his exoneration."

" 'Stolen' is a strong word," he said.

Well, DUH! she thought.

"What do you mean, 'stolen'?" he added.

"Under admiralty law, Counselor," Gracie began, choosing her words carefully and reminding herself over and over that they needed him. "How else should we look at a situation in which the owner has clearly not abandoned the wreck, has hired a salvage firm, has given no permission to anyone else to touch the wreckage, and the government does so anyway?"

"How did they inform you they were taking the wreckage?"

"How did they inform us?" She laughed. A short, singular sound of cumulative amazement and disgust carrying a far more complex message than he was willing to receive. "They informed us by creating a restricted area around the crash site and then leaving a few pieces on the ocean floor where the plane had formerly come to rest. That's how. We have no idea when they took it or where it is. The FAA could be tampering with exculpatory evidence even as we speak. After all, I gave you extensive details of that FAA inspector's hostility to the captain. They could easily damage the wreckage so that it would be impossible to determine whether a prop blade broke in flight."

"Ms. O'Brien, I can assure you the FAA wasn't responsible for taking that wreckage."

"How do you know that, Mr. Greene?"

More silence.

Too much and too harsh! she chided herself. *I'm going to lose him if I don't calm down.* But she could feel the battle between professional restraint and the supercritical desire to cut him to ribbons taking its toll on her judgment.

"Ms. O'Brien, as alien as this community seems to practitioners like yourself on the outside, the reality is that the FAA moves in a different time continuum from the rest of the universe. It would take them months to decide to salvage anything. In fact, they'd have a hard time deciding within a week to leave their building if it was on fire, for fear they might be criticized for doing it incorrectly."

"These are the same careful and probative people you work with all the time? The ones you're now disparaging?"

"I'm not going to dignify that with a response."

"Well, dignify this, if you please, Mr. Greene. Did you or did you not tell me several days ago that the FAA was conducting a vendetta of sorts and was determined to keep Captain Rosen grounded?"

"I . . . believe I said it appeared they were leaning in that direction, given my initial contacts."

"You do? You believe you said that?"

"Yes."

"Do you also believe you said these exact words: 'They're gunning for him, Gracie'? Because the fact is, you said the FAA tends to get that way with enforcement actions, and that you couldn't get even the most cursory cooperation from the FAA in Captain Rosen's case. You said, and I quote: 'It's as if they've made an agency decision to go for broke and destroy him.'"

"Well, I may have overstated the case a bit."

"Fine. We all do that at times. But would you kindly tell this poor little baby lawyer from the boondocks who doesn't understand the real world where in those statements a reasonable man or woman can find any rational room for the interpretation that a so-called delicate dance was in progress that might lead to a good solution for Captain Rosen outside of litigation?"

Now we have the long-suffering, condescending sigh, Gracie thought, listening to him shift the receiver to the other ear as if trying to gather his thoughts on how to explain nuclear physics to the village idiot.

"You clearly don't understand the process, Ms. O'Brien. You have to be very careful and diplomatic in dealing with these people. I deal with them all the time. I can't come racing in every time they take a certificate action and accuse them of malfeasance and evil intent. I'd have no credibility left if I followed your method of draw, shoot, then aim. I've developed long-standing relationships with these folks, and what you've done imperils all of that. Now I have a lot of repair work to do, just to begin with."

"What happened to being your client's advocate, Mr. Greene?" she asked quietly.

"I resent that implication, young woman," he shot back. "This is how we do it in the big city, and I agreed to help your client based on the obviously unwarranted assumption that you understood my value was more than just being an errand boy to file your papers in the Beltway. I get results over time by being careful and solicitous, and not by whacking them with a big stick at every opportunity."

There's no way I can win a battle with this windbag, she thought. *Either bare your neck, babe, or fire the bastard.*

Gracie closed her eyes and forced herself to be obsequious. *This is for the captain,* she reminded herself, letting the thought echo and grow loud enough to drown out her own fury.

"Look, Mr. Greene, I'm sorry if I've made things more difficult, but how can we not sue them? They're part of the U.S. government, and the government is messing around with the very evidence that can prove the charges they've leveled at Captain Rosen are absolutely false. Exculpatory evidence. I don't see how talking to them further is going to preserve that wreckage."

"Well, you know what? I guess that's just going to have to be your problem, Counselor, because I'm no longer a party to this."

"Excuse me?"

"I'm withdrawing right here, right now. I'll return your advance Monday."

"Now, wait a minute. Please."

"Ms. O'Brien, you're a female bull in a china closet, and it's my china closet."

"I'm hardly a bull."

"I wish you well. I wish your clients well. But I predict you've already cooked Captain Rosen's goose with what you've done. The moment you named them in that complaint, you guaranteed that the FAA will fight to the death."

"Mr. Greene, you accepted this case."

"And I am withdrawing. I am not of counsel on any filing by my hand, and I'm out of here."

"No! Please, listen to—"

The sound of a terminated connection rang in her ear and Gracie sat in stunned silence for a few seconds, feeling ill, and momentarily wondering whether to call back.

Shit!

She hated the word, but it seemed appropriate, and she decided she was far enough from any other ears to give voice to her feelings of anger and shame.

"Shit!"

Gracie sat for several minutes, breathing hard, her head pounding as she tried to push through the thicket of conflicting feelings and find something logical and rational to grab, a life ring in the rising tide of emotions that had overwhelmed her good sense and restraint.

You can't punch out the world, kid! The metaphor was sufficiently incongruous to spark a laugh amid the darkness of the moment. She realized there were tears cascading down her face, and that unblinking evidence of lost control added to the burst of self-loathing that seemed to fill the small interior of the Corvette.

Her 'Vette. Her boat. Her ego. Her expectations. Her position. All of it could collapse in a moment if she was booted out of Janssen and Pruzan. Lawyers were a dime a dozen, her salary was a rarity, and with all her new possessions, she was hanging off the edge now and wholly exposed financially, with almost nothing saved.

Why am I thinking about me? I've just imperiled the only family I've ever had.

She looked at the cell phone in her hand, the need to call April becoming almost irresistible. But April would be on the flight back to Seattle, and what could she say anyway? "Hi, old friend. My lousy judgment and combative personality have just succeeded in losing the only lawyer in D.C. who could have made the FAA change their minds. Thanks to me, your dad is really screwed now."

She laid the phone on the passenger seat and looked at the radio, wondering if the salvation of diversion would slake the pain.

No! Face this now! Figure this out! You've just started two federal lawsuits and want to file a third. What next?

A ragged breath shuddered her trim body, the feeling of fragility scaring her. *I'm not supposed to feel like such a failure at twenty-six. Wasn't it written somewhere that the enthusiasm and exuberance of youth can override anything? Focus, Gracie! Focus!*

She had the strength to survive this and win. Hadn't she survived? So many nights with her mother passed out on the couch, her father gone, the child the mother to the parent, and she'd said the same things to herself with less assurance. Survival now required self-confidence, and that self-confidence could stand on the shoulders of her past survival.

All right. So we've lost Greene. It may turn out for the best. There are other aviation lawyers in D.C., if I need one. But why do I? Finesse didn't work with the FAA. The game has changed.

Before, they had been trying to appease an agency that was angry for no apparent reason. Now they had evidence that could kill off two of the three charges, and the FAA's claim that the captain had illegally flown in bad weather had been shaky from the start.

She mentally dammed the tide of fear and ran through the things she would need to do to carry the fight to Washington. And the first step, she realized with a deep and visceral shock, would be to talk to Ben Janssen and secure permission to go. The mere thought of that unavoidable encounter made her feel cold, igniting an unfamiliar buzzing in her head.

Gracie took a very deep breath and forced her hands back to the wheel and the shift lever. The first step was to return to her office, though she had a sick feeling it might be for the last time.

FORTY TWO

M ac MacAdams selected a paperback from the rack in the concourse bookshop and turned to pay for it, noticing a lovely young raven-haired woman finishing a similar transaction next to him. The clerk slid her credit card back across the counter, the name, embossed in gold, suddenly visible.

April R. Rosen.

Mac smiled to himself, making it a point to avoid looking surprised.

He saw her stow the credit card and pull out a first-class Alaska Airlines ticket envelope that bore the same flight number as his.

Interesting. Just as I figured. She doesn't give up easily.

Mac shifted his thoughts to the sudden trip to D.C., and his wife's puzzled reaction.

"It's an unofficial mission," he'd explained. "That's why I'm flying commercially and not taking an Air Force plane."

"And, you can't tell me what it's about, of course."

"You're right. I can't."

The meeting with the Uniwave test-flight manager had been set for an hour before he had to leave for the airport. It had been almost amusing the way Dick Wilcox had sauntered into the Uniwave hangar all prepared to receive the chastened general's humble apology. A few minutes later, he was leaving in near terror with the mission of calling Uniwave's chairman to confess that he'd fabricated the whole story about General MacAdams being abusive. It had taken no more than the copies of four credit card statements with circles around charges the man had never dreamed anyone could catch. The whole thing still felt dirty and wrong to Mac, but the last thing he needed was a civilian contractor employee interfering in his chain of command, and that consideration alone justified the little arm-twisting exercise. Certainly pressuring the man with his own misdeeds was far more humane than having him fired.

Mac settled into the comfortable first-class seat. There would be a stop in Seattle in just under four hours, and then five more hours to D.C.

He watched April Rosen enter the cabin, her smile warm but subdued as she checked the seat numbers and sat a row ahead of him and across the aisle. He could see fatigue and worry in her eyes in just the brief moment that she'd glanced at him. Ironic, he thought, that she was sharing a cabin with the man who could be considered the cause of her troubles. He felt a fatherly urge to reassure her that it would be all right, and that he would make sure of it.

But there was no practical or safe way to do so, and what he was planning was already risky enough. In fact, Mac thought, there was an even chance that what he planned to do in Washington would end his career.

SEATTLE, WASHINGTON

The idea had seemed all but inspired when she was standing in her office, but now the reality of approaching the elaborate doorway of her senior partner's Medina district home felt like an act of sacrificial stupidity.

Gracie hesitated, her thoughts racing through the range of options, from turning and leaving quietly to pushing ahead and ringing the doorbell.

He's already expecting me, she reminded herself. There was no turning back.

Ben Janssen opened the door himself, his big, meaty hand engulfing hers in a not unfriendly handshake as he ushered her into a large den, warm with family portraits and framed snapshots spilling off every surface, the beamed wooden ceiling a counterpoint to the perfectly manicured, lighted lawn beyond.

She thanked him, perhaps too effusively, for agreeing to see her on a Saturday evening and he waved it away.

"Gracie, I'm always available to any of my people, junior or senior. If I can expect you to work at any hour, I can expect myself to be at the helm when you need me."

"Thank you."

"Have you heard anything from Bernie Ashad?"

"No, sir. After our conversation, of course, I've attempted no contact, but there has been nothing from his end."

"There will be, unless he returns my call first, which he won't do because I'm nowhere near as cute as you."

"Yes, sir."

He leaned forward slightly, his incredibly bushy eyebrows lowering over his deep-set eyes, his slightly craggy, squarish face showing the rigors of more than forty years of practice. Janssen, she knew, had passed his sixty-fourth birthday, but was considered as healthy as a horse.

"Gracie, I'm a very direct man. Always have been. Today's politically correct world doesn't like my style much, and I'm sure I occasionally get too close to the line."

"Sir?"

"Have I, or am I making you uncomfortable with my references to Ashad's true intentions and the sexual aura surrounding anything he does with a woman?"

"No, sir. I understand what you're saying."

He nodded slowly, studying her face. "Okay. You tell me if I go too far. Not only do I never want to field a sexual harassment suit, I genuinely don't want you to feel harassed."

"I don't, sir."

"All right. You wanted to see me."

"First, I apologize again for . . ."

He was already waving away her words. "Not necessary. We understand each other."

She licked her lips and nodded slowly. "Very well."

"If that's why you came over, then we're done."

"No, sir. There are new developments in the Rosen case, and I need to . . . ask your advice, and ask for a personal favor."

She explained her emergency filings, the loss of the D.C. lawyer, the need to take the fight to the Beltway, and the critical nature of Arlie Rosen's emotional state.

Ben Janssen sighed and sat back. "Gracie, is Rosen a client of the firm?"

"Yes, sir. Absolutely!"

"And, I assume his finances are already being drained?"

She nodded.

"What are we charging for your time?"

"One hundred fifty per hour, sir." She smiled. "I've got a way to go to get to your level of eight hundred an hour."

"But," he continued, "I get the distinct impression that these people are very close to you personally. Right?"

She nodded.

"How close?"

"I . . . never really had a family life, for numerous reasons. Arlie and Rachel Rosen have been my surrogate parents." She felt the last word catch in her throat and forced the emotion back.

"Very well. Let's do this. I'm releasing them to you individually, as your individual clients. If you need to have the firm's name for purposes of clout, then we can do that, but otherwise, it seems to me you're arguing on the merits and the firm will just cost these folks a huge amount."

"Thank you!"

"Oh, don't thank me yet. You've had your attention diverted in a way I can't institutionally allow in an associate. You have to decide that law practice, *for* the firm, comes first. But I'll allow a little adjustment time to get past this one and make your decision."

"My . . . decision?"

"I'm going to kick you out on personal leave for three weeks. I'll tell Dick Walsh. You don't need to call him. At the end of that time, you come to me at the office and tell me one of two things. You resign, or you're back to work, body and soul, with no more wild diversions."

"Okay."

"I know you're sitting there thinking, *How can he call my surrogate parents 'diversions'?* But there were better, more professional ways to handle this."

"Yes, sir."

"And, Gracie, keep this clearly in mind. We're paying you a huge starting salary, and it is not for charity. We expect you to earn every penny of it."

"Am I . . . on probation, Mr. Janssen?"

He smiled and looked at the Persian carpet for a second before looking back at her and nodding. "At the very least. I can't give you any other answer. You've blundered badly on two counts: diverting your attention from the firm and messing with a client for personal reasons—Ashad, I mean. But this will give you a second chance as well as the opportunity to clear your friends' problems, or"—he had an index finger in the air—"or send them to another practitioner better suited to that kind of matter. It's your choice, Gracie. We'd like to keep you, but there will be no more concessions. And, I might add, be very careful how you conduct yourself in this mission through the federal courts. Do not make yourself a liability to us through a tarnished reputation, or there will be no option to return."

*P*iloting her car to Seatac airport to meet April was accomplished by rote. As Gracie parked, she realized she had no conscious memory of the trip, or of much of anything since Janssen waved goodbye and closed his door physically and metaphorically. The concept of a professional purgatory filled her head, defining itself by the way she felt, which was somewhere between devastated and encouraged. She had been saved and damned in the same moment, her reputation with the managing partner a mélange of disappointment and respect, all of it leading to her professional demise if she mishandled the next three weeks.

For a while she thought seriously of quitting. It would be a simple matter to draft a brief, eloquent letter resigning from the firm and delivering it or sending it by FedEx. It would mean selling her boat and probably her car. But she could retreat without ever having to face them again. The concept, though, of what life might be like beyond Janssen and Pruzan was worse than fuzzy and indistinct. It loomed as dark and purposeless as Joseph Conrad's vision of a sailor's wrecked future in Lord Jim, a book that had always haunted her. She felt like Jim, the failed deck officer who had run from a sinking ship full of people at the moment his courage was tested.

Running, however, was not an option for her. That was cowardice and a void. Arlie Rosen, after all, was depending on her now more than ever, and she owed him and Rachel so very much.

Gracie stopped at the Alaska Airlines ticket counter and begged a gate pass from a sympathetic agent. She moved in a fog through the screening lines and out to the gate, sitting in a corner of the boarding lounge to wait for the inbound flight and watching passively as the multidimensional cross section of humanity ebbed and flowed past her. The torrent of people carried the usual stream of human emotions: the smiles at happy reunions, the tears at parting, the stoic, the dramatic, and the occasional passive face, all fascinating to her on any typical day.

But today the cavalcade failed to penetrate the black hole of doubt and apprehension that had become a vortex in her soul, a void threatening to swallow not only her sense of humor, but her sense of self.

When April emerged from the jetway, Gracie met her with a forced smile and what she thought was her usual energy. April filled her in on the meeting with Ben Cole, and Gracie reciprocated with a tale of the trip to the judge's house and the advice he'd given her.

"Washington, D.C.?" April asked in true surprise, as they reached Gracie's Corvette in the parking structure.

"Yes. Both of us need to be there, and we should leave in the morning. I've already booked a flight. We want to be in position at first light Monday."

"So, how does my presence help?"

Gracie felt the answer stop in her throat, and April noticed. She reached out and touched Gracie's shoulder as she closed the Corvette's tiny trunk.

"Gracie?"

"Yes?" Gracie responded, accelerating the intensity of her smile.

"You're not fooling me, you know."

"I'm sorry?"

"Something else has happened that's really affecting you, and you're not telling me. Is it Dad's resistance?"

"Maybe. In part," Gracie said.

"What else?"

"Let's . . . get back to my floating palace and we'll talk. I figured you could stay the night in my guest cabin."

"Yeah, that's fine, but I want answers."

Gracie took a deep breath, her eyes shifting to the concrete floor of the garage, the dam of emotion threatening to break. But once more she pulled back and smiled at April.

"Not now, okay?"

April nodded slowly as she watched Gracie's eyes. "Okay."

The short trip to Ballard and Shilshole Marina was interrupted by a brief grocery stop, but within an hour the two women had settled into the main parlor of the O'Brien yacht. Armed with fresh coffee and renewed control, Gracie related the previous hours of setbacks, trying to keep it matter of fact and professional and positive, chuckling in all the right places and making light of her own concerns. Arlie's worried daughter, Gracie figured, needed more reassurance than she did. But to her surprise, April stood without warning and pointed up the narrow stairway to Gracie's bridge.

"Come up here a minute with me, okay?"

"Sorry?"

"To the wheelhouse."

"I call it a bridge."

"Whatever." April was already up the steps and sitting on the side couch that enabled guests to sit and watch the "captain" steer the yacht when under way.

"Sit," April commanded when Gracie had joined her, standing uncomfortably by the command chair.

"Here?" Gracie asked, pointing to the command position.

"Yes, Captain Kirk. Sit, please."

"All right. I'm sitting. Now what?"

"Look out there, toward the bow. Tell me what you see."

"What?"

"Out there, Gracie. What crosses your mind."

Gracie studied the horizon, testing the various descriptive phrases she might use, none of them triggering an appropriate response.

"April, I don't know what you want me to say."

"Okay, *I'll* tell you what you see. You see the impossible incarnate, Gracie. There was no way a twenty-six-year-old newly minted female lawyer could possibly arrange financing for a yacht this big, let alone live on it, but you did. There was no way you could get that job with Janssen and Pruzan, but you did. There was no way you could get past the blows you'd had as a little girl from a disastrous family background and become a well-balanced, sophisticated, smart, and dedicated adult, who could find a way to make it into and through law school, but you did."

"April—"

"No! Now listen to me carefully. You are vastly more capable than you seem to realize or give yourself credit for, and while a little self-doubt is always healthy, I've got a news flash. You're a fallible human being and you are not going to get perfect anytime soon."

"I know that."

"No, you don't! You're acting like you should have seen everything coming. That fool in D.C. who just dumped us, your senior partner's response, the billionaire client who already sucked in two women in the firm and is obviously very good at it, are all things you couldn't have foreseen. You've done more in the previous forty-eight hours than ninety percent of the lawyers in America could have or would have done, but you're in uncharted waters, so you're kind of innovating as you go along, and that means some moves are going to be wrong."

"I'm just worried, okay? Your dad's future is at stake here."

"And yours isn't?"

Gracie looked up, thoroughly startled. A long silence passed between them as she met April's eyes, at a loss for words.

"You've pulled out all the stops for him, Gracie."

"Well . . . of course. He needed good legal representation immediately."

"No, Ms. Gracie, he needed *you!* And he needs us, along with our respective expertise and support."

"We've got to get this fixed," Gracie replied. "I'd never forgive myself if—"

"Gracie, look at me. You know, don't you, that I'm more than a little aware how much Dad—and Mom—mean to you?"

Gracie nodded and tried to speak, but the words wouldn't come.

"Sometimes," April continued, her voice softening, "sometimes I think you get a bit embarrassed by that, but we're not just friends,

Gracie. We're sisters in so many ways. They're your family, too. And I know you're in an impossible position, trying to play the probative lawyer keeping your professional distance, when you're really representing your family. And I know you're as frightened for him as I am."

Gracie sighed again, her hands clasped, her head down as she listened.

"Here's the point. Don't playact the senior lawyer with me. Save that for clients who aren't your family. I know you too well. I have faith that it's all going to work out, but you're scared to death for Dad, for your job, your reputation, and your own very human reactions. Right?"

Slowly Gracie nodded and looked up at her, her voice uncharacteristically quiet and metered. "I'm pretty frightened, April," she said, as a single tear began its journey down her cheek, tentatively at first, gathering speed until it fell away from her face and landed on the polished wood-grain surface of the instrument panel.

"I know you're scared," April replied. "I could tell the moment I walked out of that jetway that something had gone very wrong today and shaken you. And you are entitled to get shaken once in a while. So admit it to both of us, okay? Don't just give me a clinical analysis and pretend you don't need a good cry."

April leaned over and drew Gracie to her, hugging her tightly as the dam broke at last.

FORTY THREE

Arlie sat in disgust for a few seconds before deciding to search under the hood of his car for the genesis of its refusal to start. He pulled the appropriate T-handle and got out, lifting the hood, eyes falling instantly on something sitting on one side of the engine that he'd never noticed before. It was a cylindrical metallic object roughly ten inches long, and apparently part of the engine assembly. But he couldn't recall its function, or whether it could be blocking the car's starter. He reached for the object, his hand touching the metallic surface and triggering a hidden electrical circuit. The psychological impact of a small firecracker exploding from beneath the device caused him to jump back, adrenaline following the shock, a tiny burst of smoke wafting from the object and marking the reality that the harmless device had been wired to wait for his touch.

A small rod had been thrust out of the front carrying a cloth-like appendage with writing, and Arlie squinted to read the message: *Bang,* it said. *You've been warned. Next time you'll be dead.*

Arlie yanked the device from the engine and threw it angrily as far into the adjacent field as he could, then slammed the hood closed and walked quickly back to the house, shaking slightly with a confusing mix of anger and apprehension.

Rachel was standing at the center island of the kitchen when he threw open the door. She turned from the task of opening a small package and looked at him, startled at his wild-eyed appearance. "Honey? Back so soon?" she asked, continuing to remove brown wrapping paper from what appeared to be a small cardboard box.

"What's that?" Arlie asked, leveling a finger at the package, aware that his beautiful wife was inches away and pulling open the top.

"Don't know," Rachel replied. "Maybe a gift. It was on our doorstep."

"NO!" he lunged at the box as a loud crack echoed through the house.

Rachel jumped back as Arlie grabbed the box seconds too late. A similar puff of burned gunpowder assaulted his nose as he recovered his balance and turned around, his eyes meeting Rachel's, his memory recalling the horrid decapitation of one of the infamous Unabomber's victims.

"What on earth?" she managed, pushing herself back along the counter.

Arlie looked down at the box, disgusted at the small flag that had emerged: *It's Monday morning. Know where your daughter is?*

Rachel read the words as well.

"Is this some sort of stupid joke?" she asked. "If so, it isn't funny."

He was shaking his head in spite of himself. "No. No joke. It's a threat."

"From whom? About what?"

He laid the box on the counter and came to her, holding her tight, unable to stem the cascade of tears from his eyes.

"Arlie? What's going on?" she asked, her voice small and strained.

"Baby, get dressed and pack a bag. We've got to leave right now. I'll explain after we're on the road."

She pulled back, looking at him. "Where are we going, and why?"

"Trust me. I'll explain after we're in the air."

"In the air?"

"We're taking the Cherokee. Pack light. Call no one."

"Arlie—"

"Not now! Just . . . just trust me. Our lives are in danger."

The sound of gravel crunching beneath the wheels of a car was growing from the vicinity of the front drive, and Arlie grabbed Rachel's hand, leading her in a crouched position across the living room toward the bedroom, his mind fixating whether the .357 Magnum he kept under the bed was loaded.

FAA HEADQUARTERS

WASHINGTON, D.C.

Mac had never been in the office of the FAA administrator before, but somehow he'd envisioned a larger room than the one an aide was ushering him into. The FAA chief, the second woman to hold the position, got to her feet and came around the desk to shake his hand, motioning him to a large chair on the other side of the desk. Laura Busby sat in the companion chair across a small table.

"So, General MacAdams, what can I do for you? All I know so far is that you're running a very important black project, have a serious problem to grapple with, and can't tell anyone but me anything more."

He smiled and opened a leather folder to fish out a two-page briefing sheet with the essential facts, and handed it to her.

"What I can tell you is this. Your enforcement folks are inadvertently creating a major security problem and you could make it go away very quickly. Since this is a serious matter of national security, that's precisely what I need to ask you to do."

Busby, a tall, elegant former congresswoman with a full mane of silver hair and a reputation for no-nonsense decisions, cocked her head and studied his eyes.

"Specifically?"

"I need you to sweep aside an emergency license revocation and reinstate the affected senior pilot before his daughter, lawyer, and friends kick open the wrong doors and expose our project prematurely, something that would cause irreparable harm." Mac explained the basic facts and the newly obtained information on FAA Inspector Harrison's background.

"Wait," Laura Busby said, interrupting him. "You say all three charges we've raised are bogus? Support that."

Mac sighed and launched into an explanation.

She was nodding slowly. "How do you know that propellor blade broke?"

"We . . . have hard evidence. We know precisely what the wreckage looks like, and the proof is undeniable."

"I see. That's one out of three, because you haven't convinced me he wasn't illegally continuing flight into instrument conditions without a clearance, or that he wasn't drinking."

"I need you to trust me on this, since we really don't have time to go through the normal procedures."

"I'm a stickler for normal procedures, General."

"Yes, but this is an extraordinary situation. I seriously doubt you've had the Pentagon coordinator of a black project in here begging for an exception since you've been in this office."

"You might be the first. Then again, you might not."

"Well, considering the national defense harm this could do and the gross overreaction inherent in issuing an emergency license revocation within forty-eight hours of a crash based on almost nothing, coupled with the obvious personal bias of the inspector based on his own bad experience in the past, we've got all the ingredients here of a monumental injustice that needs immediate reversal, even if there wasn't a national security aspect."

Busby sighed and lowered the hand she'd been using to cup her chin.

"General, when I took over here, one of the things I pledged to my people was that the days of second-guessing and overruling field inspectors for insubstantial or political reasons were over. When I was in the House and on the Aviation Subcommittee, I got sick to death of watching the FAA mollycoddle unsafe operations because they—now we—were afraid of political backlash."

"I understand. But this involves—"

"National security. I know. I'm not unresponsive or unsympathetic, but what I'm not going to do is just sweep this aside without delving into the details."

"Time is of the essence here. The man's family has been pulling out all the stops to disprove your allegations, and they're getting uncomfortably close to us. If this thing blows into a courtroom, there is even more danger, because of possible media involvement and judicial orders we can't easily evade. This is a bum charge, and it would be beneath the dignity of the FAA to pursue this, because I promise you, on the other end you'll be mightily embarrassed. And, the damage to Captain Rosen would be immense. He's a major airline 747 captain who will stay grounded and unemployed until the license is reinstated."

She picked up the briefing papers and got to her feet, signaling the end of the discussion. "I'll look into this as soon as possible, General."

Mac stood, too, mildly alarmed at what was beginning to smell like a brush-off.

"May I check back with you this afternoon?"

She laughed and shook her head. "You are joking, right? It will take three or four days at best to get all the details assembled on this. I'll call you when I've gathered enough information to make a decision."

Mac stepped into the elevator, oblivious to the four other men and women already aboard. His focus was almost total. The danger was too real to make the foolish assumption that April Rosen wouldn't find a way through the carefully woven veil of secrecy around Skyhook, exposing things that must never come to light.

There was one ace in the hole, he knew, and if the FAA refused to cooperate, he would have no choice but to play it as a last resort. But if that moment came, he would need to be right here in Washington.

The planned afternoon return to Anchorage evaporated before

his eyes, and he made a mental note to cancel the flight reservation as soon as he returned to his hotel.

CLERK'S OFFICE, UNITED STATES DISTRICT COURT
WASHINGTON, D.C.
10:15 A.M.

Gracie checked her watch for the third time since she'd watched the clerk stamp and accept her filing of the new action against the FAA and disappear into the warrens of the court to answer her impertinent request that one of the judges hear the emergency petition within the next few hours.

She heard footsteps and saw the conservatively attired woman returning, closing a side door behind her as she approached the counter, smiling thinly. Her demeanor carried an air of resentment.

"This is a highly unusual and irregular request, you understand, Counselor."

"Yes, I do. But the situation is equally unprecedented."

"I've spoken with the appropriate parties, including Judge Walton, and I am instructed to tell you the following. First, serve the Federal Aviation Administration personally and provide return certification of that service. You may call me by phone and confirm you have it, and the judge will hear your petition then at one P.M. sharp."

"I, ah, suppose it would be impermissible to ask whether the judge is favorably inclined to such petitions?"

The smile vanished. "Ms. Rosen, Judge Walton is seldom favorably inclined to much of anything before lunch. You're lucky this is set for one o'clock."

The smile returned with a small wink as the woman turned away.

The cab ride to the FAA's headquarters was an irritating series of stops and starts through endless traffic signals flashing occasional green lights at a river of gridlocked cars. Forty-five minutes of anxiety had passed with agonizing slowness by the time Gracie escaped from the taxi and dashed into the FAA building in search of the general counsel's office. The reception was cool, quick, and seemingly unruffled, and she stuffed the signed receipt in her briefcase and rode the elevator to the ground floor to look for another cab as she dialed April on her cell phone to report their progress.

"That felt very strange," Gracie told her. "I've filed lawsuits before, but I've never had to walk into a federal agency and essentially slap them with a subpoena."

"What was the reaction?" April asked.

"Like it happens every hour."

"Gracie, I just picked up another message from Dad, directing me to stop everything."

There was a pause and Gracie cleared her throat. "Yeah, I did, too."

"So what do we do?"

"We listen to Rachel. She called just afterwards, Sunday night, and told me she holds his general power of attorney, and she's ordering me to continue full bore."

"Can you do that ethically?"

"Unless my client calls and contravenes those orders, yes."

"Thank God. I do not understand what Dad's afraid of."

"April, let me swing by the hotel and pick you up, then we go to the court and wait until one o'clock, when I get to argue my heart out for the injunction and ask for a show-cause hearing for tomorrow, if at all possible."

"We can make them move that fast?"

"It always depends on the discretion of the judges, but I've made a strong argument for imminent harm. We should get what we're after. With any luck, we'll get the show-cause hearing and some government attorney will have to come tell the court who has the wreckage and what's being done with it. In the meantime, April, I'm praying I can put enough pressure on the FAA to get them to drop the whole thing and reinstate the captain's license."

"Could it really be that easy?"

Gracie paused a few seconds too long, and knew April would interpret it badly. "Could be, but . . . I doubt it. Frankly, I'm going to have to play this by ear, April. We're in uncharted waters, and I'm a minnow challenging sharks."

iss O'Brien?"

Federal District Judge Jacqueline Walton had entered her court-room moments before, nodding to her clerk and court recorder before sitting heavily in her chair.

"Very well," the judge began. "We have before us the emergency matter of Rosen versus the United States, and I see counsel for Mr. Rosen is present."

"Yes, Your Honor," Gracie said, getting to her feet and standing uneasily behind the table normally used by prosecutors in criminal cases and plaintiffs in civil matters. She saw the judge staring directly at her from the other side of the elevated bench and met her gaze eye to eye, working hard to give no hint of how badly her insides were squirming in the heat of that judicial spotlight. The isolation was a splendid agony—a rare opportunity for a young lawyer to argue a case unchallenged by the professional wrath and constant interference of an opposing lawyer. But the advantage was all but neutralized by the intense isolation of being the sole lawyer in the courtroom. She'd been successful in fighting her way to this point, but the knowledge that the judge could bat the case away like a bothersome gnat with a flick of her gavel was a worrisome undercurrent, an unacknowledged elephant sitting on her chest.

The rows of seats in the gallery behind Gracie had no occupants, with the sole exception of April.

Gracie simulated a relaxed smile and cleared her throat.

"May it please the court, I am Gracie O'Brien, counsel for the petitioner, Captain Arlie Rosen. We are herewith presenting an emergency petition for injunctive relief in the form of a temporary restraining order, a show-cause order, and a request for an emergency show-cause hearing, all filed against the United States government, and specifically the Federal Aviation Administration, the Department of Defense, the Department of Commerce, and any other department or entity of the government having knowledge of, or involvement in, the purposeful and illicit salvage and removal of aircraft wreckage belonging to the petitioner."

The judge was nodding, her eyes on the paperwork before her.

"Miss O'Brien, is this an admiralty case, then?"

"In part, Your Honor, yes, but mostly it is a case in equity. Admiralty law only applies at threshold to the unauthorized nature of anyone disturbing the aircraft wreckage wherein there has been no abandonment, as was the case here."

"You've alleged that it's admiralty jurisdiction and equity jurisdiction concurrently, and the two cases you want to combine appear to both be in an equally confusing status."

"Your Honor, the first case against the Coast Guard—"

The judge waved a hand at her in dismissal. "I can read the pleadings, Counselor, such as they are." She removed her reading glasses and leaned forward, her face stern. "You come before this court with an armful of scattergun filings to force the government to do your will on the premise that great harm will occur if I do not immediately grant the requested relief. That's quite a frontal assault, and it carries with it a requirement for very convincing allegation of facts, not to mention at least some coloration of law. Having said that, first we need to get to the matter of whether you are even admitted to practice before this court."

"Your Honor, my application is literally before you, among the papers in this case. For the record, I'm admitted to the bar in the State of Washington and in the federal district courts for the Western District of Washington, and I'm requesting emergency admission for the purposes of this matter."

Jacqueline Walton shook her head and laughed in response. "You're presuming a lot, Miss O'Brien, coming in here and asking to be automatically enrolled and expecting us to shove aside the normal procedures."

Gracie felt her mind shift to a higher, faster level of thinking. She had researched Judge Walton the night before and knew she was tough, but she had naively let herself hope that a woman appearing before a female judge might elicit a modicum of sympathy.

"Your Honor, I would never presume to do so if this were not truly an emergency matter legitimately requiring the equity powers of this court."

"So you've said. So, tell me precisely, Counselor, why you believe there is a threat of imminent harm here that requires me to act instantly to admit you to this bar as well as enjoin the entire United States government from doing such a wide variety of things?"

"All right, Your Honor, I—"

"I mean, if some branch of the U.S. government has taken the time and trouble and spent the money and resources to raise the wreckage of your client's downed aircraft, what possible evidence do you have that leads you to the bizarre conclusion that they may be about to destroy it?"

"It's not destruction of the wreckage that concerns us, Your Honor. It's the possibility that in storing it, shipping it, hiding it, or otherwise retaining possession of it, they may move or otherwise adulterate exculpatory evidence putatively contained therein, whereas the intervention of evidence which, if intact—"

"Miss O'Brien, I do not tolerate convoluted legalese in this court when English will do nicely. Rephrase what you were saying so a normal human can understand it."

"Yes, ma'am."

The judge shook her head in irritation. " 'Ma'am' is a contraction for 'madam,' Counselor, and I am not, nor have I ever been, a madam. I am a judge. A long-suffering one in some cases, but a judge nevertheless, without regard to gender. You may address me as 'Judge' or 'Your Honor.' You will not address this court as 'ma'am.' Is that clear?"

"Yes, Your Honor. I apologize."

"And for the record, I am approving your application for admission, but I'll tolerate no flowery language. They may like that sort of verbal froth out in the ninth circuit, but I don't tolerate it here."

Gracie nodded, working hard to hide the confusion she felt, all her carefully constructed and practiced arguments suddenly verging on disarray.

Okay. Plain English, whatever that means.

"Judge, the FAA has revoked Captain Rosen's pilot's license based on the accusation that he crashed his airplane by flying recklessly. Captain Rosen, my client, in fact, had a propeller blade break in flight, creating so much damage that he couldn't control the airplane. The broken propeller caused the crash. Absolute irrefutable evidence of the broken propeller was sitting on the bottom of the Gulf of Alaska with the wreckage of the aircraft. That evidence would immediately clear my client of the main charge against him. But the government has chosen to disturb and remove that wreckage. In the process of raising the wreckage and taking it away, the government has endangered my client's ability to clear himself of the false charge of reckless flying by altering the physical evidence. If the physical evidence of the wreckage at this moment still shows his innocence, then it is vital that no one be allowed to . . . to . . . mess with that wreckage any further."

The judge raised an eyebrow and cocked her head, the slightest hint of a smile on her face.

"Did you really say, 'mess with,' Miss O'Brien?"

"Yes, Your Honor. You directed plain English, and while that expression is colloquial, it's plainly . . . ah . . ."

"Plain English. All right. Continue."

"Complicating the urgency, Your Honor, is the fact that we have been unable to discover which agency of the U.S. Government has the wreckage, where the wreckage is, and what is planned for it. The admiralty portion of this case has to do with the right to disturb or take possession of the wreckage of an airplane in international waters to begin with. First, there has been no abandonment of the wreckage by my client. Second, my client retained a salvage firm. Third, that salvage firm was illegally denied access to the waters over the wreckage by the Coast Guard. Fourth, although ownership of any registered U.S. aircraft and the address of record of that owner can be established in five minutes over the Internet by simply entering the tail number, and despite the fact that the FAA and the NTSB know well who owns that aircraft and where to find him, there has been no effort by the government to notify Captain Rosen of any intent to . . . disturb the wreckage."

"You may use the phrase 'mess with' again, if you like, Miss O'Brien."

"Thank you, Your Honor. 'Disturb' also works for me."

"Go on."

"So, we have a case of unexplained misconduct on the part of some agency of the government in failing to follow any of the established rules for dealing with the non-abandoned wreck of an aircraft, and we have a great possibility of massive harm to Captain Rosen's career and finances if the physical evidence that could clear him of the reckless flying charge is destroyed or compromised."

"There are other FAA charges against your client, I see."

"Yes, Your Honor. The FAA alleges he was drinking while flying. The blood analyses done at Anchorage Providence Hospital immediately after admission completely disprove that. The third allegation is that he was flying under visual rules, flew into instrument weather conditions, and failed to turn around fast enough. We will be able to completely disprove that when some due process is afforded my client."

"Are we now entertaining a constitutional challenge, Miss O'Brien? Are you alleging the government is acting without due process?"

Gracie caught the intent of the judge's question just in time. This was no joking reference.

Careful, Gracie cautioned herself.

"Your Honor, there is only one solitary incidence of constitutional due process that has been followed correctly up until you agreed to hear me today, and that was the formal sending of the FAA's notice of emergency license revocation. There has been no due process regarding the snatching of the aircraft wreckage, nor in the absence of notice of such intent, nor in the refusal to tell us where the wreckage is. Additionally, the reason for specifically proceeding against the FAA today is to prevent a continuation of what, in the plainest English I can manage, is a pure railroad job against Captain Rosen. The FAA inspector in Alaska held an extremely hostile interview with him, in his hospital room, on the afternoon of Captain Rosen's rescue and made it clear he was going to try to revoke his license with no supporting evidence. The conduct of the government since then has been to frustrate perhaps the most important need my client has, which is to collect and protect the evidence with which to defend himself and his right to practice his career. In other words, Your Honor, the government of the United States has actively prevented my client from showing or proving his innocence, not only in the short term, but . . . because of the serious possibility of destroying the exculp— I mean, because they may ruin the evidence, in the long term as well. So, even if we were able to secure normal due process, it may not come in time."

"That's it?" the judge asked.

"Yes, Your Honor. I believe so."

"Well, you'd best be sure. Do you have more to add to this oral argument or not?"

Gracie sighed and looked down for a moment, shuffling the papers before her and trying desperately to find anything else that she hadn't argued. It was as if she were back in law school trying to defend her interpretation against the impending onslaught of her constitutional law professor, who had been one of the most frightening, arrogant, and devastating humans she'd ever encountered.

What am I missing? It was the same question she'd asked herself in those classes as the professor paced and rolled his eyes at her stupidity.

Oh, God! Of course! "Your Honor, I'm sorry. I almost left out the basis of our adding the FAA to the TRO request, and as a respondent in the show-cause petition."

"By all means, go ahead, Miss O'Brien."

"Thank you. Specifically, we have factual reason to believe that the FAA, directly or through various staff members, inspectors, or other personnel, is actively attempting to tamper with, hide, or destroy evidence that would invalidate its enforcement actions against Captain Rosen. We believe the FAA is directly or indirectly involved in taking the wreckage, and we have reason to believe that it is hiding FAA air traffic control radar record tapes that would show the presence of another aircraft at the very place and altitude where Captain Rosen's aircraft lost the propeller blade. This belief is buttressed by the Coast Guard's confiscation of the videotapes Captain Rosen's daughter made of the wreckage before being ordered off the site, and from the fact that FAA personnel in Anchorage lied to Ms. Rosen about the ability of their radar to track an aircraft flying at the low altitudes flown by Captain Rosen just before the accident. In brief, Your Honor, we believe that there may have been another aircraft operated by, or for, an arm of the U.S. government with FAA knowledge, which may have struck a glancing blow to Captain Rosen's aircraft, leading to the loss of the propeller blade and thus the loss of the aircraft. If so, the aggressive moves to recover and hide the wreckage, suppress any videotaping of the wreckage, suppress radar tapes as well as misrepresent their contents, form a prima facie pattern of official deception. The purpose of this deception is unclear. It may be for the purpose of supporting the FAA's misguided attack on Captain Rosen, or it may be for the purpose of hiding or keeping secret some other operation that intersected Captain Rosen's flight path. In any event," Gracie summed up, "the career of an honorable and senior airman hangs in the balance with massive monetary and reputation loss, and the FAA should be denied the ability to collude in any manner whatsoever in the suppression of evidence."

"Now are you through?" the judge asked.

"Yes, Your Honor."

"All right. Counselor, the level of proof required to make a prima facie case that any arm of the United States government is engaged in illicit or illegal cover-ups is very high, and it is a burden I expected from the beginning you would have a difficult time reaching. Governmental agencies—and you've sued the Coast Guard and the U.S. Navy as well as the FAA here—seldom get the idea they can abandon the law and all accountability. Thus, if some arm of the military, for instance, did take the wreckage of your client's aircraft, there is no justification for automatically assuming that it was done illegally or for nefarious purposes, or that they will so mishandle that wreckage that evidence will be destroyed. Hollywood may make such assumptions, but rational jurists and courts do not. Second, there may be very good reasons for confiscation of an underwater videotape that are wholly unrelated to any desire to help the FAA prosecute an individual pilot, and again there is a high burden on your shoulders to make that case sufficient to justify a TRO and the attendant hearing. The fact that these things occurred is not enough. Finally, a tough FAA inspector offending your client with tough questions does not necessarily constitute prejudicial bias in contravention of due process, nor does your argument with respect to the FAA's involvement make much sense to me. They've taken your client's license because he had an accident, and they deem it to be a result of multiple violations. Despite the inconvenience of his being on the ground for awhile, there is a due process procedure for appealing that action, and you may be wasting time in starting that formal process by being here. The fact is that you've given me little reason to conclude that the FAA knows anything about the movement of the wreckage, what is or is not on radar tapes, or the presence or absence of other aircraft, other than the fact that their enforcement action might benefit from the absence of the alleged proof you claim is in the wreckage. These are rabbit trails leading in all directions, and yet you want me to accept them in a way that presumes essentially evil intent on the part of the FAA, the Navy, the Coast Guard, and God knows who else. I'm sorry, Miss O'Brien, but I—"

"Your Honor, may I add one more thing?" Gracie said suddenly, the risk of angering the judge with an interruption paling against an impending rejection of everything Gracie had tried to accomplish.

"Oh, must you, Counselor?"

"Yes, Your Honor. In direct answer to your points."

Judge Walton sighed and studied Gracie's face for a few seconds. "Very well. Go ahead. Briefly."

"The burden in an equity request for a TRO is on the moving party to state a case that, if factually true, would constitute grounds for injunctive relief. I respectfully suggest that Your Honor is raising that burden higher than the law requires only because this involves the government, and that by so doing you are demanding that I state not only a potentially viable case, but one that logically convinces this court as well. That is not the requirement I have to meet. In fact, I believe I have met the burden, Your Honor. Your detailed examination of the testimony and pleadings are to be made in the show-cause hearing, not here. There is where the court may determine whether the alleged facts I have presented are sufficiently credible. In other words, I ask the court—I plead with the court—to go ahead and issue these TROs and permit the government to answer, before simply sweeping these actions aside, leaving Captain Rosen no possible recourse if our allegations are true. The one operable question, Your Honor, should be simply this: If, by some strange anomalous and unprecedented twist of fate I'm right and the FAA has illicitly colluded through other agencies to deprive Captain Rosen of his right to due process, his right to preserve evidence, and his right to exonerate himself, is justice in any way served by cutting off the process at this point?"

Gracie felt her heart fluttering as she watched the fingers of the judge's right hand drumming on the bench, her other hand cupped under her chin as she leaned forward and stared at Gracie in thought. There was dead silence in the courtroom, except for the hiss of the air-conditioning system and the final keystrokes of the court recorder, who looked up now, first at the judge, then at the lone lawyer standing and waiting nervously for the ruling.

Another sigh from the bench. The judge's hand left her chin. The drumming stopped, as did the movement of time in Gracie's mind.

"Miss O'Brien, that argument violates my ban on flowery language, but it did contain a certain symmetry of thought. I have no doubt that my initial impression will be borne out, and that the dark conspiracies envisioned here will be shown to be nonexistent. However, in a phrase, you're right. I was about to hold you to a higher standard than necessary. I'm very much of the opinion that none of these TROs should be granted, but . . . your question of whether justice is served by dismissal is sufficiently provocative to justify a conservative course here. So, I will issue these TROs and—though it will infuriate my clerk and consternate my fellow members of this bench by interrupting the normal flow of business before this court—I'm going to set a show-cause hearing for tomorrow morning at ten. We'll see what the FAA and the rest of the government has to say."

"Thank you, Your Honor."

"I seriously doubt these TROs will survive their answers, but we shall see."

When the judge had signed the orders and left the courtroom, Gracie collected the copies from the clerk and walked carefully toward the door with April at her side.

"Gracie, what . . ." April began, but Gracie put a finger to her lips to quiet her until they were outside in the foyer. They found a bench to sit on and Gracie plopped down, her hand shaking slightly as she held the signed orders.

"That was magnificent, Gracie!" April stage-whispered excitedly, shaking her upper arm.

Gracie's eyes were closed, her breathing metered as she motioned to wait. Her eyes fluttered open at last and she looked at April and shook her head.

"We almost lost in there."

"I know, but you yanked her back to reality and won!"

"It's . . . I mean, don't count any chickens, April."

"We've got them on the run now, though. Right? Hey! Let me see at least a little victory smile."

Gracie nodded, a quick smile flickering across her face, then fading. She looked at April, her eyes haunted.

"She's right, you know," Gracie said.

"Sorry?"

"The judge. The government will respond like an anaconda with a blowtorch to its tail. We'll get a half dozen assistant U.S. attorneys in here tomorrow morning to buttress the judge's opinion that this whole thing is a delusional construct of a panicked young lawyer's mind. They'll have her convinced I've been reading too many mystery thrillers. They'll say they don't have the wreckage, they have no idea what I'm on about, and they'll claim that the FAA has virtually no knowledge of the allegations we've made, other than the fact I'm defending a dangerous man whom they've saved the public from by the license revocation. They'll point out that the blood tests in Anchorage proved nothing because too many hours had elapsed since the accident. They'll lean heavily on the visual-flight-into-instrument thing, and it's the majesty of the government's word against ours.

They'll slide, dodge, lie, wink, and roll their eyes, and in the end, she'll throw it all out." Gracie sighed. "We got the wrong judge."

"Wait a minute. Won't they have to at least cough up the tapes the Coast Guard took?"

"Oh, they'll have a story about those tapes being shipped in from Anchorage, but they'll be erased by the time we ever see them."

"Gracie, good grief! Listen to you!"

Gracie shook her head and looked down. "I'm sorry, April. We have to face reality. The only way we're going to fight this is the traditional way, using the normal FAA and NTSB appeals method. I'll have to call the captain—"

"Not with a defeatist pity party in progress you won't!"

"It's not a pity party. But . . . well, okay, maybe we can wait awhile."

"You're not going to go defeatist on me, Gracie."

"I'm not trying to be defeatist. I'm trying to be practical and think ahead to the inevitable. This . . . this was a good gamble, but we're going to lose it. I'm not saying it wasn't the right thing to do."

"Wait . . . look. Think about your own logic in there. I thought you were brilliant. But go further. If the FAA and the Coast Guard and the Air Force and Navy as a team really are guilty, as we know they are, what would you expect their lawyers to do tomorrow?"

"Sorry?" Gracie looked up, only half listening to the pep talk.

"Actually, you just told me what they'd say in great detail. So why not take the wind out of their sails and start your argument in the morning with *their* arguments. Give the judge their arguments before they do, and dismember every one of them. You get to go first, right?"

"Yes."

"Then label the arguments you know they're going to make for what they are. Lies and dodges, smoke screens and clever side steps. Convince the judge that they're simply avoiding answering the real questions in hopes she'll dismiss our case just on their say-so."

April saw the logic take root as Gracie looked up and nodded, slowly at first, a faint smile returning to her face.

"That could help, April."

"See?"

"It really could. But I've got about a week of work to do in one day." She got to her feet. "Starting with the not so insignificant task of figuring out how to serve notice on the appropriate government officials. Let's go."

"Back to the hotel? Shouldn't we eat something first?"

Gracie was shaking her head, her energy returning. "Go without me. It'll take a few hours to get these served. When I get back, just toss some candy bars and coffee in every now and then, and no matter how much I yell or beg or plead, don't let me out."

"I think I've heard that line before."

FORTY-FIVE

Gracie realized she was holding her breath as she waited for the judge to make her ruling. She glanced at April, who flashed a reassuring smile and a small nod, but the intensity of the previous ninety minutes and the energy she'd put into arguing the case were taking a toll on her ability to concentrate. She could see the government lawyers in her peripheral vision as they sat at the adjacent table shuffling papers and exchanging knowing glances. Five of them had shown up, including one newly minted lawyer as young as she. The lead attorney had forcefully argued his way through an impressive list of reasons why the judge should throw out the case and stop wasting everyone's time. There was, they argued, no jurisdiction, insufficient notice, cases wrongly transferred, an improperly admitted petitioner's attorney, procedural flaws in the complaints, and the basic fact that it was useless to order the government to produce wreckage they didn't have.

Gracie had startled the government lawyers by following April's suggestion and stating the government's arguments herself, batting them down one by one, but the judge was very good at being impassive and unreadable.

"Very well, ladies and gentlemen, I am prepared to rule," Judge Walton said suddenly, halting the monologue in Gracie's head.

"I find the plaintiff's arguments insufficient to sustain the maintenance of the various temporary restraining orders. Those orders are dissolved, and the petition for injunctions in all three combined matters is denied. These cases are dismissed."

The gavel came down as Gracie forced herself to her feet.

"Your Honor, we serve notice of intent to immediately appeal your rulings of dismissal."

"So noted," the judge said, gathering her papers and evaporating from the bench through the door to her chambers.

Once again April was at her side, but Gracie motioned her back and walked over to the lead government lawyer instead.

"You gentlemen realize this is merely the opening round?" Gracie said with a cautious smile.

The senior lawyer nodded. "We fully expect we'll see you again at some point, Miss O'Brien."

"All this is unnecessary, you know," she added.

He looked at her in silence for a few seconds, aware the other four on his team had quieted and were listening discreetly. The man was in his late forties and clearly a veteran.

"Precisely what do you mean?" he asked.

"What I mean is that a terrible miscarriage of justice is at the heart of this. All we want is Captain Rosen's license and reputation restored immediately. We're not interested in damages, or exposing whatever in the world is going on up there in Alaska, unless this drags on. But I assure you it will drag on, and we'll end up shining the light of discovery into every nook and cranny of the United States government and the United States military until we ferret it out, or until that license is restored."

"Miss O'Brien, if that statement is intended to somehow pressure us to broker a settlement of an FAA enforcement action, you're talking to the wrong guys. You should be filing the appropriate action for review of the license revocation with the FAA. It means nothing to the government whether you sue or don't sue. In fact, this has been an unnecessary waste of time, though it may have been exciting for you."

"What?"

He laughed. "I know it's always kind of invigorating, especially to folks who don't understand the Beltway. I realize that for a young lawyer, running to Washington to argue in the federal courts and sue the United States of America in any form is heady stuff, but it's seldom effective."

Gracie felt herself flushing with anger as her hands migrated to her hips unconsciously. "You think that's what this is all about? Dilettante law?"

"Well . . . these were bordering on frivolous actions, you know."

"In a word, sir, bullshit! Perhaps you didn't read the factual preamble. Instead of some silly little girl lawyer running in here to play with the big boys for the fun of it, I've got a devastated senior airline captain back in Washington state as a client who cannot understand why his government has decided to try to professionally assassinate him without evidence, without cause, and without due process."

The lead attorney glanced at his fellows and turned back to Gracie. "Look, I don't know why you took that to be a sexist remark, but I certainly didn't mean it that way."

"The hell you didn't. And even if I bought your veiled apology, you certainly meant to play the 'arrogant senior lawyer' card, though it's not having any beneficial effect on your job of protecting whatever conspiracy is in progress up there."

"Up where?"

"Alaska. Keep your phone lines open, Counselor," Gracie snapped. "I'll be back this afternoon with a new hearing notice, this time for an emergency appeal."

One of the other men snickered and the lead attorney shot his junior member a cautionary glance before turning back to Gracie.

"Miss O'Brien, please don't get your hopes up that any appellate judge is going to dignify this case with a quick appeal. That's not the way it works here."

Gracie scribbled a note and handed it to him.

"What's this?" the government lawyer asked.

"My cell phone number. When you finally realize the cover-up's about to be exposed and want to end this in time, call me." She turned and motioned to April, who'd been listening at a distance, and they headed for the door, pushing through to the foyer and onto the street as fast as possible. Gracie pointed to a Starbucks in the next block and April nodded, following her inside and paying for the two lattés Gracie ordered. They settled into a pair of rickety wire chairs in the corner.

"You look really angry," April began.

"Read that as determined to kick their superior asses," Gracie replied, immediately softening her voice with a raised hand. "I didn't mean to snap at you."

"Hey, snap away. I knew I was a surrogate just then."

"You know what's tough, April? I knew I could expect a superior attitude from anyone who showed up for the government. I *knew* it, and yet I still let it get to me."

April sipped her latté and said nothing, waiting out the progress of Gracie's thoughts as she gestured to the nearby courthouse.

"I really did expect we'd get thrown out today, you know."

"So, now what do we do?"

Gracie leaned over to open her briefcase and pull out a sheaf of legal papers in a folder that she laid before April.

"Be careful not to get any stains on these."

"What are they?"

"The appeal papers from the order of dismissal. I decided I'd better get them prepared last night."

"You mean you worked all night, right?"

"Yes. Had to. I didn't figure out the reality that we were going to get dismissed until maybe two A.M. Now I just have to find a sympathetic appeals judge on the Court of Appeals for D.C. Someone who'll hear this case immediately."

"Is that easy?"

"No. I'll have to beg and plead and hope, and I may not even get past the clerks."

"Are federal appeals court judges men?"

"Not all of them. But most are."

"How about if you wore a thong bikini and giggled a lot?"

"Yeah, right. That would enhance my image as a serious lawyer."

"Okay, *I'll* wear the thong and go with you."

"What? As a bribe?"

"It could work."

Gracie chuckled. "That's one hell of an image, Rosencrantz. Agree to hear our appeal, your honor, or April will put on some clothes."

"It's good to hear you laugh," April said. "That hasn't happened much in the last two days."

Gracie didn't answer, checking her watch instead. "I've got to call the captain, then hit the bricks. There's only one court to go to, and I need to get over there."

"What can I do to help?"

Gracie smiled and shook her head. "Just pray a little. This is a solo act. The silly little West Coast baby lawyer against the real world full of serious, experienced men ready to pat me on the head and tell me I'm in a dream world if I think I can succeed. But you know what?"

"What?"

"I can. Sometimes the good guys do win."

April gave her a quick hug and remained at the little table as Gracie shot out the front door and disappeared around the corner in search of a taxi. April pulled out her cell phone and dialed her family's number in Sequim, puzzled to hear the voice mail message. She dialed the two cell phone numbers, but there was no answer on either one.

She sat in thought for a few seconds, then checked her PDA for a neighbor's phone number and dialed it.

"I don't know, dear," the woman replied. "I think I saw them leaving a few hours ago, but I'm not sure."

April folded the cell phone, feeling off balance. There were a hundred innocent explanations for Arlie and Rachel to be out of contact, including the one they had embarrassed her with too many times regarding the sanctity of their bedroom and the theory that unmuted telephones were effective contraceptives.

But for the first time in years, the thought brought no smile to her face. The strong feeling that something was very wrong persisted.

She got to her feet and headed for the door, almost missing the buzz of the phone's vibrator and fumbling to open the device.

"Hello?"

"April? Jenny White, your parents' neighbor?"

"Yes, Mrs. White."

"I decided to come over here and have a look. April, I didn't go in, but looking through the windows, the house is empty, your father's car is gone, and . . . oh dear."

"What?"

"You know how neat your mom keeps things? April, it almost looks like someone has ransacked the house. I think I'd better call the sheriff."

General MacAdams? Laura Busby here at FAA."

"Madam Administrator. How are you?"

"Reasonably responsive to external stimuli, as I like to say."

"That's the best comeback I've heard to that question."

"We try to amuse. I'm calling about your mission to see me yesterday."

"Yes?"

"Well, it seems your Captain Rosen has sent a lawyer to town to file suit against the FAA, and although the first round was thrown out of court this morning here in the District, he's appealing that. So, bottom line, I really can do nothing about this situation while there's litigation pending."

Mac shifted the phone to his other hand. "Forgive me for countering you, Administrator Busby, but if I understand it correctly, litigation wouldn't bar you from reversing an emergency revocation unless a court specifically enjoined you from reversing course, right?"

"It's our policy, General, and it's a good one. When legal challenges are pending, I absolutely will not intervene. Too bad they did this. There might have been some wiggle room."

"I'm sorry, too," Mac replied, mouthing the appropriate niceties as they ended the call.

7:45 P.M.

Five blocks from the Willard Hotel in a small café catering to the Internet trade, Gracie plunked herself down at a computer terminal and pulled out a small steno pad and pen as she sipped a cup of coffee and nibbled a bagel. She dreaded having to tell April that all her attempts to speak directly to any of the appeals court judges had failed, even though the appeal itself had been filed. For some reason, the rebuff hadn't fazed her. Or perhaps, she thought, she was already so numb that all blows, however serious, were deflected from her psyche.

She signed into the computer with the customer code purchased from the cashier and called up several phone directory sites, checking them one by one for the home addresses and phone numbers of the various judges. For security reasons, most federal judges carefully concealed their public accessibility behind initials or unlisted numbers, but there was still enough in their biographical sketches to piece together what she needed, and one by one she found the home numbers.

Gracie took a deep breath and dialed the first judge, getting only voice mail. She disconnected and tried the second listing with the same result.

The third number yielded a suspicious wife who finally called her husband to the phone.

"Judge Summers? I am an attorney from Washington state in desperate need of an emergency hearing before your court in an appeal I filed this afternoon with the clerk. Could I please meet with you this evening and explain why this needs to be heard almost immediately?"

"What was your name again?"

She repeated the vital information, including her Washington bar card number.

"Very well. No, Miss O'Brien, you may not come to my home after hours or at any other time without invitation. I intend to complain to your bar about this ex parte contact. How dare you call me at home rather than use normal procedure?"

"Your Honor, this is a case in equity, and—"

The line had gone dead simultaneously with the returning memory of Ben Janssen warning her not to embarrass the firm.

She crossed off his name and tried to memorize the next number long enough to punch it in the dial pad, but the worry over the reaction she'd just received kept blanking her memory.

Gracie placed the cell phone on the surface of the steno pad and dialed the numbers one by one.

Once more a voice mail recording greeted her, and once more she abandoned the call without leaving a message.

There was one number remaining, and she punched it in, listening to it ring eight times before a woman's voice answered.

"Excuse me, please, but this is Gracie O'Brien, an attorney, and I need to get in touch with Judge Williamson."

"The judge is out for the evening, ma'am. May I take a message?"

"Oh, boy. He wouldn't be working in his chambers this evening would he?"

"No, ma'am. The judge is at the Mayflower Hotel speaking at a black-tie dinner."

"The Mayflower."

"Yes. You certain I can't take a message for him?"

"No, thank you." Gracie ended the call and sat in thought. The Mayflower was less than five blocks away. She scrambled to her feet and grabbed her briefcase, then sat back down and retrieved an Internet biography file on Judge Sander Williamson.

Longest sitting judge on the D.C. appellate court . . . age seventy-six . . . a maverick considered too unpredictable to have ever been in the run-

ning for the Supreme Court . . . raconteur, single . . . and where's his pic-
ture? She launched another search and found a *Washington Post* article with his picture, enlarged the image and studied it. Williamson's
face had a sharply angular look, his features Lincolnesque without
the beard.

The phone rang with April on the other end.

"Gracie, something's very wrong at home!" She relayed the sequence of calls.

"You say the sheriff found the rear door open?"

"Yes. He's not sure whether the house has been ransacked, or if
Mom and Dad just threw things around and left hurriedly. But I'm
calling everywhere."

"Keep me posted, but let me go for now. I'll explain later." Gracie grabbed her briefcase again and headed out the door, covering
the short distance to the Mayflower in less than five minutes.

From the hotel's grand lobby she moved eastward down the large
hallway, aware of the restaurant on her right and the grand ballroom.
Through an open door she could see the head table and a room full
of men in tuxedos accompanied by women in stunning evening
gowns, all of them listening intently to a speaker who was in mid-
cry, a man she instantly recognized as Williamson.

Gracie picked the rearmost door to the ballroom and had moved
inside when a large male hand landed gently on her shoulder, pulling
her back into the foyer.

"I need to inspect your briefcase and see your invitation, Miss,"
he said.

Gracie handed over the case and pretended to search her purse for
the invitation. "You know, I'm late getting here from court, and I'll
bet my senior partner is already in there at Judge Williamson's table."

"I'll need an invitation," the plainclothes officer repeated.

"What I'm trying to tell you is that I think my senior partner has
my invitation, because we passed it over the desk today in some confusion, and I think . . ."

"He ended up with it?"

"Yes."

"I have a list. Give me your name."

A blur of movement caught her attention just as she prepared to answer. Jim Riggs, the senior government lawyer she'd barked at that morning, was moving through the same portal unchallenged, with no invitation in sight.

She reached out and grabbed his sleeve. "There you are!"

Riggs stopped in his tracks as he recognized her. "Well! Miss O'Brien."

Gracie gestured to the security guard. "Would you be so kind as to confirm to this gentleman that I am, indeed, supposed to be here?"

The lawyer glanced at the security man, then back at Gracie and smiled.

"Why, of course," he said, turning to the officer. "Miss O'Brien does indeed belong here, and on top of that, she's sitting with me, where I can keep tight control of her."

The guard smiled and nodded as he handed over Gracie's briefcase and stepped back to allow her to pass.

Riggs gestured for Gracie to precede him into the ballroom, and she did so, suddenly feeling very conspicuous as she realized how underdressed she was for such an elegant crowd. He motioned her to an empty chair at one of the tables and sat down beside her, whispering a few words to the woman on his left before leaning toward Gracie and extending his hand.

"By the way, I'm Jim Riggs, Miss O'Brien, the arrogant senior sexist lawyer. Please call me Jim."

"Thank you, Jim. Call me Gracie. And thanks for helping me get in here."

"You were pretty bold to think I would do it."

"I took you for more of a chauvinist than a sexist."

"And the difference is?"

"You like girls, but you want to control them."

"I know what you're doing here, you know," he said.

Gracie looked at him, trying not to appear as startled as she felt.

"You do?"

He nodded. "I know you filed the appeal this afternoon. And I know you're here to catch Judge Williamson's sleeve."

"My, you are observant," Gracie said, her heart sinking. He was, after all, lead counsel for the opposition. "Are you worried I'll succeed?" she said, faking a smile.

He shook his head. "No, but I'm not going to let you get very far. You may not realize how improper it is to approach an appeals court judge outside of his office."

"And your point would be what?" Gracie asked. "That the Secret Service will arrest me if I try?"

"No, but if you must embarrass yourself, I'll tag along to watch," Riggs said, smiling. "Maybe I can convince him not to throw you in jail."

Ten minutes later, when the speech was over and the applause had subsided, Judge Williamson left the platform and Gracie got to her feet and moved in his direction, her eyes darting back over her shoulder to track Riggs who was indeed shadowing her.

"Judge Williamson?" Gracie said when she reached the senior jurist's side. "May I have a word with you, sir?"

The judge turned and looked at her carefully as he extended his hand.

"Certainly. And you are?"

She identified herself, aware that Riggs was standing beside her now. He could see a knowing smile on the lawyer's face.

"Jim, how are you?" the judge said as he glanced at Riggs. "What brings you to Washington, Miss O'Brien?"

"An extremely urgent legal matter against the government, Judge, which is why I'm asking the court to review a decision of the district court today denying a series of temporary restraining orders."

"Judge," Jim Riggs broke in. "I'm opposing counsel for the government, and for the record, we firmly oppose acceleration to the status of an emergency review."

The judge glanced at Riggs and nodded, returning his eyes to Gracie.

"So, you want me to hold a review right here, right now? I'm not about to do that." Gracie could see a flash of irritation flicker across his face.

"No, Your Honor!" Gracie replied. "I'm petitioning you to grant us an expedited emergency review in the next two days."

The judge studied both of them for a few seconds, then nodded. "I have people I need to talk to about other matters right now. But if you two can wait a few minutes, I'll come back and entertain the motion."

When the ballroom was nearly empty, Judge Williamson came to where Gracie and Jim Riggs were sitting and pulled out a chair. His kindly demeanor, combined with the intellectual numbness she already felt, made a succinct explanation easy, and after Jim Riggs had given an equally short summation of the government's position, they both fell silent.

Williamson nodded. "I'm going to make a significant exception to my own rule, Miss O'Brien, because of the alleged imminent harm. But I won't hear it alone. We have oral arguments scheduled in the morning on three cases, as usual, with two of the other judges and me. You two be ready by ten-thirty, and I'll see that we give you at least five minutes of oral argument and a short rebuttal each."

*G*racie returned to the Willard Hotel and stood in front of the elevator for a moment. She suddenly turned away and entered the bar to order two glasses of their best single malt scotch. She adjusted her briefcase and purse straps securely on her shoulder before lifting the drinks and carefully balancing them as she walked to the elevator, punching the button for her floor with her elbow.

"What's this?" April asked when she opened the door to Gracie's knock to find Gracie thrusting a glass at her as she walked in.

"An intermediate victory celebration before I get back to work."

April's eyes were red and Gracie felt a pang of guilt for ignoring what was obviously a growing panic.

"What's happened?" April said as she accepted the scotch.

"You first."

April shook her head. "I can't find out anything. They . . . oh, God, Gracie! They may have been abducted. The sheriff has alerted the state patrol and they're all looking for Dad's car. I'm terrified. He wanted us to stop everything by yesterday, and we didn't listen." She was beginning to lose the battle with her tears, her voice breaking. "And . . . the plane's been snatched by some powerful force, probably the Navy, and I'm thinking someone we can't fight is behind this, someone who could kill them."

Gracie put her glass down and hugged April. "Hang in there, kiddo. You've watched too many spy films. There's a logical explanation for everything, and secret agents snatching parents because they filed suits isn't one of them."

"Then where are they?"

"I don't know."

April pulled away and thanked her, downing the remaining scotch with one gulp before looking back at Gracie. "What progress have you had?"

"Nothing yet, but we've got a hearing in the morning before the federal appeals court."

"Good," April replied as Gracie held up a hand in caution.

"It's a start. A chance, April. It keeps us alive. That's all."

After a near-sleepless night of worrying about April and her parents, Gracie had managed a few hours of sleep. There had been no trace of Arlie and Rachel or their car, and the search was becoming urgent in the wake of the apparent break-in at their home.

At just before three A.M. April's cell phone had rung with an electronically challenged version of Arlie Rosen's voice on the other end.

"Dad! Where are you? Where's Mom? Are you all right?"

"I'm on the satellite phone, April. I don't have much battery. Your mom and I are okay, but we escaped in the Cherokee."

"Where are you?"

"I can't tell you that, but you and Gracie are in grave danger! Someone's trying to kill us, and they'll come after you. Have you dropped those suits?"

"We're . . . working on it."

"Oh my God, April! Listen to me. You have to make Gracie withdraw those lawsuits. We're . . . up against something we can't fight. Tell her . . . wait a minute."

"What, Dad?"

The voice changed to a whisper. "There's someone sneaking around outside this place." She could hear him whisper something about his gun to Rachel before the line went dead.

April rifled through her PDA trying to find the number of the satellite phone her father had purchased a year before, but it was no use, and the phone refused to ring.

Gracie had given up and gone to bed at four, leaving April on watch for another call. She awoke at seven feeling slightly numb but hopeful, the optimism largely slipping away as April confronted her with the decision that the suits should be withdrawn.

"Why?"

"I told you what he said. Someone's trying to kill them unless we stand down. And we could be in danger, too."

"Not in a federal courtroom. I refuse to believe that."

"Gracie, I have to order you to have them dismissed."

She shook her head, watching April's eyes flare in shock.

"Gracie, no! You've got to listen to him."

"If he calls, I'll listen. You don't have his power of attorney. Rachel does, and her last instructions to me were to go ahead. You agreed, too."

"You're not going to listen to me? I can't believe this!"

"I'm listening, but I can't stop this, and I wouldn't if I could."

"You're going to get us killed!"

"No, I'm not! You're panicking, April. Whoever has threatened the captain is bluffing."

"The house was ransacked!"

"You said yourself the sheriff wasn't sure, and . . . *and* . . . your folks weren't kidnapped. They ran."

"Gracie, Dad said—"

"He didn't say it to me! Okay? That's the bottom line. We're going to do every damn thing possible to get his license back, and I have no reason to believe that isn't the right course of action. Now, get a grip!"

April stared at her for several long seconds before swallowing hard. "You think?"

"Yeah, I do."

April nodded, her voice soft and subdued. "Okay."

*A*s Gracie pushed through the ornate double doors of the appeals court, the building itself did not seem threatening, but everything within—from the polished marble hallways to the spartan decor—was a reminder of the might and importance of what went on there. *And here I am,* Gracie thought, *attempting to bend the federal government to my will.* It was as if she had decided to attack a giant stone citadel with nothing more than logic, a hastily written brief, and her own interpretations of the law.

Gracie entered the courtroom with a squadron of butterflies performing loops in her stomach. Three judges were seated at the bench, each in an oversized leather chair. The one on the right held the lanky frame of Judge Williamson, instantly recognizable from the night before. The other two held men with stern faces belonging to Chief Judge Joe Briar and Judge Alex McNaughton.

April squeezed her elbow and broke away to take a seat in the first row of the gallery. Gracie seated herself at the counsel's table, trying not to pay too much attention to the government lawyers assembling on the opposite side, and trying to ignore the fact that there was one of her and five of them.

It's okay, she told herself. *You're ready for this!*

She would have only five minutes to argue the case and convince the men behind the bench, and yet, if she could stick to the words she had practiced, five minutes would be enough.

When the Rosen case was called, Gracie got to her feet and moved to the lectern. There was a small green light glowing inside, and when it turned yellow, she'd been cautioned, she would have one minute left. When it turned red, she would be out of time. "May it please the court," she began, "I am Gracie O'Brien, counsel for Captain Arlie Rosen, the plaintiff and petitioner in this matter. We are appealing the dismissal of the matters in my brief by the district court, and—"

"We've read your brief, Counsel," Judge Briar interrupted, somewhat laconically. "And it appears that your trial court judge, Judge Walton, clearly felt she lacked the specific evidence to justify upgrading the restraining orders to injunctions. That type of finding of fact we leave to the lower court, yet you're arguing here that her interpretation was wrong as a matter of law, because in a case for emergency injunctive relief, a court must seek to prevent imminent harm even before there is evidence that such a threat truly exists. If that were true, wouldn't it mean that any allegation of potential harm, no matter how bizarre or unsupported, would require a court to issue an injunction?"

There was a small noise behind her, and Gracie thought she heard someone moving out of the seats and back up the aisle. She glanced around involuntarily and realized with a start it was April.

"Counselor?" Judge Briar said as he tried to recapture her attention. "Are you with us?"

Gracie turned back immediately. "Sorry, Your Honor. No, in fact, we are merely stating the essence of equity jurisdiction."

"But this isn't entirely equity, is it?" Judge McNaughton interjected. "I believe part of it is admiralty as well."

Gracie quickly scribbled a note on where she'd been in her argument. Appellate judges almost never permitted the lawyers to talk without interruption, and it was terribly confusing.

"All three of the combined actions, Your Honor," Gracie began, "were primarily equity actions, with only a reference to a particular principle of admiralty law. Now—"

"Wasn't this crash in international waters, Miss O'Brien?"

"Yes, Your Honor, it was." Gracie paused, but there was no followup question. She took a deep breath and continued. "Captain Rosen is asking the court to block a harmful act, and such a request rests primarily—"

"Which request?" Judge McNaughton asked. "We've got three actions here."

"All of our requests here, Your Honor, are based on the significant potential and ongoing harm to Captain Rosen's career, his health, and his property interests. To justify a restraining order, I am required to show that if not restrained, the respondent will take actions or continue actions that will cause substantial and irreparable harm. But the burden then shifts to the respondent at the show-cause hearing to show by a preponderance of evidence that the petitioner's factual claims are wrong. If the respondent fails to meet that burden, the restraining order becomes a temporary injunction. That's the way we should have been treated by the lower court."

"And what again was this threat, Miss O'Brien?" Judge Mc-Naughton asked.

April had remained at the back of the courtroom listening to the interruptions as Gracie began describing how Arlie Rosen was being harmed. April glanced down once more at a note that had been handed to her.

Ms. Rosen, you have a visitor in the foyer who says it is vitally important that you come out right now to talk to him. He says he has material evidence pertaining to this case.

April pushed through the double doors as quietly as she could, leaving Gracie's voice behind and spotting the writer of the note immediately some twenty feet away as he sat and waited on a bench. She felt her jaw drop in amazement. "Ben Cole! What on earth are you doing here?"

He stood and took her hand, shaking it. "Trying to make up for being cowardly."

"But, how on earth did you find us?"

"I called your dad on Sunday. He told me where you'd be. Am I too late?"

April involuntarily glanced behind her at the closed double doors, then looked at him. "No! It's just starting, but . . . we lost yesterday, and this is what Gracie calls a very limited appeal."

"I'm ready to testify, Miss Rosen."

She stood, feeling stunned, and immediately wondering how to transmit the information to Gracie not a hundred feet away.

"Follow me into the courtroom," April said.

Ben hurried ahead of her and held open the door, following her inside to a spot behind the counsel tables. She saw Gracie glance around at her and raise an eyebrow. April pulled her notebook out and wrote a note.

> Gracie, Dr. Ben Cole is here from Anchorage to testify! He was on board when the Gulfstream nearly hit us, and when the Albatross was lost. He can corroborate the fact that the Gulfstream came very close to the Albatross.

April leaned over the divider and poked Gracie with the folded note until she reached down and took it, reading it quickly before glancing back to verify Ben was really there.

Gracie cleared her throat and looked up at the judges. "In the district court yesterday, the defendants were allowed to shift the burden of proof illicitly to Captain Rosen by doing little more than declaring that what we said wasn't true. They offered no proof that government vessels had not been in the recovery area. They offered no reason for confiscating April Rosen's videotape of the wreckage. They offered no explanation of why FAA radar tapes have been withheld, what's on them, and whether a second aircraft, which may have clipped Captain Rosen's aircraft, was in his way that night. They merely came in and said, 'We deny everything,' and on that basis alone, their word was taken as being more trustworthy than his. I submit that as a matter of law and equity, that is incorrect, and by itself constitutes an error requiring reversal and reinstatement of the TROs."

The light inside the podium was already yellow. Gracie glanced at it now and watched it turn red. Jim Riggs took the podium and she sat down to take notes, looking for ways to attack his arguments when the government's case was through.

She'd caught April's questioning look as she turned to sit, but there was no time to explain the futility of Cole's presence in the appeals court. She had to concentrate on the opposing argument, which began with force and precision.

Gracie heard a noise beside her and turned to find April kneeling at her side with another note.

When are you going to tell them he's here and what he's got?

She leaned down to whisper in April's ear. "I can't. This is an appeal on the law. If they reverse the lower court, then we can add his testimony."

"But he's willing to testify!" April whispered back.

"April, I've got to keep track of this. Go back and sit down."

Gracie could see one of the judges diverting his attention from the government's arguments to the whispered conversation at the petitioner's table, and she sat up instantly, feeling like a schoolgirl caught passing notes in class. She resumed her writing, aware of April's frustrated sigh as she withdrew. The thought began eating its way into her consciousness, however, that maybe somehow April was right.

Is there anything I'm missing? Gracie thought, as the government lawyer turned his attention to a list of cases that allegedly proved Gracie was wrong.

Fact presentation is to be done in the trial court. But doesn't this court have the right of original equity jurisdiction as well?

She tried to keep half her mind on the argument while the other half re-blazed its way through law school and the lessons on how the equity courts and the law courts of old England had been separate, one dealing with normal common law, the other issuing court orders and injunctions and restraining orders in equity. There was something one of her professors had taught in the third year when she'd done a directed research paper, but what was it? The lesson was hanging there, just out of reach in her mind. She thought back to that warm spring day in the professor's comfortable office, and the memory returned. "Never forget," he'd told her, "that even a federal court of appeals has full equity powers, even though they seldom use them beyond lifting injunctions or imposing stays of execution."

"And therefore, Your Honor," Riggs was saying, "not only did the trial court have the right to rule the petitioner's factual claims insufficient on their face with or without evidence, the burden of proof was theirs, and they failed to uphold it. Finding alleged facts sufficient or insufficient is a process best left to the trial court, especially in a show-cause hearing, especially since no hearing of additional evidence can be had in an appeal such as this."

Gracie was only marginally aware of standing. On one level, she had never felt more in control, but on another, she was merely a spectator to an unfolding interruption that could easily earn her an embarrassing rebuke from the bench.

"Your Honor, forgive the interruption, but Mr. Riggs is absolutely wrong, and we have just received pivotal new evidence that we need leave to introduce."

Riggs turned to her with a shocked expression, the prospect of being interrupted in an appellate argument apparently never having crossed his mind.

"What are you doing?" he asked almost conspiratorially before looking back at the judges, two of whom were exchanging puzzled glances as the third, Judge McNaughton, leaned forward.

"Counselor, if you're not aware of the protocol, you should know that we don't allow our lawyers to interrupt each other here. You'll get a two-minute rebuttal, provided you sit down. And I'd recommend a thorough review of our procedures before arguing here again."

"Your Honor," Gracie answered, moving closer to the podium and Jim Riggs's side. "This actually *is* an appropriate interruption. May I tell the court why?"

"No!" Riggs thundered as he recovered from the shock. "Sit down."

"That will do, Mr. Riggs. We're capable of giving the same orders from up here," Judge McNaughton said. "Miss O'Brien, if you persist in this affrontive behavior, we could consider a contempt citation to bring you under some modicum of control. I prefer hog-tying misbehaving lawyers, but case law, and our esteemed chief judge, seldom allow it."

"Your Honor, this court has original equity jurisdiction and can hear new evidence in the form of a new witness, and here we have a doozy."

An immediate commotion broke out at Jim Riggs's table and the bench simultaneously as one of the judges began banging his gavel while the other two exchanged some hurried words. Judge Williamson finally quieted his two colleagues with hand gestures and took the floor.

"Miss O'Brien, we're intrigued by your risk-taking here in insisting on educating us as to the scope of our jurisdiction, but if you haven't noticed, there is no witness stand in this court."

"No, Your Honor, but this court's jurisdiction is not defined by furniture."

There were renewed protests punctuated by Jim Riggs's giving voice to the urgent buzz of advice from the other lawyers at the government's table.

"Your Honor, we must protest the interference with our time for argument—"

"Wait a minute, Mr. Riggs," Judge Williamson said. "We do have the authority to add to your allotted time, you know. You'll get your additional minutes." Judge Williamson turned back to Gracie, who could feel icy cold adrenaline in her bloodstream with the recognition of possible real danger.

"Now, Miss O'Brien. Please continue."

"When our courts were created by the constitution and formed by congressional action, federal appellate courts were limited to hearing disputed matters of law only on appeals from normal legal matters. But equity jurisdiction has always been an uneasy mix, an additional duty for the courts, as it were, and there was never any prohibition in the enabling legislation nor in the rules of this court that suspended the duty of an appeals judge to consider equity pleas. In fact, any one of you may hear a matter in equity and even compel testimony, if you so choose, and the fact that it is not often done does not mean that you do not possess the authority. A breakthrough witness has just walked into the courtroom with vital evidence that wholly contradicts the government on several key points, and what he will say under oath will prove the justice and applicability of the restraining orders that were issued, then vacated by the lower court."

"You . . . are alleging that we have the discretion to hear original testimonial evidence, Miss O'Brien, even though our procedures and rules do not permit it?"

"Yes, Your Honor. You may issue injunctions and restraining orders just as a federal district judge may, and your powers are not limited to that in equity."

Jim Riggs was on his feet again, but Williamson warned him to stay quiet with a quick tilt of his head. Gracie held her breath, thoroughly alarmed at what she'd just done, and only marginally aware of more noises and commotion from the back of the courtroom.

Riggs had reached the breaking point.

"Your Honor, I move for a brief recess."

Judge Williamson smiled an amazed smile over the top of his reading glasses.

"A recess in an appellate argument, Counselor?"

"Yes, Your Honor. The United States would appreciate a recess and opportunity to converse about this extraordinary circumstance in chambers."

"Really? Well, I think," Williamson continued, "that given the wholly unprecedented nature of the last few minutes, that would be a wise idea. I remind counsel for the petitioner that holding this hearing in the first place was an extraordinary concession to the justice of the matter. So, we will . . ."

Judge McNaughton whispered something to Williamson, who nodded.

"Oh, yes. We are going to take a short recess and meet in chambers, but first, Miss O'Brien, precisely what are you requesting?"

"That I be allowed to swear in Dr. Ben Cole of Uniwave Industries in Anchorage, Alaska, who is in the courtroom, and examine him on the issue of his presence aboard a government project aircraft on the night Captain Arlie Rosen lost his aircraft, permitting him to testify as to the high probability that Rosen's aircraft was actually clipped by the aircraft Dr. Cole was in."

There was a gavel banging away and a scowling Judge Mc-Naughton was holding it as he turned to his colleagues, then back to the lawyers.

"Fifteen-minute recess to chambers."

"All rise," the clerk called as the judges got to their feet and filed out.

Gracie could feel her heart pounding as she glanced at Jim Riggs, expecting him to turn and charge her with angry protests.

But he had turned and gestured to someone behind her, and Gracie turned as well in time to see one of three men in business suits nod to Riggs and begin to make his way toward the government lawyers' table.

April, too, was in motion, coming to Gracie's side with a wide-eyed Ben Cole in tow.

"What's happening?" April asked as Gracie ran her hand through her hair and shook her head.

"I think," she said, shaking her head, "that I just screwed up big time. But I'm not sure."

FORTY EIGHT

M ac MacAdams waited while the guard verified his name and identification, then opened the gate to the front drive of the White House. The meeting he had requested was a huge risk, but it had to be done. His call earlier in the day had been received with consternation that a potential leak had occurred, but the news that Ben Cole himself had arrived in Washington with an obvious intention to violate the secrecy agreement he'd signed meant they had to take action, and the authority for what had to be done could only come from one source.

Mac walked into the main foyer, unable to keep his eyes off the artifacts of living history that defined the American form of self-governance.

A Secret Service agent with the cold, expressionless eyes of a cobra nodded to him as he showed his pass and turned down a familiar corridor, checking his watch as he passed. The appointment was in exactly eight minutes, and he intended to arrive as the second hand hit the twelve.

UNITED STATES COURT OF APPEALS
FOR THE DISTRICT OF COLUMBIA

An assistant clerk appeared at Gracie's side from nowhere.

"Miss O'Brien, your presence is requested in the judges' conference room. Please follow me. Dr. Cole? You, too."

Gracie shot a "stay here" glance to April, who nodded and sat down at the petitioner's table, watching Gracie and Ben following the clerk as if they were being escorted the last mile to a gas chamber.

Judge Williamson was waiting in what appeared to be a large boardroom. Jim Riggs was already there, pacing along one wall and looking agitated. The three men Gracie had seen in the back of the courtroom were standing near Riggs.

"Miss O'Brien?" Judge Williamson said.

"Yes, Your Honor?"

"We remain in recess, but we're extending that recess to a matter of hours. These gentlemen will explain. We will resume when you return."

"I'm sorry, Judge . . . return?"

But Judge Williamson had already turned and left through a side door as Jim Riggs began speaking.

"Miss O'Brien, we need you to come with us to a little meeting a few blocks away."

Gracie leaned against the back of a chair and stared at Riggs, squinting as if trying to see through a ruse.

"Go where?"

"I can't tell you until we get there. Dr. Cole comes, too."

"What are you trying to pull, Mr. Riggs?"

Jim Riggs chuckled tiredly. "I assure you you're not in any danger. We're not going to shanghai you or molest you or rough you up or anything."

"So, where are we going?"

"Miss O'Brien," one of the men said. "I'm Special Agent Breck of the Secret Service. Your presence and Dr. Cole's are requested across town in a matter of great urgency. Miss Rosen, too."

"Gracie," Riggs continued, "the court will stay in recess on this matter until we get back."

Gracie noted the shift to her first name.

"Do we have a choice?" she asked after studying their eyes.

"Ma'am," Agent Breck said, "we were sent here to bring you to a meeting. We were not instructed to accept no for an answer."

"Gracie," Riggs continued, his voice conciliatory, "Judge Williamson knows and approves of this. Please."

Gracie knew she looked grim as she and Ben joined April in the backseat of a black government town car, with Agent Breck in the right front seat and another agent at the wheel. She knew enough about the physiology of Washington, D.C., to recognize the names of the streets, but her concentration was on April and Ben as they talked quietly. The car pulled up to a heavy gate, which was quickly pulled open, and they motored into an underground alcove and were ushered out of the car. An interminable series of corridors followed, the decor becoming gradually more plush before one final door was opened and Gracie found herself motioned to a seat in the Cabinet Room. Jamison Hendee, the President's chief of staff, walked in, his face instantly recognizable. He introduced himself and sat across the table.

"Well, we have a problem, folks, but fortunately, we also have a potential solution. We brought you here, by the way, at the specific request of the President."

"I don't understand," Gracie began, glancing at the equally stunned expressions on the faces of April and Ben Cole.

"I have before me three very determined people," Hendee said. "But your determination has all but compromised a very important government project."

Another man had quietly entered the room. An Air Force general, Gracie noted. He sat down on Hendee's side of the table, several chairs to one side, and merely nodded at them.

"Miss O'Brien, first I want to congratulate you on wrestling the federal judiciary to the mat in only three days."

"Excuse me?" Gracie said.

The chief of staff chuckled. "May I call you all by your first names?"

There was a murmur of agreement from Gracie and April, quickly followed by Ben.

"Good. Gracie, I never went to law school, but I know enough about the courts—and I've got a few real lawyers around here who've confirmed this to me in the last half hour—you just turned the tables on us in that courtroom."

"Sir, I . . . really don't understand."

"You were supposed to lose, Gracie. Oh, there was no fix. Not even the White House can get away with monkeying with the courts, thank God. But Riggs and everyone else assured us that even though you'd found the one maverick judge in the federal court system who would agree to hear your appeal in an off-the-wall way, you'd never win. But you skunked them, and lawyer Riggs over there had to go to plan B."

"I skunked them?" Gracie repeated.

"Damn right. I don't know word for word what you said in there, but Riggs had the authority to call a halt to it if for some strange reason he felt you might win, and that's why we're here. I know you don't understand what the hell I'm talking about, so let me explain. Any details I give you are top secret. This is about a major military research and development project called Skyhook. Dr. Cole knows the details very well, since he's the chief software engineer. And you three were about to blow the whole project wide open."

April was nodding. "Were we right? Did my dad hit a government aircraft?"

"We believe he did. And if you kept pressing for information on that military aircraft, you'd eventually get the press interested and destroy a billion dollars of effort to maintain secrecy."

"Then, my father *has* been falsely accused," April said.

"Perhaps. But my first concern, and the President's concern, is the fate of Operation Skyhook, and that fate now rests in your hands. All three of you. In fact, poor General MacAdams over here has been sweating bullets trying to find a way to help your father and you, April, without compromising the project, but when you two turned out to be such excellent sleuths hot on the trail of the truth, Mac was forced to bring this back to where it all began, in the Oval Office."

"Mr. Hendee," Gracie began, "with all due respect, there was no justification for the FAA revoking Captain Rosen's license."

The chief of staff smiled thinly. "Well, that's not entirely true, Gracie. As I understand it, the FAA has substantial reason and hard evidence to suspect that he was drinking and flying, as well as a substantial case against him for potential violation of the air regulations governing visual flight. And there's another charge I can't recall. But I *do* believe that the FAA's shameful rush to revoke Captain Rosen's pilot's license was uncalled for, and that's the mistake that's brought us together."

"So," Gracie replied, leaning forward, her hands open in a questioning gesture, her words careful and calm, "why *are* we here, sir? What do you want us to do, and what is the government willing to do in return to correct this injustice? Because regardless of what the FAA's out-of-control inspector says, Captain Rosen was not drinking and did not violate the rules."

Hendee looked at April and nodded. "Maybe. Okay, Gracie. Let's deal. We have a project of great national interest to protect, and if that takes reinstating a single pilot's license before we're sure of the facts, thus overruling and embarrassing the FAA for the greater good, then we're prepared to do it."

"You mean," Gracie said, leaning back slightly and trying to restrain herself from smiling, "if we drop our lawsuits, you'll reinstate Captain Rosen's full license?"

"In a nutshell, yes."

"And . . . with no record of any of this?"

"As if it never happened."

"And, what else do we have to do?"

"Just return to the court and withdraw all your actions with prejudice and give me your solemn word as American citizens that you will take the classified details I'm about to give you to your graves. Not even Captain Rosen can know."

Gracie looked at April, who glanced at Ben Cole, who looked at Gracie, and all three began nodding simultaneously.

Jamison Hendee nodded in response. "What I'm going to tell you now is top secret. Dr. Cole knows all of it, but you two ladies have signed no secrecy agreements and are not subject to military law, so if you want to walk out of here and call Sam Donaldson or Ted Koppel, we can't stop you. But, your country is relying on you to understand this very delicate situation. May I have your solemn agreement to maintain secrecy?"

Gracie raised her hand before April could reply. "Sir, what about the wreckage of the Albatross? We need it returned intact. That wreckage has the proof—"

"We don't have it, Ms. O'Brien."

Gracie shook her head. "That's not true, sir. It was removed from the ocean bottom."

"Indeed. But we didn't take it. No arm of the U.S. government or military took it."

"With all due respect, sir, someone isn't telling you the truth."

Hendee was shaking his head. "Yes, they are. Take this to the bank, Gracie. We don't have the wreckage, and if you make the return of what we don't have a condition, Captain Rosen will remain unlicensed until he can disprove the charges."

Gracie and Jamison Hendee locked eyes for what seemed an interminable period before she looked down and nodded. "Okay."

"Absolutely, okay," April echoed. "But, there's something else that needs resolution." She described Arlie Rosen's panicked escape from Sequim and the report that someone had rifled their house. "I'm terribly worried about him."

Jamison Hendee's expression grew dark. "I can assure you, April, that no one has been authorized to break into your house, or even surveil your father."

"My dad's scared to death and running."

"We categorically did nothing to cause that, but we're sure as hell going to look into it." He scribbled a note and looked at the three of them in turn. "Do we have a deal? I have to know before I tell you what Skyhook is all about."

"We have a deal," Gracie said, echoed by April and Ben Cole.

"Very well. Several years ago, after the attack on America, the World Trade Center destruction and the hit on the Pentagon, a defensive idea to protect military aircraft was hatched, which started very badly. At first, there were those who thought that we could install automatic systems that would allow air traffic controllers to land hijacked Air Force and Navy craft remotely. We quickly realized that air traffic controllers are not pilots and have a very different skill set. If we tried to use them for such recoveries, we'd end up killing just about everyone involved and probably take out a few cities in the process. The plan grew more sophisticated very quickly, and by the start of the next year, we launched a deep black project, which, April, your dad unfortunately stumbled across when his airplane apparently struck, or was struck by, a converted business jet being used in the tests."

"The Gulfstream."

"Yes. The system we were testing will allow a special command post somewhere in the U.S. to take over control from any U.S. military aircraft and have qualified pilots fly it back safely to any airport on earth, whether the pilots are incapacitated, hijacked, or whatever."

"So, the Gulfstream my dad hit, that was in the wrong place?"

"Yes. The damage that proves both aircraft touched was illicitly repaired on the Gulfstream and this fact was hidden from General MacAdams at Elmendorf Air Base until just a few days ago." He briefly explained the sudden loss of control of the Gulfstream and the fact that it had left the restricted area, which had been improperly reserved in the first place, so Arlie Rosen would not have had any way of knowing about it.

"I knew he wasn't being reckless."

"You know the FAA administrator is somewhat independent of presidential control, but she's not an idiot, and when I got her in a hammerlock a few minutes ago by phone, I got her to agree to reinstate your dad's license."

"Thank you, sir!" April said, but Hendee held up his hand.

"Gracie, here, was about to accomplish the same thing through the judicial route. She wins, the court orders the files opened on Skyhook, and the project is massively compromised. We don't want the bad guys to know our Air Force jets can be taken over by remote control."

"But this way there's no record?" Gracie said.

"Right. The court's still in recess, Gracie. You can go back there and push ahead and win, and your country will lose. But if you go back in there and move for a dismissal, we can ask them to seal what little record there is and the program stays secure. That's the choice you've got to make."

Gracie nodded slowly, her eyes huge. "Mr. Hendee, as I said, it's a deal."

"Then I'll make the call," he said, standing, "as well as find out whether someone under our control threatened your father. Dr. Cole? I'm going to send these two folks back to court. Would you stay with us a few more minutes?"

Gracie got to her feet and raised her hand for Hendee's attention. "Part of the agreement, sir, is that Dr. Cole's career will not be damaged."

Jamison Hendee laughed. "Don't worry. You have my word that no software engineers will be harmed in the making of this deal."

*W*hen April and Gracie had been escorted out of the Cabinet Room, Jamison Hendee motioned Ben to follow him through a series of doors ending in a startlingly familiar office.

"Have a seat," Hendee offered, gesturing to a pair of facing couches. Ben gingerly lowered himself into one of them, popping back to his feet as the President of the United States came into the room, shook his hand, and sat in a chair by the fireplace, regarding Ben skeptically. "Sit, please, Dr. Cole," the President said, motioning him back down. "You've been both a bad-boy thorn in our side and a hero, Ben. But now you're going to tackle a higher duty."

"Sir?"

"The true aim of Skyhook, Ben, is so secret that even the Secretary of Defense doesn't know its full scope. Everyone else but General MacAdams and a few staffers have been told that Skyhook concerns only military aircraft. Well, I launched it to cover more than that. I launched this project as the last line of defense to forever prevent a repeat of September Eleventh. Fact is, the Boomerang Box you've helped to design is scheduled to be installed on every civilian airliner as well."

Ben Cole came forward on the couch, his eyes wide. "Really?"

"All of them," the President replied. "My goal was simple. With every U.S.-registered airliner secretly equipped, if one ever gets hijacked by two-legged animals wanting a cruise missile, we literally take control from the ground and fly it someplace safe. We may lose people aboard in some sort of bloodbath, but the plane won't have to be shot down over American cities, and we may end up saving everyone on board. The plan includes pilots standing by twenty-four–seven in a newly designed facility at Offit Air Force Base in the old Strategic Air Command headquarters bunker."

"This . . . wasn't an Air Force project, then?"

"We'll equip our major Air Force assets, like the B-1 and B-2 bombers and C-17 transports, too, just as you were told. But the civil fleet is included as well. We've installed eight remote-control cockpits down there and trained a cadre of Air Force pilots to operate them. Three of those cockpits match Air Force aircraft. Five of them match airliners like the Boeing 757 and 747, the MD-80s, and Airbus products." The President paused, watching recognition grow on the faces of the people before him.

"I had no idea!" Ben said. "I . . . I found some strange reference information in the code about the civilian fleet and was afraid it might be evidence of an attack."

The President smiled. "No, just evidence of our secret intentions. And you almost blew our cover with your dedication to finding out why that extra code was there."

"And the airlines . . . don't know?" Ben asked.

The President shook his head. "No. They know we've got a rack already built into the equipment bay of every airliner in America. All FAA-licensed maintenance people have been trained that to disturb that rack or the black box installed there is now a federal felony offense. But they think it's only an emergency communications device that lets air traffic controllers see and hear what's happening in the cockpit of a hijacked airliner. Well, that's right, it will. But that's not the whole story. Once the new boxes are in place, we'll have full standby recovery control."

The look on Ben Cole's face was ashen, and the President noticed.

"Ah . . . Mr. President . . . if we're talking about using this on commercial airliners, I have to tell you I have grave doubts about the reliability of this system." He described the problems with the tests, and the fact that even though the Gulfstream's loss of control was due to a bad autopilot, the Boomerang Box had been unable to seize control each time.

"You're saying it's not ready for prime time?" the President asked.

"Yes, that's exactly what I'm saying, with apologies to the general," Ben added, glancing toward MacAdams.

Mac nodded.

"So happens," the President said, "General MacAdams over there has already briefed me on the level of risk we'd be taking putting these boxes in place right now in the civil fleet, and how rushed the tests have been.

"Mr. President, I . . . I just don't see how we can be sure an airliner can be recovered with enough assurance. We need more time, and the pressure has been far too great."

The President had his hand up. "I have a radical idea about how to handle this, but I've also decided that you're such a tenacious guy, if I didn't bring you in on my plan, you're liable to louse it up and get yourself thrown in the pokey by going public."

"Sir, that problem with Captain Rosen is solved, so I . . ."

The President was shaking his head. "No, this is different. If you truly believe that this system is too unreliable to be installed in the civilian fleet and somehow the project leaked, you could, with the best of intentions, do great harm by telling the world we had a dangerous system on every airliner."

"I guess I'm confused, sir."

The President chuckled. "So was Mac at first. Okay. We agree the system isn't ready to install in airliners, right?"

"Yes, sir."

"All right, and I've decided that the system, if delayed in secret, will leave an exposure to terrorism I don't want after spending billions to develop this fix. But I've also come to believe that the deterrent factor is greater than the actual operational value. Ben, ever see those little signs in people's yards that say they're protected by such and such security company?"

Ben nodded.

"If you're a burglar, you can't be sure if they really do have a system or not, so maybe it's best not to chance it. Deterrence. So with Skyhook we let it leak that we're installing it, we confirm that we have it on every airliner, we let the pilot unions and the airlines howl with fury, and we stand firm. Anyone planning a hijacking will be on notice that their best efforts can be thwarted by a turn of a switch. So instead of having to seize control someday of an airplane already full of dead and injured people with hijackers in the cockpit, we'll stand a good chance of not having the hijacking attempt in the first place. In the meantime, we'll go ahead with the Air Force system when you're sure it's ready."

"I don't have the authority to make that determination, Mr. President."

"Yes, you do. Joe Davis is retiring as of now. You're taking over."

"I am?"

"Provided you agree with all this."

"And, Uniwave gets enough money to survive?"

"The check's in the mail. We'll keep them afloat, because I may actually decide to put them in later on."

"So, we leak information that the Skyhook system—the Boomerang Boxes—are deployed, but we secretly leave them out?"

"When the media breaks the story we leaked, we announce openly that yes, in fact, the Boomerang system does exist and is operational, and that no future hijacker will ever be successful taking over an airliner. We put on a show and demonstrate the system for the world's media. The deterrent effect is nearly one hundred percent, we've saved billions, and we don't run the risk of losing an airliner to an electronic glitch, which, if I understand your worries, is your greatest nightmare."

"Yes, sir, it is."

The President stood up. "Obviously, Ben, you can tell no one else in this life. Not those two determined young women, not your coworkers, not any future wife or lover. No one. Only a handful of people other than us will ever know the truth."

Ben stood and took the President's hand. "You have my word, sir."

*F*or April and Gracie, the ride back to the appeals court was taken in stunned silence. Three times April started to pull her cell phone from her purse and call home, but each time the presence of the agents in the front seat intimidated the effort.

Only Jim Riggs was in the courtroom representing the government when Gracie returned to the counsel table. She glanced at him and read in his pleasant expression the phone call he must have received from the White House. There would be things he did not know, of course, but what she was about to present would be no surprise.

They stood as Judge Williamson entered by himself.

"We're back in session, and I understand, Miss O'Brien, that you have another unique motion to present?"

"Yes, Your Honor," Gracie said, mentally toying with the words she had never expected to use. "I doubt Mr. Riggs will object to this, since it's a motion to dismiss. The petitioner hereby withdraws the petition and requests an order of dismissal."

"With prejudice?" Williamson asked, smiling at the deer-in-the-headlights look on Gracie's face.

"With, sir. We won't be refiling."

"Very well," the judge continued. "Case dismissed."

Jim Riggs was at Gracie's side when the judge departed, his hand outstretched and a smile on his face.

"Very nice job, Gracie, on everything you did. You're an impressive opponent with a great future."

"Thank you," she replied, still feeling as if she were seeing him and the courtroom through several feet of water.

April hugged Gracie tightly as she left the counsel table, neither of them noticing that Ben had just returned to the court. "I wonder if I could buy the two of you dinner this evening?" Ben asked.

Gracie shrugged. "I don't see why not. When do you have to go back to Anchorage?"

He smiled. "Now that I've got reason to believe I won't be arrested, I can catch a flight anytime I wish. And you? When do you go back to Seattle?"

Gracie had found a bench in the hallway. "Scarlett O'Hara's words come to mind: I'll think about that tomorrow." She sat and looked over at Ben Cole. "It may take a lifetime for me to grapple with what's happened in the past two hours."

"One hour and twenty minutes," Ben corrected.

She laughed. "Yeah, I forgot. You're an engineer."

"But I'm recovering," he chuckled, wondering how becoming a high-power executive would feel.

"By the way, Ben, why did you come?"

"I guess I just couldn't picture myself living with the consequences of not doing something for April's father and . . . for my project. Too much was wrong. Too many strange things were happening. I didn't know whom to trust."

"Well, that's one problem solved, right?"

He grinned. "I'd say so."

Gracie looked around at April, who was on her cell phone, then back to Ben as she put a finger to her lips. Ben nodded as April folded her cell phone and came over to sit beside them.

"I can't reach them on the satellite phone or the cell, and I'm out of ideas."

"Well, I'm not," Gracie said, pulling out her cell phone.

"What are you doing?" April asked.

Gracie finished a string of numbers and punched the transmit button before looking up with a smile. "Sending him a message. You've forgotten he never goes anywhere without his beeper."

At first, Bernie Ashad's voice failed to register. Gracie pushed her cell phone closer to her ear as she followed April and Ben out of the federal courthouse into the roar of Washington midday traffic.

"Excuse me, who is this again?" she asked, hunching over. April noticed and caught Ben's elbow, and both of them turned to wait for her.

"This is your client, Ms. O'Brien," the voice said. "Bernie Ashad. Remember me? The guy with the ships." There was a chuckle in the voice she could hear over the background noise.

Gracie snapped to full alert. She could see the scowling face of Ben Janssen in her mind as she raced to think of an appropriate— and safe—response.

"Mr. Ashad, I believe the firm has handed your . . . affairs off to one of the partners."

There was laughter on the other end. "Yes, I'm well aware that Ben is telling wild stories about my defiling all of the women at Janssen and Pruzan, and I can tell you it's all nonsense. But, if I in any way made you feel uncomfortable, Miss O'Brien, when I proposed a dinner, I humbly apologize."

"None required, sir."

"Your senior partner thinks he's a guardian uncle and monk rolled into one."

"Well, it was gracious of you to call—"

"Wait, Ms. O'Brien. We do have some unfinished personal business."

Oh no! He's going to proposition me anyway. Gracie felt the adrenaline pumping into her bloodstream.

"Your friend's airplane that crashed in Alaska. You wanted me to try to get one of my ships involved."

Relief chased the adrenaline. "Oh, yes! Of course. I really appreciate your considering that, Mr. Ashad, and I apologize to you for making an inappropriate request of a client."

"Nonsense. But now that we've been successful, we need an address."

"I'm sorry?"

"I must apologize for being slow to call you. Actually, I called several days ago to talk to Ben Janssen about another matter and he handed me my head over the idea that I had carnal designs on my female lawyer. So, I put the whole thing out of my mind and forgot to check with my captain about it, and I didn't realize until this morning that he'd been successful."

"Successful? I don't understand."

"We recovered the wreckage of your friend's airplane, Miss O'Brien, and I need to know where to send it after my captain puts it on a barge, or ashore."

"*You* recovered it?"

"Yes. Isn't that what you requested?"

Gracie straightened up in confusion and glanced at April with wide eyes, gesturing silently to the phone.

"Yes . . . yes, it is. I had no idea that was going to be possible."

"It was very little trouble. Our ship loitered for about an hour, I think, to grapple it aboard, then sailed right on as scheduled. Not a problem. But now he's in port in Tacoma and needs to get it off the deck."

"May I have your number and call you back in ten minutes?"

He recited the same number clearly displayed on Gracie's phone, and she thanked him and disconnected.

She leaned against the wall of the adjacent building to catch her breath. April moved toward her in alarm.

"What? *What is it?*"

"They were telling the truth, April."

"Who?"

"The government. Our government. I hauled them halfway to the Supreme Court and they were innocent all along."

"What are you talking about, Gracie?" April asked, holding her forearms.

"It was one of Bernie Ashad's ships that fished your dad's Albatross out of the Gulf of Alaska."

"*What?*"

Gracie was nodding. "The U.S. government never touched it."

*A*rlie Rosen's voice on the other end of Gracie's cell phone was a wonderful sound.

"I got your message, Gracie. It's truly over?"

"We won! The FAA is withdrawing their allegations."

"How?"

"I can't tell you for certain," she said, carefully composing her words. "But I think they simply got scared at a high level of how this would look if they were wrong and we got a major court decision out of it."

There was a tired sigh on the other end. "I can't tell you how grateful I am."

"Where are you, Captain?"

There was a hesitation. "Up in Canada. On the west coast of Vancouver Island. Someone was chasing us."

"I heard. That will stop now, too, whatever it was about."

"Are you sure, Gracie?"

"Yes. Absolutely. Highest authority."

"Because we're armed and safe up here."

"You're armed?"

"Yes."

"In Canada?"

"Yes."

"Captain, get the hell out of there! Fly back immediately. Unless you somehow cleared a hunting rifle with customs, you can't have guns up there and I don't want to have to bail you out of a provincial jail."

SEATTLE, WASHINGTON
FOUR DAYS LATER

Gracie knew better than to read too much into Ben Janssen's voice, but it was hopeful that her call for an appointment on return to Seattle had been so cheerfully received.

She used the circular stairway from her floor to the top floor and rounded the corner to Janssen's huge office, wondering how closely Ben Janssen might have read the e-mail memo she'd sent from Washington reporting the call from Bernie Ashad in excruciating detail.

"Well, well, Gracie!" Janssen said. "Come on in. Home from the wars, I see."

"Yes, sir."

Janssen had left his desk to greet her with a handshake and a pat on the shoulder. He motioned her to a dark burgundy leather divan, and settled into an adjacent matching chair around a low coffee table.

"Tell me what transpired in your case for Rosen," he said, smiling at her, his demeanor one of ease as he sat back, hands behind his head, and waited for her to chronicle the sequence of events. When she was through, she added the fact that the wreckage had never been in Navy possession, and Janssen nodded, dropping his hands to his lap as he leaned forward.

"Did you feel a little silly?" he asked, nailing her emotions.

"Yes."

"Don't. We do the best with the facts we've got, and I would have arrived at the same conclusion."

"I appreciate that, sir."

"I know a bit more than you think about this," he added, his smile triggering the unsettling thought that somehow her body language had transmitted a state secret learned in the Oval Office.

"You do?"

"Well, I do have a few friends in both low and high places, and one of them called me the other day to say that a particular lawyer from my office had suddenly appeared before him like a sort of feminine cloudburst. Fact is, he said you'd chased him down at a formal dinner, gently but effectively twisted his arm, gained the unprecedented honor of being added to an appellate argument schedule at the last minute, something even solicitor generals can't do, and filed a well-reasoned brief."

"Judge *Williamson?*"

"Exactly. Sander Williamson. I went to law school with the old reprobate."

"So, he called you?" she asked in stunned affirmation.

Ben Janssen was enjoying the moment and nodding. Either a good sign or one of impending execution, meaning she had no idea why he was in such a good mood.

"Yes, he called me, all right. He said one Gracie O'Brien presented herself at argument well groomed, well prepared, poised, fearless, and factual, all attributes he admires. And, he says you virtually stood the court on its head by reminding them of something all three judges had apparently forgotten for years, that not only do they, in fact, possess primary equity jurisdiction concurrent with their appellate role, but they can hear something as obscure as a plea for interlocutory decree even in the matter of a temporary restraining order."

"They were surprised?"

" 'Stunned' would be a better word. Sander called your use of the argument as nothing short of brilliant. He was very impressed, and convinced."

"He understood we had settled with the FAA conditioned entirely on reinstatement of Captain Rosen's license?"

Janssen smiled again. "Well, let's just say he understood that would be the only reason you'd back off and move to dismiss."

"Good."

"Which was very fortunate for you and your client."

"The settlement? Yes. It was."

"No, actually, Gracie, I mean the fact that you were able to move for dismissal was very fortunate on a separate plane."

"I don't understand."

"Well, you panicked the government into settling because they were convinced you were going to win and embarrass them. That's very clear. But although Sander Williamson was convinced, and the government lawyers and the FAA were convinced, the other two judges up there held the trump card. According to Sander, they agreed they had the power to consider your petition and issue an interlocutory order, but they weren't convinced the case justified it. In other words, Gracie, you would have lost."

She felt suddenly very cold inside as Ben Janssen continued.

"But, what I'm most delighted to hear is that one of my team did such a great job of thinking on her feet in the face of extreme intimidation and with little experience. Well done."

"Thank you, sir."

"Oh, one more thing." He got up and moved with suprising agility to his desk to retrieve a thin manila folder, which he laid in Gracie's lap before sitting again.

"What's this, sir?"

"A pathology report. You never did get the matter of drinking and flying resolved for Captain Rosen, did you?"

She shook her head.

"And I imagine that's still rattling around in your head, and perhaps shading your formerly pristine view of the man with latent suspicion?"

"Oh, I know he wasn't drinking. That's not like him."

"Bullshit, Gracie. You're talking to a recovering alcoholic. The propensity is always there."

She looked at her senior partner in silence for a few moments, her heart sinking. There was something in the folder that she didn't know about Arlie Rosen, and she hadn't processed the small bomb he'd already tossed.

Janssen shifted in his chair and leaned toward her. "Gracie, I know how much this fellow means to you, so I had one of our investigators take a look. He found Rosen had suffered a few deep cuts the night of his crash, and there was considerable blood left in his exposure suit. The Coast Guard had retained them both. There's a sophisticated little test that can be run in certain cases to get a snapshot of the alcohol content of spilled blood at the time it was spilled."

"You . . . he ran the test? He found enough blood?"

"Read," Ben Janssen directed. Gracie opened the folder and forced her eyes to focus. The blood-alcohol percentage of Arlie Rosen's blood within a few minutes after the accident was precisely zero, and she was losing the struggle to hold back tears.

"Have you made your decision?" Ben Janssen added suddenly.

"I'm sorry? Oh! Yes. I dearly want to stay."

"Wonderful, because we dearly want to keep you."

"But . . . I have one request. You gave me three weeks off, and I'd like to take one more and make it a total of four. I . . . really need to spend some time with friends and decompress, and then come back and hit the deck running. I understand that none of the time will be paid."

He stared at her in silence for a few seconds before laughing and shaking his head. "You're a born litigator, Gracie. Just like me. You'd negotiate with God for a better deal at the very moment he was holding open the pearly gates for you."

"Then, I can have the time?"

"Do I have a choice?"

"No, sir."

"Then go. See you back here at the end of four weeks."

She stood and shook his hand. "And . . . I assume you'll have the velvet handcuffs waiting?"

"Absolutely. You just think you're ever leaving these offices again."

ANCHORAGE, ALASKA

General Mac MacAdams settled into one of the huge, leather wing-back chairs facing each other in front of a roaring fire in his den and lit the cigar he'd just selected from a small humidor. A snifter of his best cognac sat on a side table. He glanced around at the warmth he knew was reflected throughout the stately home built as the commanding general's quarters by the Army Air Corps at Elmendorf Air Force Base a half century before, and sat back, enjoying the aroma of the Indian Tabac Churchill.

"This is a fine cigar, even if it does have a somewhat politically suspect cigar band," a male voice intoned from the recesses of the other wingback chair.

Mac turned to the visitor. "You know, don't you, that I'm going to need your services for at least another year or two?"

"I expected that," the other man replied. "What with all the civilian airliner installations you have to complete, as well as those in the military fleet. I figure you'll have to ride herd on Uniwave for some time. The little mafia-style muscle they put on Captain Rosen is just a small example. Chairman Martin is a loose cannon on a rolling deck."

"A bit harsh," Mac replied. "What was the final word on that, by the way?"

There was a laugh from the other chair. "Frustrated ex-CIA covert-ops guy named Todd Jenkins decided to solve our problem by threatening Captain Rosen. Even put a bullet through his car for emphasis."

"Martin ordered that?" Mac asked.

"No, no! It's the Thomas Beckett syndrome. Jenkins knew that Will Martin was upset by the Rosens' trying to defend themselves, so he figured that's what the king wanted. He's now enjoying an early retirement."

Mac remained silent and took another long puff on his cigar and turned his head toward the man. "You need a light for that cigar, Colonel, or are you just wanting to get acquainted with it better?"

"Would it offend you if I smoked it later out by the lake?"

"Which lake?"

"Any lake. We have a bunch up here."

"Of course not. You're welcome to take it with you."

The other man raised his glass and drained the last drops of the cognac, a broad smile on his face. "Top quality, Mac. I'm thankful I never fell into alcoholism. I'd hate to miss such a smooth, silky taste."

"You know, I could still try to get you on a fast track to brigadier general," Mac said.

The Air Force colonel chuckled, shaking his head. "Please, not that! They forced me to be a full colonel, Mac, even though I've spent my entire career hiding out in the intelligence community so I wouldn't have to wear a uniform. I don't want to wear stars. I just want to be where I can see them at night. Which is right here in Alaska."

"You said you were going to take a month or two off. You taking a vacation?"

"No. Going home. There's someone I need to see, and she's been without me for too long, although she may not share that opinion."

"Where is she?" Mac asked. "In Fairbanks? Seattle?"

There was the sound of rustling leather to the side of Mac's chair, as the visitor rose to his feet and turned toward Mac.

"No, Mac. Kotzebue. She's gone back to our home village to teach."

"Way up there?"

"You forget, General. Underneath this covert-ops exterior, I'm also a stealth Inupiat." Nelson Oolokvit smiled broadly as he shook Mac's hand. "Thanks again for the dinner and the hospitality."

When the front door to the MacAdams's base home had closed behind him, Nelson walked to his car and paused to look up, immensely pleased to see a blazing canopy of stars twinkling overhead in the crisp air of a crystal-clear night. He checked his watch. In a few hours, Ben Cole would be arriving home on a late-night Alaska flight from a week-long cruise vacation. Nelson had agreed to meet him curbside, bringing along with him a large, bossy, and sometimes irritable feline named Schroedinger, who'd been his houseguest while Ben was gone.

And Old Man Schroedinger would be looking for his dinner.